Deborah Alcock

The Czar

a tale of the time of the first Napoleon

Deborah Alcock

The Czar
a tale of the time of the first Napoleon

ISBN/EAN: 9783337349721

Printed in Europe, USA, Canada, Australia, Japan

Cover: Foto ©Andreas Hilbeck / pixelio.de

More available books at **www.hansebooks.com**

THE CZAR.

TIMELY AID.

THE CZAR.

A Tale of the Time of the First Napoleon.

SWEET COUNSEL TO A MOURNFUL HEART.

T. NELSON AND SONS,

LONDON, EDINBURGH, AND NEW YORK.

THE CZAR.

A Tale of the Time of the First Napoleon.

By the Author of

"THE SPANISH BROTHERS,"

&c.   &c.

London:

T. NELSON AND SONS, PATERNOSTER ROW.

EDINBURGH; AND NEW YORK.

1895

Contents.

CONTENTS.

THE CZAR.

CHAPTER I.

A SLEEPING VILLAGE.

THE nineteenth century was still very young; its eventful day—that day whose sunset we have yet to see—had but lately dawned upon the world. There were regions, even in Europe, where, for any illumination brought them by the age, the hand of time might have been put back for centuries. In the vast monotonous plain around Moscow the ancient,—Moscow the holy, with her "forty times forty churches,"—Russian serfs tilled the corn-fields of their lords, trembled beneath the knout and the plitt, ate their kasha and drank their kvass, and enjoyed the simple luxuries of their stoves and their vapour-baths, just as their fathers and fathers' fathers had done for generations.

In that land of sameness, where received types repeat each other to weariness, with almost as little variety in the works of nature as originality in those of man, the village of Nicol-ofsky was a fair sample of a hundred others. It belonged to Plato Zoubof, one of the favourites of Catherine II., who had bestowed it upon him with the adjacent lands and the "bodies and souls of men" it contained. Out of these he contrived to

wring no inconsiderable revenue; but he never honoured Nicolofsky with his presence. A steward managed everything,
unfortunately for the peasants, or mujiks, who were treated
with much more severity than their brethren whose natural
lords dwelt "among their own people," and cultivated relations
with them usually kindly, often even paternal. From the
mujiks of Nicolofsky heavy dues were exacted, and much
labour required in the corn-fields of their lord. In harvest-
time they were often forced to toil the whole night long, and
any shortcoming was cruelly punished. At this very epoch
a series of enlightened enactments, tending to ameliorate the
lot of the serf and to prepare the way for his complete emancipation, were emanating from the supreme authority in the
state; but from these Nicolofsky had as yet received little or
no practical benefit, except, indeed, the deep conviction, which
sank into the heart of the mujik, that his lord the Czar loved
him and cared for his welfare.

Still, as the proverb tells us, "The holy Russian land is
large, but everywhere the dear sun shines." Many a gleam of
sunlight, from the mercy of Him whose compassions are over
all his works, brightens even the lot of servitude, that looks,
and rightly looks, so dark and so degrading to the thoughtful
observer. Had such an observer visited· Nicolofsky on the
bright afternoon of one of the Church holidays in the late
Russian spring, he would have found some difficulty in remembering, and perhaps as much in persuading the mujiks, that
they were an oppressed and miserable race.

Youths and maidens, boys and girls were crowding to the
birchwood to enjoy their favourite pastime of the swing. Nor
were the older villagers unrepresented — at least so far as
regards the men. Many a grave, bearded mujik keenly
enjoyed the motion without labour so dear to the indolent and
excitable Russian, although the women for the most part
remained at home to prepare the tschi (or cabbage soup)

for the festive evening meal. The young people, as they passed along, made the air resound with their sweet national songs, chanted in parts and with wonderful grace and harmony.

The company of children seemed to follow the guidance of one of their number, whom either his position or the choice of his companions had made a leader amongst them. At twelve or fourteen the little mujik is often a very handsome lad, as may be seen from the boy postilions of St. Petersburg. And a most favourable specimen of the class, if indeed he belonged to it at all, was the fair-haired boy who stepped so proudly along, quite conscious of his superior dignity, and conspicuous in his new caftan of bright blue, bound round the waist with a crimson sash. He held by the hand a little girl, very pretty, though not so gaily clad. She seemed to be his especial charge; and when the spot in the wood where they meant to pursue their sport was reached at last, the other children crowded around them, and, like juvenile courtiers, emulously tendered their help to make a swing for "Barrinka," the little lord, who had promised to swing Anna "Popovna," the priest's daughter. These swings were made very easily, by bending down and tying together the flexible elastic branches of the giant birches.

Barrinka, however, wanted to do all himself, and he did it quickly and neatly. He had just, with boyish gallantry, placed his little companion in the seat prepared for her, when an older lad pushed rudely through the group of children, and coming up to him laid his hand on his shoulder. "Get into that seat and swing yourself, Ivan Barrinka," he said. "To-day Anna Popovna belongs to me—not to you."

Ivan shook off his hand, and for a moment they stood motionless, looking each other in the face. Strong was the contrast between the fine, delicate features of the one, and the rough, dogged, determined face of the other, which seemed hewn out of his native granite. Evidently this was not by any means their first quarrel.

"Hold thy peace, one-eared Michael," Ivan answered at last. "I tell thee Anna wants me to swing her—*me*, and not thee."

"Let her say so, then.—Is that true, Anna Popovna? Didst thou not promise me yesterday, after church, that I should swing thee to-day—I, and no one else?"

Thus appealed to, the little girl behaved very like a grown-up daughter of Eve. She pouted, blushed, stammered, and seemed to hesitate between her two cavaliers, neither of whom she wished to offend. At length she said, "If you wanted so much to swing me, why were you not here in time, Michael Ivanovitch?"

"Easy for those who have naught to do to blame those who work hard. I had water to fetch and wood to cut for the mother," said Michael, the widow's son.

"Well, it was a pity, since you stayed away so long, that you did not stay altogether, and leave us in peace," Anna rejoined in a pettish tone.

This exasperated Michael, and not without reason, if all were told. "You did not say that to me, Anna Popovna," he cried, "when I went to seek you in the snowstorm, you and your brother the Popovitch, and lost my left ear to save you." Then he turned fiercely upon Ivan, as upon a foe more worthy of his wrath : "It is all your fault, Ivan Barrinka. I am quite tired of you and of your pride. Lord though you may be, you shall not lord it over me. And, after all, who knows who and what you are? I'm sure I don't. Do you know yourself? Answer me that. Whose son are you?"

"It is you who are proud, Michael Ivanovitch. Since that wonderful snowstorm you were out in there has been no bearing with you. One would think, from the airs you give yourself, that no one ever had an ear frozen before."

By this time the loud voices had attracted the attention of

the other boys. Leaving their swings, they came crowding around ; and as soon as they understood the cause of the dispute, they all turned with one accord upon Michael, threatening him with condign punishment if he did not forthwith let Barrinka have his way, whatever that way might be.

But Barrinka no longer cared for the pastime. Michael's taunt, " Who knows who and what you are ?" had struck home. From infancy the pet and plaything of the village—every wish anticipated, every caprice borne with, he had been surrounded with an atmosphere of deferential affection. He could not but know that he differed from all around him ; a mystery hung about his birth, which, through injudicious and mistaken kindness, had been neither wholly concealed nor yet frankly revealed to him. All his little playfellows had fathers and mothers. It is true they were beaten sometimes, while *he* was never beaten. Still, it seemed to him a strange thing to have no father or mother. He called the starost, or elder of the village, in whose house he had been brought up, " bativshka " (little father), and his wife, " mativshka " (little mother), but that was not by any means the same as having a father and mother of his own.

" Take the swing if you like it," he said to Michael. " I care nothing about it. I shall do something by-and-by much better than anything you have ever done in your life."

Leaving the children behind him in the wood, he bent his steps homeward, regardless of the regretful looks sent after him by blue-eyed Anna Popovna, who saw that her little cavalier was sorely vexed, and would gladly have comforted him. Two longings filled his childish heart,—to be able to tell Michael and everybody who he was, and to be the hero of an adventure more wonderful than Michael's wanderings through the snow in search of the priest's children. Michael had been out in a snowstorm and lost an ear ! In comparison with such a hero the little lord felt himself a very child.

He soon came in sight of the double row of brown wooden cottages that called itself Nicolofsky. These cottages, or izbas, were built of the trunks of trees laid one over the other, with the interstices stuffed with moss. There was a church, also of wood, but larger and better built, with a bell suspended from a fine elm tree close to it. Two of the izbas were better than the rest, and belonged, one to the starost, the other to the pope, or parish priest, Anna's father. That of the starost boasted a porch, with ornamental wooden pillars and quaint carvings. It had a substantial chimney built of good bricks, and secure well-glazed windows to keep out the intense cold of the Russian winter. Indeed all the cottages were more comfortable than they looked.

Ivan entered, and dutifully made his bow, as he had been taught to do, to the holy picture which hung in the corner, with a lamp burning before it, since this was a feast-day. The contents of the izba were extremely simple. The most conspicuous object was the stove, with a wide shelf or platform over it, upon which the family usually slept; a handsome carved chest contained the clothing used upon festive occasions, and there were besides a few stools, a table, an arm-chair, and some wooden cups, platters, and cooking utensils. The vapour-bath, that indispensable Russian luxury, occupied an outhouse.

An old woman stood over the fire, diligently stirring a capacious caldron, from which there issued a very savoury steam. The family the starost had to feed was not a small one,—three grown-up sons, with the wife and child of one of them, found shelter beneath his roof.

"You are cooking tschi for our supper, mativshka," said Ivan.

" And what better dish could I be cooking, my little dove? 'For tschi, folk wed,' says the proverb."

" When I am old enough I will wed Anna Popovna."

"Hush! hush! My darling must not talk so. He is worth a thousand Popovnas."

"One-eared Michael does not think that."

"Who cares for one-eared Michael?"

"But, mativshka, to-day he asked me who I was, and I—I had no answer."

"No answer! Why, every one knows who you are. You are our dear little lord."

"But whose son am I, mativshka? That was what he wanted to know."

"Ask the father, boy, ask the fatner. As for me, why, 'A word is not a bird: if it flies out, you'll never catch it again.'"

Old Feodora would not have thought it any harm to put her nursling off with a string of falsehoods, if they had occurred to her at the moment, or if she had thought them necessary; for these poor, "dimly-lighted souls" had little idea of the value of truth. But Ivan's history was now so much an "open secret" in the village, that she saw no reason why the boy should not know it himself, since he was twelve years old, and very intelligent. Still, she was afraid to tell him anything without her husband's knowledge and concurrence.

Soon afterwards the starost came in—an imposing and venerable figure, his long, gray beard nearly covering the breast of his caftan. He would have parted with his head quite as readily as with that beard.

As soon as he had made his reverence to the sacred picture, seated himself in his chair by the stove, and exchanged his formidable (and fragrant) boots of Russia leather for a pair of lapti, or bark slippers, Ivan stood up before him, and put the question directly, "Bativshka, whose son am I?"

"Great St. Nicholas! what has come to the boy?" the starost exclaimed; then he looked perplexed, and hesitated for an answer. His wife leaned over the back of his chair and said a few words in a low voice, and a whispered discussion followed, during which Ivan waited patiently. Presently Feodora returned to her cooking; and the starost solemnly crossed his breast with the thumb and two fingers of his right hand, then taking from his pocket a medal with the effigy of his patron saint upon it, he brightened it with a rub against his sleeve, and said a prayer to it, or to the personage it represented. Having thus prepared himself, he told Ivan to sit down at his feet.

"My child," he said, "since you wish to know, I will tell you to-day what name you have a right to bear; but pray to your saint day and night that the knowledge may work you no harm."

"Why should it work me harm, bativshka? Is it that I am the son of a bad man?"

"God only knows that. What I know is that you are the son of our lord and master."

"Not of Zoubof! no, no!" cried Ivan, wondering.

The old man replied by a gesture of supreme contempt: "*Zoubof!* He is of yesterday. Such as he come and go and are forgotten, like last year's snow. But you, Ivan Barrinka, you are the son of our true lord, our master in God's sight—a great boyar,* a prince who can trace his lineage back to the days of Rurik. Yes; you are the son of"—here he paused and bowed his gray head reverently—"of Prince Pojarsky."

Ivan was impressed by the solemn tone in which these words were spoken. He waited in silence for a few moments, then he questioned in a low voice, "And who is Prince Pojarsky?"

"He and his have been the lords of Nicolofsky and the lands around it for generations and generations, even before the old times when the Poles conquered Muscovy. But in the days of the great Czarina Catherine, who rests with God, our lord and your father, being a young man, full of pride and loving plea-sure, must needs go forth to travel in strange lands. For you must know, Ivan Barrinka, that there are other lands in God's

* Nobleman

world besides holy Russia, and that the peoples thereof do not obey our lord the Czar, but have kings and rulers of their own. This is hard to believe; but Pope Nikita says so, and, moreover, the soldiers tell us of them when they come back from the wars. Besides, I have seen Nyemtzi* myself—Frenchmen and French-women, who had not a word of good Russian, but spoke an out-landish tongue of their own. What is sad to think, our lord and your father not only went amongst these foreigners, but gave his hand in marriage to one of them. Not that I have anything to say against the beautiful, gracious lady, your mother. The good saints rest her soul! Mativshka loved her well, and God knows she served her faithfully. But amongst her kinsfolk must have been some who were the devil's children; for they rose against their own king, and, horrible to tell! they slew him. Moreover, they did not do it secretly and in darkness, but openly, in the face of day, on a scaffold, as if he had been a thief or a murderer. Truly they are strange people, those Nyemtzi.

"Let us hope that evil men slandered our lord to the Czarina when they said *he* bore part in such wickedness. But at all events she believed the tale. When he came back to St. Peters-burg, and dared to show his face at the Hermitage (the great, beautiful house where our lady the Czarina lived), she scathed him with the lightning of her anger. It is even reported that she said to him, '*Pachol!*'†—the word you would use to a dog if you were angry with it. Straightway he was sent an exile to Siberia, and all he had was taken from him and given to Plato Zoubof. Better had they laid him in his grave at once. The beautiful young lady, your mother, quickly died of grief, and mativshka, who was your nurse, brought you home to her own people. For a long time we hid you carefully, and guarded the secret jealously amongst ourselves; for we feared the new lord Plato Zoubof, and still more the steward Dmitri

* Foreigners.   † Get out!—Go out from my presence in disgrace.

—a hard man, who has no pity.   But now both know you are here, and care nothing for it.   'What is it to us?' they say. So that now, without fear, you may call yourself, and be called by every one, by the noble name you have a right to bear. Only remember, Ivan Barrinka, that although you are the son of a boyar and a prince, the same God made us and you, and the poor man's soul is worth as much in his sight as your own."

Ivan answered not a word.   As one overpowered, he threw himself face downwards on the earthen floor, and lay there absorbed in thought.   But at last he raised his wondering, child-like face, full of the brightness of a new idea.   "Bat-ivshka, people sometimes come back from Siberia, do they not?"

The old man shook his head.   "They who go are as the sand," he said; "they who come back may be reckoned on your fingers."

"But I remember the time of the Czar's coronation—four—five years ago, was it?   I was quite a little boy then.   Many exiles came home from Siberia; and you went to the Moscow road to see them pass, and the people wept for joy, you said. I wanted to go, but you would not bring me, saying I was too young.   If these exiles came back, then why not my father?"

"Ah, you cannot understand.   That was quite another matter.   The late Czar, Paul Petrovitch, who reigned after the Czarina Catherine, was somewhat stern and hard.   Doubtless God sent him to punish the great nobles for their sins.   He banished many of them to Siberia; but the Czar that now is, whom God preserve! pardoned them all, and let them return home.   Yet some offences there be that find no pardon ever, except in the grave;—and to the exile's resting-place the grave is always near."

Ivan's next thought was a more childish one.   "Bativshka,"

he said, after another silence, "I should like to tell all this to Anna Popovna and to Michael Ivanovitch. Still, although I am the son of a boyar and a prince," he added presently, "I shall not be quite happy, not *quite*, until I have taken a longer journey than ever Michael did, and have had something happen to me much more wonderful than getting frozen and losing one of my ears."

CHAPTER II.

IVAN'S ADVENTURE.

"Adventures are to the adventurous."—CONINGSBY.

IVAN BARRINKA, or Ivan Pojarsky, as he may now be called, was a genuine child of Russia. His nature was quick, mobile, restless, passionate. He was capable of strong determination, but capable also of changefulness and inconstancy, because the mood of the moment always seized upon and swayed his whole soul. But he was all this only in the germ, for his was as yet the unawakened, undeveloped mind of a child. The simple-hearted guardians of his infancy had given him all they could—food, shelter, and tenderness; and this not only without hope of reward, but during some years under absolute terror of discovery and punishment. But they could not give him the instruction to which his intelligent mind would have so eagerly responded. No one in the village, except the priest, knew the mysteries of the Russian alphabet; and Pope Nikita, like most Russian priests, was in no real sense a pastor or a teacher, but rather a machine for performing the numerous ceremonies of his Church. All that could be said in his favour was, that if he did little good, he did little harm. Neither from him nor from the starost did Ivan learn any religion except a series of outward acts and postures, of bowings and crossings, and formal repetitions of "Gospodin pomilvi,"* with a respect for sacred pic-

* "Lord, have mercy upon me."

tures, and a vague reverence for God, for the saints, and for the Czar. He never dreamed that any of these mysterious, far-away powers should influence his daily conduct, though he did believe that his patron St. John (Ivan is the Russian form of John) might help him in a time of need; because, when he had the measles, a picture of the saint had been blessed by the pope and laid on his breast, and straightway he began to recover! It was mournfully significant of the kind of instruction he received, that he had but one and the same word to designate the divine Being and the "gods of silver and gods of gold" that too often, in the popular estimation, usurped His place. If any one had asked him, "Who made you?" he would have answered, "Bog;" and had the question followed, "What is that in the corner, before which the candle is burning?" he would still have replied, without hesitation, "It is Bog."

A few childish legends of the saints, a few stories of "kikinoras" or goblins, formed the staple of the "folk lore" that circulated round the stove during the long winter evenings. The Bible narratives, so familiar and so fascinating to the English child, were almost unknown to Ivan; nor did exploits of the heroes of his own country hold the place they sometimes do on the lips or in the hearts of the people. Hence, when the starost told him that he was himself the heir of one of the noblest of Russian names, no answering chord resounded in his heart. The revelation, that ought to have moved him so deeply, failed of its due effect, because his ignorance did not supply the background that was needed to throw it into relief. He had always known that he was something other, something greater than those around him; but beyond that he had no power of measuring social distances. Princes, boyars, all who were not mujiks, were alike to him; just as it seemed to him nearly the same thing to go to the Moscow road, to Moscow itself, or even to St. Petersburg. Therefore, after spending a little vague, half-comprehending wonder upon the starost's story, his mind reverted, as days went on, to what was at this period his ruling idea—the hope of rivalling and surpassing Michael in some deed of daring, and consequently in the regard of Anna Popovna.

It was not for his advantage that his kindly foster-parents never exacted from him any of the labours that fell to the lot of the little mujiks, his play-fellows. "Prepare to die, mujik, but till the soil," says the Russian proverb; and certainly where there is no other education an early apprenticeship to manual toil is rather a blessing than otherwise. Ivan's idle hands and restless feet were left quite at liberty to obey all the suggestions of his active, untaught mind; while his naturally brave disposition was rendered still more fearless from the fact of his never having been, upon any occasion, punished or even thwarted or reproved.

One summer morning, just as the first faint streaks of dawn began to brighten the cottage window, he rose softly from his sleeping-place on the shelf above the stove. All the rest had worked hard the day before, and were slumbering soundly now; so he dressed himself quietly, and going to the great carved chest lifted the heavy lid with difficulty and took out and put on his rough sheep-skin coat, or shuba; then he drew on his warm boots of Russia leather lined with fur; next, he cut for himself with a hatchet a great piece of sour black bread, and tied it in a cloth as provision for the way; lastly, he went to a secret hiding-place of his own and transferred to his pocket his greatest treasure—a silver rouble mativshka had given him. Having done all this, he was hurrying forth with quick noiseless footsteps, when he remembered an omitted duty. Returning a step or two, he took his stand before the picture in the corner, made a reverence, and repeated a hasty prayer; then, with a brave heart and a quiet conscience, he went forth in search of what fate might bring him,—a little knight-errant going to look for adventures.

He passed through the sleeping village, with the familiar

brown cottages on either side of him looking peaceful and home-like in the morning twilight. The church-bell in the tall elm-tree seemed to beckon him near; he could scarcely resist the temptation of climbing the tree, seizing the rope, and astonishing the village with an untimely peal. Only the reflection that this would inevitably bring his own adventure to an abrupt conclusion stayed his hand. Leaving the houses behind him, he passed through fields rich with waving corn, then through pasture-lands, from which he emerged at length upon a bare, monotonous, sandy plain. Now, for the first time, he ventured to beguile his way with a song; and his clear, ringing, childish voice sounded far and wide, yet failed to reach any human ear. Nor would it have fared otherwise with a cry for help, however shrill and agonized.

Ivan, happily, did not think of this. Fleet of foot and light of heart, he pursued his course, still singing as he went, until village, corn-fields, and birch-woods were all left far behind him. And now, wherever he looked, he saw nothing but a dreary waste of sand, with here and there a few patches of stunted herbage, and at rare intervals a solitary pine or a little cluster of birch-trees. The stillness was absolute: the children of the air eschewed that land of barrenness, and the beasts of the field seemed also to have abandoned it. None of the gentler races that man has succeeded in taming found pasture there; and fortunately wolves were extremely rare, though not quite un-known. Ivan never dreamed of them; his one concern was to keep the road, for so he called the track made by the wheels of the rude waggons which brought the produce of the corn-fields to the river Oka. He knew that a ferry-boat crossed the river, bringing adventurous travellers to the great Moscow road on the other side. This road was the goal of his ambition. As already intimated, no clear distinction existed in his mind be-tween the Moscow road and Moscow itself, the holy city towards which the heart of every Russian yearned with reverent love and passionate longing. It was their Jerusalem, "beautiful for situation, the joy of the whole earth." Even ignorant little Ivan had heard of its wonders and its glories; and he fancied that if once he gained the road he might see in the distance the gilded spires and domes of the Kremlin gleaming in the sun. Michael had never seen so much as that, nor been so far from home!

The sun, in Russia such a rare and much-prized guest, was prodigal of his favours that day, and shone forth from a cloudless sky. Ivan had equipped himself for a winter journey, and about noon he began to grow hot and weary. No shelter was near him, so he sat down on the sand, rested a little, and ate some of his bread; but he longed in vain for a draught of kvass* to finish his repast, nor could he find a single drop of water anywhere. He rose unrefreshed and pursued his way; but, in spite of all his childish courage, the utter loneliness of the dreary waste around him began to tell upon his spirits. He sang, he shouted, he talked aloud to himself, merely for the comfort of hearing his own voice; until by-and-by he became too weary for these exercises—all he could contrive to do was to keep moving on with a kind of dogged determination. Once and again was he tempted to turn back and give up the adventure; indeed, he would have done so, only for the thought, "If I come back having seen nothing, Michael will jeer me, and Anna Popovna will join in the laugh."

At last he grew so tired and frightened that he threw himself on the ground in a kind of despair, made the sign of the cross, said a prayer to his patron St. John the evangelist, then fell into a state of drowsiness, and lost all sense of time, until, after an interval of perhaps an hour, he was aroused by the sound of voices.

Never had human voices seemed more welcome. Ivan started to his feet, and saw to his great delight a party of five

* A light, sour beverage, made by pouring water upon flour or meal.

or six mujiks, carrying large baskets of cabbages and other vegetables. Greetings were soon exchanged. His new friends told him that they were journeying from a distant village to a fair at Kaluga, a town on the other bank of the Oka. They intended, after crossing the river, to travel all night, that they might reach the fair with their merchandise early the next morning. They took the tired little wayfarer by the hand and helped him on, encouraging him with kind words, and telling him they were now not far from the ferry.

At last the river appeared in the distance, glimmering in the light of the rising moon. "Look," cried his companions, "yonder is the Oka." But Ivan was by this time too weary to care; he could scarcely keep his eyes open and his feet moving.

They drew nearer and nearer. The river was as broad as the Thames—a fine sheet of water, with green banks on either side. From these there came a hoarse, monotonous sound—the croaking of innumerable frogs, which some one has unpoetically called "the nightingales of Russia." Soon a brown wooden shed came into view, where the men said they would find kvass, and perhaps even vodka.* This roused Ivan, who was still tormented with thirst. He saw the moonlight upon the waters; the grassy sward beside them; the rough boat-house, out of which a withered old woman, with a red handkerchief wrapped around her head and a torch of pine-wood in her hand, came to meet the wayfarers.

There was no boat to be had, she said; her son had not returned, though she expected him before sundown;—she could not think what detained him. The peasants were grievously disappointed. The sale of their merchandise depended on their reaching the fair in good time, so their vexation was quite natural. It was somewhat allayed, however, by the offer of vodka, that charmer so fatally dear to the heart of the mujik. And their weary little companion was not quite forgotten.

* Brandy.

"Give the little one a taste, mother," they said.   "Poor child, he is ready to faint."

It was to the honour of the people of Nicolofsky that, though themselves no patterns of sobriety, they had at least kept the destroyer from the young lips of their nursling. Ivan turned from the fiery beverage with loathing, and asked for kvass. "Here is no kvass," said the old woman roughly.   "No man would be fool enough to drink it who could get vodka. But you can have water, if you like."

With this he was content. He wrapped himself up in his shuba, lay down beside the fire in the shed, and was soon fast asleep; while the mujiks sat outside talking, laughing, singing, and drinking vodka.

CHAPTER III.

SOMETHING WONDERFUL HAPPENS TO IVAN.

"Dir ist dein Ohr geklungen
  Vom Lob das man dir bot,
Doch ist zu ihn gedrungen
  Ein schwacher Schrei der Noth.
Der ist ein Held der Freien
  Der, wenn der Ruhm ihn kränzt,
Noch gluht, zu dem zu weihen,
  Das frommet und nicht glänzt."—RÜCKÄRT.

HEN Ivan awoke it was broad daylight; the shed was empty, and all around him still and silent. After a few moments of bewilderment, he remembered where he was, and a sudden terror seized him lest the boat might have come and gone, and his companions have crossed the river without him. So he threw on his shuba and hurried out. They were standing on the bank, watching eagerly for the boat—or rather for the boatman, of whom as yet there was no appearance, though they were tantalized by the sight of the empty boat lying high and dry on the opposite bank. Their irritation increased every moment, and curses were not wanting, which lost none of their effect uttered in that hard, resonant, metallic language.

At this point a new wayfarer joined the group. He came with long strides, as one in eager haste, and his annoyance at the delay seemed even greater than that of the rest. He was a fine, active, young fellow, neatly dressed, and with a mason's trowel stuck in the sash of his caftan, where all the others carried the indispensable axe. Seeing no sign of the approach of a boat, he grew pale, and ground his teeth with angry disappointment.

"Just like my luck!" he muttered. "As well throw myself into the river at once, as wait here much longer."

"Patience, friend," said the oldest of the mujiks. "Are we not all in the like case? Nay, we are worse off than you, for we have waited here all night."

"Worse off! you little know! With you it is a matter of a few kopecks; with me it is life and death. If I am not at Klopti by sundown, there is the knout for my back."

"Why? In Heaven's name, what have you done?"

"Done! nothing in the world but work at my trade, and pay my obrok truly to my lord" (for he was one of that numerous class of serfs who were permitted by their lords to work on their own account, upon payment of an annual tax, or *obrok*). "But he raised my obrok three times, until at last I could scarcely live, and was left no chance of saving a rouble or two for the future. Then last summer I fell from the scaffolding of a house I was building, and was sore hurt. Only that the people I lodged with were good Christians, it would have gone ill with me. But I recovered, thanks to my patron St. Stefen; and when the spring came on I got work again—government work too, which is well paid. I made up my obrok, and then —why then, my brothers, the world went well with me, and my heart was light. Little Katinka, the daughter of the kind soul that took care of me while I was ill, was the prettiest girl in the quarter, and good and pure like a candle of white wax made to burn before the picture of a holy saint. So we gave each other our troth ; and I think the Czar himself on his golden throne was scarce happier than I. But five days ago there came a messenger from Klopti to call me home at once. My lord wants to make him a new house, and must needs have me to build it for him and to teach the men of the village to build also.　It was sudden ; but my lord does not think much of us poor people—God forgive him !"

"But, brother ;—what is it you call yourself?" asked the mujik who had spoken before.

"Stefen Alexitch, at your service."

"Well, then, Brother Stefen, why did you not set out at once? You would have been by this time at your journey's end."

"I know it. Indeed I was wrong, very wrong. But the very next day was Katinka's feast-day, and as I knew only too well that I was never likely to look on her sweet face again, I was tempted to stay, just that I might dance one more measure with her. I thought I could have walked more quickly. And now this cursed delay ! God grant my lord may not lose patience altogether, and wreak his vengeance on my poor old father and mother ! That would be worse than the knout across my own shoulders."

Stefen's narrative elicited many expressions of compassion.

"Poor lad ! thy case is hard indeed," said one.

"Ah," sighed another, "how true the proverb, 'Heaven is high, and the Czar far off.'"

But at that moment a third exclaimed joyfully,—

"Look, brothers !—the boat at last !"

So it was. At first it was seen to shoot rapidly across the strong current of the river ; but by-and-by the rower seemed to flag, and his strokes grew uncertain and unsteady.

The mujiks were too glad to see him on any terms to be critical about the quality of his performances. They crowded to the river's brink, that they might be ready to spring into the boat the moment it touched the land.

Ivan took advantage of the confusion to steal up to Stefen and slip his silver rouble quietly into his hand. "Take it," he whispered. "It is all I have ; but you can get a fairing with it to send to Katinka."

It was poor consolation; but he meant it well, and Stefen's sore heart was soothed by the gentle touch. He bent over the boy and kissed him. There was no time to do more; if they wished to get places in the boat, they must hasten.

The boatman, meanwhile, was volubly explaining the cause of his delay, his speech thickened with much vodka. A party of boyars—*very* great boyars, high and mighty excellencies—had come to the post-house on the Moscow road, and the post-master had kept him busy going on their errands, both last night and this morning. It was easy to see in what coin his services had been paid for; he had taken so much vodka that he was scarcely able to row the boat at all, and, moreover, it was too heavily freighted for safety, not to say for comfort.

Ivan had never been on the water before, and he soon became thoroughly frightened; not without reason. When they reached the middle of the river the boatman showed himself so manifestly incapable that Stefen offered to take the oars. Russian peasants are usually good-tempered, even when under the influence of vodka; but the boatman, unhappily, was surly and dogged by nature, and rudely refused to yield his place. For a few minutes Stefen waited quietly; then seeing that the man was allowing the boat to drift, to the peril of all their lives, he made an attempt to take the oars from him by force. The boatman resisted, and a struggle ensued, from which Ivan hid his face in terror; for now the two men were standing up, striking and pushing each other wildly, while the frail, heavily-laden boat swayed and rocked beneath their reckless feet. One was drunk, the other angry and "bitter of soul." At length Ivan heard a heavy plash close beside him. Hastily uncovering his eyes, he saw the waters closing over the luckless Stefen, and uttered a cry of horror. To his great relief, however, Stefen rose again to the surface, and one of the mujiks, seizing an oar, held it out to him. But either he had lost his presence of mind, or, more probably, his head had been hurt by the boat in falling. At all

events, he made no effort to grasp the oar; and the mujiks—
ignorant, stupid, and awkward, though not lacking in kindliness
—gave him up for lost.   Indeed, their own situation was critical
enough ; but they got to the shore somehow.

The boatman was sobered by the shock, and almost stupified
with grief for what had happened.   But the others crowded
round him, and urged him to go and seek for poor Stefen's
body, that he might at least be buried like a Christian.   This
he consented to do; and the task of finding it proved un-
expectedly easy, for a miniature island, in the midst of the
river, with a single tree growing upon it, had arrested the
body as it was borne downwards by the strong current of the
stream.   The group on the shore waited in mournful silence
while the boatman and two of the mujiks went and returned,
bringing with them their solemn freight, which they laid sadly
and reverently on the fair greensward, beneath the happy
morning sun.

All crossed themselves and murmured a prayer for his soul ;
and the oldest of the mujiks detached a little sacred picture
from his own neck and laid it on his breast.

It was Ivan's first meeting face to face with the king of terrors.   The form so lately full of life and energy lay stiff and
rigid ; while the brow, the cheek, the lips—when he saw the
strange and solemn change that had swept over all these, his
young heart could bear no more, he lifted up his voice and wept.
His tears unlocked the floodgates of the general sorrow ; all the
mujiks standing around him wept and wrung their hands, like
the grown-up children that in truth they were.

Just at that moment, as if to throw into strongest relief the
contrast between life and death, between earth's brightest sunshine and her deepest shadows, a young boyar from the party
at the post-house came riding rapidly over the smooth greensward.   Drawing near the weeping group, he checked his horse
to a foot-pace, and Ivan turned and looked at him.   There was

no splendour in his dress—an officer's uniform, gray in colour and plain in fashion. But his face, which seemed to bring the glow and glory of the morning with it, held Ivan's gaze with a kind of fascination. Features almost perfect enough for the deathless marble of a Grecian sculptor might have worn no charm to his untrained eye, if they had not also beamed with a kindness and gentleness that took his heart at once. That bright, young face—the first beardless manly face he remembered to have seen—left itself for ever on his mind. It was destined to be the inspiration of his life; and when death closed his eyes, he had scarcely a dearer hope than to see it once again in the morning of the resurrection.

The boyar, meanwhile, had come quite close to the group ere he appeared to perceive distinctly the cause of their distress. But no sooner had he done so than he sprang from his horse, flinging the bridle to Ivan, who proudly accepted the charge. The next moment he was bending over the lifeless form; the next, he turned and said cheerfully to the mujiks standing near,—

"My children, this is not death. We will save him yet."

They were speechless with amazement. Was this stranger a holy saint, a worker of miracles? They knew at least that he was a nobleman and an officer, whom fortunately every instinct of their nature, every habit of their lives, taught them to obey without a question. Rapidly singling out two or three of the most intelligent-looking, he set them to work— working with them himself as Ivan, used to the dawdling, dreamy ways of the mujiks, had never in his life seen any one work before. By magic, as it seemed, poor Stefen's dripping clothes were removed, and he was wrapped in the warmest garments the mujiks could contribute for the purpose—Ivan, amongst others, gladly offering his little sheepskin shuba. Then the cold and rigid limbs were gently chafed, a work of time and patience. Those who were helping did mechanically whatever they were directed to do, while the rest looked on in a kind of wondering stupefaction. How could even a boyar expect to bring a dead man to life?

After a considerable time had been spent in this manner, the whole party from the post-house came up, boyars and servants, all on horseback. Instead of calling upon their companion to join them, as Ivan rather expected them to do, the boyars at once dismounted and joined *him*, leaving their horses on the road in the care of the servants. One of these drew near Ivan, and attempted to take his charge from him; but he resisted.

"No," he said. "My boyar's hand gave this bridle into mine, and into no other but his will I give it back again."

"Let the boy alone, Ilya," cried another of the attendants, with a good-humoured laugh. "Let him keep his luck. It may not come twice in his life-time."

After that Ivan could not so easily see what was happening, though he watched intently and with the keenest interest. "His boyar" seemed to refer the matter, as to a person of superior authority, to a very tall, very stern-looking individual, who examined Stefen carefully, putting his hand on his heart and on his wrist. Presently, and rather to Ivan's horror, he drew from his pocket a sort of case, out of which there flashed a bright instrument of steel, like a thin sharp knife, and with this he proceeded to inflict a deep cut upon Stefen's arm; while, far from objecting, the young boyar carefully held it for him, and then produced a fine white kerchief of his own, which he gave him to bind the wound. *

But still the pale, cold form lay there stiff and motionless. Was it death? or was it only a death-like swoon? It was the nobles who were busy now, chafing the cold hands and feet, and using every other possible means to restore animation; for the peasants had given place to them, and stood aside, silent and wondering spectators of the scene.

* Of course this would not be done *now*. But the scene is given exactly as it occurred.

Time passed : life and death were struggling for the mastery, and the conflict was tedious and protracted. It was no even contest. From the first, victory seemed to incline to the side of the sable king. The chance of life, always desperate, lessened apparently with every minute, and when the minutes grew to hours it seemed to vanish altogether away. At last the tall surgeon shook his head, and turning to the boyar said something in a foreign tongue that evidently expressed despair. But *he* would not admit the thought. Ivan knew not, of course, what he said in answer, but it was easy to see that he had steadfastly resolved not to abandon hope, and that he was entreating, urging, even commanding the rest to continue their efforts.

Apparently for no purpose but to please him they obeyed. An interval followed of renewed exertion, though of ever-waning hope. At length, however, the surgeon's instrument flashed out once more, and almost immediately afterwards a thrill of emotion passed through the entire group. One shuddering sigh, one faint, low groan was heard from the lips that had seemed to be sealed for ever in death. "Thank God!" said the boyar, raising the military cap from his stately head with its clustering chestnut curls. "This is amongst the brightest days of my life." Ivan stood near enough to see that his blue eyes were full of tears.

Whilst they gave Stefen a little vodka, and prepared a kind of litter in which to carry him to the post-house, several other persons came up, including the priest and the starost of the nearest village; for some of the mujiks had gone away and spread the story of the strange things they had been witnessing.

Then to Ivan's young eyes the scene became confused. Much happened that he could not exactly understand. But Stefen was alive—that at least was certain, for he saw him try to kiss the hand that had so patiently drawn him back from the gates of the grave. And now, for the first time, the thought occurred to Ivan that his triumph over Michael would be complete and glorious. Michael assuredly had never seen a dead man brought to life again !

At last the great people seemed to be preparing to pursue their journey. Ivan watched "his boyar" as he talked for some time to the priest and the starost, who stood before him with uncovered heads and an air of the deepest reverence; then, seeing him look for his horse, he led his charge forward, and held the stirrup gracefully while he mounted. He got a word of praise for his "long patience," and a bright piece of gold glittered in his hand.

"Take me with you, my boyar," he cried, with a sudden impulse. "Let me serve you; I would *love* to do it."

"My child, you shall serve me one day—not yet," said the boyar, smiling.

A few moments more, and the stately cavalcade had moved away. Ivan stood in silence, unable to withdraw his gaze from the retreating figure of his hero until it was lost in the distance.

The white-haired priest came up to him and laid his hand on his shoulder. "My lad," he said, " do you know who has spoken to you—whose horse you have had the honour of holding ?"

"Yes," said Ivan, wakening out of a dream; "no—yes—at least I know it was a boyar, a great, and good, and splendid boyar, with the face of an angel. I love him !"

"Then pray for him all the days of thy life, for know that he is none other than thy sovereign lord and mine, the Czar Alexander Paulovitch."

Ivan stared, then burst out laughing. "You are jesting with me," he said. "Nay, father, I am only a boy, but I know better than that. I am quite twelve years old, and I know very well that the Czar lives in St. Petersburg, and wears a golden crown, and sits upon a throne, and all the boyars stand uncovered around him."

"Still, I tell thee truth. That handsome young officer was the great Czar himself—the lord of all the Russias. To prove my words—I am a poor man, but I will give thee twice, three times its value for that coin in thy hand, which his hand touched."

Ivan shook his head. "No, no, father; I don't believe a word of your story; but I love my boyar, and I will not give away his gift. He said I should serve him one day, and I mean to do it. Though, to be sure," he added, thoughtfully, " I might almost part with it for poor Stefen's sake, and to do a good deed. How will he dare to meet his master's face—later than ever now ? "

" Never trouble thyself for thy friend Stefen; he is rich enough this day to buy his freedom, if he will. He who gave him back his life has taken care to make that life worth the keeping."

" Then he can marry Katinka ? "

" He can marry whom he pleases. Our lord the Czar never leaves anything half done."

"Oh ! what a good day it has been ! " and Ivan, in his own estimation far too old to be deceived by an idle story, was by no means too old to leap and dance for very joy.

" You believe *that*," said the priest; " then why do you doubt the rest of my story ? "

" Because," returned Ivan, " I have wit enough to know that the great Czar, who 'is God upon earth,' as the proverb says, would not care for the life of a poor mujik, and toil hard to save it, as my boyar did this day."

" Well, fools will be fools while the world lasts. Here, take thy shuba ; Stefen left it for thee when they brought him to the post-house. Go thy ways ; and God teach thee that it shows more wit to believe what one is told than to question it."

" Good day, father," returned Ivan ; " I am going home—to Nicolofsky, where people speak the truth to their neighbours."

With this parting shaft, he drew on his shuba, and turned his steps homewards, highly pleased with his adventure. What a story he would have for the starost and mativshka, for Pope Nikita and one-eared Michael, not to speak of Anna Popovna, by no means the least in his estimation !

He crossed the river without delay—the ferry-boat and the penitent ferryman being this time both in readiness—and then he resumed his journey on foot. As he walked, he ate the remainder of his bread; for he had tasted nothing that day, and it was now long past noon. With a happy heart he pursued his way until about sunset, when fatigue obliged him to stop and rest. He lay down under a solitary fir-tree, intending only to indulge in a short—a *very* short slumber. But nature proved too strong for him : when he awoke again the sky was flushed with the light of early dawn. The remainder of his task was quickly accomplished : he walked into the starost's cottage as the family were sitting down to their morning meal of kasha, or stewed grain.

Warm was the welcome and great were the rejoicings that greeted his appearance. The poor people had been sorely terrified by the mysterious absence of their nursling, and they had sought him far and near, through the birch-wood and the corn-fields, and even for some distance in the waste. They were preparing to renew the search that day with anxious and foreboding hearts.

Almost all Nicolofsky crowded to the starost's cottage to congratulate Ivan and to hear his wonderful story. Certainly, he had attained his object, if that object was to make himself the hero of the village, and totally and for ever to eclipse the exploits of Michael Ivanovitch !

But Ivan was no more the thoughtless little lad who set out two days ago in search of adventures. His young heart had awakened from the sleep of childhood ; new feelings, vague and dimly comprehended, were beginning to stir it. As he trod his homeward way, full of all the wonders he had witnessed, a voice seemed to murmur within him, "And I, too, am a boyar." What did it mean to be a boyar?   He had no words in which to express his thought; but the dawning light of a grand truth, faint and far off, shone upon him from the face of the first boyar he had ever seen, as it bent anxiously and tenderly over the mujik's senseless form—that to be greater than all the rest meant to do good to all the rest.

He told his adventures modestly and truthfully.   What he had done with his silver rouble he told no one, but he showed the gold piece that had been given him with proud pleasure, and asked the starost to make a hole in it, as he wished to keep it always, and to wear it on the ribbon round his neck with the little iron cross put there at his baptism.

He told what the priest had said to him, adding, however, "But of course he was mocking me; no one could believe such a foolish story as that."

Every one present agreed with him, except Pope Nikita, who pondered awhile, and then said thoughtfully, "Who knows? it may have been.   After all, One greater than the Czar put his hands upon the poor sick folk and healed them." *

* Alexander's part in the adventure told above is historically true, even to the smallest particular. The only liberty taken has been that of transferring the scene from the bank of the Wilia to that of the Oka. The story became known in England through a private letter, and the Royal Humane Society sent the Czar a medal—rather a singular "decoration" for a monarch. He "accepted it with a noble and modest simplicity," and profited by the circumstance to introduce a similar society into his own dominions. For the description of his personal appearance one contemporary authority amongst many may be cited: "Malgré la régularité et la délicatesse de ses traits, l'éclat, la fraîcheur de ses teints, sa beauté frappait moins à la première vue que cet air de bienveillance qui lui captivait tout les cœurs, et du premier mouvement inspirait la confiance....Il avait l'œil vif, spirituel, et couleur d'un ciel sans nuages ; sa vue était un peu courte, mais il possédait le sourire des yeux, si l'on peut appeler ainsi l'expression de son regard bienveillant et doux....Son front chauve, mais qui donnait à l'ensemble de sa figure quelque chose d'ouvert et de serein, ses cheveux d'un blond doré, arrangés avec soin comme dans les belles têtes des camées ou des médailles antiques, semblaient faits pour recevoir la triple couronne de laurier, de myrte, et d'olivier."

CHAPTER IV.

IVAN'S HORIZON WIDENS.

O child ever dreams of being grateful for food and shelter, unless taught by the sad experience of destitution. The little guest expects to be welcomed to the feast of life, and even assumes that the board has been spread on purpose for him. Ivan was no exception to the rule : hitherto he had received the devotion and tenderness of those around him as a matter of course ; perhaps indeed he was in danger of exacting them as a right, and of becoming, as he grew older, proud and overbearing. But now a change had come. If he knew that he was noble, he had also gained a glimpse of the great truth that " Noblesse oblige." He had begun to reflect, and to some purpose.

" Bativshka," he said one day to the starost, " why was it you were afraid to let the lord Zoubof or the steward Dmitri know who I was ?"

" Because they might have killed you, Barrinka, out of spite and jealousy, knowing that your father was our lord before Zoubof came."

" But would they have done anything to *you*, bativshka, for taking care of me ?"

" Oh ! as to *that* I don't know. Perhaps I might have had the knout."

Ivan bent down and kissed the old man's hand.

The next morning, when the family rose early to begin the toils of the harvest, Ivan rose with them. " I am going to the field," he quietly observed, putting on his oldest garments.

All protested, especially mativshka, whose love for her foster-child amounted to weakness.

" Dmitri and Vasil and little Peter are going, and they are all younger than I am," said Ivan.

" But *they* are only little mujiks," she answered. " They must work hard for their bit of rye bread and their bowl of kasha. It was for that God made them."

" Boyars work too ;—I am a boyar," said Ivan, raising his fair head proudly ; and he went with the rest.

To do him justice, he bore himself bravely in the field, although the unaccustomed toil wearied him quickly, and it was tantalizing to find himself so easily outdone by Michael's stronger limbs and more practised hands. Yet, after all, it was no great hardship to bind the sheaves along with Anna Popovna all the morning, and at noon to share with her his dinner of okroshka.*

But harvest-time does not last for ever. At length all the sheaves were gathered in : the wheat to be sold for the profit of the lord of the soil ; the rye to be transformed into the black bread, the kvass, the kasha, which were the staple of the mujik's diet ;—for, as they said themselves in one of their terse though homely proverbs, "Wheat picks and chooses, but Mother Rye feeds all fools alike." Then the long blank winter settled down over Nicolofsky, which, like the rest of Russia, "lay numb beneath the snow" for many a month in the year.

During this silent, dreary season the industrious fingers of the girls and women found occupation in spinning and weaving. The lads too made lapti, wove rude baskets, and prepared fire-wood ; and these occupations were often pursued in social gatherings, and lightened with jest and song and story. Still

* A kind of cold soup made of kvass, with small pieces of meat in it.

there was abundant leisure, in which the young people amused themselves with games of babshky—little pieces of mutton bone, which they used as English children use nine-pins—while their elders sat beside the stoves, and too often enlivened their gossip with much vodka. In this respect, however, Nicolofsky contrasted rather favourably with other villages, since the starost and the pope were both temperate men and set a good example.

They were great friends, and during their long confidential talks one question often came uppermost, What was to be done with Ivan when he grew up? In a country like Russia, where sons almost invariably followed the calling of their fathers, and every man's position was assigned him by the fact of his birth, it was peculiarly difficult to find a niche for a waif like Ivan. A mujik, of course, he could never be; nor a priest, since he was not a popovitch, or priest's son; nor a merchant, that would have been a terrible degradation for one who was born a boyar; nor a soldier, for his village friends had not the influence necessary to procure him a commission, while had he been drawn for a recruit they would at once have provided a substitute. But Ivan was not old enough to share these perplexities. The knowledge that he was by birth a boyar, with the desire, sincere though ignorant and wavering, to be worthy of his destiny, sufficed him for the present.

Thus two long winters passed away. A second spring had come, heralded by the eight days of drinking and carousing which the Russians call the Mässlanitza, or "Butter-week." Then the long fast went slowly by. At last came the crown of the Russian year, with Easter eggs, and joyous greetings, and manifold festivities.

One fine evening, a few weeks after, a kibitka, or rude one-horse vehicle, drove up to the starost's door. Its occupant, a well-dressed man, whose hair and beard of iron gray showed him past the prime of life, flung the rope that served him for a rein on the horse's neck, and entered the izba. He first made his reverence to the sacred picture in the corner, then courteously saluted the starost and his wife, who, without speaking, placed some bread and salt on a carved wooden trencher and offered them to him. He tasted both; and this indispensable ceremony performed, he began at once to make known his errand.

"God save you, Alexis Vasilovitch!" he said to the starost. "Do you chance to remember in your early youth one Feodor Petrovitch, who was born here?"

"Feodor Petrovitch?" repeated the starost, stroking his beard meditatively.

"Feodor Petrovitch?" cried his wife. "Yes, I think *I* remember him. Had he coal-black hair, and eyes like an eagle's?"

"That he had; but the hair is now snow-white, and the eagle eyes—well, no marvel, they served him fourscore years.— I am his eldest son, Ivan Petrovitch."

"Ah, I too remember him now!" said the starost, "though, like my wife, I was but a child when he went away. Many a time our old folk have told us how our good lord, Prince Pojarsky, the last but one, took such notice of him on account of his bright face and clever ways—how he had him taught to read and write and to count up money. At last he took him away somewhere, so that after he came to man's estate Nicolofsky knew him no more."

"All quite true. The prince sent him to Moscow, and when his education was finished he gave him a sum of money to trade with. My father quickly doubled it; and, unlike most men, he brought every kopeck honestly to his lord. 'Go on and prosper,' said the prince. 'Take that money with thee and double it again.' He did so. Then said the prince, 'Feodor Petrovitch, thou hast paid me thy last obrok. From this day thou art free.' He divided the money into two parts, declaring himself well satisfied with half, and leaving the other half to my father to start with on his own account. Large hearts had the Princes of Pojarsky, one and all, God rest their souls! From that day all things prospered with my father; and now he and his have silver and gold more than enough for their needs. For he has sons and sons' sons, all prosperous—one here and one there, as God wills. About fifteen days ago, tidings reached him, through Dmitri, Zoubof's steward, which filled his aged heart with joy. The grandson of our lord is living still, and among you. I am come the bearer of my father's earnest prayer that you would give the boy to him. It will be his pride and pleasure to have him taught all that a young noble ought to know, and so to maintain and provide for him that he may go without shame among his equals, and live the kind of life that is right for such as he. And I, the son of Petrovitch, say that therein my father will do well. Since every rouble and kopeck we have came from Prince Pojarsky, it is right that some should go back to his heir. But my father prays of you to send him the little lad at once, while yet he can see his face, for God's hand is fast drawing down a curtain over his aged eyes. What say you, Starost Alexis Vasilovitch?"

The starost paused. At length he said firmly, though in a broken voice—"That we love our little lord too well not to send him with you—ay, and that thankfully, though it wrings our hearts to part with him. Ah! here he comes himself.— Ivan Barrinka, this good man will take you with him to Moscow the holy, and make of you that which it is your birth-right to be."

Petrovitch gazed admiringly on the tall, graceful figure of the handsome lad, now about fourteen, and looking considerably older. "Praise be to God!" he said. "That is a goodly shoot from the old stem."

Ivan's face changed rapidly from pale to red, and from red

again to pale.   At last he said, " Bativshka, I will do what *you* think I ought."

" Then, dear child, you will go from us ; for like should ever dwell with like."

But the old foster-mother lifted up her voice in lamentation, mingling her tears for her " little dove," her nursling, her treasure, with regrets that his shirts were not in order, that the new socks they had been knitting for him in the winter were not finished, and that his boots wanted mending.

" We will see to all that in the city, good mother," said Petrovitch, unable to repress a smile, as he pictured the extraordinary transformation Ivan's outer man would have to undergo before he could take his pleasure in the Kremlin gardens with the *élite* of Moscow society.

Hospitality is a plant that flourishes luxuriantly in Russian soil, and seems to find the smoky atmosphere of the izba as congenial as the clearer air of the palace.   It was with great difficulty that Petrovitch could fix his departure for the next day but one ; but a single day of rest for himself and of preparation for Ivan was all that the starost's importunities could obtain from him, since he knew his father's anxiety about the result of his mission.

That evening, in the starost's cottage, there was much baking of wheaten bread, of cakes called kissel, and of greasy, indigestible pastry called pirogua.   There was also a great slaughter, —a sheep, a couple of sucking pigs, and quite a multitude of fowls were sacrificed on the altar of hospitality ; for the whole of Nicolofsky would no doubt *assist* at the festival of the next day, not in the French, but in the English sense of the word. Huge buckets of kvass were of course prepared ; and it might have been better if this harmless beverage had not been supplemented by a plentiful supply of vodka.

Next day began, not unworthily, with a service in the church, a kind of farewell to Ivan and compliment to Petrovitch.   But its remaining hours were wholly given up to revelry, and it is to be feared that but few sober men went to rest that night in Nicolofsky. Meanwhile Ivan bade farewell to the friends and playfellows of his childhood. With Anna Popovna his parting was a tearful one. He kissed her again and again, and vowed that he would come back and marry her as soon as his beard was grown.

"God be praised!" said her mother, who was standing by. "See how St. Nicholas protects the innocent, and will not let him take the sin of a false vow upon his soul! He does not dream, poor child, that his beard will never grow at all, since he is born a boyar, who will have to shave it off every morning —worse luck for him."

But the saddest and most tender farewells were spoken at daybreak on the following morning, when Ivan was kissed and wept over by his foster-parents, and by all their immediate family. His own eyes were dim as he took his place in the kibitka beside Petrovitch; and when he turned to look his last upon the brown cottages of Nicolofsky, he could scarcely see them through his tears.

"But the winds of the morn blew away the tear." By-and-by Ivan cheered up a little. He roused himself to listen to his companion's stories of the great city, and began to be interested, and even to ask questions.

There was not much in the incidents of their journey to engage or rivet his attention. They crossed the Oka upon a raft —horse, kibitka, and all—but not at the spot so well remembered by Ivan as the scene of his adventure. After that came the long monotonous Moscow road, where everything seemed to Ivan always the same. Only that his senses assured him he was moving, and that rapidly, he would have fancied himself fixed in the centre of the same horizon, which was revolving around him eternally and unchangingly. Plains of sand, forests of birch or pine, went by in endless succession, merely diversified here and there by some pasture lands, or by a brown village built upon the pattern of Nicolofsky. On one occasion, however, they passed a company of horsemen carrying long lances, and clad in gray cloaks, with ample hoods drawn over their heads.

"Who are these?" Ivan asked with interest.

"Cossacks. I suppose they are going to join the army. They had better have stayed at home now that peace is being made with the French. That unlucky peace!" he grumbled, touching his horse rather unnecessarily with his long whip.

"Why do you say that? I thought peace was always a good thing. We have a proverb in Nicolofsky, 'A bad peace is better than a good quarrel.'"

"A bad peace with your enemies sometimes means a worse quarrel with your best friends.—On, my little pope! Now, now, my beauty, my darling, mind what you are about. Gee up, you barbarian!" This to his horse, the wheel of the kibitka having stuck fast in a deep rut. A touch of the whip, this time in earnest, and the horse bounded on, freeing the wheel with a jolt that brought Ivan to his feet, and shook peace and war alike out of his thoughts. But Petrovitch, more accustomed to the ordinary incidents of travel, presently resumed the thread of his discourse.

"What does peace with France mean? War with England, for one thing. And that—what does that mean? Our ports shut up, our trade destroyed. No market for our timber, our corn, our tallow, our furs. Ruin, ruin!" groaned the merchant.

"I have heard of France," said Ivan. "But England—what is that?"

"England is a great, rich, beautiful country, with the sea like a wall of defence built by the hand of God all around it. The King of England hates Napoleon, and has sworn before the picture of his saint never to make peace with him."

" I have heard of Napoleon too," said Ivan. " The recruits who left our village said they were going to fight against him. Pope Nikita thinks he is a magician."

" Pope Nikita thinks truly. It is said he has for his wife a beautiful lady named Josephine, who transforms herself at will into the likeness of a white dove, flies into the midst of his enemies, hears all they say, and comes back and tells her lord.* No one can resist him; the Emperor of Austria and the King of Prussia are both at his feet, and he has conquered all the other kings and dukes of the Nyemtzi, except the King of England."

" But the Czar—why does not the Czar send his soldiers and tell them to kill him ?" queried Ivan.

" Not so easy !" Petrovitch answered with a short laugh. " However, there is little to be said after all. Russia has fought him long and well. If the devil helps his own, what can good orthodox Christians do ? Think of Austerlitz, Eylau, Friedland—blood and tears have flowed in torrents. I know a widow who lost her two sons at Austerlitz. Another ;—but why speak of these things ? War is always terrible."

" Then why don't you wish for peace ?"

" A *good* peace might be very desirable, but save us from a peace that will ruin our commerce !" cried Petrovitch with energy. " The Czar has evil counsellors around him who are persuading him to that sort of peace. Perhaps, indeed, Napoleon has bewitched him with his sorceries. Who knows ?"

Having thus uttered, not merely his own sentiments, but those of Moscow and her merchants upon the subject of the Treaty of Tilsit, at that time in progress, Petrovitch relapsed into silence. The only part of his discourse that greatly impressed Ivan happened also to be the only part of it which had

---

* This fable was extensively believed in Russia, and not exclusively by the lower classes.

not at least a considerable substratum of truth—the story of the beautiful lady who could transform herself into a white dove. The rest he understood very partially.

After a journey of many days, a happy change came over the spirit of what had almost seemed to Ivan a long and dismal dream. The dreary expanse of sandy waste was succeeded by a green, fertile, well-cultivated plain, diversified by the gentle slope of wooded hills and the gleam of a winding river.

At last, one evening, they reached the summit of a lofty eminence. Petrovitch, who was on foot leading the horse, turned suddenly to Ivan, and said in a tone of solemnity, "Take off thy cap, Ivan Barrinka, take off thy cap, and thank God for thy first sight of holy Moscow!"

Any traveller might have thanked God for the beauty of that sight. Dome and cupola, minaret and tower, shone beneath them in the evening sunshine, giving back its rays with dazzling brightness from their gilded tops; and some there were which flamed like balls of fire suspended in the air. The brightest and most varied of colours—green, purple, crimson, blue—relieved and diversified the gleaming gold of the cupolas and the burnished lead of the roofs, which looked like silver. Beyond the bewildering glories of the Kremlin, whose feet were kissed by the bright waters of the winding Moskva, the great city stretched away into the distance. To the eye there was no limit: streets and squares and gardens, gardens and streets and squares; here a castle, there a blooming terrace; yonder a painted gateway, everywhere light and colour, and shining metallic surfaces that reflected the sun. "Forty times forty churches" pointed upwards with their "silent fingers," as if to remind the dwellers in that city of palaces of the yet fairer city which is eternal in the heavens, even the new Jerusalem, with its streets of gold and gates of pearl.

Ivan crossed himself. "Beautiful! beautiful!" he murmured, as he gazed like one entranced on the scene before him.

"Upon God's earth there is no spot like that," said Petrovitch, stretching forth his hand and pointing to the city. "'If I forget thee, Jerusalem, let my right hand forget her cunning.' God keep Moscow the holy, Moscow the beautiful, the ancient city of the Czar, the fairest jewel of his crown, the apple of his eye!"

CHAPTER V.

PETROVITCH.

> " Oh, but soon ye read in stories
> Of the men of long ago;
> And the pale, bewildering glories
> Shining farther than ye know."

OUR travellers had still a long drive before them after they entered the stately gate called "the Gate of Triumph." The ancient capital of the Czars enclosed, within the vast circumference of its painted walls, gardens, orchards, terraces, even parks and pleasure-grounds, in this as in other ways resembling an Eastern city. In due time, however, the merchants' quarter was reached, and Ivan Petrovitch drew rein before the gateway of a long, low, wooden building, or rather range of buildings, painted in various colours. He was evidently expected and watched for; quite a crowd of men, women, and children, servants or members of the family, hurried out to meet him, and his young companion shared the welcome and the greetings that followed. Ivan Petrovitch, however, took him by the hand, saying to those who were pressing around them, "Stand back, brothers and sisters; no one should speak to the little lord until he has been presented to our father."

He led Ivan into a spacious room or hall, of which the furniture, though far from answering to Western ideas of comfort, showed conclusively that wealth was not lacking, for vessels of silver, rugs of costly fur, and rich Turkish carpets were there in abundance. But Ivan scarcely noticed anything, except the great arm-chair at the upper end and the venerable figure of its occupant. "My father," said the younger Petrovitch, as he gently placed the boy directly in front of him, "I have brought thee our little lord."

The old man rose slowly from his chair, leaning upon his staff. His hair was white as snow, and so was the beard which reached nearly down to his waist. His large, dark eyes, once so full of fire, were dim with age, but an ardent soul glanced forth from them even yet, and they had, moreover, a wistful, pathetic look, as if seeking the light which was fading from them. "God be gracious to thee, Prince Ivan Ivanovitch Pojarsky," he said solemnly, laying his hand on the young fair head which was bowed before him in instinctive reverence. Then he kissed the boy, and having seated himself once more in his chair, drew him close and examined his features. " Like his grandfather, my dear friend and master," he said at last.

It was evident, from the silence which followed, that thoughts of other days came crowding fast upon the old man's memory. But he soon aroused himself from his reverie to bid Ivan welcome to Moscow, and to commend him to the care of the members of his family who had gathered around them.

These now came forward, drew Ivan gently away, and lavished upon him every kindness and attention that could be devised. He was charmed with his new friends, and quickly and easily took his place as the honoured guest of the great heterogeneous household united beneath the roof of its venerable head. There were sons and sons' sons, daughters-in-law and grand-daughters, and quite a tribe of servants, forming altogether a little clan rather than a family. This large household had all the necessaries of life in abundance, and many of its luxuries, though only such as the old Muscovite manners and traditions fully sanctioned. For Petrovitch was an autocrat in his own house, though usually a just and generous one. Woe to the son or grandson of his who should presume to "deface the image of God" by shaving his beard, to exchange his caftan for a French paletôt, or to lose his roubles and peril his soul at the fashionable game of loto! This strong personal government was the secret of the domestic peace which, on the whole, prevailed in the household, notwithstanding the many different elements of which it was composed.

There was only one person who ventured to take liberties with the patriarch—to tease him, coax him, sometimes even jest with him, always to claim his caresses as a matter of right, not, like the others, as a rare, occasional favour. This was little Feodor, a bright, black-eyed boy about three years younger than Ivan. The mother of this favourite grandson had been the only daughter of Petrovitch, and she was dead. Much of the old man's heart was in the grave with her, nor could his seven brave and prosperous sons wholly supply her place.

Ivan's first days in Moscow were spent in viewing its wonders, under the guidance of one or other of the Petrovitch family. Feodor was often with him, and soon became his particular friend ; for his playfellows at Nicolofsky having been dull and slow, the overflowing merriment of his new acquaintance was a welcome change. He was shown the marvels of the Kremlin,—its palace, its three cathedrals, its bell-tower of Ivan Veliki, to the top of which he ascended and beheld the panorama of the city stretched out beneath him like a picture. He saw also the great Cathedral of St. Basil, in the "Beautiful" Place outside the Kremlin wall. He saw the Chinese city and the dwellings of the Tartars ; he wandered through the streets and rows of the Grand Bazaar. In fact, he saw so many wonderful things that his power of wondering was exhausted, and he soon ceased to be much impressed by any of them.

Each time that he returned from one of these expeditions, old Petrovitch would call him to his side, and make him sit where he could see his face. One evening he said to him,

"God make thee as brave and true as thine ancestor, the great Prince Pojarsky, who delivered Moscow from the Poles."

"Who was he? I have never heard of him," said Ivan.

"Is that possible? Poor child! did no one ever tell thee that story, so glorious for thee and thine? Know, then, that about two hundred years ago the Poles conquered holy Russia. The whole country was at their feet, in great misery and trouble, and no man dared resist them. Prince Pojarsky lay on his bed in his own castle, sick as it seemed unto death. But God put it into the heart of a poor man working at his trade in Moscow, a butcher named Minim, to save his country. He first went to all the great people of the city and of the surrounding country, and got them to promise men and money. Then he went to Prince Pojarsky, and stood before him like a messenger from God. 'Rise,' he said; 'go forth and conquer the Poles. God will strengthen thee.' 'But soldiers are needed, and arms,' said the prince. 'All are ready,' answered the courageous citizen. The prince arose from his bed of sickness, and, trusting in God, put himself at the head of the men of Moscow. He gained a glorious victory, and the sword of the Poles was broken for ever in Muscovy. That is the man whose name you bear, and whose blood is flowing in your veins, Prince Ivan Pojarsky!"

"He was splendid!" said Ivan with kindling eyes; "I am proud to bear his name."

Petrovitch felt shocked by the disclosure of Ivan's ignorance of the history of his native country, that country which was to himself the object of proud and passionate love.

"Can it be," he said to him the next day—"can it be that no one has ever even told you about the great Czar Peter?"

"I have heard of the Czar Peter," said Ivan: "he ordered all the mujiks to cut off their beards, threatening to cut off their heads if they refused. 'God will make your beards grow again,' he said; 'but will he do the same for your heads?'"

Petrovitch built a long and interesting narrative upon this

very meagre foundation of historical knowledge.   He had little
Feodor for a listener as well as Ivan, and the intelligent questions of the boys drew out the information he loved to impart.
Especially graphic was his account of the Swedish defeat at
Pultowa, and the horrors of the retreat that followed—horrors
that seem to have prefigured those of a yet more awful retribution near at hand, though still wrapped in the mysterious veil
of the future.

> "File after file the stormy showers benumb,
> Freeze every standard sheet, and hush the drum ;
> Yet ere he sank in nature's last repose,
> Ere life's warm torrent to the fountain froze,
> The dying man to Sweden turned his eye,
> Thought of his home, and closed it with a sigh :
> Imperial pride looked sullen on his plight,
> And Charles beheld, nor shuddered at the sight."

Then, gradually bringing down the narrative to more recent
times, he told of the great Czarina Catherine—of the splendours
of her court and the triumphs of her arms—especially of the
conquest of Poland, in his partial eyes only a just retribution
for the past wrongs, and a glorious achievement of the prowess
of holy Russia.   At last, though with some reserve, he spoke of
the short, sad reign of the Czar Paul.   "God sent him for our
sins," he said.

This reserve only piqued the curiosity of the boys.

"It is true he wrought much evil," he admitted, in answer to
their questions ; "but still his heart was good.   It was his head
that went astray.   Oh, my children, there are sorrows in the
world darker than you have ever dreamed of !   Seems it sad to
you to sit as I do now, and see the beautiful light of God's
world fading from me day by day ?   What is that to the desolation, the anguish, when God lays his hand upon the immortal
light within and turns it into darkness ?   The Czar Paul was
not himself when he sent half his nobles to Siberia, shut up
his own son in prison and threatened his life—ay, even the life
of the Empress.   His true self fought long against the demon

that possessed him. Many a time did he listen to his son, though he never loved him, when he dared bravely to plead for and shelter the victims of his wrath. More than once he said regretfully, after some unusual outburst of violence, 'I wish I had consulted the Grand Duke Alexander.' But such a state of things could not go on. The end came."

"What was the end, dädushka?" queried Ivan. (Dädushka, "little grandfather," the term of endearment constantly used by Feodor, was often adopted by Ivan.)

"Do not ask me of the end," said the old man very sorrowfully. "It was said in official proclamations, it is still written in printed books, that 'the Czar Paul Petrovitch died of apoplexy.' But all the world knows that is false. Some there are, too, who will have cause to know it when they come to stand before the judgment-seat of God."

"He was murdered," said Feodor with decision. "That is what *I* have always heard."

"Were the people sorry for him, or glad of his death?" asked Ivan.

"Glad exceedingly. They were delivered from a reign of terror. Yet there were men who loved the Czar Paul truly —who love him still, and will take that love with them to the grave. One such I know—my good friend and patron, from whom I have received many favours, Count Rostopchine. He kept proudly aloof from the court of the new Czar, would hold no communication with him, and take no favour from his hands—hands which, he dared to hint, were not pure from the stain of a father's blood. When the great battle of Austerlitz was lost, Count Rostopchine said, 'God would not prosper the arms of a bad son.'"

"How angry the Czar must have been!" said Ivan. "He ought to have sent him to Siberia, to repent of his insolence."

"He did not send him to Siberia, nor have I heard that he was angry. It is the guilty who are angry, and from that stain the soul of Alexander Paulovitch is white as the snow from heaven.—Of the necessity of removing the Czar Paul from the government, and placing him under restraint, there was no shadow of doubt; and to that he had given his consent—*only to that.* When he knew what had been done, his horror and anguish were unbounded. At last he was not so much persuaded as compelled to take up the blood-stained sceptre which the conspirators laid at his feet. I saw him myself, on the day of his coronation, yonder in the Cathedral of the Assumption, and sadder face have I never seen upon living man than that young handsome face of his. Often yet I seem to see it, and to hear the very tones of his voice, as, kneeling before the altar, he recited the solemn coronation prayer: 'May I be in a condition to answer thee without fear in the day of thy dreaded judgment, by the merits and grace of Jesus Christ thy Son, whose name is glorified for ever with thine, and with that of thy holy and life-giving Spirit.' God fulfil that prayer! Amen."

A brief silence succeeded the sublime words, uttered so reverently; but presently the old man resumed :—

"Six short years only have passed since then ; but I charge you two, who are children now, to lay up in your hearts the things that have been done in them, and to tell them to your children and your children's children. The Czar Alexander Paulovitch has freed the Press, has abolished the secret police, has refused to make use of spies. He has utterly forbidden every kind of torture as a blot upon humanity. He has also forbidden the confiscation of hereditary property."*

"Dädushka "—it was Ivan who spoke now—"I do not understand what you are talking about. What are those things which you say he has forbidden?"

---

* It is, perhaps, scarcely probable that a man of the character and position of Petrovitch, an "old Muscovite" and a *protégé* of Rostopchine, would have appreciated these liberal measures. But Petrovitch is supposed to be unusually thoughtful and enlightened. Upon other points, especially upon the French war, he is made to share the usual sentiments of his class.

"Ah, child, I forgot. So little do you know as yet of wrong and cruelty, that the story of the efforts to redress them falls without meaning on your ear. But the young do well to remember much they cannot understand. As for me, I was born a serf, like my father and my father's father; and these lips of mine shall be silent in the grave ere they forget to praise Alexander Paulovitch. Before his time we were bought and sold like the beasts of the field. You might read a notice in the window of a shop, 'To be sold :—An active and capable servant, and a good milch cow. Inquire within.' This he forbade; forbidding also the removal of peasants from the land. He permits and encourages the nobles to set their serfs at liberty whenever they will; and if they are without land, he himself advances them money to purchase their homesteads. He has deprived their lords of the dangerous privilege of sending them to Siberia without a trial; nor dare any one, however rich or great, use his serfs with harshness or cruelty. Amongst many stories of his interference on behalf of the oppressed, I remember one concerning a great lady, whose name I will not tell you, as she lives in this city. From that love of money which the priests tell us is a root of all evil, she neglected her sick and aged serfs, and allowed them to suffer from want. The Czar heard of it, and he sent his own physician to minister to these poor suffering peasants, whom no man cared for. Dr. Wylie—so they call him—a shrewd, clever Scotchman, took care to order his patients so many expensive remedies and comforts that the princess, by the time she had paid for wine and wheaten flour, and I know not what besides, had also learned the useful lesson that nothing costs so dear in the long run as a duty neglected. Nor has the Czar given the mujik that which costs him nothing. He refuses absolutely to grant men as serfs to his courtiers; and thus he has dried up the unfailing stream of wealth wherewith all the Czars that went before him have enriched and rewarded their servants without impoverishing themselves. God give it back to him in the prayers of the poor! Moreover, I have heard that every year, out of his own treasure, he lays by one million of roubles to aid in the fulfilment of his beloved and cherished dream—to make the body of every mujik on the soil of holy Russia as free as his soul is already in the sight of God."

The rapt, kindling expression of his face as he spoke thus impressed the children deeply. He seemed to be gazing far away into some " white starry distance " where he could see the fruition of that glorious dream. But gradually the light faded, and the shadow passed once more over the aged face.

" Who shall see that day ? " he murmured sadly. " Not the old ; their work is quickly over, while God's work goes on but slowly. No, not the old ; they are content to lie down in hope, waiting for what God will let them see in the resurrection morning. But the young.—He is young yet, this Czar God has given us, whose youthful dreams are not of pleasure, or conquest, or glory, but of loosing the heavy burdens, letting the oppressed go free, and breaking every yoke. Shall it be given to him to see the desire of his heart ? It may be—before his hairs are white as mine. But it may not. I have heard the priests say that, after all, it was not Moses who led the children of Israel into the Promised Land."

Ivan and Feodor waited in respectful silence until his reverie was over. Then Ivan began to question him upon a subject about which he was interested, and indeed perplexed.

" Dädushka, why do you seem to think the Czar ought not to have made this peace with Napoleon for which all the bells in the city have been ringing ? "

" There be many reasons, boy—good reasons and bad, noble reasons and selfish. Of the selfish reasons I need not tell you. You are now surrounded by merchants ; you will soon be surrounded by nobles. No doubt you will hear lamentations enough from both—for the luxuries wherewith English commerce supplied the tables of the one, and the gold with which it filled the purses of the other. But what, perhaps, you will never hear, is the truth that lies buried beneath that stream of idle talk. Have you ever, in Nicolofsky, listened on winter nights to the low howling of the wolves amidst the snow? There is a horrible story I remember hearing in my childhood about a woman—a mother—who was making a winter journey in her sledge with her five little ones. Perhaps you too know the tale? The famished pack with their demon voices howled around her sledge. To save all the rest, as she fondly dreamed, she sacrificed one child, her youngest. Then a moment of respite, a verst or two gained upon the savage pursuers—a wild, fleeting gleam of hope. Then—*then;*—but I need not go on. She reached her journey's end alone, to die the next day, accursed and broken-hearted.* Forget the story if you can, but remember the awful lesson. The taste for blood grows with what it feeds on, and the doom of the coward only comes the more quickly from his guilty efforts to avert it. The French are wolves, and Napoleon is a demon. Already has he devoured the nations of Germany, and it has but whetted his appetite for fresh victims. He deceives the Czar—who is young, and likes to think others as true and generous as himself—with his offers of peace. But the peace he offers is only from the lip out; for he hates us, and he will never cease to hate us. Why not? We stand upright, while the other nations—all except the English—bow down and kiss his feet. But they are all infidels, those Frenchmen. They believe neither in God, nor saint, nor devil. Therefore I think that if we had put our trust in God, and gone to war with them again, he would have protected holy Russia, the land of his people and of his orthodox Church."

Old Petrovitch, in speaking thus, expressed the thoughts and feelings of the mass of his countrymen. They were ignorant and superstitious, but they were devout. They believed in

* Readers of Mr. Browning's "Dramatic Idylls" will remember "Ivan Ivanovitch."

"the God of Russia," and in the Czar as the first of his servants. A time was drawing near when this belief of theirs should be tried in the furnace heated seven times. The trial proved beyond a doubt that metal was there, genuine and enduring; but how much was the pure gold of faith, and how much the iron of a fierce fanaticism? There is one test potent to divide between the gold and the iron. The fanatic may endure like a martyr and fight like a hero; but when the battle is past, and the victory won, he will trample on the fallen like a tyrant;— for his God is the God of vengeance. But while the man of faith can suffer and fight, and that with a heroism as undaunted, he can also pardon;—for his God is the God of mercy, and He whose "right hand holds him up" makes him "great" with " His gentleness."

CHAPTER VI.

IVAN'S EDUCATION.

" Our young people think they know everything when they have learned to dance and to speak French."—Words of the Emperor Alexander, quoted by Madame de Choiseul-Gouffier.

ETROVITCH the merchant would have thought himself greatly lacking in his duty towards Ivan the boyar if he had suffered him to remain beneath his roof. As soon as he had provided him with a fashionable outfit—that is to say, an outfit composed of garments fashionable in Paris three seasons previously—he transferred him to the palace of a widowed lady of rank who had promised to act as his guardian. He was to associate with her sons, and to share with them the instructions of the French tutor whose services were then considered indispensable to every young Russian of noble birth. For these advantages Petrovitch paid very liberally: in many families, even of the highest position, good silver roubles were not as plentiful as they were desirable, and were not likely to be rejected when they presented themselves for acceptance.

Feodor was deputed to accompany Ivan to his new home, since the elder members of the family did not care to present themselves. It must be owned that the little Russian, in his glossy blue caftan of the finest cloth and his bright silken sash, had the advantage of his companion, who looked as awkward as a naturally graceful boy could contrive to do with his limbs confined in the tightest of French garments.

Having reached the stately painted gateway of the Wertsch family mansion or palace, the two boys were admitted by the porter and led across an ample courtyard into a large saloon furnished in a manner utterly strange to Ivan. As no one was there, he had time to indulge his wonder and curiosity. Chairs and tables, divans and ottomans, with many other objects, of the uses of which he had not the slightest conception, were scattered about in profusion; the woodwork was painted rose-colour or lilac, and lavishly adorned with gilding, while the numerous cushions were covered with a kind of tapestry of a shining gray. At one side of the room a row of slender shafts, rose-coloured and tipped with gold, supported climbing-plants in luxuriant flower; at the other, three large windows looked out upon the terrace and the pleasure-grounds beyond it. Ivan thought these windows were open, and was stepping confidently towards one of them, when Feodor pulled him back with a laugh. "Take care, Prince Ivan," he said; "that is one great sheet of glass. I have seen such before; they cost—oh, I know not how many roubles. But come, let us look at the orangery;" and he pointed to a trellised door at the farther end of the room.

Here a fairy scene met their view. Oranges gleamed amidst dark glossy foliage like "golden lamps hid in a night of green;" heavy clusters of grapes, purple and amber, hung high above their heads; peaches, apricots, and plums ripened temptingly beside them—for in that ungenial climate many fruits that grow elsewhere in the open air require the protection of glass. Wonderful was the wealth of flowers, all of which were new to Ivan. Sheets of blossom—gold, and purple, and scarlet, azure, and creamy white—wooed his delighted gaze; and ever and anon he paused as some rare peculiar beauty, rose or lily, geranium or costly orchid, attracted his eye with the richness of its colouring or the grace of its form.

But this was not the first " orangery " (all greenhouses were then called orangeries in Russia) which Feodor had seen, and he had no objection to show off his larger experiences before his senior and his superior in rank. He could even name to him a few of the flowers. "Look here," he said, as he paused before a plant laden with clusters of graceful bells, their dark crimson sheaths half concealing cups of white faintly tinged with rose-colour; "that is called fuchsia. There is one of the same kind in the Kremlin gardens. Last winter's frost nearly killed it; but it lives still—a thick, stunted, hardy bush, with little red flowers, as unlike as possible to this one. That is like me, and this one before us is like you, Prince Ivan. You are going to be put in the orangery, because you were born a boyar; while I am left outside in the frost and snow. After all, I had rather be myself than you. It is hot here in the orangery, and there is not room enough—one could not run or play in comfort."

He was about to try the experiment by indulging in a race from one end of the tiled passage to the other, when a strange figure was seen approaching them. It was that of a young lad with flat, ugly Tartar features, and very fantastically dressed. He was one of those Calmucks whom the Russian nobility had a singular fancy for keeping in their houses as pets; although, as they grew up, they often proved very troublesome to their patrons. With a grin and a bow he informed the boys that the countess was ready to receive them, and invited them to follow him into her presence. Having passed once more through the saloon, they entered a boudoir richly furnished and adorned with hangings of blue and silver. An elderly lady, dressed in exaggerated French fashion, reclined on a couch. Her appearance was not improved by two rows of teeth dyed an ebony hue, a curious Russian custom of the period. She played with a fan, which was rather useless in that climate, while she conversed in French with two gentlemen in frock coats who sat near her. When Ivan entered, she languidly extended her hand, glittering with jewelled rings, and addressed some words to him in the same tongue. He looked embarrassed, but the ready Feodor came to his aid. "Pas Français, madame," he said.

The Countess Wertsch accordingly condescended to the use of her native language, in which she bade Ivan welcome cordially enough. She then gave him a French *bonbonnière*, and told him to help himself and his companion to its contents, while she continued her conversation with her guests. Ivan could not help thinking, from the manner of the speakers, that this conversation had reference to himself, and he was beginning to grow hot and uncomfortable, when Feodor effectually diverted his thoughts by taking out his pocket-knife and cutting upon one of the bonbons—a large almond covered with chocolate—a striking likeness of the countess's rather peculiar face. He was on the point of indulging in a laugh which might have had awkward consequences, when a young man, dressed *à la française*, and carrying in his hand a long pipe tipped with amber, lounged into the room.

"This is Adrian, my eldest son," said the countess, turning to Ivan. "You are to be fellow-students, so you ought to be friends.—Adrian, this is Prince Ivan Pojarsky."

Adrian made a bow, and addressing himself to Ivan, asked if he had seen the new piece at the French theatre.

Ivan, who thought he meant a new part of the building, answered with simplicity, "I do not know; everything I see here is alike new to me."

"Then I shall have the pleasure of introducing you to a great many things," said Adrian, with a smile, and, by way of a further overture of friendship, he took out and presented a jewelled snuff-box. Ivan supposed this to be another kind of *bonbonnière;* but fortunately for himself he was not attracted either by the look or the odour of its contents, and declined with thanks.

At length the older guests took their leave, and the countess turned her attention to the boys. She seemed struck with the appearance of Ivan's little companion, and asked him many questions, which he answered with a grace and sprightliness that interested her still further.

"I should like to keep both of you," she said to Feodor. " Will you stay with me, and become my little page of honour? I will have you taught French, and you shall be always with your friend Prince Ivan."

" I thank you, madame," Feodor answered gravely. " But I cannot leave my grandfather. I belong to him, and I will stay with him always—*always*," he repeated with earnestness.

" But, my little lad, your grandfather is very old. Some day he will die, and then what will become of you ? "

" When he dies, I will die too," said Feodor resolutely, with a glow in his dark eyes.

" Wait, boy, till you are ten years older," laughed Adrian, " and for no man in the world will you say as much as that. As for a woman—well, I know not ; you may have your fever-fit like another, and get over it, and laugh at it."

Feodor gave him a surprised, incredulous look, and repeated quietly, "When he dies, I will die too." Then, turning to the countess, he took his leave in words he had been carefully instructed to use : " May I be permitted to kiss your hand, madame ? My grandfather will expect me at home."

She responded graciously, and asked Adrian to take him into the orangery and give him some fruit. Ivan went with them, being anxious to see the last of his little friend. They passed a half-opened door, which the boys had not noticed before. Within was a kind of oratory : sacred pictures glittered in frames of gold and silver adorned with jewels, and lights were burning before them in massive silver candlesticks. Adrian turned in, but not to make his reverence, as the boys supposed. On the contrary, he deliberately used one of the candles to light his pipe. Ivan and Feodor were both horrified, and Ivan said, "How can you do that? The saint will be angry, and some harm will happen to you."

"My dear innocent babe, when you know a little more you will believe a little less. Ah, here comes *Mousié*, our French professor.—M. Thomassin, here is your new pupil, Prince Ivan Ivanovitch Pojarsky."

A dapper little Frenchman glided noiselessly towards them, and bowed profoundly. But the ceremony of introduction accomplished, Adrian went off with him, much to the relief of the boys, whom he left in the charge of a servant, bidding him supply Feodor plentifully with fruit.

That day was the beginning of a new life for Ivan. His versatile, imitative Russian nature stood him in good stead. Ashamed of his ignorance of what Adrian and Leon Wertsch knew so well, and perhaps with the same feelings of emulation towards them as of old towards Michael, he devoted his quick intelligence and his retentive memory to two branches of study, —the French language and the art of reading. The average Russian is a remarkably good linguist, and Ivan was much more than an average Russian. It very soon became unsafe for "*Mousié*" to say anything in his presence which he was not intended to understand; nor was it long before he could read sufficiently well to amuse his leisure with the worthless sentimental romances then, unhappily, popular in Russia.

In other ways his education made rapid progress. He soon appreciated the attractions of the French theatre; he learned to like the taste of champagne; and cards and loto were substituted for the homely babshkys of his childhood. Under the tutelage of M. Thomassin—as worthless and unprincipled a Frenchman as ever professed and propagated the doctrines of Voltaire— the Wertsches were growing up into frivolous, dissipated young men of fashion, and open scoffers at what they styled a stupid and antiquated superstition. Their mother, a thoroughly ignorant woman, with a thin veneering of showy accomplishments, was a little horrified when their contempt for things she had been accustomed to revere was manifested in her presence; but she supposed that all must be right which was taught them by a fashionable French "professeur." At all events, they only did like other people in the *beau monde*, and its opinion was her idol.

Once only did Ivan see her really provoked. He often visited his kind old friend Petrovitch, as indeed for every reason he was bound to do. The easiest way of reaching or returning from the merchants' quarter was by crossing the river, in summer by a ferry-boat, in winter on foot or in a sledge. Once, however, just when the ice was beginning to break, and the passage was difficult and rather unsafe, Ivan stayed with the Petrovitches for dinner, and came home in the evening in a drosky by a longer route. The countess, before his return, had been a little alarmed for his safety, but was much more annoyed when he made his appearance and explained how his day had been spent.

"It is well enough to *visit* people like the Petrovitches," she said. "But to *eat* in their house! such a thing is never done in the world—*never!* For Heaven's sake, Ivan, do not let any one know of it. You would be talked about."

Adrian, who was present, took Ivan's part. "After all, mother," he said, "in St. Petersburg his Imperial Majesty has been known to drink tea in the house of a merchant."

"His Imperial Majesty," replied the countess with solemnity, "had better take care of himself."

"Which," returned Adrian, "he is abundantly able to do."

"Of course, Ivan," Madame Wertsch resumed, "you can go to the Petrovitches at proper times and in a proper way, when the old man wishes to see you."

"He will never see me again," Ivan answered sadly; "he is quite blind now."

One incident of his first winter in Moscow shocked Ivan considerably, though it made scarcely any impression upon those around him. Coming out at midnight with the Wertsches from a sumptuous entertainment at the palace of a friend, they found their little postilion lying dead in the snow, close to the horses' feet, with the reins still wound around his stiffened arm. The child—a mujik of twelve years old, chosen for his beauty—had fallen from his seat overcome by cold and fatigue, and the coachman, himself half frozen, did not know what had happened until too late to help him. Such accidents were of daily occurrence, Ivan was told, during the frosty weather. No one seemed to think much about it; he was only a mujik, one of the "black people," in the eyes of the fashionable world little better than beasts of burden. But Ivan was haunted for weeks with the dead face of the pretty boy, to whom he had often given a few kopecks to buy sweetmeats. Another face came before him too with a reproachful, accusing look—the face that he had seen bending compassionately over the senseless form of Stefen Alexitch. Ivan often looked for that face in public places, in fashionable assemblies, in church; but it is needless to add that he looked for it in vain.

About two years after his arrival in Moscow, Ivan made an expedition to Nicolofsky to visit his old friends. Although scarcely sixteen, he already considered himself, and was considered by others, quite grown up. The young Russian of that day ripened early into manhood: fifteen was a usual age for entering the army, and education was then considered complete. Still, though he thought himself old enough for any adventure, Ivan might have postponed his journey for another year, had not the proprietor of a neighbouring estate, who was going to spend the summer at his country house, obligingly offered him a seat in his carriage.

He had provided himself with gifts for all his friends, and ransacked the "Silver Row" in the Great Bazaar for the prettiest ear-rings and bracelets he could procure for Anna Popovna. The welcome he received was everything that could be desired—affectionate, enthusiastic, and admiring. There was but one exception. Michael Ivanovitch scowled upon him with undisguised ill-humour. He would like to know what brought him there, he was heard to mutter; adding that the less boyars and mujiks had to say to one another the better for both. Otherwise, his visit was a complete success. He returned to Moscow fancying himself desperately in love with Anna Popovna, and the hero of one of his favourite romances, in which princes sighed for shepherdesses and queens wedded clowns. An attack of fever, which he had shortly afterwards, and which kept him for some time confined to the house, gave him leisure to indulge his dreams and reveries.

As he grew older, the works of Voltaire and Diderot began to replace in his esteem the flimsy, unreal productions of the novelists. M. Thomassin's only genuine love was a love of pleasure, his only genuine hatred a hatred of religion. Consequently he taught his pupils just enough to make them sensualists and scoffers like himself. He bid fair to succeed as completely with Ivan as he had done with Adrian and Leon Wertsch; indeed Ivan would probably go farther than they, because his nature was stronger and his character more energetic. What has no root is easily displaced. The religion of Ivan's early years was a mere superstition, a matter of outward forms and observances; therefore, when he ceased to attach importance to these, he lost everything. "From him that hath not shall be taken away even that which he *seemeth to have.*" There was no mental conflict, there were no keen and bitter searchings of heart. From a dead faith he glided almost insensibly into a dead scepticism, and by neither the faith nor the scepticism had the profound slumber of his soul been at any time disturbed.

He continued to attend the numerous church services because

others did so, and because the exquisite music (in the Greek Church entirely vocal) and the gorgeous ceremonial gratified his taste. He also observed, at least as strictly as those around him, the long and severe fasts of the Church; availing himself, however, of such evasions as were sanctioned by custom: "name days," for example, which happened to fall in Lent were sure to be honoured with a double measure of feasting.

Meanwhile his emotional nature craved excitement and his mind needed occupation. Genuine, earnest study under a competent teacher he would have thoroughly enjoyed; but the Greek and Latin lessons with which M. Thomassin supplemented his instructions in French were very superficial and perfunctory. Fortunately he had another master for Polish and German; and with these languages he took some pains, because a knowledge of them was necessary in order to obtain a commission in the army. But even in these his interest was slight; for at present he found the attractions of the ballroom and the gaming-table far more powerful than those of the library.

The narrow world of pleasure in which he lived thrilled but faintly to the shock of those mighty impulses that were moving the great world around him. Now and then he heard the strife of many tongues which accused the Czar of blindness for having made peace with Napoleon at all, and of weakness for keeping that peace in spite of numberless provocations. In those days, any one who heard the talk of the *salons* in Moscow and St. Petersburg might have thought it the easiest thing in the world to measure swords once more with the conqueror of Austerlitz. Ivan shared the sentiments of those around him, and accordingly he was overjoyed when at last, in defiance of Napoleon, the ukase was published which reopened the trade with England under the protection of neutral flags, and foreign luxuries appeared once more upon the table of the noble, while foreign gold glided quickly into the purse of the merchant.

He shared, too, the universal indignation at Napoleon's
atrocious spoliation of the Duke of Oldenburg, the Czar's
brother-in-law, perhaps the most flagrant of his many violations
of the Treaty of Tilsit. Ivan was breathing an atmosphere
highly charged with electricity, and full of the indications of
an approaching storm ; but he knew not the signs of the times.
Besides, how was it possible that he, whom competent judges
were calling the best dancer in Moscow, and who was the
acknowledged favourite of fortune at all games of hazard, could
disquiet himself about the designs of Napoleon and the prospect
of a war with France ?

CHAPTER VII.

"Still the race of hero-spirits
Pass the lamp from hand to hand;
Age from age the words inherits—
' Wife, and child, and fatherland!'"

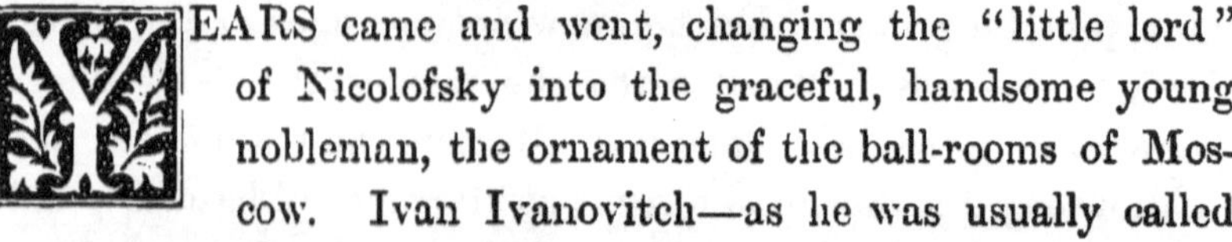

YEARS came and went, changing the "little lord" of Nicolofsky into the graceful, handsome young nobleman, the ornament of the ball-rooms of Moscow. Ivan Ivanovitch—as he was usually called by his numerous friends, such use of the father's Christian name being accounted the best style and the highest courtesy in Russian society—had now completed his education. He spoke French, the French of the *salons*, in perfection; he played the violin; he danced with exquisite grace; he was an adept at cards and loto.

This last accomplishment was a dangerous one. Diderot's famous saying, "Russia is rotten before she is ripe," had but too much truth in its application to the higher classes. A superficial foreign civilization too often covered without eradicating the barbarism from which the nation was only emerging, and thus the vices of the one state of society were added to those of the other. In the brilliant circles where Ivan moved, no form of vice was rare, except perhaps intemperance. The noble did not usually misuse his champagne as grossly as the mujik did his vodka; but this was the only particular in which he set his poorer brother a good example.

The most fashionable vice of the Russian nobility at this
period was the perilous excitement of the gaming-table. In
this, as in other things, the licentious court of Catherine II.
had been to the whole empire a very seed-plot of corruption.
It is recorded that on one occasion the Empress herself had
been unable to obtain a glass of water, so engrossed were pages,
equerries, ladies-in-waiting, even grooms and porters, with their
cards and their dice. Things were altered now. Alexander
neither played himself, nor permitted any one to play for
money within the precincts of his palace ; but when once evil
seed has been sown, who can eradicate the crop that springs
from it ?

Adrian Wertsch was now a tchinovik ; that is to say, he had
obtained a place under government which gave him an official
tchin, or rank, corresponding to a particular grade in the army,
the standard of all honour under the military despotism of the
Czars. Leon had a commission, and had recently joined his
regiment. Like every one else, he was greatly excited by the
prospect of the war with France ; but, like nearly every one,
he thought the vast army Napoleon had been collecting was
intended to winter in Germany, and that the grand drama
for which all the world was looking with strained eyes and
eager hearts would not be played out until the following
summer.

About Ivan's future there was some perplexity, but of a
kind which no one was in a hurry to solve. His education had
begun very late, and his present life of elegant dissipation was
very pleasant. Still, when Count Rostopchine became Governor of Moscow, early in 1812, Ivan's friends thought it well to
present him, acquainting the count with his position as the
penniless heir of a great though proscribed name. But
Rostopchine was a Russian of the old school, in whom the
proverbial " Tartar " was very near the surface. He surveyed
Ivan critically, from his perfumed hair to his silk stockings

and jewelled shoe-buckles, and muttered contemptuously, as
he turned away, " Dandified French coxcomb !"   To Count
Rostopchine the French, with all their works and ways, were
anathema.

Ivan's heart was not broken by this repulse, though he took
his revenge for it in a clever lampoon, much applauded in the
salons.   He plunged the more madly into every form of excitement and dissipation.   For a while fortune continued to smile
upon him, and all things went well ; his heart was glad, his
laugh light, and his step elastic.

But a bitter hour came at last.   One night the debts scored
against him upon the gaming-table grew and grew, until the
total became absolutely alarming.   Of course he was plied with
the usual arguments, " Go on ; your fortune will change,—you
will retrieve all ; "—and, of course, he yielded.   The fascination
of companionship was upon him, and the yet more potent spell
of champagne completed his infatuation.   So far as he was able
to reflect at all, the very thoughts that ought to have checked
his madness only stimulated it.   He could not bear that his
associates should taunt him with cowardice, but it was still
more intolerable that they should suspect him of poverty.   The
fear made him desperate, and he went on wildly and recklessly,
lavishly increasing his stakes, lest any one should surmise the
truth—that he was risking more than he possessed.   But at
last that very fear arrested him when on the brink of ruin.
Seeing him so heavy a loser, his friends came forward with
offers of assistance, which they urged, nay, even pressed upon
him.   But he rejected all.   Not to these would he become a
debtor ; for what hope could he entertain of repaying them ?
There was only *one* in all the world to whom he could turn for
real help in the hour of need.

It was not until the next morning that he fully realized his
position.   He awoke unrefreshed from a short feverish sleep,
and drank the tea his valet brought him, but could not eat

Fortunes ten times larger than the whole sum of his debts changed hands continually over the card-tables of Moscow and St. Petersburg. But all things go by comparison, and what would have been little indeed to the lord of broad lands and toiling serfs, was much to the "merchant's pensioner," as Ivan bitterly called himself. He had no alternative but to go to Petrovitch, confess his folly, and throw himself upon the generosity of his kind old friend. This, to a youth of his spirit and temper, was a cruel humiliation. All his manliness, all his independence of character revolted from the task ; and it was equally abhorrent to his pride. Both the good and the evil in him were at war with the necessities of his position ; but both had to give way. He dressed himself quickly, left the Wertsch mansion without speaking to any one, hailed the first drosky he saw, sprang in, and gave his directions,— choosing the longer route to the merchant's house, that he might avoid the ferry with its possible delays. The driver, as he settled himself in his seat and grasped more firmly the long ropes that served him as reins, leaned over and asked him, "Gospodin,* have you heard the news ? "

"Curse the news ! " said Ivan petulantly. "Drive quickly, isvostchik,† and I'll double thy fare."

Yet absorbed as he was in his sordid, selfish trouble, he could not fail to see that some extraordinary change had passed over the city. At the street corners and in the thoroughfares persons of all classes were gathering in groups, talking and gesticulating. A few had letters or printed papers in their hands ; but those who could read were a small minority, and by far the greater number were discussing what they had heard from the lips of others. Now and then Ivan wondered languidly what had happened ; but his thoughts always slipped back to subjects of more pressing interest. What should he say to Petrovitch ? and what would Petrovitch say to him ?

* Lord, or Sir.   † Driver.

It was a glorious morning at the end of June,

> " The very city's self was filled
> With the breath and the beam of heaven."

Fair shone the gilded cupolas of the Kremlin, brightly gleamed the silver Moskva, and the gardens and terraces were blooming with a thousand flowers. Never had the old city looked more lovely, with the strange peculiar charm of its quaint barbaric magnificence toned and softened by those sweet influences of sun and air that touch the responsive earth like the benediction of Heaven. On that day Ivan scarcely noticed its beauty; but in after years the memory often returned to him,—like the last happy, untroubled look we have seen on some beloved face, ere it is dimmed by those shadows of disease and pain that prelude the darker shadow of the grave.

At length he reached the house of Petrovitch, dismissed his drosky, and walked in. He was accustomed to enter the old man's presence unannounced, to be recognized by the sound of his footsteps, and affectionately welcomed.

It was now almost four years since Petrovitch had become totally blind. God's hand had touched him gently, and the touch softened and ennobled him. The interests of commercial life, the buying, selling, and getting gain, which once occupied him so intensely, had faded from him now; and if still he ruled his household with a strong hand, it was less by fear and more by love. Feodor had learned to read on purpose to while away the long hours for him, though there were not many books in the Russian language likely to interest him. For romances in the French style, whether translated or imitated, he cared nothing at all; history, which he would have greatly enjoyed, had still to be naturalized in Russia; and, unhappily, the best Book of all was then locked away from the Russian in a casket of which the key was well-nigh lost—the old Slavonic tongue, more unintelligible to Petrovitch than the English of Chaucer would be to us. But a friend of his, Pope

Yefim, a priest of much more than average intelligence and seriousness, used often to visit him, and to tell him Scripture narratives, and repeat for him prayers or passages from the Psalter. "I can no longer raise my eyes to the holy pictures," Petrovitch was wont to say, "so I must learn to lift up my heart to God."

To-day Ivan found him surrounded by several members of his family. His eldest son stood before him; two or three others, sons or grandsons, were at hand; and Feodor, now a fine lad of sixteen, had perched himself as usual upon one of the arms of his chair.

"Father, your will is law," Ivan Petrovitch was saying. "Still it is rather hard upon me to be chained to desk and ledger because I am the eldest son, while sons, nephews, and grandsons are doing their duty."

"Thou too wilt be doing thine," the old man returned. "What if it be a harder one? Is it thy part, or mine, to choose?—But hush! are not the footsteps that I hear those of my lord's grandson?"

Ivan came forward, and the usual greetings were exchanged, though on his side in a tone of embarrassment, which did not escape the quick ear of Petrovitch.

"Prince Ivan," he said, "you are in trouble. Do you wish to speak with me alone?"

Petrovitch usually gave Ivan the title of prince, although, on account of his father's disgrace and his own equivocal position, the heir of Pojarsky had forborne to assume it in general society—a modest reticence which Petrovitch not only approved, but had himself actually recommended.

"It is true, dädushka," Ivan answered frankly; "I wish to speak with you alone."

At a sign from Petrovitch the others left the room, and without waiting for Ivan to begin, the old man said, "I know what you feel. Speak freely. What can I do for you?"

Ivan was greatly surprised at this address. Which of those who were present last night, he asked himself, could possibly have told the story of his folly, and how could it have found its way so quickly to the ears of Petrovitch?

"I do not think you *can* know what I feel," he began humbly; "I am so utterly ashamed of myself. You have so often warned me to be moderate in play, and as often have I made the best of resolutions, and I meant to keep them faithfully, but—"

He came to a sudden stop, astonished, even terrified by the change that swept over the sightless but expressive face of Petrovitch. Disappointment, sorrow, anger chased each other rapidly, like clouds before a stormy wind; then all these passed away and were succeeded by something too sadly like contempt. Ivan stood in silent embarrassment, unable to proceed with his story.

But he had said enough. After a pause, Petrovitch spoke in a cold, constrained voice, "So *that* is your trouble, Prince Ivan? You have lost money at play. How much?"

"Eight thousand seven hundred and fifty roubles," said Ivan in the low tones of penitence and shame.

"Silver or paper?"

"Paper," said Ivan, rather more cheerfully. There was an enormous difference in value between the two, although in neither case would the sum have been a large one in the eyes of extravagant Russian nobles.

"Do me the favour to call Feodor; you will find him in the next room."

Ivan obeyed; and Petrovitch, taking a key which hung round his neck, gave it with a few directions to his grandson.

Something in the old merchant's manner made Ivan stand before him in silence, without venturing a word of explanation or of defence, until Feodor's return.

The boy gave his grandfather a roll of bank-notes, clean and crisp, and immediately left the room.

In perfect silence the old man handed the notes to Ivan, who tried to express his thanks; but Petrovitch stopped him. "The money," he said coldly, "is a matter of indifference to me. You are more than welcome to it, Prince Ivan." Never until to-day had he addressed him in such a tone.

Ivan drew near, knelt down before his chair, and took his hand affectionately. "Dear old friend," he said, "I see that I have wounded you. Forgive me, for my grandfather's sake, —and for my own, for I love you truly."

The aged face quivered with suppressed emotion, yet Petrovitch drew his hand away. "You cannot love me, Prince Ivan Pojarsky," he said, "if you love not the land of your fathers."

"The land of my fathers!" repeated Ivan in surprise. "What can you mean?"

"Stand up, Prince Ivan," continued the old man, still speaking with sternness; "the posture of a suppliant does not become you. Do you think it is anything to me that you have lost a few thousand roubles at play? Do you think that if you needed my whole fortune I would heave a sigh or shed a tear as I gave it into your hands? But it *is* a grief to me, beyond sighs and tears, that trifles such as these should occupy the heir of Pojarsky when the foot of the enemy is on the soil of holy Russia."

"*What?*" cried Ivan, springing to his feet in amazement.

"Can it be possible you have not heard?" asked Petrovitch, the heavy cloud of displeasure beginning to clear from his brow. "At daybreak this morning the tidings came. They have crossed the Niemen, those barbarous hosts that own no God in heaven, no king on earth save that monster from the abyss they call Napoleon. They come—in the stillness and darkness I seem to hear their footsteps across plain, and forest, and river. They come to trample down the soil of our father-land, to water it with blood, to waste our fields, to burn our villages with fire, to make our wives widows, our children orphans; ay, and to do yet darker deeds than these, deeds which I have no words to tell. The storm has been gathering long; and now, at last, the thunder-cloud has burst upon us! My country, O God, my country!"

"But our cause is just," said Ivan. "Surely every Russian will fight to the death."

"This, indeed, will be a death-struggle," Petrovitch resumed. "Do you not understand? It is all the world against holy Russia—all the world, except England and Spain: England, far away, safe within her God-given rampart of crested foam; Spain already bleeding beneath the talons of the vulture. Russia, Russia only, stands upright, and refuses, as Pope Yefim expresses it, to bow the knee to the Baal, or rather to the Moloch of France. Therefore, the conqueror has forced the conquered to join his standard, and it is not only the legions of France who are pouring across the Niemen, but Prussians, Austrians, Saxons, Westphalians, all the men of Germany who are Napoleon's subservient though unwilling slaves; Poles, ever eager to trample on our pride and profit by our mis-fortunes; ay, even Spaniards, dragged from their vines and their olives to fight for the tyrant they detest." He paused, then went on again in a sadder tone and with even deeper feeling—"If in this dark hour God had but been gracious to us, and given us a bearded Czar!"

"A bearded Czar!" Ivan repeated in perplexed surprise.

"Yes. Do you not remember the words of the great Czar Peter? 'If ever again a bearded Czar shall sit upon the throne of Russia, all Europe may tremble.' He meant a true Muscovite Czar—stern, hard, and strong, like Ivan the Ter-rible long ago, somewhat like Count Rostopchine now. But instead of such a hero as the Czars of old—with the world in arms against us, God in his inscrutable providence has seen fit to send us Alexander Paulovitch."

"But, dädushka, the people love him."

"*Love him?*—with all their hearts. The men of Russia are not wood or stone. They love him well enough to be true to him to the death, if only he dares to be true to himself and to them. But that is too much to hope. All things must do after their kind. Does the antelope of the desert confront the tiger in his den, and tear from him his blood-stained spoil? Do men take the fine gold out of the furnace to forge it into their weapons of war? or the silk of China to spin into the cable that holds the ship of war to her moorings? But, Prince Ivan, I am talking wildly, perhaps idly and sinfully. Forget what I have said. After all, Alexander Paulovitch is the Lord's anointed."

"And you know that, since last April, he has been in the field with his army—where he ought to be."

"Where he ought *not* to be!" thundered Petrovitch angrily. "What we ask from our Czar is not the cheap courage of the recruit, whose one virtue is to stand and be shot at, but the far higher courage to think, to decide, to act for fifty millions of men. 'Thou shalt not go forth with us to battle,' said the men of old to their king, 'that thou quench not the light of Israel.' God put the heart of man in the very midst of his body, to send the life-giving blood to the strong hands, which in their turn are meant to defend it from scath and harm."

"True;—and it occurs to me," said Ivan quietly, "that my place is with the hands."

The face of Petrovitch actually lighted up. "Thank God for that word!" he said. "But I expected no less from Prince Ivan Ivanovitch Pojarsky."

Ivan had entered the house of Petrovitch that day a reckless, frivolous youth, capable indeed of nobler things, but absorbed in the pursuit of pleasure and in the petty, selfish troubles

it entailed upon him.   He left the presence of his aged friend
with the heart, the purpose, the thoughts of a man.   He felt
the ennobling glow of patriotic fervour.   His country was in
jeopardy, and he was ready to give his life for it.   He thought,
as he turned his steps homewards,—

" This is enough to make my brave ancestor, the great Prince
Pojarsky, arise from his grave to fight for holy Russia.   From
his grave?   There are living graves, far off in drear Siberia :
will the dead arise out of *these*, I wonder?   Dear, unknown
father—unknown, yet not forgotten—if still you see the sun
and breathe the air of this world, how would you rejoice to
come back and cover your stained name with glory !   But I
scarcely dare to hope your life has lingered on through all
these weary years.   If not, then mine are the only veins in
which the blood of Pojarsky is flowing.   Oh that I could win
our ancient honour back again ! "

CHAPTER VIII.

A NATION'S TRANSPORT.

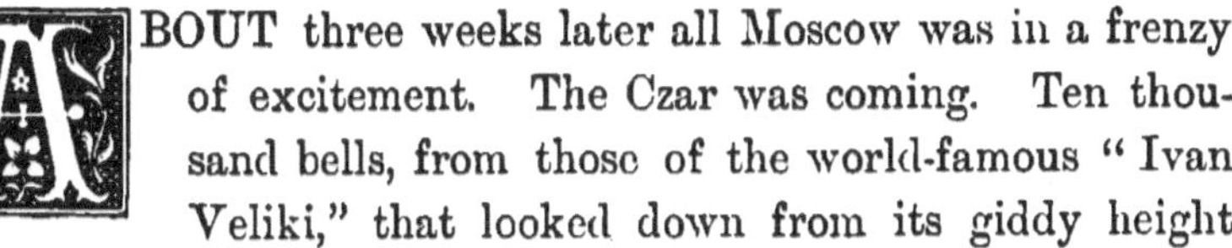

BOUT three weeks later all Moscow was in a frenzy of excitement. The Czar was coming. Ten thousand bells, from those of the world-famous "Ivan Veliki," that looked down from its giddy height upon the domes of the Kremlin, to that of the most obscure of her fifteen hundred churches, were clamouring their sonorous welcome. Cannon were ready to thunder a greeting yet more deafening, though far less musical; and the nobles and clergy were preparing a grand procession to meet their sovereign at the Smolensko gate. Meanwhile the people poured forth in a dense, tumultuous crowd to watch for his approach. Long and patiently did they wait; and the shades had fallen deep over the city, in which that night there were but few sleepers, when at last continued shouts and "houras" announced his appearance. Happy was he who could catch, through the darkness, even a glimpse of the unpretending open carriage, drawn by four unbroken horses from the steppes of Tartary, in which the Czar was wont to travel.

It had been a bitter sacrifice to Alexander to forsake his

armies, now face to face with the enemy, and retrace his steps to the centre of his dominions. But his generals had said to him, "Sire, your presence here paralyzes the army; it takes fifty thousand men to guard you;" and he was forced to acknowledge the justice of their remonstrances: a chance bullet —perhaps a bullet which was *not* a chance one; for Napoleon was no chivalrous antagonist—might at any moment leave Russia a prey to untold confusion.* On the other hand, a new army was urgently needed, and none but the sovereign could raise it; men's hearts everywhere were failing them for fear, and none but the sovereign could inspire them with hope and confidence. So "the great heart" returned "to the midst of the great body."† For the present.

On the morning after the arrival of the Czar in Moscow, Ivan was walking in a fashionable street called the Arbatskaya, not far from the Kremlin. Adrian Wertsch and two or three other young noblemen were with him. Like all the crowd amongst which they were moving, they had donned their richest and gayest dresses. Every one wore a festive air, and seemed to be making holiday in honour of the presence of the sovereign.

"Come, Adrian Nicoläitch," said young Kanikoff, the very person to whom Ivan had lost so many of Petrovitch's hard-earned roubles—"come, tell us how much of the show *you* saw last night."

"As much as you did," was the laughing answer; "or as our friend here, Ivan Ivanovitch."

"Oh, as for me," said Ivan, "*I* am born under an unlucky star. I am destined never to see his Imperial Majesty. During one of his visits to the city I was ill; during two I was absent; and last night, all I could contrive to see was the head of one of his horses."

---

* His heir would have been the wayward, eccentric Constantine, who, in such a crisis, could not have maintained his position for a month.

† De Maistre.

"Better luck another time. Stay, I really think we are going to have it now. Hark! listen to those shouts. What a throng there is though—all the 'black people' in Moscow pressing about us!—Come, come, good people; if it *is* the Czar, still you need not crowd us in this way. There is room enough in the world for all. Stand back, I say!—Ivan, take care of your purse!"

"No need," laughed Ivan; "there is nothing in it."

"Hush! he is coming. Off with hats and caps.—Yakovlef, of what are you thinking? Do not kneel, man; he has strictly forbidden it."

"Great St. Michael!" exclaimed Wertsch in another moment, "what a disappointment, and what fools we have all been making of ourselves!—Be quiet there, good people, and save your throats until you have something to shout for. That is *not* his Imperial Majesty; it is only one of his aides-de-camp, with some other person belonging to the suite."

"Eh bien!" said Kanikoff. "It is no wonder the servant was taken for the master. He is handsome enough for that." And he gazed in undisguised admiration at the splendid figure of the young aide-de-camp, with his plumed cap in his hand, and a galaxy of jewelled orders glittering on his breast, as he bowed gracefully to right and left in acknowledgment of the salutations of the crowd.

"That is Prince Ouvarov," said Yakovlef. "You seem to admire him."

"Who could help it?"

"Not the ladies of St. Petersburg, at all events. It is said he breaks a score of hearts every season. Once the Czar himself read him a lecture; and I am told he answered, with the utmost *sang-froid*, 'How can I help it, your Imperial Majesty? The ladies are such fools about me.' But would you believe it?—in war he is the Archangel Michael himself. He led the hussars at Austerlitz; and at Erfurt Napoleon asked, 'Which is the brave general who punished my infantry so sorely?' This young gallant, as beautiful as a girl, and as daintily curled and perfumed, stepped forward and said quietly, ' Je, sire.' ' You may not speak very good French, but you are a very brave officer,' said Napoleon, taking his hand kindly."

"Have a care, Yakovlef. If the people hear us talking of Napoleon, ten to one they will tear us to pieces."

"Not they, while the Czar is here.—Ivan Ivanovitch, what ails you? You seem lost in a dream. Wake up, my friend."

Ivan started.

"True enough," he said ; "I feel in a dream. I am perplexed, haunted, by the face of that man."

"Of Ouvarov?"

"No; of the other who rode beside him. That tall, gaunt, foreign-looking man. I have seen him before ; I am sure of it. But where? when?"

"I should think," said Kanikoff, "that you would care very little to see him again. He must ride out with Ouvarov on purpose to illustrate Beauty and the Beast."

"Ivan would like well enough to see him if he were ill," Yakovlef interposed. "That is the Czar's physician—Dr. Wylie, a Scotchman, very clever, but very ready with his lancet, they say. He has been accused of cutting off a man's head to cure him of a headache."

"The head of the man who allowed him to do it could have been little loss to its owner," laughed Ivan. Then he repeated thoughtfully, "His lancet ! I am sure I have seen him with a lancet. Of what can I be thinking?"

He was interrupted by Feodor, the grandson of Petrovitch, who pushed his way through the crowd to the group of young nobles. The handsome, dark-eyed lad, in his blue caftan and crimson sash, looked to no disadvantage amongst them. They all knew him, and greeted him with kindness, if also with a little condescension.

"I am so glad I have found you, Prince Ivan," said the boy breathlessly. "My grandfather thought you would like to see the benediction of the Czar with the holy picture. His friend, Pope Yefim, is to take part in the ceremony, and he says he can secure you a good place."

Ivan gladly accepted the offer; and in the short conversation that followed, the merchant's son was able to contribute materially to the information of his social superiors.

"Pope Yefim has seen a copy of the letter which the Patriarch wrote to the Czar," he said. "He was not able to come himself—for you know, gentlemen, he is nearly a hundred years old, much older than my grandfather—but he writes that it grieves him to the heart he cannot see the face of his sovereign—that face which is to him 'as the face of Christ.'"

Neither speaker nor hearers were startled by the expression which to us seems to border on the profane. But the profanity was unintentional, and the passionate loyalty utterly sincere.

Feodor went on—"He has sent him the sacred picture of St. Sergius, from the Troitza monastery. You know, gentlemen, that is the picture which the Czar Alexis and the great Czar Peter carried into battle, and it always gave them the victory. Though, my grandfather says, it is not the holy picture that gives the victory, or even the holy saint, but God himself."

"Thy grandfather seems to be a wise man," said Yakovlef. "But I wonder what the Czar himself thinks of the matter. People used to call him very enlightened, quite a philosopher, a disciple at heart of Voltaire and Diderot. I warrant me they are right, and he believes little enough."

The last remark was intended for the nobles, but it reached the ear of Feodor, who, to every one's surprise, both understood and answered it.

"The Czar," he said reverently, "must believe very much in

God, for he cares very much about the poor, whom God has made."

"God give him the victory over his enemies!" said Kanikoff; and the little group responded with a hearty "Amen!"—for, "beneath all the foam and sputter" of their light and careless talk, it was true that "the heart's depths boiled in earnest."

Such a benediction as the Czar was about to receive is often bestowed, in the Greek Church, even upon private persons who have in view some important enterprise, or wish to offer some particular supplication or thanksgiving. It is called a Molében; and it would be a beautiful and touching ceremony, but for the baneful influence of that superstition which too often leads its votaries to worship and serve the creature more than the Creator. Usually, most of the prayers are addressed to the guardian angel, or to the saint with whose picture the votary is blessed—the picture being then given to him as a kind of talisman.

The benediction was to take place on the 27th of July, and early in the morning Ivan entered the Church of the Assumption, the sacred spot where the holy anointing oil had been poured upon the head of the Czar. Pope Yefim had found for him a quiet niche, from whence he could witness the whole of the ceremony. He had room to stand or kneel: in Russian churches the worshippers never sit, however protracted the services may be. From his place of waiting he heard the tumult, the shouts and cheering, which welcomed the Czar as he approached. He knew that now he was ascending the "Red" or "Beautiful" Staircase, by which, upon state occasions, the Czars were wont to enter the cathedral; but he could not know that he was "followed by an immense crowd, who wept, and blessed him, and swore to defend his empire with their lives."*
He knew that now this Czar would take his stand, as other Czars had done, upon the summit of the staircase, to allow

* Madame de Stael, " Dix Années d'Exil."

the people beneath "to see the light of his eyes ;" but he could not know as yet how profoundly the mighty heart of that people was moved, "as the trees of the wood are shaken with the wind."

Clear and sweet as the song of angels rose the ringing treble of the boyish choristers, who welcomed the Czar as he entered— "Blessed is he that cometh in the name of the Lord !" The violet robes of the bishop and the assistant priests—the flash of innumerable jewels upon mitre, pall, and crozier—the faint perfume of incense—the sparkling drops of holy water flung from vessels worth the ransom of a king,—all these held the senses of Ivan, and wholly filled for a time his imaginative and impressible heart.

Meanwhile, the man who was the centre of all this pomp, and whose manhood for Russia in that solemn hour was more than worth it all, stood reverently in his place while the officiating bishop sprinkled him with holy water, or touched his forehead, his lips, his breast with the sacred picture. As the eyes of Ivan rested on that stately figure, peerless in its grace and majesty, a kind of awe stole over him. All the old superstitious reverence of the Russian for the Czar, who is "God upon earth," came upon him. It seemed almost an irreverence to raise his eyes to the face of the monarch ; he could scarcely dare to do it.

But a " Gospodin Pomilvi" of exquisite sweetness from the choir drew away his thoughts for a moment, and involuntarily he glanced towards the spot whence the sound proceeded. Then, once again he looked where all else were looking ; and suddenly a strange thing happened to him. As in a dream, he saw—instead of the gorgeous, dimly-lighted church, the gleaming vestments, the drooping banners—a green bank beside a river, a group of peasants, a cold and rigid form, a noble, compassionate face bending over it. He heard a voice that said, in tones of courageous hope, " My children, this is not death.

We will save him yet." For he knew that his boyar and the Czar Alexander Paulovitch were the same. Only, it seemed to him that now it was holy Russia that was lying numb and prostrate, and that the Czar had pledged himself to save. He would do it. From that moment Ivan never doubted it.

Besides the great ceremony of which the world was talking,* another, known to one only, took place in the church that day. Ivan drew out the piece of gold his boyar's hand had given him, and which, ever since, had hung round his neck. He kissed it, and made a solemn vow upon it, " Faithfully to serve my Czar; to live for him all my days; and, if God will, to die for him."

Yet once more his eyes sought the face of his sovereign, and never wandered from it until the service was concluded. But little could he guess what was passing in the soul of which that expressive countenance was sometimes the too faithful index.

Alexander's own hand has sketched for us in a few slight touches the conflicts of that period. Not then, nor ever, so far as we know, did the thought of St. Sergius, or of any other human mediator, interpose itself between his soul and the Divine Presence. But for some time past he had been wrestling hard in secret with questions which go down to the very roots of a man's being. Was there a God in heaven whose ear could be reached by that cry from human lips, " Gospodin Pomilvi"? And, if so, was he the "invented God," the " God afar off" of the deist and the philosopher; or the God of the Bible, the Father of our Lord Jesus Christ? Already these questions were answered for him, almost with assurance; but there still remained another. Would this God hear and help a man who was kneeling before him on behalf of fifty millions of other men whose destinies were committed to his keeping? Would he deign to touch him with his hand, to strengthen him with his strength? In those days the soul

<hr>

* An eye-witness tells us "how the image of St. Sergius was presented to the young Czar, whose handsome face, surrounded by the old banners in the dimly-lighted church, had a most picturesque effect." (See the " Memoirs of Madame Junot.")

of Alexander was feeling after God, if haply he might find him.

The service over, Ivan repaired to the Hall of Nobles, as one whose rank entitled him to find entrance there. He had to content himself with an obscure place in the crowded assembly, where he could not see the Czar, although he could hear his voice. In a noble address, Alexander laid before his subjects the full extent of the public danger. He concealed nothing; the strength of the invaders, the position of the army, its perils, its resources, its needs, all were revealed with a large-minded candour which would have honoured the constitutional monarch of a free people. In conclusion, he said that he " regarded the zeal of the nobility as the firmest support of the throne. In all times and on all occasions it has proved the faithful defender of the integrity and glory of Russia." Here his voice thrilled, faltered with emotion, and he paused amidst a universal cry that seemed to shake the massive roof and walls of the grand old hall—" Ask what you please, sire; we offer you everything."

One of the nobles proposed the gift of a serf in every twenty-five; but a chorus of eager voices interrupted, " It is not half enough !" Finally, one serf in every ten, ready armed and equipped, and provided for three months, was unanimously voted for the service of the Czar.*

While all this went on, Ivan sat in his place, silent and sad at heart. *He* had nothing to give,—nothing but his life; yet that, perhaps, might count for something hereafter.

In the meantime, a scene equally significant was taking place in the adjacent Hall of Merchants. Old Petrovitch repaired thither with the rest, leaning on the arm of his youthful guide Feodor, his eldest son, who ought to have accompanied him, being absent at the time. " I cannot see the face of the Lord's

* All these particulars, as well as those of the meeting in the Hall of the Merchants, are historical.

anointed," he said, "but I can hear his voice." This assembly, like the other, was densely crowded. Feodor contrived to find standing room upon the edge of a seat; and from this vantage-ground he was able to look over the heads of the throng of grave, bearded merchants. "Grandfather," he whispered, "the Czar is not here; only the Governor."

"God save his Excellency Count Rostopchine! Hearts of steel, such as his, are sorely needed now," the old man responded.

"But we can see *him* any day we like. It is the Czar we want to see," grumbled Feodor.

"Patience, boy; he is coming," said one of the merchants near them. "And, while we wait for him, it is *his* words the count is going to give us, not his own."

This was true. Amidst a hush of eager expectation, the Governor rose and read aloud the address of the Czar "to our ancient city and metropolis of Moscow." It contained the same explanations and appeals which at that moment in another place were falling from his own lips; and concluded with an earnest exhortation to prepare for "that defence which must now shield the babe at the mother's breast, and guard from sacrilege the tombs of our fathers. The very existence of our name in the map of nations is menaced. The enemy denounces 'Destruction to Russia.' The security of our holy Church, the safety of the throne of the Czars, the independence of our ancient Muscovite Empire, all call aloud that the object of this appeal may be received by our loyal subjects as a sacred decree. May the filial ardour spread itself from Moscow to the extremities of our dominions; and a force will then assemble around the monarch that may defy the thousand legions of our treacherous invader. The ills which he has prepared for us will then fall upon his own head, and Europe, delivered from slavery, may then celebrate the name of—"

"Alexander!" The words sprang from the lips of Feodor

Petrovitch, the youngest there, who spoke aloud the thought that thrilled in every heart, and knew not that he spoke until he caught the reproving looks of some of those around him. In the meantime Count Rostopchine calmly completed the sentence as it had been written—" Europe, delivered from slavery, may then celebrate the name of Russia."

Scarcely had he concluded, when the Czar himself stood amongst them, and with a few eloquent words wound up to its highest pitch the enthusiasm of the audience. Amidst the tears and acclamations which followed, the venerable chief of the merchants * stood up in his place and subscribed his name for the gift of fifty thousand roubles—two-thirds of his fortune. Others gave in similar proportion ; and Petrovitch was surpassed by none in self-sacrificing liberality. Feodor, under his directions, wrote his name upon the list of subscribers. When he had done so, he turned to his grandfather—" Dädushka, I think you must give the Czar something more even yet."

" Even sons and grandsons ?" said the old man, with a smile that had in it a little sadness and a great deal of resignation ; " well, I shall not refuse."

" *Even me ?*" said Feodor, nestling close to him and putting his arm caressingly about his neck. But Petrovitch did not answer.

" The people were willing," even beyond their power, so that three days afterwards the Czar published a ukase, not to ask for gifts, but to limit their amount. "The nobles literally gave him Russia," wrote the Sardinian ambassador to his sovereign. "They melted into tears ; in short, sire, there never was anything like it. The merchants have given him ten million roubles, and lent him fifty or sixty million."

But the mass of the people—peasants, mujiks, serfs, who tilled the soil—what part had they in this splendid outburst of

* Elected annually from their own body. His munificent donation was paid the next day.

loyal and patriotic enthusiasm? Napoleon expected that these "oppressed and degraded slaves" would hail him as a deliverer —would rise everywhere in revolt, and massacre their tyrants. Very different was the fact. When the time came for the serfs voted by the nobles to be levied from their estates, and when the vast crown lands had also to contribute their proportion of recruits, there was weeping and wailing in the izbas of every village from the Neva to the steppes of Tartary. But it was not, as in other days, the conscript who mourned his hard lot, and his mother, his sister, his betrothed who made sore lamentation over a separation probably life-long. It was the one *not* chosen who mingled his tears with those of his friends and parents, because he might not go and shed his blood for the Czar and holy Russia. Glad was the young recruit as he donned his simple uniform—a gray caftan, with loose trousers and a crimson sash; and proudly did he wear on the front of his gray cap the imperial badge, "a brazen cross surmounting a crown over the letter *A*." First and highest the cross, symbol of the Christian faith; beneath that, the imperial crown of Russia; again beneath that—Alexander.

But although putting himself, as he was wont to do, in the lowest place, and when possible out of sight altogether, the strong personal love with which Alexander had inspired his subjects counted for more, in that hour of a nation's conflict and agony, than the traditional religious veneration of the Russian for his country and his Czar. Well was it for Russia, and for Europe also, that the Czar God had given her was Alexander Paulovitch. It was not only that he had been, since the beginning of his reign, "perfectly just as emperor, singularly generous as man;"* not only that he was richly endowed with all those brilliant and fascinating qualities which take the eye and win the suffrage of the multitude. The secret of his influence lay deeper. God had given him a gift more

* Madame de Stael.

precious still. He had touched his heart with "the enthusiasm of humanity." This autocrat of fifty millions "loved his brother whom he had seen," even when as yet he knew not the divine Father "whom he had not seen." The hand that toiled so hard to bring back the perishing mujik from his death-like swoon was well used to deeds of beneficence. Of these a hundred stories might be told : at that time they *were* told, not only in the salons of St. Petersburg, but beside the stove in the izbas of many a country village. Everywhere the mujiks said, "Our lord the Czar loves us." And everywhere, as long as the world lasts, love will win love.

CHAPTER IX.

CLEMENCE.

"Vive, vive le Roi!
A bas la République!"—Vendéan War-Song.

IT is the fair and pleasant land of France—a land of corn-fields and orchards and sunny garden-plots, where quiet villages nestle in shady nooks, and old châteaux stand proudly amidst their sheltering woods. You feel everywhere that this land has been for many a century tilled and cared for by the hand of man; that generation after generation sleeps in peace beneath the shadow of its gray old churches. Long ages of toil and civilization have left their impress here, and the present is the heir of a glorious and venerable past.

Yet, perhaps no country has ever suffered more. War after war has swept over it; cruel oppression made the Revolution a terrible necessity; and, again, the excesses of the Revolution made men forget the crimes of the despotism that engendered it. And in the days of which we write there brooded over all the portentous shadow of another despotism—almost crushing enough to recall the worst days of Louis, falsely called the Magnificent, and of his thrice-accursed successor.

Still, even in those evil times many a secluded nook seemed to be hidden in the hollow of His hand, so quietly did it slumber throughout all—escaping not indeed occasional suffering, but anything like general ruin.

One such nook—a little pastoral village not a hundred miles from Paris—had in its immediate neighbourhood a spot yet more secluded, where a noble family of the " old *régime*," who otherwise might have wandered homeless exiles from their native land, found a welcome refuge. The simple four-roomed cottage, with the vine trained over its tiny porch, would have been an unpretending dwelling for the village smith or carpenter. Yet few could have looked on it attentively, even from the outside, and none could have entered it, without feeling sure that its inmates inherited the traditions of centuries of refinement and cultivation.

The morning sun of one of the earliest days of 1812 was streaming into the little porch. The weather was mild and beautiful—unusually so for the season. One person was enjoying it thoroughly—a lad of about seventeen, who reclined in the porch, intent upon a book, while the sunshine streamed brightly over him, and the breeze gently lifted his soft brown hair. The expression of his face was rather sweet than strong —his forehead was good, his eyes large and dark, his mouth well-formed and sensitive, but lacking as yet the look of resolution that might come with riper manhood.

So absorbed was he in his book that he did not hear an approaching footstep; but then it was a very light one. The young girl who came out from the parlour to join her brother was his senior by a year, and looked even more. She was tall, but her slight figure was well formed and graceful. Her eyes were dark, like her brother's; and her hair a glossy brown, very fine and soft. It did not wave or float, but was neatly coiled about a head which might have served a sculptor for his model. There was no weakness in the delicate lines of her face, though there was much tenderness. Her complexion was pale; but there was in her cheek a hint of possible colour, which came and went with every passing emotion. No one thought of calling Clémence de Talmont pretty, but in the

eyes of the few who loved her she was beautiful as the dream
of a poet.

"Henri," she said, in a gentle but decided voice—"Henri."

He looked up slowly, and said with a reluctant air, "Surely
it is not time for breakfast."

"Mother has had her coffee, and yours is ready whenever you
wish for it.   It is not *that*—"

"I had rather wait," said Henri, ignoring her last words. "I
want to see the end of Pizarro's expedition;" and he turned
over a page of his book.

"What are you reading?" asked Clémence, suppressing something like a sigh.

"Les Incas de Marmontel—a beautiful book," he added,
rousing himself. "Those old heathen monarchs, who lived for
their people, tried to make others happy, placed their glory
in being loved, not feared, *ought* to have had a better fate."

"I think *you* might find a better book," returned his sister,
with a slight tinge of asperity. "Marmontel was a friend of
the Revolution—a philosopher, a deist."

"Ah, sister mine, you would rather see me reading the Con-
fessions of St. Augustine," said Henri with a good-humoured
laugh. "But there is a time for all things; and I cannot
think ill of books that make me love God, and his beautiful
world, and the creatures he has made."

"True, brother," said Clémence earnestly and with a rising
colour; "only take care that the God you love is the God of
the Bible and the Church, not the God of the philosophers and
the *savants*.   But "—after a pause, and with a change of tone—
" but, Henri, will you not run down to the village before our
mother leaves her room, and see whether there is any placard
on the Mairie?"

Henri closed his book and stood up, the anxiety in his sister's
face reflecting itself, though faintly, upon his. "Why such
haste?" he asked.

"Babette told me this morning that she hears there is a new 'senatus consultus.'"

Henri's thoughts turned rapidly from the mild sway of the Incas, of which he had been dreaming, to the iron despotism of Napoleon, for him no dream, but a stern and terrible reality. "If there were twenty conscriptions," he muttered hastily, "you know I am under age."

"I do *not* know it," Clémence answered. "The curé says he fears all are liable who will complete their eighteenth year in 1812. That is why I want you to go and see whether the placard is there, before we alarm our mother. But take your coffee first, brother. I will bring it to you, if you like."

She brought him a cup of fragrant café-au-lait, and a fresh roll, prepared that morning by her own hands. He had just begun to eat and drink when a voice from an adjoining room—like her own, gentle and musical, but decided—called, "Clémence."

"Don't delay about the Mairie," she said as she hastened in. "I will tell our mother you are going for a walk."

Grave, sweet, and dignified was the lady who stood at the table in the little parlour. Her face was worn and pale ; the hair that appeared beneath her snowy cap was slightly silvered; and in her demeanour something of antique stateliness combined with the peculiar and inimitable grace of the old *régime.*

A dress of purple brocade, rich and stiff, lay on the table before her. "Come here, Clémence," she said ; "I want to make this dress fit you."

But Clémence shrank back. "Oh no, no, mother!" she said, with an air of pain.

"But yes," returned Madame de Talmont, in a quiet, peremptory voice. "Not a word, my daughter ; it is yours." And seating herself, she took up a pair of scissors, and began to rip off some antiquated trimming from the sleeve.

Clémence felt almost as if a living thing she loved was being hurt. Tears quivered in her eyes, and the colour rose to her cheek as she laid her hand on her mother's arm. "Mother, listen to me," she pleaded. "Do not touch that gown. It would never suit *me*. Is it well, think you, that I should go to mass on Sundays looking like a princess, while the few who know of our existence know also that we have scarcely bread to eat from day to day? Is it suitable? And besides, dear mother," she continued timidly, "you know I do not love gay clothing. I do not think it becomes a girl who, however unworthily, still desires and endeavours to lead a religious life."

"Be as religious as you please, my dear daughter," said Madame de Talmont, with a slight smile, "but be dutiful also, and believe that I know how Mademoiselle de Talmont ought to appear at mass much better than she does herself."

"Mother, that is not all," Clémence resumed. "I had rather keep that gown of yours all my life as it is now. It is part of my childhood; and, mother dear," she continued sadly, "there is so little of our childhood left to Henri and me. One of the earliest things I can remember is your showing that dress to me and telling me how my father brought it home to you the first time he went to Paris after his marriage, and how you wore it when you stood at the window of our old château in the Bocage, and watched him as he rode out with his men to join the Royalists."

"The last time I ever saw him—until I stood beside his death-bed. Ah, my child! that war in La Vendée has broken many a woman's heart."

"Still, mother, it was a *just* war. My father did well to die for his King."

"That is understood.   My children and I have a consolation denied to those whose dear ones perish every day in the frightful wars of this Corsican usurper.—But do not trouble thy heart about the old gown, Clémence.   Silk and brocade and such things fade and perish and are lost; but thy father's last look as he rode away—*that* remains, *that* is mine for ever.   Does not the Bible say that 'the things which are seen are temporal, but the things which are not seen are eternal'?"

"Yes; but—is *that* what it means, mother?"

"That may not be all it means, but it may mean that too."

Clémence yielded.   She was accustomed to give way to her mother; and indeed it is not usually the strong in heart who dispute pertinaciously about trifles,—like good soldiers, they reserve their fire until the right moment.   A consultation followed; and certain mysteries of cutting and placing, of letting out and taking in, were decided upon and arranged. While they were discussing the pattern of the sleeves, Madame de Talmont paused to ask, in a kind of parenthesis, "What has become of Henri?   I have not seen him this morning."

"He has gone for a walk."

No more was said until the ladies had entered upon the mechanical part of their task, and deft, skilful fingers were busy with needles and thread.   Then Madame de Talmont resumed, "Is it a fancy of mine, or is it true, that Henri becomes every day more like our cousin Louis?"

"That, of course, I cannot tell," Clémence replied, smiling, "since, as you are aware, mother, I have never seen Cousin Louis; though I find it hard to believe that.   From my earliest childhood I have thought of him and pictured him, until he has become a kind of friend to me—like the saints, or the holy recluses of Port-Royal."

"He was no saint, my daughter," returned Madame de

Talmont rather bitterly. "And an evil friend he proved himself to thy dear father."

"Yet, mother, he must have been one of the most lovable of men."

"He was fascinating, I do not deny. Besides, he was the head of our house—or, at least, he became so on the death of his father. And thy father could never forget that his own orphaned childhood and youth had been protected by the parents of Louis, and surrounded with an atmosphere of love and tenderness. Often has he talked to me of his happy boyhood at Vernier, where he and his cousin Louis were like brothers, and Victoire was the cherished sister of both."

"Cousin Victoire! Ah, mother, I wish you would tell me more about her. I have always felt such a romantic interest in this beloved and beautiful sister of Cousin Louis, and yet, somehow, I know very little about her."

"There is little to know, child," said the mother, with perhaps a shade of embarrassment.

"One thing perplexes me," Clémence resumed thoughtfully. "I remember to have heard you say that for generations the first daughter of our house has been always called Victoire. Now, *I* am not Victoire. Nor do I bear your name, mother, nor that of my father's mother, Léonie."

"Child, ere thou wert born, the name Victoire had become a sound of woe to thy father's ear. Once, perhaps, it may have been too sweet;—I cannot tell. Brought up together as they were, and with the grateful, reverential love he bore to all the De Talmonts of Vernier, it would have been but natural if— Still, when all things changed—"

"Mother, how was it that they changed so sadly? What could Cousin Victoire have done to grieve my father? As for Cousin Louis, I know that he became a Jacobin, a *bonnet rouge.*"

"Too true. Louis de Talmont—the child of a family of

unstained honour and unshaken loyalty, the nephew of the gallant prince who died so nobly on the scaffold for his King* —betrayed every sacred memory of the past, every holy hope for the future. I marvel that the dust of his ancestors did not rise from the battle-fields of their country to curse the wretch who bore part in the murder of his King." A red glow suffused the pale cheek of Madame de Talmont as she spoke, showing how hotly the fire of passion burned beneath its covering of proud and dignified self-control. With this lady of the old *régime* the affections of the heart were strong, but the traditions and prejudices of a class were stronger yet.

" But Victoire ?" Clémence ventured after a pause.

" Ah, Victoire ! Poor child ! she was more sinned against than sinning. But her life was wrecked ; and that sin lies at the door of Louis de Talmont. In those early days of the Revolution many foreigners came to Paris. With one of these, who was young, brilliant, wealthy, and noble, Louis formed, after his fashion, a violent friendship. M. le Prince, as we used to call him, had a fine figure, a handsome face, and the most splendid diamonds I have ever seen. But *there* was an end of his perfections ; and great as they may have been, they could scarcely atone for a head and heart as empty as air. Being a stranger, with nothing to lose, and no knowledge of our past to restrain him, he went farther than even his misguided teachers. There was no excess of the mob, in those evil days, in which he did not bear a part. In the Jacobin halls his voice was the loudest, his counsel the most violent ; and ever on his lips was that misused, delusive cry, ' Liberty, Equality, Fraternity.' It was to this man that Louis de Talmont must needs give the hand of his sister, the cherished daughter of his house."

" Poor Victoire ! How terrible for her ! How miserable

---

* He fought in the Vendéan War, and was taken prisoner and executed by the Republicans. He said to his judges, " J'ai fait mon devoir ; faites votre métier."

she must have been! And this foreign prince—did he perish on the scaffold, like our Cousin Louis?"

" No; he escaped that fate. When the storm he and his friends had evoked passed beyond their control, and the Revolution began to devour its own children, he found safety in flight."

" And Victoire?"

" His wife went with him. I believe he took her to his own country. It is but justice to say that he seemed to love her well. But her place here knew her no more; she has been dead ever since to all who held her dear. Her name has passed into eternal silence. And when God gave you to us, your father said to me, 'M'amie, for many years now the world has been talking of nothing but peace and love and the universal brotherhood of man; but because in the brotherhood of man men have forgotten the Fatherhood of God, their peace is ending in war, and their love in hatred such as earth has seldom seen. By the time this babe is a woman grown, perhaps once again the world will have tired of war and *victory*' (only in this way did he utter the name), 'and may be glad to be reminded of the existence of such things as clemency and forgiveness; so I propose that we call the daughter of our house Clémence.' Accordingly, Clémence you are."

" It is quite right, mother. I like my name. Clemency should always follow victory.—Ah! there is Henri. His step is tired and slow."

Henri came in, and in the old ceremonious way kissed his mother's hand and asked after her health. But the look that passed between them showed that although Madame de Talmont loved both her children intensely, her son was the very joy of her existence; while on his part, the love of his mother was the strongest passion that had yet found entrance into his young heart. His face was pale and anxious; indeed it wore almost an expression of terror.

" What is the matter?" his mother asked presently.

" Nothing particular,—nothing much," said Henri.

" Whatever it is, speak, my son,—and at once," said Madame de Talmont imperatively.

" There is a placard on the Mairie announcing that the drawing for the conscription is to take place next Thursday. It is as the curé told us: all are liable who will be eighteen in the course of the year."

Both his hearers grew pale, and the work fell from their hands. After a short pause his mother said, " It is plain you will have to attend. God grant you may draw a good number. But, at all events—" She remained silent for some moments, then she added, in a voice which struggled hard to be calm, " Bring me my desk, Clémence ; we must be prepared for the worst."

Clémence obeyed mechanically, while Henri stood silent and listless, watching her movements.

" Henri," resumed Madame de Talmont, " I am going to write to our good friend Grandpierre. *Should* the worst happen, you must escape, and go to him through the forest. He will shelter you."

" But, mother, mother "—the lad's colour came and went, and a quiver ran through his frame—" the risk is terrible."

" To *him?* He will venture it, for the House of Talmont, for his King, and for his God."

" To us all. Do you know how they deal with the *refractory*, as they call those who try to evade the conscription, and with their families ?"

Madame de Talmont raised her thin hand with a peremptory gesture, " Not another word, Henri. It concerns not thee or us to measure the danger ; the duty is all with which we have to do. I can bear to think of thee pining on bread and water, with a bullet chained to thy foot, and thy head shaved like a convict's ; I could *not* bear to know thee in the camp of the

Corsican tyrant, fighting to fasten his iron yoke upon the necks of free men. How could I look upon thy father's face in heaven, if I had reared and nourished his son for *this?*"

"But oh, mother, it is *you* I think of—you and Clémence."

"Whatever cross God lays upon us he will give us strength to sustain. Go, my children, and pray to him. I must be alone while I write this letter, for it will need to be very cautiously but very distinctly worded. The posts are not safe."

CHAPTER X.

> " Our God upon the cross,
> Our king upon the scaffold; let us think
> Of these, and fold endurance to our hearts."

CLEMENCE went into her own room, and Henri followed her. The chamber was severely simple, but scrupulously neat. The narrow bedstead might have suited a nun, and the table and chairs were of unpainted deal : but an ivory crucifix, exquisitely carved, hung over the bed; and the white-washed wall was adorned with a little tier of book-shelves, constructed by Henri, and containing a select and precious library—the " Augustinos " of Jansenius, the works of Arnauld, Nicole, and other divines of the school of Port-Royal, the sermons of Fénélon, and the letters of Madame Guyon. Most precious of all was De Sacy's translation of the New Testament; and next to this inestimable treasure, the volume best beloved and most carefully studied by Clémence was the Port-Royal edition of the " Pensées de Pascal." Many a line, marked by the hand of the thoughtful young student, showed her sympathy with the soul of the great teacher. Her heart, like his, had turned from all that earth could give to seek a more enduring rest and a better portion. Had she found it ? At least she had found much that was unspeakably precious—a God to be loved and served with all her mind, with all her soul, and with all her strength. But she had been taught to dwell rather upon his commandments

than upon his gifts, and was still far from recognizing, with St. Augustine, that he himself must give that which he commands. She had seen the mystery of the cross, but dimly and afar off, reading therein rather the exceeding sinfulness of the sin that had to be atoned for, than the unutterable greatness of the love that atoned for all. Consequently, her religion was one of surrender and renunciation, not of joyous acceptance and activity; death to the flesh was her watchword rather than life in the Spirit. The air she breathed was bracing and invigorating, but it was cold and sunless. If it were the will of God that Henri should become a hunted fugitive, that he should be arrested as "refractory," and should perish miserably in a fortress dungeon, there was nothing for her to say but this, "It is the Lord; let him do what seemeth him good." And having said it, she would still be an unprofitable servant. Her heart, it is true, would be broken; but what mattered that to any one?

While such thoughts passed through the mind of Clémence, Henri stood in silence, leaning against the little latticed window, and looking out upon the peaceful country landscape. At last he spoke. "They are gay enough in the village," he said. "They do not seem to dread the conscription half so much as they did last year. In fact, this new war is very popular. Mathieu Féron, who was standing in his father's forge when I went by, said *he* would be glad to be drawn; and Jacques Bonin, and that other lad who is with him, were of the same mind, saying they would like nothing better than to go and give the Russians a good beating."

"What miserable folly!" said Clémence with bitter sadness. "What have the Russians done to us, that the blacksmith's son and the butcher's boys of Brie should be eager to go and kill them?"

"I daresay you know as well as they do," returned Henri.

"'It is in his heart to pluck up and to destroy kingdoms not a few,'" Clémence quoted. "But, Henri," she added, with a sudden gleam of hope, " may not good for *us* spring out of this madness of theirs? Might we not, even if you draw a bad number, find a substitute? You know there is nothing we would not part with to raise the money—*nothing.*"

Henri shook his head. " Last time," he said, " the price went up to three thousand francs, and beyond it. Indeed, it was difficult to get one at any price. But that is not all,"—he lowered his voice : " Clémence, I have reason to think M. le Maire means no good to me."

She started. " Why do you say that?" she asked, with a quick fading of the new-born hope.

" Quietly as we have lived here," Henri resumed, " we are not quite unknown. Every one is aware that I am the son of Henri Charles de Talmont, who died for his King in La Vendée. I have no favour to hope. On the contrary, I think M. le Maire would be glad to see me with a musket on my shoulder."

" If that be the case," Clémence returned sadly, " at least we may thank God that he cannot tamper with the numbers."

" The numbers we are to draw? They matter less than you think. The lists *must* be filled up ; and so many young men have been taken already that few enough are left to choose from now. In any case, our little village will have to contribute its full quota ; and even should *I* succeed in escaping, some other luckless lad will have to go in my place."

" It is not the misfortune of serving as a soldier that you want to escape, but the dishonour, nay the sin, of serving a usurper."

" But, Clémence "— He paused.

" Well, brother?"

" It is no sin to fight for France,—for France, not for Napoleon."

" There is no France," Clémence returned proudly—" no

France that we can recognize apart from the King of France, Louis Dix-huit."

"Of whom *I* know no more than Féron or Bonin knows of the Emperor of Russia."

"What does that matter? What do you mean, Henri?"

"That we think Féron and Bonin a couple of fools because they are longing to go and destroy the Emperor of Russia, about whom they know nothing. Are *we* so much wiser if we let ourselves be destroyed for a king of France about whom we know just as little?"

"Not for *a* king of France, but for *the* King," Clémence answered gently. "And not alone for the King, but for truth, and loyalty, and God."

No more was said; for at that moment they heard the voice of Madame de Talmont, who, having finished her letter, called her daughter to read it. Henri stood yet beside the window; but it was not the quiet wintry scene without which was passing before the boy's anxious eyes. He saw instead his mother's peaceful home invaded by ruthless soldiers; he heard the clank of their spurs, the tread of their feet upon the stair, their oaths, their threats as they sought everywhere for him, the fugitive. He saw—he heard much more—his dwelling given over to pillage—*that*, perhaps, might be borne; but his mother, his sister, exposed to all the wrongs and insults a lawless soldiery could inflict, and *had* inflicted in like cases! No; he could not risk it. Not for all the kings of France that ever wore a crown! Better serve Napoleon—better a thousand times! And, after all, what was Napoleon—what were emperors and kings, to him and his? What was death on the battle-field? He had always heard that such a death was honourable and noble, and at all events a man could die but once. But the deserter's fate was only terrible; suffering without glory, "the pang without the palm." From those dreary fortress prisons where the "refractory" toiled in the garb of convicts, fed on bread and water, with shaven heads and fettered feet, no man ever came forth alive.

Days wore on, bringing the dreaded morning that was to decide the fate of the conscripts. Madame de Talmont wrapped her mantle around her and took the arm of her son. Clémence also was prepared to accompany them to the village. Henri, who looked very pale, attempted a remonstrance. " The place will be crowded to-day," he said. " It is not fit for *you*, mother, or for Clémence."

But they would not listen. " There is no country lad," said his mother, " who will not have his people with him to-day to learn his fate ; and shall De Talmont go to the drawing alone, as if no one cared for him ?"

As they passed along, they could not avoid hearing the mocking remarks which were exchanged by the peasants of Brie when they saw the proud aristocrats, whose lives had flowed on for years beside yet apart from their own, forced at last into fellowship with their neighbours by a common hope and fear. The silk of Madame de Talmont's mantle, well-worn yet unmistakably elegant, rubbed against the homespun gown of the baker's widow, and both faces were pale with one anxiety.

" Ah, madame, there's little chance for us this time," said Widow Simon. " *They* like it, the young folk. *They* know no better. But God help the old !"

A crowd of women were standing together in the town hall, while the young men went inside into the mayor's office to draw each his number from the box. Without, in the village street, a band was playing martial airs, and people were shouting, " Vive l'Empereur !"

Every minute or two some one came out of the office, swaggering or downcast, as the case might be. Widow Simon's son had drawn a very high number, which made him comparatively safe ; and Madame de Talmont felt glad ever afterwards that she congratulated the mother. Mathieu Féron came out waving his cap triumphantly, and shouting, " Vive l'Empereur ! I am going to fight the Russians ! Hammer and tongs, good-bye !"

Then Henri came. He was calm, but a few shades paler than before. He showed his number—*eleven*. No one spoke; but a moment after Clémence touched his arm and whispered hurriedly, " Come out into the air. Our mother is growing faint."

" Let us go home," said Madame de Talmont, sighing heavily. The crowd was increasing every moment, and the din and tumult were deafening. With some impatience Henri pushed aside those who stood in his path, and there was a sharp ring in his voice as he said, " Make way, make way, good people !"

" Oh yes ; make way for the new conscript. How well M. de Talmont will look in the awkward squad !" cried some one.

Féron had crossed the street to the little inn opposite the Mairie, and was about to drink the Emperor's health in a cup of good red wine, a practice much in favour with the conscripts, but before tasting it he pushed through the throng, and offered the brimming goblet to Henri. " Drink, M. de Talmont," he said. " We are all comrades now, and the sooner we learn good fellowship the better."

Henri pushed the cup aside without a word ; but Clémence spoke gently to the village lad. " It is not that my brother would not drink with you, Mathieu," she said ; " but he is troubled just now, and so are we—like your mother and your sisters."

No other word was spoken until the De Talmonts reached their home, and even then very few. Madame de Talmont and Clémence arranged everything, and Henri seemed quite passive in their hands. According to their plan, he was to leave the cottage after nightfall, and travelling on foot by unfrequented ways, to try to reach the neighbourhood of their old home in the Bocage, where the faithful Grandpierre, who had been their father's steward, would receive and protect him. A little money and a change of linen were concealed about his person, but on no account must he look like a traveller. So long had Madame de Talmont contemplated the necessity for this journey that she was able to give her son the fullest and clearest directions.

At length all was done. The last meal was eaten together, or at least a pretence was made of eating it. Henri embraced his mother, and received her parting blessing; then Clémence, wrapping a shawl around her, said, "The night is fine; I will go with you to the stile of the far corn-field."

They walked along in silence. They had worlds to say to each other, and this might be their last opportunity on earth, yet neither found a word. Not until the parting-place was reached did Clémence whisper, as she slipped a purse into her brother's hand, "There are five napoleons, Henri; you will be sure to want them. And oh! write to us as soon as you can. I will try to cheer and comfort our mother. Just one word more, dearest of brothers. Pray to God, seek to have him for your friend; then, whatever happens"— But here her voice failed utterly.

Henri threw his arms around her, and his voice was hoarse and changed, very unlike his own. "Clémençe," he said, "pro- mise me one thing."

"Yes."

"That, *whatever happens*, you will not hate or curse me, or call me traitor, but forgive and love me still; that you will plead with my mother to forgive me"—

"Forgive you! love you still! What can you mean, Henri? It is not possible we should ever change to each other. Not— *possible*," she sobbed, clinging to him, and straining him to her heart in an embrace that seemed as if no power on earth could sunder it.

Somehow or other Henri freed himself at last.   He said in a kind of choked whisper, " Remember my words.   Good-bye, and God—your God—bless you."   One last lingering look, and he turned away, ran quickly down the sloping corn-field, and was soon lost to sight.

But he did not take the path that Clémence supposed.   He returned to the village by a circuitous route, and about midnight tapped gently at the curé's door.   The priest was evidently on the watch, for he opened the door and admitted him at once, then shut and bolted it, and extinguished the light he had kept burning in his window as a guide to his expected guest.

CHAPTER XI.

ONE OF HALF A MILLION.

IT was evening in a crowded barrack-room in Paris. Recruits, not yet clad in uniform, but wearing the blouses or the coarse fustian jackets they had brought from their native villages, chatted, drank, quarrelled, or dozed upon the benches or about the floor. One noisy fellow was singing the Marseillaise at the top of his voice, another was defying any man in France to beat him at single-stick, but by far the greater number seemed dispirited and utterly weary.

A young lad had seated himself at the table, beneath one of the lamps which, at long distances, lit up the darkness of the great bare room. Writing materials were before him, and he had begun a letter, but paused, as if unable to proceed, and shaded his face with his hand. Presently the tears dropped slowly down between his fingers, blistering the paper; then once more he seized the pen, and wrote eagerly and rapidly:—

"Dearest mother, forgive me. I could not—no, I could not expose you and Clémence to the terrible sufferings inflicted upon the families of the refractory, even if, for myself, I was strong enough to encounter the horrors of a convict prison. There was no way but the way I took. M. le Curé answered for me

to the maire, and concealed me in his house until marching
orders came. As we started in the gray dawn of a winter's
morning, I hoped to pass unnoticed; but so many villagers
were there to bid farewell to their friends, that I know you
must have heard all. Mother, Clémence, pray for me; and
oh, mother, forgive me if you can! It is not for Napoleon I
am going to fight, but for France."

"Conscript, do you want that letter put into the post to-
night?" asked a short, thick-set, red-haired man with a corporal's badge on his sleeve; "because, if you do, I am going
out, and I am a very obliging fellow."

Henri looked up quickly. He might perhaps have doubted
the corporal's word, but five or six other letters which he held
in his hand seemed to corroborate his statement; besides, he
knew that for him there would be no leave to go out that
night.

"Then I shall be very much obliged to you, corporal," he
said.

"Quick with you then. Sign your name and give it to me.
I cannot wait all night. You may make my compliments to
your sweetheart while you are about it, however."

Henri hastily folded and sealed his letter, and put it in the
corporal's outstretched hand.

"Peste, man!" said the other impatiently; "where is the
postage?"

Henri took out half a franc. "That is it, I think," he said,
without noticing the signs one of his comrades was making to
attract his attention. The corporal flung the coin upon the
table, and caught it again, as if to try whether it was genuine,
muttered a curse, and went his way.

"Fool!" said Henri's neighbour. "Did you not see he
wanted something to drink? What else should he take your
letter for? Look out for yourself on parade to-morrow; he
will do you a mischief if he can."

"And who cares?" cried the chanter of the Marseillaise. "We want no aristocrats among us. 'Çà ira! çà ira!'"

"We want no bad companions either," said Féron, who was standing near, "so you may keep your breath for your eternal 'Çà ira,' Guillaume St. Luc." Then, going over to Henri, he sat down beside him, and laying his hand on his shoulder, said in a low voice, "Keep up your heart, M. de Talmont. Who knows but you have a marshal's bâton in your knapsack?"

Henri felt grateful for the kind words, and perhaps yet more so for the form of address, which had not fallen upon his ear since the miserable morning when he marched out of Brie—a conscript. He placed his white, delicate hand in the rough palm of the blacksmith's son. "You are a good comrade," he said.

"I vowed you should find me that, the day Mademoiselle Clémence spoke to me so kindly," returned Féron.

"But as to the marshal's bâton," resumed Henri, "that is a fine story. Six feet of Russian clay to lie in is what more of us are likely to get, I fancy."

"No good comes of burying ourselves before we are dead," returned the cheery Féron. "Of course, some are killed in every war. It is their luck. If a Russian bullet has my name upon it, why, then, I shall have the consolation of falling in the greatest war of the greatest captain that ever lived. I shall see his eagles flap their wings over Moscow and St. Petersburg. I shall die in the hour of victory, and I shall die shouting, 'Vive l'Empereur!'" In fact, the last words so nearly approached a shout already, that they were taken up and re-echoed by those around.

Then Féron resumed his low tone. "M. de Talmont, may I give you a word of advice?"

"Certainly, comrade."

"When you hear other people shouting, always shout too; and the greater fools you think them, the louder you ought to shout, if only by way of drowning their foolish voices."

For the first time since the day of the conscription Henri laughed; and Féron presently continued, "But as for me, I do not shout 'Vive l'Empereur!' like a fool. I know very well what I am about. I am only a conscript, it is true, but I am a soldier. The whole world is before me, and if I am brave, active, and resolute, the marshal's bâton is no impossible dream for me. If we had lived in the old times, M. de Talmont, you would have ridden a fine horse and worn a beautiful sword; and I should have been like the dust beneath your feet—a private all my days, and no more. Thanks to the Revolution and the Empire, we have changed all that; so now we can be good comrades, as you have been kind enough to say."

Good comrades they were through many a dreary day of drill and marching. At first the physical hardships of his life weighed so heavily upon Henri that thought and feeling were almost crushed into silence. When he halted for the night, after a long day's march, he was scarcely conscious of anything except weary limbs and blistered feet. During his stay at the depôt in Metz, where the conscripts had to go through some preliminary training, things were scarcely better. The moral and the mental atmosphere of the barrack-room were alike abhorrent to his refined, sensitive nature; while the cruel and degrading punishments that followed any failure in skill or quickness on the parade-ground, forced him to bend all his remaining energies to the task of avoiding them. No answer to his letter from Paris ever reached him, and this added to the dull apathy that was creeping over his soul. His mother, he feared, was implacable. And Clémence?—perhaps his mother would not allow her to write, perhaps she herself was too deeply offended to make the attempt.

At last marching orders came once more. Strange to say, from that day the heavy cloud of gloom that hung over Henri began to lighten. Change of scene proved a tonic, and as he grew accustomed to long marches he ceased to suffer so greatly from fatigue. Like other young conscripts who did not droop and fail utterly, he gradually plucked up strength and spirits. As he was uniformly gentle and courteous—no ordinary merit in a French soldier of the Empire—he often met with much kindness from the families upon whom he was billeted; and the extreme youthfulness of his appearance gained many friends for him. By the time he reached the headquarters of the imperial army, the profession into which he had been forced was rather an object of indifference than of detestation to him. When the recruits were reviewed by Napoleon in person, he remembered the sage advice of Féron, and did not imagine that a cry of " Vive l'Empereur !" from the lips of a De Talmont would awaken the slumbering dust of his ancestors. Moreover, he could not but gaze, with a kind of fascination that had in it as much of admiration as of horror, upon the face of the man whose will at that moment was the most stupendous force in all the world. Henri de Talmont did not love Napoleon Buonaparte—he feared him, perhaps he hated him—but, like almost every other man in Europe, he believed him irresistible. There was a sense of exhilaration in the universal feeling that to march under him was infallibly to march to victory. Some faint reflected glow from the enthusiasm of all around could not fail to reach him and to awaken stirrings of the martial ardour that slumbered in the son of a long line of gallant warriors.

An unknown unit in a regiment of infantry—young recruits who as yet had won no laurels—Henri de Talmont marched one day over a temporary wooden bridge which had been flung by French pontoniers across the Niemen. " Now, mes enfants," their captain said, " you are standing upon Russian ground."

They cheered, embraced one another, and shouted until they were hoarse, " Vive l'Empereur ! vive Napoleon ! A bas les

Russes!"   Henri shouted as loudly as the rest; while, at least
to the human eye, coming events cast no shadow before, nor
was there any foreboding voice raised to whisper, as that vast
and gallant host passed by,—

> " The snow shall be their winding-sheet,
> And every turf beneath their feet
> Shall be a soldier's sepulchre!"

CHAPTER XII.

" The might that slumbers in a peasant's arm."

 GREAT battle, and a great victory—this was what Henri de Talmont, in common with the six hundred thousand fighting men who crossed the Niemen under Napoleon, fully expected to see. Young hearts kindled, young blood grew hot at the thought; while the veterans of Lodi, of Austerlitz, of Jena, saw their cherished laurels fade and pale before the lustre of those with which they hoped soon to adorn their victorious brows. And then how royally would the treasures of Moscow and St. Petersburg recompense all their toils !

But there was no great battle. The Russians, under Barclay de Tolly, retreated without fighting, skilfully drawing the enemy after them into the immense and dreary plains of the interior. Then followed a succession of marches, as wearisome and far more monotonous than those by which the recruits had reached the headquarters of their army. The weather was hot and sultry—a curious first experience of the climate of Russia—and both men and horses suffered from the want of water. Other wants, too, were supplied but carelessly, or perhaps not at all. Many a conscript lay down supperless night after night beside the fire of his bivouac, to sleep away his hunger as best he could. It is said that some even died of starvation, while others found unwholesome nutriment in the unripe corn and the raw vegetables that grew along their route. Nor did the knowledge that the general of his division was feasting upon sterlet and champagne make the hard, insufficient fare of the conscript more palatable. "It is the soldier's own fault if he wants anything in an enemy's country," was a maxim often repeated; but what can the soldier do when the people flee at his approach, carrying off or destroying everything they possess, and the country, at best but thinly inhabited, is left a desert around him?* Yet it must be owned that the French had themselves to thank for some of their privations, since those peasants who did not flee at their approach were plundered, beaten, ill-treated, perhaps even murdered.

One day Henri accompanied a detachment of his regiment which was sent out on a foraging expedition. They were under the command of Seppel, the corporal who had undertaken to post Henri's letter in Paris; but he was a sergeant now, and rode a good horse, while the others tramped wearily on foot. After a long march through a dreary country they saw, towards evening, a brown village surrounded by promising corn-fields. "Courage, mes enfants," cried Seppel; "here is luck for us at last. No doubt food and water, ay, and brandy too, are to be found yonder."

They marched across the fields, trampling down the standing corn without remorse. Henri and some of his comrades were hungry enough to pluck the unripe ears and to eat them as they passed, like another company strangely opposite to these in their character and their place in the world's history.

As they approached the village, they became aware that its inhabitants had not only seen them, but were prepared for their approach. A crowd of men and boys, armed with axes, pitchforks, and reaping-hooks, came towards them with loud cries and intentions evidently the most hostile.

* Alexander would not allow the country to be laid waste before the invaders; but government stores were destroyed or carried away, and private individuals voluntarily did the same, to a great extent, with their own possessions.

Seppel caught hold of a tall, gaunt soldier, whose white uniform gleamed conspicuous amongst the blue tunics of the rest, and pushed him to the front. "Here, Klinki, Schlinki, or whatever your unpronounceable name may be, tell these beggars in their own jargon that we want food for man and horse, and that if they give it, in plenty and at once, we will do them no harm."

The Pole—who had been brought with the party to act as interpreter, as he happened to know a little Russian—tried to gain a hearing; but in vain. So the Frenchmen drew their swords, and a brisk fight began. Suddenly, however, Seppel observed something which made him call upon his men to stop. He saw a party leaving the village and proceeding towards the adjoining birch-wood, and he rightly conjectured that these were the women and children under the escort of some of the men who had remained behind for the purpose. In fact, this had been from the first the design of the villagers, and the attack had been only a feint made in order to gain time for its execution. Seppel raised his hand, pointing to the retreating group. "Fire, mes enfants!" he cried; "fire yonder—upon *them!*" They were just within musket-range, and the sharp, ringing sound of the shots was followed by heart-rending cries.

There was no more thought of resistance. The village lads threw down their extemporized weapons, and hurried to the assistance of their friends. Soon the whole party, their movements quickened by terror, had disappeared into the wood, carrying with them their wounded, perhaps their dead. "Was not that well done?" laughed Seppel. "I knew they would go to look after the women at the first cry."

Thus Nicolofsky was taken by the French. The victors were soon busy exploring the deserted cottages in search of food and vodka. Other things too were needed.

"Here, blacksmith," said Seppel to Féron, "look after my horse. He has cast a shoe."

"Yes, sergeant," returned Féron coolly, "if you will find me a hammer and tongs, and a nail or two."

"Is that my business, stupid? Go and look. These fellows have horses, so they must have smith's tackle somewhere about."

"And they call this conquering a country!" grumbled Féron as he walked away. "Well, it may be glorious, but it is not particularly convenient or amusing."

At that moment there was a joyful shout from some of the party. Very few fires were burning in the village on that warm summer evening, but in one of the two largest cottages the great stove had been lighted, and a capacious caldron of tschi was simmering over it. The French soldiers fully appreciated the national dish of the Russians, and found the prospect of an abundant and savoury supper very agreeable.

"Here is one good thing for me," said Féron, glancing at the fire. "Now for hammer and nails.—Talmont, you lazy fellow, don't stand there gazing at nothing, but come and help me to find them."

But when they stood outside together, Féron's tone changed. "M. Henri," he said in a quick, eager whisper, "show me your musket."

Henri did so with a smile.

"Ah!" said Féron, looking relieved, "then after all you *did* fire. I feared you would not, and I was going to give you a word of advice."

"I *did* fire," answered Henri in a low voice,—"in the air. What *else* could I do, Féron? they were women and children."

"Well, perhaps *I* did not shoot very straight either; still we are in an enemy's country. Why did not the Czar do whatever the Emperor wanted him? But take care, M. Henri; that old fox Seppel is no friend of yours."

They entered another cottage in search of what they wanted, and Féron struck his foot against a small bucket full of some liquid. "Ha! what have we here? Vodka, I hope." He stooped down and tasted it, but got up with an air of disgust. "No such luck. Only frog's ratefia" (so the French called the kvass of the Russians). "How could any poor wretches be expected to fight with such stuff as that in their insides?"

"Let me have a pull at it," said Henri. "I am thirsty enough not to despise even frog's ratefia. Do you think Seppel means to stay here all night?"

"He ought not; but if he finds vodka I would not answer for the consequences. And certainly it is growing very late."

Féron at last succeeded in finding the tools with which the villagers performed whatever rude blacksmith's work they needed. Then he rejoined his companions, who were just beginning to help themselves to the supper which had been prepared for very different guests by the priest's wife. The cottage was that of Pope Nikita, and the day happened to be the name-day of Anna Popovna.

A good store of vodka had been found, and with this help the soldiers soon forgot their troubles, past, present, and to come. They ate, drank, and made merry; and the sergeant, far from being any check upon their mirth, drank more deeply and talked more boisterously than any of them. The night closed over them unawares, and of course there was now no question of leaving their comfortable quarters until the morning.

Féron had brought in his hand a small piece of iron, as well as the hammer and tongs he had been using. He had a jesting dispute with one of his comrades, who called in question his capabilities as a blacksmith. "Blacksmith, indeed!" said Féron. "That's nothing. I am quite an artist, messieurs. At Brie I was accounted a connoisseur—an ornamental worker in brass, iron, and the other precious metals."

"A fine story," laughed Henri, who was greatly the better for his comfortable meal. "At Brie your crooked nails were a joke for the whole village."

"Don't talk, but let us *see* what you can do. Give us a specimen," said a conscript, a timorous little fellow, who was unpopular in the regiment because of his habit of shifting off his work upon his comrades.

"Yes, I will," returned Féron. "I'll make an iron to brand you with when you are caught trying to desert, as you are sure to be one of these days."

A general laugh followed this retort, then silence fell over the group, while Féron hammered away at his task, and most of the others began to doze in their places. When at last he held up triumphantly, in proof of his skill, a finely-formed branding-iron with the letter N upon it, his companions were far too sleepy to give him the applause he expected.

One hour—two hours passed away. All were sleeping now, even the sentinels Seppel had placed outside as a matter of form. The village of Nicolofsky was as still as it was wont to be in the noon of a midsummer night. If a sound of weeping and lamentation came, softened by distance, from the adjacent birch-wood, it failed to disturb the sleepers. But the short summer night was soon over, and the dawn began to creep in, cold and gray.

Its first faint light fell upon the figure of a mujik, who traversed, with stealthy, silent footsteps, the deserted street of his native village. As he passed the church he noticed that the door had been forced open—though it was again roughly secured on the outside. He removed the fastening and looked in. The spirit of wanton outrage, only too common amongst the French soldiery, had made Seppel choose that sacred place as a stable for his horse, and the animal was eating corn out of a consecrated vessel placed upon the altar.* Michael Ivanovitch ground his teeth, and his dark cheek flushed ominously; but he passed on, for his heart was full of a great, deep anguish, before which every other emotion paled and faded.

---

* These outrages, and others yet more revolting, were constantly committed by the French in Russia.

That which, at the risk of his life, he had come to fetch, was not in the desecrated church. It had to be sought for in the very place where most of the French soldiers had taken up their quarters for the night—the cottage of Pope Nikita. The door of the cottage was half open, and he saw that the floor was covered with sleeping forms clad in the blue tunic of the French infantry. What matter to him? Blotting out that sight, he saw the wistful, longing look in the dying eyes of the girl he loved, and, before him, the sacred picture her faltering accents had entreated him to bring to her. Thank God, there it hung yet—on the cottage wall, in the right-hand corner. Could he tread amongst those sleepers without awakening them, and reach it?

His step was noiseless as the footfall of the desert panther, and the French were weary with marching, and most of them heavy with vodka. He had grasped his prize—he stood with his hand on its frame, and a momentary throb of triumph in his sorrowful heart, when suddenly a head was raised; some one more wakeful than the rest had seen the intruder. In an instant the alarm was given, and the whole group were on their feet; in another, a dozen strong hands were laid at once upon Michael Ivanovitch.

He struggled desperately, but what could one man do against a dozen armed with swords and bayonets? He would have been cut down almost immediately, had not Seppel, very sensibly, called upon his men to spare his life and secure him as a prisoner. "He may serve for a guide, or at least give us some information," he said. Then he summoned the Pole to act as interpreter, taking the precaution to make another man —Féron it happened to be—stand before the prisoner with his loaded musket pointed at his breast. "He looks dangerous," he observed.

There was not much to be read in Michael's stolid, determined face, as the light of the early morning shone upon it.

He had placed the sacred picture in the breast of his caftan; but seeing the musket, he took it out and laid it on the table. "They shall not harm *that*, at all events," he thought.

"Tell him," said Seppel to the Pole, "that if he fails to satisfy us, we will shoot him; but that if he behaves well, we will spare his life."

The Pole interpreted, and Michael answered coolly, "Nitshevo."

"That means," the Pole explained, "'It is no matter. I do not care.'"

"Ask him," pursued Seppel, "what brought him here."

Michael, as soon as he understood the question, pointed to the picture.

Seppel laughed incredulously; and the Pole inquired of his own accord, "Is that the whole truth, Russian?"

"Da," returned the prisoner.

"He says, 'Yes,'" the Pole explained.

"Tell him he is a liar," said Seppel.

A scornful smile was the only answer, and Seppel tried another course. "Ask him," he said, "how far it is from this place to Klopti."

He did so; but Michael answered nothing.

"Tell him he must take us there to-day."

Still no answer.

"Tell him if he chooses to behave in this way he has not two minutes to live."

"Nitshevo," was the only reply.

This went on for some minutes, every inquiry being met by a dogged silence, every threat by "Nitshevo." At last Seppel lost patience, and told Féron to fire upon the prisoner.

But Féron disliked the task, for he rather admired the courage of the Russian. He slowly laid his finger on the trigger of his musket, then withdrew it again. This he did twice, keenly watching the countenance of the prisoner, which showed no perceptible change. All the French soldiers had now crowded around them, and were watching the scene with interested faces.

"Do not kill him, sergeant," pleaded one.

"He is a brave fellow. Try something else first," said another.

Seppel paused, and a new thought occurred to him. "Ah, yes," he said, "these Russian slaves understand nothing except it comes to them through their bodily feelings. They are accustomed, I suppose, to be treated like beasts of the field.—Pole, tell him he is our prisoner; *that*, at least, we will make him know.—Féron, put down your musket, and bring that branding-iron I saw you make last night; there is enough fire yet in the stove to heat it red-hot."

Féron obeyed without hesitation, even with alacrity; for it seemed to him much better to brand a man on the hand than to shoot him through the heart. So the letter N, fashioned in sport the night before, was used in earnest now. It came down with burning pain, and left its mark, indelible for ever, upon the unresisting hand of Michael.

For a moment his strong frame quivered, but his lips were silent, pressed closely together. Then he turned to the Pole, and, for the first time speaking of his own accord, he asked him, "What does that mean?"

"It means that you belong now, soul and body, to our Emperor, the great Napoleon. That which you bear on your hand is his mark—the first letter of his name."

Michael smiled slightly, and advancing to the table, laid the wounded hand upon it. (Féron not unintentionally had made choice of the left one.) Then with one blow from the axe which he drew from the sash of his caftan, he severed it from his wrist. "Take what belongs to your Emperor," he said, turning proudly to the astonished group. "As for me, I belong altogether to the Czar."*

* A fact.

A thrill of involuntary admiration passed through the spectators, and for some moments no one spoke. Meanwhile, in the calm summer sky outside, the sun was rising, and its first red beams flashed through the little window upon the homely features of the serf, which shone with a courage and devotion that were almost sublime.

"Cut him down!" cried a solitary voice, that of the conscript who, the night before, had challenged Féron's skill. But half-a-dozen other voices cried, "Shame!" while Seppel himself seemed to hesitate, and stood with the air of a man perplexed and confounded.

In the meantime Henri de Talmont, who had hitherto taken no part in the scene, walked boldly up to the prisoner. He held in his hand a fine white cambric handkerchief, which he wound carefully about the wounded arm. "As you love your Czar," he said gently, "so we Royalists in France loved our King."

The words, of course, fell meaningless upon the ear of Michael; but the tones in which they were uttered, and the action which accompanied them, were abundantly intelligible. The eyes of the Russian serf and the French gentleman met with a look of comprehension and sympathy.

"Shall we let him go?" Seppel asked at length. "What say you, mes enfants?"

There was now not one dissentient voice, and Seppel turned to the interpreter. "Tell him, Pole, that we Frenchmen know how to respect a brave enemy. He is free."

Michael heard, bowed his head gravely in acknowledgment, took up the sacred picture with his remaining hand, and walked slowly out. He scarcely noticed the ringing cheer which the excitable Frenchmen sent after him. Their applause was nothing to him: it could not bring back the young life of his betrothed, flowing forth so quickly through the wound their guns had made last night. Enough if he might but be in time to see her once again, and to comfort her dying moments with the treasure he had risked so much to procure.

When he was gone, Seppel stretched his limbs once more before the stove, and said half to himself with a meditative air, " After all, I begin to doubt whether we shall succeed so easily in conquering these Russians."

CHAPTER XIII.

"Vengeance, deep brooding o'er the slain,
Had locked the source of softer woe;
And burning pride and high disdain
Forbade the rising tear to flow."

IT was evening. Ivan Pojarsky sat alone in the saloon of the Wertsch family mansion. The costly furniture with which it was strewn had that indescribable air of neglect and forlornness which household goods assume when death, or sorrow deep as death, broods over their owners. There was disorder too: chairs had been dragged carelessly about, and their rich and delicate coverings soiled and crumpled; while a beautiful climbing plant, laden with rare flowers, lay unheeded on the floor beside the broken shaft that had been its support. A costly buhl table near Ivan's chair had the remains of his last meal upon it.

Within the apartment all was still,—Ivan sat motionless and silent, his head resting on his hands,—but without there was a hoarse, continuous, never-ending murmur, made up of many sounds. There was the tramp of armed men, heavy and monotonous. There was the roll and rumble of ten thousand wheels —wheels of every sort and description, from those of the ponderous waggon laden with the goods of an entire household to those of the light telega, from which every now and then a scout was imparting to the breathless crowd his tidings that the standards of Napoleon had been seen at such or such a

point of the Smolensko road. Mingling with and following
the stately rhythmic march of the disciplined hosts was the
tread of innumerable footsteps—footsteps of women and little
children, of boys and aged men, who were leaving with breaking hearts the only home they had ever known. And if the
weeping and wailing, the sighs and groans and cries, which
filled the clear September air did not rise above all other sounds,
it was only because the things most deep and real are ofttimes
the last to meet the eye or reach the ear—except, indeed, the
ever-present eye and the ever-listening ear of Him who notes
" the sob in the dark and the falling of tears."

Suddenly Ivan raised his head and looked around him. The
last few weeks had changed him wonderfully. He appeared
several years older—no longer a stripling, but a man, with a
man's responsibilities, thoughts, and duties. There was in
his young face a look of sternness, as of one who had to do
hard things and to bid others do them; there was the high,
courageous, half-defiant air of one who dares death cheerfully,
even joyfully, and also an expression of proud though mournful satisfaction. For had not he, a youth scarcely twenty,
been intrusted with a terrible secret, been charged with a desperate but honourable mission ?

" Beg pardon, gospodin," said a servant, entering. Ivan
was now virtually the master of the household, for both the
Wertsches were with the army—Adrian serving as a volunteer,
Leon as a lieutenant of hussars. " Here is a mujik," continued
the servant, " who wishes to speak with your excellency."

" Send him in," said Ivan quickly. " And—stay a moment,
Joseph. What does your wife say of her mistress ?"

" The countess, gospodin, will not hear reason from my wife,
though she has been waiting upon her these twenty years,
any more than from your excellency. ' The French,' says
my lady, ' will never enter holy Moscow. They dare not.'
I must own, Lord Ivan, that Maria thinks this very hard;

because if our lady the countess will not be persuaded to go away, as all other folk are doing who have brains in their heads, she—my wife I mean—must stay, too, of course, and be murdered by the Nyemtzi."

"Murdered by the Nyemtzi shall *our* women never be, Joseph," said Ivan, with a flash in his eyes. "At the worst, we know what to do. Tell thy wife the countess must be induced to quit this house before to-morrow night. If she will not leave the city, like a sensible woman, at least she must go to the Devitshei Convent, and Maria must go with her. I suppose even the infidel French will scarcely outrage *that* asylum. Meanwhile, send in this mujik; perhaps he brings tidings."

A tall figure entered, with a bandaged arm, and wearing a rough, soiled caftan, and heavy Russia leather boots that left their traces on the inlaid floor.

Ivan looked up, started, hesitated, then exclaimed in great surprise, "Michael Ivanovitch! One-eared Michael!"

"One-handed Michael now, at your service, Ivan Barrinka; and well if *that* were the only loss I had to tell of."

"Have you come from Nicolofsky?" asked Ivan.

"Yes, I come from Nicolofsky. Barrinka, the Nyemtzi have been there."

"Ah!" cried Ivan. "Curse them!"

"I have done with cursing them, Ivan Barrinka—I cannot find words—so I leave them to God. He knows what wages they have earned, and he will pay them one day. But as for me, my heart is hot and dry, and unless I can go and fight and kill some of them I shall die."

"What has happened, Michael? what have they done to you?"

"At Christmas I was to be married to Anna Popovna. You remember her, Ivan Barrinka?"

"*Remember* her!" cried Ivan angrily. "Of what are you dreaming, Michael? Do you not know that I—I—"

" Oh, I forgot—it seems a thousand years ago," said Michael, in a sad, dreamy voice. " Besides, it was never anything but child's play with you. Ivan Barrinka, we quarrelled in the old days, you and I. She used to like you better than me, because you were handsome and a boyar. But that is all over now. We shall quarrel no more, for Anna Popovna is with the saints. The Nyemtzi have killed her."

Ivan's agitation was extreme. He still fancied he loved the village girl, no real passion having as yet taken possession of his heart to " put the old cheap joy in the scorned dust." In wild excitement he strode up and down the room, uttering incoherent lamentations and cursing the French; but at last he stopped before Michael and asked briefly, in a choking voice, " How ?"

Michael's grief had been his companion for weary days and nights—he was used to it now, so he answered very quietly, " One evening we saw the blue-coats coming, and some of us went out to show fight and keep them off a little, while the rest convoyed our women safely into the wood. But the scoundrels saw them, and fired. The distance was long, and they did not take good aim. Only two shots told: one of them wounded the lad we used to call little Peter rather badly in the shoulder; the other—killed her—"

" At once !"

" She lived some hours. She did not suffer much. She died—in peace." Michael spoke with difficulty, and in a low voice. There was a pause; then he resumed, taking a picture from beneath his caftan and showing it to Ivan, " Her last look was fixed on *this*. Her father gave it to me, because I brought it to her from his house, where the Nyemtzi were."

" Did the French stay there for the night ?"

Michael nodded.

" Then what were you about, Michael Ivanovitch," cried

Ivan with sudden energy — "what were you about that you did not set the village on fire and burn it over their heads?"

Michael's remaining hand fell by his side with a gesture of mingled admiration and regret. "Great St. Nicholas!" he exclaimed.

"Well?" said Ivan.

"We never thought of it," cried Michael. "Would to God we had! What a sight it would have been!"

"You may yet see a greater, Michael Ivanovitch."

There was silence, and the tumult outside became audible once more to both.

At last Michael resumed. "I am forgetting what I came for. Since that night my head is confused. I live those last hours over and over again. I hear nothing, I see nothing except that bed of leaves in the forest, and the torches flickering upon those sad faces all around, and that one sweet white face—except when I sleep and dream of killing Frenchmen. Ay, killing Frenchmen, that is it! Ivan Barrinka, I come here to beg of you—if you like it, on my bended knees—to speak one word for me to our lord the Czar,—only one word."

"My good friend—for my friend you are, in the love we both have for the dead—I would speak a hundred if I could; but the Czar is in St. Petersburg, and I am here. I scarce hope ever to see again the face that is to us all as the sun in the heavens."

"Then give me a written word for him. You are a boyar, and can do it."

"Nay, I should not presume so far. He does not even know of my existence—*yet*." The last word was spoken proudly, with an evident under-current of meaning. "But what is it you want, Michael?"

"See, I have lost my left hand."

"Another French outrage?"

"Yes, and no. When I went to fetch that picture, they

caught me, and put their Emperor's mark on my hand. Was I to carry *that* with me all my life, and after my life in the resurrection, before the judgment-seat of God? I had a good hand still, and a good axe in it, and with these I struck off what they had defiled. Now there is not an inch of me that does not belong to the Czar."

"Nobly done, brother!" cried Ivan, embracing him. "I am proud of my old Nicolofsky playfellow. Michael, will you cast in your lot with me, and let us serve the Czar together?"

"Ay, Barrinka; but there is the difficulty. No use in *my* offering myself for a recruit. No officer would take me, because I want my hand. That is why I pray you to ask the Czar to let me fight for him in spite of that loss. You could tell him I would serve him so faithfully."

"I can show you, even now, a way to render him signal and splendid service; but it is hazardous, *very*. It is scarce likely we shall live to go through with it; but, Michael, if we do, I think the Czar will have cause to thank us."

"And shall we kill plenty of Nyemtzi?" Michael asked eagerly.

"We shall deal their Emperor a blow he will never forget." Ivan sat down before him, looked at him in silence for some moments, and then, apparently changing the subject, he asked, "Are you not surprised at the condition in which you find the city?"

"What condition?—Oh yes; I saw crowds of people going away." Then, looking up—"But is it true, is it *really* true, Barrinka, that holy Moscow is to be given up to the infidel Nyemtzi?"

"Too true. A great battle was fought a few days ago at Borodino. The French say they won, and we say we won; but, however that may be, the result is for us as bad as a defeat. Marshal Kutusov says it is now hopeless to think of defending the city. All day our soldiers, with breaking hearts, have been marching through on their way to Vladimir."

"And without fighting? Ivan Barrinka, it is too bad! So those accursed Nyemtzi will have it all—the glorious, beautiful city of the Czar; the tombs, the treasures of his fathers; the forty times forty churches, the holy pictures of the saints! Woe, woe! Why have we lived to see such days?"

"Listen, Michael," said Ivan, arresting the hand with which he was tearing his beard. "Listen to me. The Nyemtzi shall *not* have it."

"What do you mean, Barrinka?"

"This. We will do for holy Moscow—our beautiful, our beloved—what a father would do for an only daughter, a husband for a wife, a brother for a sister, if there were no other way to save them from those accursed Nyemtzi—our own hands will deal the death-blow."

"How?"

"What should *you* have done with Nicolofsky while the French were in it?"

"Holy saints! Then you mean to burn the city?"

"These hands of mine will fling the brand into this house, which has been my home ever since I left your village. Nay, more, I am one of the directors of the secret band commissioned to spread the conflagration."

Michael stared at him in amazement, but did not speak.

Ivan resumed: "Perhaps you will think me dreaming—at least you will wonder by what authority I tell you these strange and awful things. I was a boy when last we met, Michael; indeed, until six weeks ago I was little more. Then the war broke out, and the Czar came here. I saw him; not for the first time, Michael Ivanovitch, for it was he—he and no other —whom I saw in my childhood's days ministering to poor unconscious Stefen on the bank of the Oka. My heart went forth to him at once, laid itself at his feet, vowed to serve him until death."

"So? Then *you* fight for love, Ivan Barrinka. *I* fight for hate."

"I too, after what you have told me to-night," said Ivan, with flashing eyes.   He continued more calmly : "Then I went to the governor, Count Rostopchine, and told him my story. I said that, though my name was of the noblest, I had not, like other boyars, lands, or serfs, or gold to give to the Czar ; I had only a strong heart, full of devotion.   He answered me, for he saw I was in earnest, 'Such hearts are what we want now.'   Then he told me what to do.   At first, Michael, I was horror-stricken.   I had rather have been burned at the stake myself.   But he assures me there is no other way of saving holy Russia and the Czar.   Moreover, most of the nobles, and all the merchants except seven, have resolved upon the sacrifice of their property.   Loss of life we will try to prevent."

"I suppose all good Russians, save those who, like you, have work to do, are leaving the city ?"

"Almost all ; except the ' black people,' who think they have nothing to lose and perhaps something to gain by the confusion. A few others are remaining on various pretexts ; for instance, Countess Wertsch, the owner of this house, obstinately insists upon staying, positively refusing to believe that the French will enter the city—a great embarrassment to me, since I cannot burn the house over her head.   I must get her away somehow.   For this and other matters I need advice from my good old friend Petrovitch, and I mean to go to him at day-break.   You shall come with me ; I should like to tell him what you have done, Michael."

"Anywhere with you.   There will be plenty of work for us, and plenty of danger too.   All the better for me.   But *you* will be sorry to part with life, Ivan Barrinka."

For a moment Ivan's face assumed a grave and thoughtful expression ; then it gradually lighted up, until it absolutely glowed with enthusiasm.   "If I fall," he said, "Count Rostopchine has promised to name me to the Czar."

CHAPTER XIV.

THE FORLORN HOPE.

"Oh, sweet and strange it seems to me, that ere this day is done
The voice that now is speaking may be beyond the sun,
For ever and for ever with those just souls and true;
And what is life that we should moan? why make we such ado?"

THE two young men wore out the short summer night in earnest talk. Neither thought of sleep; but Ivan was careful to provide a comfortable repast for Michael, and was by no means reluctant to share it. Very early in the morning they set out on foot for the merchants' quarter. The shades of night had brought no repose to the doomed city; hour after hour the living tide flowed on without pause or respite, and Ivan and Michael found it extremely difficult to thread their way through the dense confused mass of vehicles and foot passengers that crowded every street.

At last they reached the dwelling of Petrovitch. The doors were all open. Unhindered and unannounced, they walked into the great hall. Here they found the whole family assembled. In the midst sat the patriarch, with silver hair and beard, and large, wide-open, sightless eyes. His face was as calm and almost as colourless as that of the dead; but its look expressed the steadfast high resolve of a "living soul," the heir of a deathless immortality.

All around that calm centre there was profound agitation. Women were weeping and wringing their hands; and those "tears of bearded men" which are so rare and sad to see were flowing without restraint. One of the sons of Petrovitch—in the green uniform of a Russian grenadier, his military hat, with its long black feather tipped with white, laid beside him—was sobbing bitterly himself, while he tried to comfort a little girl whom he held in his arms. Another young soldier, almost a boy, seemed to be imploring the interference of his mother, who was sitting a little apart, her face covered with a kerchief. At one side of the old man's chair stood his eldest son, with a look of indignant appeal and remonstrance; at the other knelt Feodor—and *his* face no one saw.

"Welcome, Prince Ivan!" cried Ivan Petrovitch as soon as he perceived his entrance. "Come hither and speak to our father. It may be he will listen to you, as the son of his ancient lord."

"Is that Prince Ivan?" asked the old man. "Son of my dear lord, ever welcome in this house, yet give us leave, I pray you, for a little space, for this is a bitter hour to me and to all of us. I am bidding farewell to every one in whose veins my blood is flowing. By-and-by I will talk once more with thee."

Ivan would have withdrawn, from a feeling that the scene was too sacred for any not immediately belonging to the family; but the eldest son of Petrovitch appealed to him once more. "Have you not a word—you whom he loved so dearly—to persuade him against flinging his life away?"

"My son, I am not flinging my life away," the old man interposed. "That would be a sin. I am only laying it at the feet of the God who gave it. He has given me a message for these Nyemtzi, and shall I spare to deliver it?"

"But how is this, dädushka?" asked Ivan gently, as he drew nearer to the weeping group. "How is this? Do you not go, with these your beloved ones, to a place of safety?"

"I go indeed to a place of safety, but not with these. My resolve has long been made; nor is it for thee, Prince Ivan, nor for you, sons and grandsons, true and well-beloved though you are, to change it now.   Here have I lived, and here will I die.   The Nyemtzi shall enter holy Moscow only over my body."*

" A vain sacrifice, useless as it is cruel," said Ivan Petrovitch in a broken voice.

" My son, it is neither.   I have no strong arm to fight for the Czar, but I have yet a voice with which to hurl defiance against his enemies.   It is the mightiest of all voices, though it makes no sound—the voice of blood.   My blood shall cry to the invader from the gate of the city I have loved: ' It is but vain the labour that you take to conquer this land for your Prince.   A land where youth and manhood arm to resist you, while old age dies beneath your feet rather than submit to your sway—such a land is unconquerable.'   Therefore, my children, no more words.   They are but needless pain, and time presses. I think my soldier lads should even now be rejoining their regiments.   Are you all here, my brave boys whom I have given to the Czar?"

The sergeant of grenadiers answered for the rest, "Yes, my father, all."

" Four sons and nine sons' sons—thirteen in all—have I given to our lord.   Soldiers of holy Russia, fight bravely ; and may God prosper your arms and give you the victory!   I doubt not he will, for your cause is just."

" My father, ere we go," said the sergeant, advancing and kneeling before him, " bless thy sons."

In a voice tremulous with deep feeling the solemn patriarchal blessing was given.   One after another the members of the family advanced to receive it: first the soldier sons and grandsons, keeping down their emotion with manly self-control; then Ivan Petrovitch, and a few others whose circumstances

---

* The story of Petrovitch is historical.   Scarcely anything has been added, and only a few rather improbable details have been omitted.

had prevented their volunteering with the rest; lastly the women and children. But Feodor did not stir from his place, until at length the old man called him by name. Then he slowly rose and stood before him.

"Son Ivan," said Petrovitch, "come hither and take this boy's hand in thine. Children, you know that little Feodor is all God has left with me of Maria Petrovna, the daughter of my old age, the one white dove in our falcon's nest. Be tender with him, all of you; and thou, Ivan, take care of the lad, and be to him a father in my place.—Feodor, my little Feodor, Maria's son, God bless thee!"

"Kneel, boy," whispered Ivan Petrovitch almost angrily, as Feodor, like one in a trance, stood motionless, with his passive hand in his uncle's.

The boy obeyed mechanically. The aged eyes of Petrovitch were full of unaccustomed tears, and his voice faltered, grew almost inaudible, as he murmured the words of blessing over that beloved head. But Feodor showed no sign of feeling, except that cheek and lip were white as marble.

Ivan Pojarsky, who, though he had withdrawn into the background, had not left the place, observed him with sorrowful wonder. "The boy," he thought, "will soon forget the old man, who will die with a prayer for him upon his lips."

Once more the aged voice was heard. Petrovitch arose slowly from his seat, and lifted up his hands over the group. "Now farewell, my children, and God bless you. May he grant us in his mercy a joyful meeting in the home above, the abode of the righteous, where no enemy or evil thing can enter. Go in peace."

Sadly and slowly, one by one, they turned away. Ivan Pojarsky followed, to assure his weeping friends that he at least would do all he could for the comfort and protection of their father. There were servants, too, who purposed remaining in the house for the present; and to these was intrusted the task of consummating the sacrifice by setting fire to what had been the happy home of three generations.

With a feeling akin to awe Ivan returned to the side of the now solitary old man. He was almost ashamed to bring his personal difficulties and perplexities before him. A reverent, tender compassion for the silver hairs so soon to be steeped in blood filled his heart, though even this was dominated and subdued by the over-mastering enthusiasm that possessed him, rising higher and higher every moment. Before that tide of passionate loyalty and patriotism all else gave way. It seemed easy and natural—and oh, how beautiful!—to die for the Czar and holy Russia.

Petrovitch, of his own accord, asked him about his plans and purposes. He knew already what a commission Rostopchine had intrusted to the young man ; and Ivan, though thoroughly master in outline of the *rôle* he had to play, was glad to consult his aged friend upon certain questions of detail. After discussing the directions he had to give to the criminals who were to be released from the various prisons to aid in the terrible work, he spoke of the unaccountable obstinacy of the Countess Wertsch, and of the difficulty in which it placed him.

But instead of expressing indignation at the old woman's folly, Petrovitch answered gently, " My boy, be patient with her. Remember all her days have been spent here. To her, as to others, the ruin of holy Moscow is like the fall of the sun from the noonday sky. Should the need to remove her actually arise, God will show you what to do. But wait. Where we stand now, hours do the work of years."

" Dädushka, there is another thought in my mind of which I want to tell you. I talked it over last night with my old friend Michael.—Ah, where is Michael ?" said Ivan, who in the excitement and confusion of the last two hours had totally forgotten his companion. " No matter," he continued, " I shall find him by-and-by.—Say, dädushka, would it not be a pity these infidel Frenchmen should enter the Kremlin without so much as a musket-shot to bid them welcome ?"

" But what would you do, my son ? Remember the lives of Russians are precious."

" I should peril no life which would not be just as sorely perilled elsewhere; but I think that, with the help of the work-men who are still on the spot, and a few of the lads whom I know to be ready for any wild work, I could give a fair account of some of Napoleon's advanced guard."

" Well, since Count Rostopchine has left the city, every man may do that which is right in his own eyes.   Have you arms ?"

" Plenty; and I, as well as the other directors nominated by the count, have his authority to distribute them as I see fit.— Ah, Pope Yefim, is that you ? So you have not left us yet."

" Not yet, nor ever," said the priest as he advanced and saluted first his aged friend, then Ivan.

" I thought all the churchmen were gone already, or going to-day," observed Ivan.

" It may be so," returned Pope Yefim, " but, whosoever goes, sorrow and death remain."

" *Remain !*" cried Ivan.   " It is their carnival."

" Well, then, may not one of God's humblest ministers remain also, to pray beside the sorrowful and to bury the dead ?"

" My dear pope, the part you have chosen is noble, but most perilous."

" I scarcely think so.   All civilized nations respect Religion and her ministers.   I have heard that Napoleon said to one of our popes, who bravely presented himself before him to plead for his flock, ' You have done well.   Your " Bog" is the same as our " Dieu." ' "

" Whose altars the French have cast down, and whose wor-ship they have forsaken; therefore they shall not prosper," said Petrovitch.   He added after a pause : " My friends, I am solitary now. Stay with me for a little while. And if Prince Ivan will forget his worldly rank in the presence of great Death, who makes all men equal, I pray you both to partake with me of what may be to all of us our last meal upon earth."

Ivan readily consented; and the attendants left in the house, who watched carefully over their aged master, served a comfortable repast. One of them informed Ivan that his servant was in their quarters, awaiting his orders. Michael had been a deeply-moved spectator of the parting between Petrovitch and his family. He had been seen coming out of the hall with a sobbing child in his arms, a little great-grandson of Petrovitch, whom he was trying to comfort. Afterwards he fraternized with the attendants, who were mujiks, like himself, and to whose inquiries he answered simply and briefly that he was Prince Ivan's servant.

The hours wore on. At last Ivan and Yefim were obliged to depart—Ivan to his work in the city, the priest to one of the numerous services of his Church.

Then for the first time Petrovitch knew himself indeed alone. To darkness he was accustomed now, but the strange unwonted stillness "ached round him like a strong disease and new." No kindred voice would break the silence ever again upon earth. Such had been his deliberate choice, and he must bear it. But his strong heart sank lower and lower yet, even to the very depths—those deepest depths of all, which only strong hearts know how to sound.

"Out of the depths have I cried unto thee," said one of old, uttering the experience of ten thousand tried and sorrowful hearts. Very earnest was the cry that went up that bitter hour from the soul of Petrovitch. It was not his first cry to God; for the hand that had drawn a veil over the eyes of his body had been gradually and gently opening the eye of his soul to another and holier light. What though, at the best, that light was dim and clouded? It was enough for his needs;

and in this hour of lonely anguish it shone out with greater clearness than ever before. "I am a sinful man," thought Feodor Petrovitch; "and now the last hour of my long day of life has struck. I am going into the presence of God. But there is the dear Bog Sūn,* and the cross, of which Pope Yefim talks. I hope to be forgiven for the sake of what He suffered there, and to see His face with joy in the resurrection."

Then thoughts of the past chased each other quickly across his mind, like clouds across a summer sky. All the events of his life seemed to crowd upon him, and to pass in review before him " like a tale that is told." First came visions of his early years, — his village home, his boyhood's friends, his dear lord, Prince Pojarsky, with the face of Ivan grown older; then his own struggles as a man,—his efforts to secure an honourable place in the world, to gain wealth, character, and the esteem of all. But these things flitted lightly by, and did not stay. What came and stayed, fresh and vivid as though he saw them even now, were the faces that he loved—faces over which the grave had closed long ago. " Yesterday they seemed so far; to-day they are close at hand. I shall see them before another sun has set," he thought. The wife of his youth came back, young and fair as on her bridal day. Scarce younger and not less fair, so like that they seemed to mingle into one sweet all-pervading presence, was that child of his heart, so tenderly loved, so deeply mourned. As the Hebrew patriarch, casting a retrospective glance over his long and weary pilgrimage, rested the wistful gaze of his dying eye upon one chief unforgotten sorrow—" *As for me*, when I came from Padan, Rachel died by me in the land of Canaan"—so it was with Feodor Petrovitch. A passionate yearning swept over him to see his daughter's face, to hear her voice again.

By-and-by another change came. It was no longer faces that haunted him, but voices—voices and footsteps. The little feet

* **God the Son.**

of his grandchildren pattered around him; he heard their merry shouts, their ringing laughter at their play. He felt tempted to call them; he almost believed that if he called they would come to him. At last he heard the footstep that he loved best—so plain, so near, that he thought he must be dreaming. How strangely fancy must be cheating him! Surely that *was* Feodor—*his* Feodor—trying in jest, as he was wont to do, to steal upon him unawares and surprise him. Surely, as in the old happy days, the boy had slipped off his lapti, and was stepping softly and noiselessly upon the rugs that strewed the floor. Surely he was close to him now—his breath was touching his very cheek. All unconsciously the name escaped his lips, and he called aloud, "Feodor!"

"*Dädushka,*" the voice he loved seemed to answer.

"O God!" sobbed the old man, for the first time completely unnerved, "leave me my senses. Do not let me lose myself in vain delirious dreams. Grant that I may give up my soul to thee in peace."

"Dädushka, do not be afraid. It is I—it is your little Feodor." And now he knew it was no dream, for Feodor's arms were around him, Feodor's face was buried in his breast.

"Did you think I could leave you, dädushka? Did you think I could really go away with the others? Of course I pretended to go; but I watched my opportunity, slipped off, and came back to you as soon as I dared. I have been hiding ever since."

"My child, my child, I must send you from me."

"Dädushka, you must not, for I cannot go. Listen—I have sworn upon bended knees before the picture of my saint that where you die there will I die also."

"My boy, I cannot have it—the old have so little life to give, the young so much!"

"Dädushka, I will not live after you; for am I not yours altogether? My mother is dead, and my father too. You have ever been to me instead of both. I have nothing in the world but you. But what need of words?" said the boy, drawing up his slender figure to its full height; "*I have sworn.*"

Petrovitch could not see how his young face glowed, and his dark eyes shone like lamps of fire; but he heard the tones of his voice, which had in them the ring of a steadfast purpose, not proud or self-confident, scarcely even passionate, only full of a quiet resolute persuasion that he was doing something to which God had called him.

The old man's reverence for the sanctity of an oath was rendered stronger by a tinge of superstition. Moreover, he thought this world—where apparently and for the present the infidel Nyemtzi were victorious—not such a safe and happy home that true hearts need mourn to leave it. Perhaps it would even be well for him to take his dearest treasure with him to the better land, and bring Maria Petrovna the little one she had intrusted to his care. Thus it was that when once more Feodor whispered softly, "And I too, dädushka,—I am glad to die for the Czar," he only answered, "For our monarch, our country, and our God. May he accept the sacrifice, and receive our souls into his kingdom."

Just then a servant hastily entered the room. "Father," he said, in great agitation, "a horseman is galloping through the streets, crying aloud that the French are coming. Their standards may be seen, he says, upon the Sparrow Hill. And, father," he added, "the kibitka is ready, according to your orders."

"Then give me thine arm, Feodor," said the old man rising. "Our hour has come."

CHAPTER XV

THE MARTYR CITY.

THE slow hours that had dragged their weary length since the evacuation of the doomed city began, seemed a lifetime to Ivan. He almost felt as if the suspense, the dull, hushed lull of expectation that was not hope and yet was scarcely fear, would never end. But the end came at length, and from that hour events followed each other with tremendous, bewildering rapidity.

Ivan was in the Kremlin, distributing arms to the workmen whom he found there, when some one cried that the French were fording the Moskva (the Russian general, Miloradovitch, having broken down the bridges). Ivan sprang to the nearest point of observation, and saw some horsemen in fantastic uniforms, and bringing with them a couple of guns, actually crossing the stream. A personage, splendidly attired and surrounded by a brilliant staff, was directing their movements, and apparently preparing to follow them. This, though Ivan knew it not, was Murat, King of Naples, who was leading the French vanguard, thirsting for glory and plunder, and already devouring with covetous eyes the fabulous treasures of the Kremlin.

Ivan returned to his companions. " God has delivered them

into our hands," he said. "We will let them cross the ford, and then—"

What followed may be learned from Murat's own confession found in an intercepted letter to his wife. "Never in my life," wrote the King of Naples, "was I in such wild danger." First a sharp fire of musketry saluted the advancing French; then the workmen and the populace sprang upon them "with maniac fury," and fought "like demons." The two pieces of cannon which Murat had with him, and which were loaded with grape-shot, eventually decided the contest, but not until a colonel of engineers and a large number of soldiers had fallen.

After the fray Michael saw Ivan, covered with dust and mortar, leaning against a wall which had just been struck by a shot. "Are you hurt, Barrinka?" he asked.

"No," said Ivan, shaking the mortar from his clothes; "I am all right. And you too, I hope? We must not throw away our lives, Michael; there is too much still to be done. Come with me to the prison."

"Anywhere with you, Barrinka. See, though I could not use a gun, I have killed Nyemtzi." And Michael triumphantly displayed a short sabre dyed with blood.

"Where did you get that?" asked Ivan.

"Took it from one of themselves. That is French blood upon the blade," said Michael, with an air of intense satisfaction.

The Wertsch palace was directly in their way, and Ivan went in, saying, with a determined air, "I will hear no more excuses from the countess now. Go she must; her hour has come."

Her hour had come—in a sense other and more solemn than Ivan meant. The waiting-woman Maria met him in the saloon, and told him with many tears that her mistress was dying. At the tidings that the French had actually entered holy Moscow, so terrible was her agitation that she had broken a blood-vessel, and was now beyond the reach of human aid.* Ivan despatched a messenger for Pope Yefim—the only priest he knew who had not left the city—while he himself hastened to the side of the dying woman, to whom he thought his presence might be a comfort.

He was too late. The countess had sunk into a state of unconsciousness, and only faint occasional sighs showed that life lingered still. As he stood in the darkened room beside the motionless form, thoughts of death, at once more solemn and more true than any that had come to him before, stole into his heart. There was a sense of reality about this slow sinking of the powers of nature which he had not felt in any of the wild and stormy perils he had braved and was braving still. That living soul, that personal mind and will, but yesterday so pronounced and active, where was it? Whither was it going? Ivan did not know. With him all the future was mist and fog—"a land of darkness, as darkness itself." And for a moment his strong heart almost quailed as there swept over it those old yet ever new apprehensions and doubts, those

> "Blank misgivings of a creature
> Moving about in worlds not realized."

But this mood passed as quickly as it came. He dared not linger; every moment was of importance now. With one sad look of farewell he went his way, and was soon absorbed in preparations for the great and terrible sacrifice which was approaching so quickly.

He did not forget to send a messenger to the dwelling of Petrovitch to learn the latest tidings of the heroic old man; and was told that he had left the house, with his grandson Feodor, on the first intimation of the approach of the French.

The first regiment of Frenchmen who advanced that day along the great Smolensko road to the Gate of Triumph could

* Her persistence in remaining in the city and her death are historical.

have told Ivan something more. Just outside the gate, under a green and spreading oak-tree, sat a venerable old man, with hair and beard of silver whiteness; while beside him stood a slight, tall stripling of some sixteen summers. The boy held a gun in his hand, and as the French advanced, he took deliberate aim at their leader, who was conspicuous on his stately horse, his plumed cap waving in the wind. In a moment more the horse was riderless and the plumes were trailing in the dust.

This was the signal for a dozen Frenchmen with drawn sabres to spring at once upon the old man and the boy. "It is I whom you ought to kill," cried Petrovitch; "for it was I who armed him and bade him fire upon you." Feodor meanwhile took two pistols from his belt and discharged them against his assailants; then drawing a poniard, he defended his aged grand-father, until at last he fell overpowered by numbers and covered with wounds. Nor did the snow-white hairs of the patriarch save him from the same fate.

It is said that an hour afterwards Napoleon passed the spot attended by his staff. With a look of horror he turned away and drew his horse to the other side of the road, saying to those around him, "Such a venerable old man! It was a cowardly murder."

Night fell over the doomed city, and a full moon illumined its fair minarets and domes with a robe of silver light. But to the French, as they entered, it seemed like the deserted camp of the Syrians—"Behold, there was no man there, neither voice of man," except a few trembling servants, who led the conquerors into the abandoned dwellings of their lords, and showed them the rich furniture, the costly provisions, the rare wines which they had left behind them. In some cases even the unfinished embroidery of the ladies was found lying as it had fallen from their hands.

Yet the city had not surrendered to the enemy. No one brought the keys to Napoleon; no one entreated his mercy or deprecated his vengeance. The strange silence touched even his haughty soul with surprise and misgiving. In all Moscow there remained not one person with whom he could communicate, not one of sufficient importance to answer his inquiries or to receive and execute his commands. The only official he could find was the director of the Foundling Hospital, who had refused to desert his helpless little flock at the coming of the wolf.

The Bourse and the buildings around it were already wrapped in flames when the French entered the city; but the immense extent of Moscow prevented anything like a general alarm, and the first four-and-twenty hours of the Occupation passed quietly away. On the following night, however — a night much to be remembered in the annals of Russia, of Europe, and of freedom, that of the 15th of September—the sad Russian host on its weary march, and the immense crowd of weeping fugitives that followed it, beheld a sight magnificent indeed but most terrible. A sheet of flame, fanned by a tempestuous wind, grew and spread until it wrapped the wide extent of the devoted city like a shroud of fire. The entire horizon was illuminated. Three quarters of a league away men could see to read by the lurid light. Nor did the dawn of day bring any respite to the horror. The sun turned sickening from the scene, its pale beams unable to contend with that fierce red glare. Another sun arose, and yet another;—still the conflagration raged. It took six awful days and nights to consume that holocaust, the grandest the world has ever seen. But when at last the flames died slowly out, nine-tenths of the ancient capital of the Czar were laid in ashes.

CHAPTER XVI.

ALEXANDER.

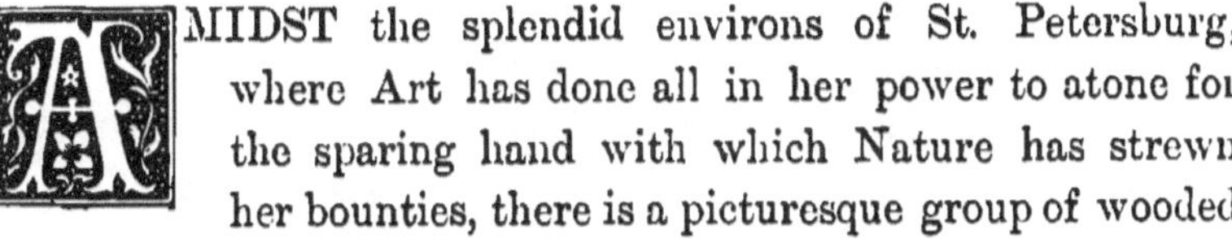

MIDST the splendid environs of St. Petersburg, where Art has done all in her power to atone for the sparing hand with which Nature has strewn her bounties, there is a picturesque group of wooded islets embraced by the clear blue waters of the Neva, and conspicuous for the splendour of the "datcha," or country houses, which adorn them. One of these islets, called Kamenoi-Ostrov, or the stony island, contains an imperial residence, a castle surrounded by gardens; and here, while Moscow was still in flames, arrived Colonel Michaud, the eminent Sardinian engineer, with a sad and heavy heart.*

He had travelled with the speed and almost in the style of a courier. When he alighted from his unpretending vehicle at the castle gate, he saw that the place had a deserted look; and only a single Cossack, who happened to be on duty as sentinel, perceived his approach. Although the Emperor was still here, even his very guards had been despatched to the seat of war. Michaud briefly gave his name, and asked for an audience.

He was introduced at once into the cabinet of the Czar. Alexander looked worn and anxious; young as he was, a few

---

* The conversation which follows is given as it was recorded by Michaud himself. All the details in this chapter are historical, without any admixture of fiction.

threads of silver showed themselves already in his chestnut hair. He saluted Michaud courteously ; but asked immediately, with a keen and searching look, " Do you not bring me sad tidings, colonel ? "

" Very sad, sire ;—the evacuation of Moscow."

" Have they given up my ancient capital without a struggle?"

" Sire, the environs of Moscow offer no position in which we could hazard a battle with our inferior forces. The marshal* thought he did well in preserving your army, whose loss without saving Moscow would have been of the greatest consequence ; and which, by the reinforcements your Majesty has just procured, and which I met everywhere along my road, will soon resume the offensive, and make the French repent of invading Russia."

" Has the enemy actually entered the city ? "

" Yes, sire. At this moment Moscow is in ashes. I left it in flames." Here Michaud stopped abruptly, for the agony depicted on the Emperor's face, " the expression of his eyes," completely unmanned him,—he could say no more.

It was Alexander who, after a few bitter moments, and maintaining his self-control with a strong effort, resumed the conversation.

" I see that God requires from us great sacrifices. I am ready to submit to his will. But, Michaud, tell me frankly, what of the army? What do my soldiers say upon seeing my ancient capital abandoned without a struggle? Must not this have exercised a most disastrous influence upon the spirit of the troops ? "

" Sire, may I speak to you quite frankly, and as a loyal soldier ? "

" Colonel, I have always required this frankness ; now I entreat of you to use it. Hide nothing from me: I desire absolutely to know the truth."

* General Kutusov.

"Sire, I left all the army, from the generals to the meanest soldier, possessed with one overpowering and terrible fear—"

"How? Whence these fears? Are my Russians overcome by the first misfortune?" the Czar interrupted with emotion which even he could not restrain, and which, as Michaud says, "altered for a moment the noble calm of his fine features."

"Never, sire!" resumed the colonel. "Their one fear is that your Majesty, out of kindness of heart, may be persuaded to make peace. They are burning to fight for you, and to prove their devotion by the sacrifice of their lives."

At these heroic words the light flashed once more across the clouded face of Alexander. "You reassure me, colonel," he said. "Well then, return to the army. Say to our brave men, say to all my subjects wherever you meet them, that if I had not a soldier left, I should put myself at the head of my dear nobles, of my faithful peasants, and expend to the uttermost the resources of my empire. They are greater than my enemies think. But if it be the will of God that my dynasty shall cease to reign upon the throne of my ancestors, then—after having done all else that man can do—I will let my beard grow to *this*," said Alexander, placing his hand upon his breast, "and I will eat potatoes like the lowest of my mujiks, rather than sign the humiliation of my country and of my dear people, whose sacrifices for my sake I appreciate." Here his voice failed : it was easier to speak of his own ruin than of the love of his subjects. Greatly moved, he turned away from Michaud, and walked to the other end of the cabinet. But he came back almost immediately with long and rapid strides, and a face that had quickly changed from a deadly pallor to a fiery flush. Pressing his hand on the arm of the officer, he said, "Colonel Michaud, do not forget my words; perhaps one day we shall remember them with pleasure. Napoleon or I—I or Napoleon —we can no longer reign together. I know him now; he shall never deceive me again."

"Sire," cried the colonel joyfully, "your Majesty signs in this moment the glory of the nation and the deliverance of Europe."

His words were true—with this qualification, that the glory of Russia and the deliverance of Europe were not the work of a moment, but of long months of patient, heroic resolution. Alexander had not wished for war—perhaps, indeed, he had striven too long to avert it. Personally, in his earlier years, he admired Napoleon : the fact is undeniable, though it has been the subject of much exaggeration. From the dawn of manhood his favourite dream had been of a universal and durable peace, and he imagined he saw in the victories of Napoleon so many steps to its attainment. What are now called "Les idées Napoléoniques," seem to have captivated for a season this young, ardent, somewhat visionary mind. But the veil once torn from his eyes by the insatiable ambition and the repeated perfidies of the French usurper, thenceforward it was between them war to the death.

When Napoleon suddenly poured his enormous hosts across the Niemen, Alexander at once and emphatically announced his resolution, "I will not sheathe the sword while a single foreigner remains in arms upon the soil of Russia." At that moment the eyes of all Europe were upon him, and neither friend nor foe believed it possible that he could make good his word.

"Napoleon," said an astute observer, "thought he could terrify the Emperor of Russia by his menaces without drawing a sword ; he thought he could make him lose his head by beginning the war suddenly in the midst of negotiations ; he thought he could end that war by a single battle. But nothing happened that he thought."* In a letter written by him about this time, which was intercepted and brought to his rival, were

* De Maistre.—Sir Robert Wilson, an Englishman, was of great use in this crisis as the friend and counsellor of Alexander.

these words: "Alexander is a child. I will make him weep tears of blood." Alexander upon reading it remarked : "He said to me himself that in war determination always carries the day. We shall see who has the most determination, he or I."

But the determination of the strongest heart might well have quailed before the perils that beset the Czar in this solemn crisis of his own and his people's history. Six hundred and fifty thousand fighting men had crossed his border under a leader hitherto invincible, whose name was the terror of the civilized world. No man felt more keenly than Alexander his own inferiority to Napoleon as a general. The bitter memory of Austerlitz, his "unfortunate day," never left him. Nor had he any commander whose surpassing merit might inspire the army with confidence. The excellent Barclay de Tolly had unfortunately become so unpopular both with the army and the nation, that Alexander, though with much regret, was obliged to remove him. Of his successor, the aged Kutusov, he had no very high opinion; but when everything depended upon the cordial support of his people, he was in a manner obliged to consult their wishes.

Meanwhile the French were marching onwards into the very heart of the country. The retreat of the Russians before them was no doubt a master-stroke of policy, but to the sovereign of Russia it was unutterably painful. From the thought of the suferings of his people,—the murders, the plundering, the desolation,—his sensitive heart recoiled in horror. Nearer and nearer came the fiery deluge, leaving a track of ruin behind it. Consternation seized his counsellors, his court, his very family. The foreign envoys at St. Petersburg packed up their effects in readiness for an immediate flight. Even the Grand Duke Constantine made the hard task of the brother he idolized harder still by assuring every one that the French would inevitably conquer, —it was hopeless to resist them. He called for peace, it was said, "as men call for water in a conflagration."

To aggravate and crown all this misery, dejection, and terror, came the overwhelming tidings of the destruction of Moscow. In some ways it was a calamity more bitter, more crushing than that of St. Petersburg would have been. While the one was the official capital, the other was the real heart of the old Muscovite empire. Here the Czars were baptized, were crowned, were buried; here were heaped all the treasures, were concentrated all the glories of their past. It was their holy city, their Jerusalem. No one knew as yet that its destruction had been a signal act of patriotism and self-sacrifice; almost all the world, including the Czar himself, believed that the French had consummated their atrocities by setting fire to the city. Nor could he or others foresee the future, or discern at once amidst the dust and smoke of the conflict that the victory, in truth, was won. The final hour of Napoleon's triumph had struck, but the toll of fate was audible neither to friend nor foe; and to Alexander and to Russia the day that saw the fall of Moscow seemed the darkest that had ever dawned upon them.

In the heart of Alexander it left "a profound and bitter sorrow," which neither time, nor victory, nor glory could ever wholly obliterate. Long afterwards, when conquered France offered the conqueror pecuniary compensation, he answered with proud sadness, "Gold can never give me Moscow back again." Yet not for one moment did his courage fail or his determination falter. His wife implored him with tears to make peace, or to allow her to leave the empire. His mother, less submissive, actually prepared to go. He gently dissuaded her from a course so injurious to the interests of the country, and at last, when she refused to listen, he said firmly, "I have entreated you as a son; I now command you as your sovereign. You shall not go." Amidst the universal panic he alone stood firm. Naturally susceptible, tender-hearted, perhaps even irresolute, the hour of trial found him undaunted as the fiercest of his barbarian ancestors. Like the delicate mainspring of some complicated machine which sustains a pressure that would shatter a bar of iron, so this fine sensitive nature assumed the best attributes of strength, and bore up triumphantly against a world in arms.

Amongst the first words which he addressed to his people after the fall of Moscow were these :—"An oppressed world looks to us for encouragement, and can we shrink from the honourable mission? Let us kiss the hand that selected us to act as the leader of nations in the struggle for independence, and contend with courage and constancy to obtain a durable peace, not only for ourselves, but for those unhappy countries forced by the tyrant to fight in his quarrel : it is glorious, it is worthy of a great nation, to *render good for ill.*" The proclamation ends with a prayer :—" Almighty God, is the cause for which we are battling not just? Cast an eye of compassion on our holy Church. Preserve to this people its courage and constancy. Suffer it to triumph over its adversary and thine. May it be in thy hand the instrument of his destruction ; and in delivering itself, redeem the independence of nations and of kings."

Here we recognize the secret of Alexander's strength. He knew himself in the hands of God ; he and his people were instruments to do his will.

Some years later he said to a friend, " The conflagration of Moscow illumined my soul." It certainly marked a crisis in his spiritual history ; but with souls the sudden illumination of a tropical sunrise is the rare exception, while light " increasing more and more unto the perfect day" is the ordinary rule. From Alexander's earliest years it had seemed as if God was drawing his heart towards himself. While yet a little child he would rise from his bed at night, and kneel unbidden to ask forgiveness for some childish fault. Then and throughout his life his tenderness of heart was remarkable. He "never willingly hurt any living thing ;" and so beautiful was the influence he exercised over his wayward brother Constantine, that a plan for having the latter brought up amongst Greeks as their future sovereign was abandoned, because it was wisely concluded that no political advantage could counterbalance the loss of Alex·ander's example and companionship.

Unfortunately, the Empress Catherine had intrusted the education of her favourite grandson to freethinkers like herself, of the school of Voltaire and Diderot.   He was early taught to look upon all forms of religion as antiquated superstitions, useful, perhaps, for the vulgar, but beneath the notice of the wise.   His natural benevolence was not discouraged, but justice and humanity were inculcated to the utter exclusion of piety.

With such an education, and while yet a boy, he was launched upon the troubled sea of one of the most dissolute, frivolous, and vicious courts in Europe.   He did not wholly escape contamination, but all the dreams of his youth were noble and lofty.   To be the benefactor of his kind, to free the oppressed—such were the visions he nursed in solitude or breathed into the ear of a sympathizing friend during the long walks in which he delighted.   The voice of God was never quite silent in his heart. He himself says that with regard to religion, "things were at the court of St. Petersburg very much as everywhere else—many words, but little meaning; many outward practices, but the holy essence of Christianity was hidden from our eyes.   I felt the void in my soul, and a vague presentiment accompanied me everywhere.   I went—I came—I sought to distract my thoughts."

The void within of which he spoke was deepened by sorrow. During the reign of his father, who disliked and dreaded him as a rival, his position was both difficult and painful.   Personally, he was submissive and patient; but he was brave in interceding for the oppressed, and in using for the good of others any measure of authority that was allowed him.   After four years, the tragedy which terminated the reign of the unfortunate Paul placed the imperial crown upon the head of Alexander, but cast a shadow over his life which never wholly passed away. To his latest hour, in every period of sorrow or despondency, "the agony returned." It was not exactly remorse, for he was guiltless; but it was poignant grief and horror. It deepened that inherited tendency to morbid gloom and depression which perhaps, even amidst the happiest surroundings, might have developed as years went by.

In one of these sorrowful moods he confessed his dejection to an intimate friend, hinting that he envied him his unfailing cheerfulness. Prince Galitzin told him in reply that he had found in the Bible the source of true comfort and happiness. The story was a remarkable one. Early in his reign Alexander nominated Galitzin "Minister of Public Worship." "But I know nothing about religion," objected the Prince, who, like his master, had been educated in an atmosphere of French infidelity. "That is a point in your favour," replied the philosophic Czar. "It will secure your impartiality. You have only to hold the balance even, and do justice to every one." But Galitzin, not quite satisfied, asked Archbishop Plato to recommend him some book which would give him a knowledge of religion. The venerable metropolitan advised him to read the Bible; which he did, at first very reluctantly, afterwards with ever deepening interest and profit.

Alexander determined to follow the example of his friend, and next day surprised the Empress Elizabeth by asking her to lend him a Bible. She gave him a French copy of the Sacred Word—De Sacy's translation, printed at Cologne—and it became thenceforward his inseparable companion. For a long time he was haunted by sceptical doubts; but he persevered in his study, and the shadows that obscured his soul gradually and slowly passed away.

Notwithstanding the general unbelief and indifference of the higher classes, there were at that time in the Russian court a few " devout and honourable women," who were earnestly seeking light from above. To these the Czar was an object of interest, as " not far from the kingdom of heaven." When the French war was impending, and the burden of anxiety from which few hearts were free was known to weigh most heavily upon his, a message, which proved to be indeed from God, came to him through one of them. It was the night before he started for Vilna, and, according to his usual custom, he was spending it in transacting business, content to find what sleep he could in his open carriage while dashing at headlong speed through the country. As he was diligently arranging his papers, a lady entered his cabinet unannounced, and looking up in great surprise he recognized the wife of his Grand Marshal, the Countess Tolstoi. She apologized 'for her unseasonable visit, and put a paper into his hand, which she entreated him to read, saying he would find true comfort there. His unfailing courtesy led him to accept it and thank her; and she withdrew. He put the paper in his pocket, resumed his occupation, and thought no more of it until, after two days and nights of rapid travel, he changed his clothes for the first time. Upon removing his coat he found it, and saw that it was a copy of the ninety-first psalm. He lay down; but, worn out with fatigue, was unable to sleep, so he called his chaplain and requested him to read to him. Strangely enough, the portion which the priest selected was that very psalm, and the Czar was greatly impressed by the coincidence.* The glorious words of promise, so exactly suited to his need, were received with simple faith. From that day forward he said of the Lord, " He is my refuge and my fortress: my God; in him will I trust."

His study of the Divine Word became more earnest and

* Another story is told, connecting Alexander's first acquaintance with the ninety-first psalm with Prince Galitzin, but that given above seems on the whole to be preferable.

systematic : from this period until the end of his life he read three chapters daily, even under the most difficult circumstances, " when the cannon were thundering about his tent." He prayed constantly, " using no form," as he said himself, " but the words which God's Spirit taught him, according to his needs." And he sought to conform his conduct to the will of God, so far as he understood it.

This was not done without a struggle. His life had not been blameless, and much once dear had to be surrendered. But henceforward his court became a model of purity ; and moreover his fear of God showed itself in an increase of gentleness towards man. He made great efforts to control his naturally passionate temper ; and if, after this period, he was betrayed into a hasty expression, he would frankly apologize, not only to a member of his suite, but even to the humblest of his attendants.

He had always known that his enormous power was intrusted to him for the good of others, not for his own happiness or glory. " Fifty millions of men are worth more than one man," had been an axiom with him from the beginning of his reign. But now he knew himself the steward of God, responsible to *him* for its exercise. " You should be in my place," he said to a friend, " to understand what is the responsibility of a sovereign, and what I feel when I reflect that one day I must render an account of the life of every one of my soldiers."

Amongst the commands of Christ which impressed him most deeply were these : " Love your enemies : do good to them that hate you." He learned to forgive personal injuries, " which in other reigns would have drawn down thunder." One instance amongst many may be given. Admiral Tchichagof, one of his ministers, quarrelled with his colleagues, and at length withdrew to Paris, where he said many bitter and injurious things about the Czar, which were all reported to him, and probably exaggerated. Just before the outbreak of the war, Tchichagof's wife died, and, in accordance with her last request, he brought her body to St. Petersburg for interment. He wrote to the Czar to inform him of his return and its reason ; and Alexander replied by an autograph letter, which Tchichagof showed in confidence to his friend De Maistre. "What a letter!" wrote the Sardinian ambassador to his sovereign. "The most tender and most delicate friend could not have written otherwise." And he said to Tchichagof, as he handed back the precious paper, "You ought to die for the prince who wrote you that letter." An interview followed, in which the reconciliation was cemented. "I know what you have said of me," said Alexander, "but I attribute all to a good motive." Need it be added that henceforward Tchichagof served him faithfully?

But what of the French—of Napoleon? What of his desolated country, his murdered subjects, his fair and favourite city laid in ashes? Could these things be forgiven? Or is it true, as many would tell us, that the precepts of Christ are admirably suited for women and children, perhaps, at the utmost, for men in their private relations each with the other, but a nullity or a failure when applied to larger scenes and interests, utterly ineffectual to guide and control the statesman in his cabinet or the monarch on his throne? We shall see how far the story of Alexander answers this question.

For two or three years he might truly have been said to "abide under the shadow of the Almighty," although not as yet did he "dwell in the secret place of the most High." He trusted in God, he sought to obey Christ, long before he knew him as the Saviour upon whom his sins were laid. Again, to use his own words, "I did not arrive there in a moment. Believe me, the path by which I was conducted led me across many a conflict, many a doubt."

The light that shone within him was like the slow dawn of a Northern day—

> " An Arctic day that will not see
> A sunset till its summer 's gone."

Those were indeed the beams of the sun which flooded the whole horizon, gladdening the heart of every living thing; but the sun itself was still unseen, because as yet unrisen. Its light was there; its glory was yet to come.

CHAPTER XVII.

IN THE CAMP.

ONE evening towards the end of October, and just when the first snow of the year was beginning to fall, Ivan Pojarsky and Michael Ivanovitch entered the head-quarters of the Russian army at Tarovtino. Their fleet Arabian horses were flecked with foam, for they had traversed the ten leagues which divided them from Moscow without once drawing rein. As they dashed along, they shouted to all whom they passed, " Napoleon has quitted Moscow ! " and answering " houras " and cries of joy cheered them on their way.

" Bring us at once to Count Rostopchine," said Ivan to the soldiers who crowded around them. " He is here, is he not ? "

" He is here, gospodin ; but the Marshal—"

" With all due respect to the dignity of his Highness the General-in-Chief, our business is with the Count, brothers," returned Ivan.

He was accordingly conducted to the presence of Rostopchine, who, after a lengthened interview, dismissed him to seek rest and refreshment, desiring him to return early in the morning.

Rostopchine's aide-de-camp offered his hospitality, and Ivan thanked him courteously, but inquired whether Captain Adrian Wertsch, of the Moscow militia, was not then in the camp. The aide-de-camp answered in the affirmative, and agreed to bring Ivan to his tent, though very reluctantly ; for he was sorry to lose the honour and pleasure of entertaining one who could give him so many interesting details about the French occupation of Moscow.

Adrian was standing outside his tent when Ivan approached, and he greeted him with joyful astonishment, as one risen from the dead.

" I did not think to see your face again," he said.

" Life is still left me," returned Ivan in a broken voice ; for, after so many horrors, the sight of a familiar face proved at the moment almost more than he could bear.

" Come in," said Adrian, drawing his arm affectionately within his own. " A good draught of champagne is what you want now."

" Will you tell your orderly to take care of my friend Michael Ivanovitch ? He has behaved like a hero."

" Certainly."

Adrian gave a few rapid directions, then led Ivan into his tent, and before he would listen to a word, poured for him a sparkling goblet of the beverage which he considered a panacea for all the ills, mental and bodily, of the noble, as vodka was for those of the mujik.

Ivan needed the stimulant, for he was worn out with fatigue and excitement. He said, as he finished the draught, " You got my letter, Adrian ?"

" Yes. My poor mother ! "

" No one was to blame. We did all we could, but nothing would induce her to leave the old home ; and when the French entered Moscow, the shock was more than she could bear. We buried her honourably, by the side of her husband, in the Church of St. Eustacius. Pope Yefim performed the funeral services."

"That was nobly done, Ivan, and I thank you most heartily. —By the way, your friend Pope Yefim has made himself famous."

"How? By remaining in the city?"

"By daring to celebrate, with a solemn service, the Czar's coronation day, under the very beard of Napoleon.* We have all heard of it."

"He never supposed he was doing anything extraordinary. The Prior of the Dominican Monastery, whom he consulted, agreed that he was right. I can tell you, Adrian, that good man himself was by no means in love with his countrymen. Though his religion is their own, and he kept his church open the whole time of the Occupation, scarcely a Frenchman darkened its doors, except a few officers of noble birth belonging to the old *régime*. As a rule, the soldiers of Napoleon are infidels. Sometimes, out of curiosity, they would stray into our churches. On the coronation day, a poor young fellow, a mere lad, stole into Pope Yefim's church, and was near paying dearly for his rashness; for a party of mujiks set upon him after the service, taking him for a spy. They might have killed him; but—strangest chance of all—my friend Michael, whose thoughts by day and dreams by night are only of slaying Nyemtzi, interposed to save this one, saying he knew him, and had received a kindness at his hands. I spoke to the youth, and he told me he had been religiously brought up, and said the very sound of a church-bell, and the sight of men kneeling in prayer, seemed to do him good, though he could not understand a word of the service."

"A queer taste," said Adrian, shrugging his shoulders. Then to his orderly, who had just entered the tent, "Bring us the best supper you can get, and more champagne."

"Adrian," asked Ivan, "where is Leon?"

Adrian's face assumed a sorrowful expression. "Gone to

* A fact.

our mother," he answered. "He was wounded at Borodino, though not severely. He insisted upon going out again, and met his death in a skirmish ten days ago."

Ivan felt and showed real sorrow. Of the two companions of his youth, Leon had been his favourite, and he could not hear unmoved the tidings of his death. "Death—death everywhere," he murmured sadly.

"Come, my friend," said Adrian kindly, "you must not give way. It is only the fate of war. You have been so long in that horrible den of a city that your nerves are shattered. Take some more wine."

"That horrible den!" Ivan repeated. "A lair of wild beasts! Such it has been indeed. The count, who is as hard as *this*," laying his hand upon Adrian's iron camp-bedstead, "has been asking me for reports and descriptions. I cannot describe, I can scarcely even report facts. Picture to yourself nine-tenths of the town in ashes—or in charred blackened ruins — with thousands of the wretched inhabitants, who could not, or did not, make good their escape, wandering about homeless and starving, filling the air with their lamentations. Then think of the French, like a host of demons turned loose upon their prey, ransacking the smoking ruins in search of plunder. I have seen the gold-laced uniform of the general and the woollen jacket of the private side by side, contending for the spoils of our desolated homes; while all the dangerous classes, all the thieves and ruffians who are to be found amongst the scum of the populace in every great city, joined them in the horrible work and added to the confusion and misery."

"Did not Napoleon shoot or hang a great number of our people?"

"If you call three hundred a great number; so many at least he executed as incendiaries—and indeed most of them were taken in the act. They died in silence, without asking for mercy, and without accusing any one as having instigated them to the deed."

"How did *you* escape?" asked Adrian.

"There was little difficulty in escaping. It was easy enough to hide in the ruins or in the cellars, many of which had been left well stocked with provisions when the city was abandoned. But have you heard about our wounded men?" he asked, with a return of animation, and even of something like cheerfulness.

"No; I have heard nothing."

"The count was obliged to leave two thousand men, who were too desperately wounded to bear removal, concealed in the cellars of the city. Here they managed to drag on their lives, though in a state of extreme wretchedness. We found them out, and used to bring them food and other comforts. That work was even more hazardous than setting the city on fire; for discovery would have cost, not our lives alone, but theirs. Napoleon's last act before he left the city was to order ten sick men, found in a cellar, to be shot."

"Wretch!" cried Adrian, clenching his hand.

"The half has not been told you, or you would find no name to call him by," returned Ivan fiercely. "He has defiled our holiest sanctuaries; he has torn open our imperial tombs; he has stabled his horses in the church where our Czar was crowned; he has carried everything away upon which he could lay his sacrilegious hands, even to the cross upon the tower of Ivan Veliki, and the Tartar banners which hung as trophies in the Arsenal. Well may Count Rostopchine curse him, as only he knows how to curse. But those wounded— we contrived somehow to keep them alive; and I think a goodly number may be saved yet. I asked the count not to lose an hour in sending them succour."

"I hope he has had the grace to do justice to your courage and your exertions."

"He has condescended to approve my conduct," said Ivan

with modest satisfaction. "And now he offers me three things, by way of recompense, as he is pleased to say. If I choose to return with him to the city, he will give me an appointment in the civil service, with the rank of titular counsellor, which, as you know, answers to that of senior captain in the army."*

"Surely you will not do that! You could not sheathe your sword *now*," Adrian exclaimed.

"So much I said to the count; and he answered that, if I pleased, he would request the marshal to put me on his staff."

"Capital! What more could you desire?"

"He made another proposal—to send me to the Czar with the report of what I had seen and done."

"And which did you accept?"

"*The last*," said Ivan. At that moment a sound, dull, prolonged, and loud, like distant thunder, smote upon their ears. Again it came, and yet again, making the air tremble around them and the earth shake beneath their feet. "What is that?" cried Ivan.

"Not musketry or cannon," said Adrian, with a look of alarm and perplexity. "We are tolerably familiar with those sounds. *This* is different."

"More like an explosion—if so, a terrible one. Perhaps a great powder magazine. But where?" mused Ivan.

Adrian hurried out in search of information, and soon returned to tell his friend that the noise evidently came from the direction of Moscow. More than that no one knew.

Morning brought the explanation. Ivan was still enjoying the profound slumber of youth and weariness, when a brother officer of Adrian's rushed into the tent. "The Kremlin is destroyed!" he cried. "That demon Napoleon had it undermined before he left, and last night it was blown into fragments!"

* The ninth of the fourteen official Tchinns, or ranks, recognized by the Russian Government. Each rank in the army has a corresponding grade and title in the civil service.

"The Kremlin?—Impossible!" cried Adrian, who was dressing for parade.

"Too possible, and too true," said his informant. "A messenger from the city has just arrived to bring the tidings to the marshal and the count."

Meanwhile Ivan, who had been suddenly awakened, started up in horror, exclaiming, "The Czar! oh, what will it be to *him*?"

"Blown into fragments, did you say?" returned Adrian. "Utterly impossible! The masonry is as solid as the rocks beneath our feet, and the walls of the arsenal are three yards in thickness."

"Those walls are now level with the ground," said the officer; "and the palace—the Czar's ancient palace—is in ruins."

Ivan uttered a bitter cry, and Adrian asked breathlessly, "What of the churches?"

"One of them, I have not heard which, is thrown down. The mines were fired by slow-consuming fusees; and our men, who arrived just before the messenger left, were beginning a perilous search for powder, to prevent further mischief, if they could."

"But," said Ivan, who had risen now,—"but there must be a mistake somewhere; for the French kept their own sick and wounded in the Kremlin, and I happen to know that those unfit to be moved were still there when I left the city. That Napoleon could have exposed *them* to a horrible death is simply inconceivable."

"Yet too true," the officer answered. "He has sacrificed his own helpless followers to his revenge and hatred. For this barbarous deed can have had no other motive. There was nothing to be gained by it."

Adrian laid his hand upon Ivan's shoulder. "Do not go to St. Petersburg," he said. "Stay with us, and fight. We will pay this Napoleon double for all his atrocities."

"I wish his neck were *there*," said Adrian's comrade, grinding the earth with his strong heel. "But I would not kill him," he added, after a pause. "No. I would drag him in chains to the feet of the Czar, and let *him* kill him with his own hand."

"I think," said Ivan slowly and with deliberation,—"I think every Russian, from the Czar himself down to the lowest mujik, should swear a solemn oath not to sheathe the sword until we have taken such vengeance upon Napoleon and his Frenchmen as the world has never yet seen."

"So be it," said Michael, who came in while he was speaking. "I, a mujik, will be the first to swear.—Barrinka, what is the name of Napoleon's great city, where he has his palace and all his treasures? Suppose the Czar were to make a blaze of *that* some day! It may be. God is just!"

CHAPTER XVIII.

TWO IMPORTANT INTERVIEWS.

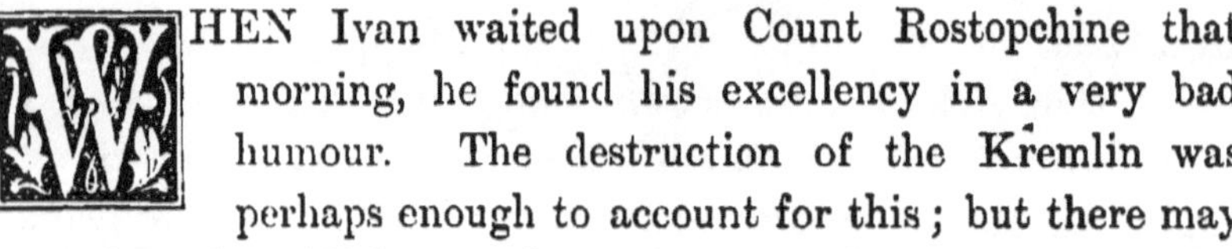

HEN Ivan waited upon Count Rostopchine that morning, he found his excellency in a very bad humour. The destruction of the Kremlin was perhaps enough to account for this; but there may have been in addition an altercation with Marshal Kutusov—not a very rare occurrence, for between the general-in-chief of the army and the governor of Moscow there was no friendship. Ivan found the count surrounded by the members of his suite, to whom he was giving directions in preparation for an immediate return to the city.

" Do you come with us, Ivan Ivanovitch ?" he asked abruptly, and of course in Russian, the only language he would tolerate in his presence, although he himself spoke and wrote French with elegance and precision.

Ivan saluted him with due respect, but answered in the negative.

" Ah ! then I shall have the trouble of speaking to the marshal about you," returned the count, with an air of annoyance, at which Ivan was scarcely surprised, for Rostopchine's manner on the preceding evening had made him fully aware that he desired to retain him in his own service. So he answered deferentially, " Instead of imposing that trouble upon your excellency, I shall avail myself of the third proposal you did me the honour to make, and very humbly entreat of you to intrust me with despatches for his Imperial Majesty."

Ivan was utterly amazed at the count's reception of this request. "Then you are as great a fool as I took you for the first day I saw your face. And," added Rostopchine, with one of his resounding Russian oaths, "you could not possibly be a greater!"

Such an address from such a personage, and in the presence of a score of witnesses, might well have disconcerted an older man than Ivan, especially as he could not in the least imagine the cause of it. But to every one's astonishment he stood his ground, and answered with the utmost coolness and self-possession, "Your excellency's opinion may be correct, but it must have some better foundation than my choosing to embrace an offer which you yourself condescended to make to me last night."

"He sees no difference between last night and this morning," remarked Rostopchine, turning to his officers, but speaking in a voice quite loud enough for Ivan to hear. "He is in a mighty hurry to go and tell the Czar that the Kremlin is destroyed." Then addressing Ivan directly—"I understand you perfectly, young gentleman : you prefer the air of a court to that of a camp, and had rather dangle your feet in the Czar's ante-chamber than use your hands fighting the French."

If Ivan had not just been performing most hazardous services with signal intrepidity, he might have been angry. But he knew that no one present doubted his courage for an instant, Rostopchine perhaps least of all. So he only bowed, and answered with extreme *sang-froid*, "That being the case, when shall I have the honour of waiting upon your excellency to receive your commands for St. Petersburg?"

"I will send them to you in half-an-hour ; you need not show your face here again."*

* Any one who has read the letters and proclamations of Count Rostopchine, will be aware that the violence of language attributed to him is very far from being exaggerated.

Ivan returned to the tent of his friend with, strange to say, a more cheerful air than when he left it. He seemed to be rather exhilarated than otherwise by his encounter. "Every one knows the count's temper," he said, after detailing the adventure. "I was not going to lose the reward of all I have passed through during the last six weeks for a few rough words. Only for the hope of seeing the face of my Czar, and telling him I tried to serve him faithfully, I should once and again have lain down to die."

"It is well known," answered Adrian, "that Count Rostopchine does not love the Czar—but he loves Russia." Then, to Ivan's surprise, Adrian told him that he himself hoped to be the companion of his rapid journey to St. Petersburg. His mother's death had left the pecuniary affairs of the Wertsch family in confusion, and of course the intervention of "government" was necessary for their arrangement. Amongst other matters, the term of years for which one of their estates had been granted by the crown was now expired, and a new grant would have to be solicited. While Ivan was engaged with the count, Adrian had asked for and obtained a short leave of absence, that he might take advantage of his friend's telega; for Ivan, as one travelling upon public business, would be authorized to require, at every post-house, the swiftest horses that could be obtained.

This explanation had not long been finished, when a fine young man, the son of Rostopchine, entered the tent. He brought Ivan his father's letter to the Czar, and the other documents necessary for his journey. Then he offered him a supply of money, which Ivan, under the circumstances, was glad to be able to decline — the contents of a purse of ducats, found accidentally in one of the abandoned palaces of Moscow, sufficing for his present needs. Lastly, young Rostopchine lingered to say, "My father desires me to tell you that he has mentioned you to the Czar in very handsome terms, though not more so than you have fully deserved."

Ivan was touched by this magnanimity, which was quite in keeping with the character of the fiery and prejudiced but honest and generous old Muscovite. He answered gratefully: "I beg of you to present my very humble thanks to his excellency, and to assure him I shall never forget the trust he has reposed in me."

Ivan, Adrian, and Michael were soon seated in a rough, light telega and dashing across the country, under the guidance of a practised driver, at a speed that almost anticipated the age of railways. Until they passed beyond the theatre of war, they had a guard of flying Cossacks; after that, they were left to their own resources. They travelled day and night— Ivan anxious and rather melancholy, Adrian enlivening their way with his conversation. As they were drawing near their journey's end, he took occasion, from some remark of Ivan's, to explain to him the views of General Kutusov with regard to the war. "Russia, says the marshal, is making herself the champion and the martyr of Europe•; and scanty thanks will Europe give her for the same when once the common danger is over. These English, Germans, and Swedes are glad enough to see us shedding our best blood to overthrow the despotism of Napoleon and secure the general freedom; but when the work is done, which of them will have the grace to be grateful to us? Rather will they envy us the very glory we acquired in fighting their battles. Hence the marshal would not be at all averse to an honourable peace, if such could be had; and they say the Czar has had to interfere more than once to prevent his opening negotiations with the enemy—"

"Of which the enemy would be only too glad," said Ivan. "Our friend Yakovlef, who, as you are aware, was detained in Moscow by the illness of his uncle, was taken before Napoleon, who cajoled and threatened him by turns to try and induce him to bring a letter from him to the Czar. But young Yakovlef stood firm ; in fact, he told Napoleon he could not presume so far, if his life depended upon it. The Czar's refusal to receive any proposition whatsoever from the French is absolute. But surely I see buildings in the distance, and smoke.—Isvostchik, can this be St. Petersburg ?"

"Yes, gospodin, this is St. Petersburg." Then, being himself a native of Moscow, "But it is *not* Moscow the holy. Ah! Moscow the holy will be never more what she was in the old days."

None of the party, except the driver, had seen the new capital before. Adrian was full of natural curiosity and interest in all that met their view as they drove along ; while Michael was busy wondering whether the Nyemtzi would come here also, what sort of defence could be made if they did, and whether a great many of them would be killed. But Ivan grew silent and absorbed, and looked very pale. "I verily believe," said Adrian, turning to him suddenly, "that you are seeing the horrors of Moscow over again."

"No," returned Ivan—"no. I was not thinking just then of what I have seen, but of what I am about to see."

"You are about to see the thing you have been longing for through all your toils and perils. Rouse yourself, man ! Of what are you afraid ?"

"Of the face of Majesty," said Ivan to himself ; though to Adrian he only answered, with a rather nervous laugh, "First interviews are trying." Yet he knew that this was not, for him, a first interview with his sovereign. He felt beneath his doublet for the precious piece of gold, the cherished souvenir of his boyhood, as if to assure himself that the great Emperor, into whose presence he was going, was really the kind young boyar who had promised that he should serve him one day.

"Dear Barrinka," pleaded Michael, "do not forget to tell our lord the Czar that a mujik who has lost one hand desires his leave to fight for him, and that he will serve him *so* faithfully. At the camp," he added, "they laughed at me, and told me I would never make a soldier. But the Czar will listen to *you*."

Ivan smiled doubtfully. In his heart he wished that the poor mujik's childlike idea of his sovereign had been his own also. Then he saw Michael take out his beloved picture, and, fastening it before him on the telega, address to it his prayers for the success of his young lord's mission. "The saint and the Czar are equally real to him," thought Ivan, "and he would address either with equal reverence and equal confidence."

His reverie was interrupted by the voice of the isvostchik. "This is the square of the Admiralty, and there is the great Czar Peter," said he, as he pointed out the celebrated equestrian statue where the father of modern Russia perpetually climbs the rock and treads the serpent beneath his horse's hoofs.

They drove to an inn, where Ivan merely delayed to make those changes in his dress which etiquette imperatively demanded, and then, leaving his companions to await his return, took his despatches to the Winter Palace. There he was fortunate enough to find the Emperor, who had just returned from Kamenoi-Ostrov.

In less than two hours Ivan came back to the inn. Michael had gone out with the isvostchik, but Adrian was waiting for him, and met him with an air of some anxiety. "Is it well?" he asked briefly.

"Well?—oh yes, *very* well," Ivan answered. He spoke in an abstracted voice, but there was a new light in his eyes, and his face was flushed and excited.

"I cannot make you out," said Adrian, looking at him with surprise and curiosity. "If it were possible, I should say that you look at once ten years older and ten years younger than you did two hours ago."

"Two hours! It ought to be ten years, if all— O Adrian!"

he broke out suddenly, and with uncontrollable emotion, "the half was not told me! He is grand—beautiful! There is only one thing more I want now—*to die for him.*"

The sorrows of the last two months had done somewhat to deepen the slight nature of Adrian. He was no longer disposed to scoff at everything. "I guessed ' le séduisant,' as Czernichef calls him, would fascinate you," he said. "But, now you *have* returned, I will own that I wished you better news to bring him than that of the destruction of the Kremlin. Evil tidings do not always insure their bearer a good reception."

"I think he was prepared," Ivan answered. "At all events he betrayed no emotion; only saying very calmly, 'It is the will of God!' I think he grew pale, but even of that I cannot speak certainly, as at the beginning of our interview I scarcely dared to raise my eyes to his face. But all changed when he spoke of Moscow, and questioned me about the things I had witnessed there during the Occupation. I could see that much was new to him, and even startling, and that my account of the conflagration moved him deeply. Then all fear passed from me, save the fear of giving pain to him. His intense gaze seemed to draw the whole truth from my lips, even in spite of my will; but it was hard to tell of the burnings and plunderings, and of the starved, homeless, despairing people. Once or twice my voice dropped so low that he had to ask me to repeat my words; for you know he is somewhat deaf. But when I told him of the wounded men whom we found in the cellars and tried to keep alive, his face lighted up, and he thanked me —yes, thanked *me*," Ivan repeated, raising his head proudly; though almost immediately he allowed it to sink again, while a vivid flush passed over his features.

"Tell me the rest," said Adrian eagerly.

Ivan struggled with some feeling which he would not, perhaps could not express. "It is almost too sacred," he said at last. "But I will tell you; only, never speak to me of it again. Even now I look back upon what I said with amazement. Evidently Count Rostopchine has been generous, and has spoken highly of my services in his letter. His Majesty observed that heroism and fidelity appear to be hereditary in my family; and asked me whether I was not the representative of the great Prince Pojarsky, the deliverer of Moscow. I answered, 'Sire, I am his descendant; I know not whether I am his representative.' He inquired my meaning, and thus it came to pass that I talked to him about my father."

"About your father!" Adrian repeated in great astonishment. "You amaze me! You and I have lived together for six years, and never have I heard you so much as name him."

"No; never to any one around me—scarcely even to dear old Petrovitch. Yet to my sovereign, in one hour, the whole secret of my life flashed out, I know not how. I told all;—how ever since I heard the story of my birth in early boyhood, I dreamed of that exiled father, dwelling forlorn and solitary in the frozen desert of Siberia; how I longed to seek him out and comfort him, and even dared to cherish the hope that one day I might win his pardon and restore him to his home. But, even as I spoke thus, a sudden overwhelming sense of the presence in which I stood swept over me. I was confounded, struck dumb, paralyzed with the sense of my own boldness. At last I stammered, by way of excuse, 'I implore of your Majesty to pardon me; you can understand how the sad fate of a father must shadow the life of a son!'"

Adrian uttered a groan of dismay. "Most luckless of men!" he cried. "Never in all your days did you make a blunder until that moment. My friend Ivan, it is clear you are no courtier; you may as well give up the game at once and come back to the camp with me."

"Why so?" asked Ivan, terribly disconcerted. "What have I said amiss? I don't understand—"

"You don't understand! Have you forgotten the fate of

the Czar Paul, and the unfortunate circumstances under which his majesty began his reign ?"

" Utterly !" cried the horror-stricken Ivan, growing red and pale by turns. " Oh, what have I done?—I never dreamed of any sorrow save my own." But after a long pause he resumed, with a look of returning composure: " I think he did not misunderstand me. It is true I saw a look of pain pass across his face, and I wondered at it for a moment. But his manner to me grew even gentler than before. He asked me what my father's supposed crime had been, and I told him frankly. Then he said, ' He shall be sought out and restored to you, *if* he be not already beyond our reach;' and he added, ' Beyond the reach of God he cannot be. Is it not so?' I thought he waited for an answer, and I said, ' Yes, sire.' That was nearly the end. He told me I should receive a communication to-morrow through the Governor of St. Petersburg, General Soltikoff. Then I kissed his hand; and the gentleman-in-waiting, who accompanied me to the gate of the palace, asked for my address. Now, Adrian, you know as much as I can tell you. But," he added to himself, " not *all ;* the look, the tone, the manner, these are mine, mine only. These it is that give me the precious sense that I myself—Ivan Ivanovitch Pojarsky---am recognized, thought of, cared for."

CHAPTER XIX.

> " I sang the joyful pæan clear,
>   And, sitting, burnished without fear
>   The brand, the buckler, and the spear—
>
> " Waiting to strive a happy strife,
>   To war with falsehood to the knife,
>   And not to lose the good of life."

HE following morning brought Ivan a request, equivalent of course to a command, that he would wait upon General Soltikoff. The Governor of St. Petersburg was a veteran approaching his eightieth year, and much and deservedly respected both by the sovereign and by the people. He received Ivan with remarkable courtesy. Although the ante-chamber was nearly full of persons awaiting an audience, and some of them were evidently of high rank, he sent for him almost immediately, and introduced him to his son and to others who were with him in the cabinet as a young nobleman who had acted a most heroic part during the Occupation of Moscow. Then addressing Ivan himself, he said, " The Emperor has commended you to my particular care. I am authorized to offer you at present a nomination for the Chevalier Guard."

This was a great honour. In this splendid corps every private was a noble of the highest birth and a Knight of Malta. Upon state occasions the members formed the monarch's guard of honour; they had the *entrée* to the receptions at the palace;

they dined at the imperial table. Their uniform, upon which fabulous sums were expended, was a mantle of scarlet, with a massive silver cuirass bearing a large Maltese cross in relief; and the trappings of their priceless Arabian horses glittered with gold and jewels. Ivan, knowing all this, remained silent, his face a curious mixture of intense gratification and extreme embarrassment.

The kind old general beckoned him nearer and spoke in a lower tone. "I believe I understand your feelings, my young friend. You are thinking of the expenses the gentlemen of the Chevalier Guard usually take pride and pleasure in incurring— of their armour, their horses, and so forth. Upon that ground you need hesitate no longer. His Imperial Majesty has requested me to attend to all your requirements."

"His goodness overpowers me," said Ivan with emotion. "But, my general, that is not my only nor my chief reason for hesitation."

"What other can you possibly have? My own grandson would give one of his eyes to be in your place."

"My general, Napoleon is near Moscow, and the Chevaliers of the Imperial Guard are, I believe, in St. Petersburg."

"So that is your objection! But they have not been there always, and they are not going to remain there now."

"Is it not their duty and their honour to remain near the august person of their sovereign? and that—"

Soltikoff interrupted him with a smile. "Make your mind easy, my young friend. The red mantles of the Chevalier Guard will soon have the opportunity of acquiring a deeper dye. Already they have received their marching orders, and in a few days they start for the seat of war. There is barely time for your equipment and your investiture, if you wish to go with them."

"*Wish it!*" cried Ivan, with kindling eyes. "Whilst Napoleon—who has spoiled Moscow and burned the Kremlin—still sets his foot upon the soil of holy Russia, I could not support life without doing all that one man may do to drive him thence with infamy."

"My brave boy, I share your feelings. I could wish myself two score years younger to take my place amongst the combatants. Nor is mine," he added, "the only heart that throbs with the soldier's longing. But too gladly would he who is the highest of all stand this moment in the van of all, did not the bonds of a sacred duty detain him here."

"My general," said Ivan, "I am overcome with gratitude. The honour of serving my sovereign, in the position he has assigned me, is beyond my utmost dreams."

"Then that is settled. Here is my son, who is anxious to take possession of you. He will introduce you to the Commandant of the Knights of Malta."

At a sign from his father, the younger Soltikoff came forward, and cordially invited Ivan to his house. Seeing him hesitate for a moment before replying, he said, "Perhaps you have friends with you?" Ivan mentioned Adrian Wertsch, who was immediately included in the invitation. He then remembered Michael, and turning once more towards the general, craved permission to add a few words. This being readily granted, he told the mujik's story; and the poor fellow's courage and devotion touched both the Soltikoffs.

"I think," said the general, "we might put him into the artillery. He could help to serve a gun. Send him to Colonel Tourgenieff; my son will give you the address."

The days that followed were "marked evermore with white" in the calendar of Ivan Pojarsky. His host introduced him to the best society of St. Petersburg; he became acquainted with the Galitzins, the Tolstois, the Narishkins, the Gagarines, and was welcomed everywhere as a young man who had done much that was heroic and seen much that was interesting. He was presented to both the empresses;* he attended an imperial recep-

* The Empress Mary, the mother of Alexander, and the Empress Elizabeth, his wife.

tion at Kamenoi-Ostrov, offered his humble acknowledgments to the Czar for his kindness, and had a few gracious words addressed to him in public, which at once raised to the highest point his popularity with the great world.

But he could not help observing that this was a world strangely unlike that which he had known in Moscow before the war. The reckless extravagance, the heedless gaiety, the wild dissipation of those days seemed to be no more. Over many of the noble houses where he visited the angel of death had already spread his wings,—a son, a brother, a nephew had fallen at Smolensko or Borodino; while over all there brooded the apprehension of the same dread visitation, producing, if not melancholy, at least seriousness. Ladies of fashion, instead of playing cards or loto, prepared lint for the wounded or garments for the perishing. Great efforts were being made for the relief of the sufferers in the terrible tragedy of Moscow; and Ivan rejoiced to see immense convoys of clothing and provisions setting out from the new capital for the old.

Troops of all kinds were coming every day to the city, or leaving it for the seat of war. Ivan's friends pointed out to him, with justifiable pride, the excellent equipment of the soldiers, and told him of the unwearied exertions of the Czar to supply the whole of his enormous army not only with the necessaries, but even with the comforts of life. " Every man in the service," it was said, " has his fur pelisse, his warm boots, even his warm gloves."* Infinite care and pains were expended upon the commissariat; and depôts of all kinds of provisions were established wherever they were likely to be needed.

In a few days Michael came joyfully to inform "Barrinka" that he had attained the desire of his heart. " Praised be the great St. Nicholas!" he said, " I am to be a gunner. My officer tells me that after a little training I shall be able to pull a thing they call the lanyard. It makes the gun go off, and

* De Maistre.

kills the Nyemtzi." But no earthly happiness is ever without alloy, and Michael's was not an exception. There was one hardship, in his own estimation very serious, to which he had to submit. "Barrinka," he asked, "why must our beards be cut off before we go to fight the Nyemtzi?"

"It has been always done," said Ivan. "It is the custom. Besides, do you not know it makes you a free man? The very hour your beard is cut, you cease to be a serf; you have no longer any lord on earth except the Czar."

"I do not care to be a free man," grumbled Michael; "and I do not see why I must part with my beard, which God gave me. It is very hard."

Ivan laughed. "My dear lad," he said, "you have given your hand for our lord the Czar; you are ready to give your life for him; then why do you grudge him your beard?"

"Do you call it giving to *him*?" asked Michael. "That makes a difference certainly. Though I cannot see what the Czar wants with my beard, still, if it be his Majesty's pleasure, he shall have it."

Shortly afterwards he paid Ivan another visit. Great was the transformation in his outer man. The cherished beard was gone; he wore, instead of his caftan, the green uniform of a gunner; and he was already beginning to acquire the indefinable but unmistakable air of the trained soldier. "Only think, Barrinka," he began eagerly;—"I am afraid you will not believe me, but I am ready to swear it is true upon the picture of my saint. Besides, all the men in our corps heard it, and can tell you I say nothing but the fact, just as it happened."

"But you have not yet told me what the fact is. What has happened to you, Michael?"

"The Czar has spoken to me," said Michael with beaming eyes—"the Czar, his very self."

"How?—when?—what did he say?" cried Ivan, now thoroughly excited.

"He came to-day to inspect our corps—'recruits for the artillery service,' we are called. You will not need to be told that every man of us did his best, and that we made the air ring with our cheers and 'houras.' When the parade was over, I saw him speaking to our captain, who looked towards me, and then called me forward. 'Your Imperial Majesty,' says he, 'this is the man.' 'Give me your hand, my brave lad,' says the Czar, taking in his own this very hand of mine that you see now. 'I know how you lost the other, and I honour your courage and devotion. You have been tried and found faithful.' I fell on my knees and kissed the hand that held mine; which would be honour enough for such as *you*, Barrinka, not to speak of a poor mujik like me. Then he said to all of us, 'You have done well, my children;' and we answered with a shout, 'Father, we will do better next time'* So he rode away, — God bless him! — and the rest all crowded round me, embraced me, and wished me joy. Now my one hand, which he has touched, is quite as good as two."

Ivan shared the joy of his humble friend. He himself was beginning to learn some lessons which were new and strange to him, and which perhaps the miseries he had witnessed and the sorrows he had experienced had been preparing him to receive. In the circles where he moved now there was no longer any scoffing at religion, but rather a devout and reverent acknowledgment of the hand of God. Most of the nobility were diligent in their attendance upon the church services; but some ladies, and a few men of the highest position, were spoken of in the hearing of Ivan as remarkably pious. Foremost amongst these were the Princess Metchersky and the Countess Tolstoi, Prince Alexander Galitzin, and the Sardinian ambassador De Maistre. No reproach was implied or intended; their piety seemed to be rather considered as a distinction,

* The custom upon such occasions.

and it was usually added that they stood high in the imperial favour.

On the last evening of his stay in St. Petersburg, Ivan saw one of his acquaintances—a nephew of the Grand-Marshal Tolstoi, and like himself a member of the Chevalier Guard—sitting apart absorbed in a book. The stirring romance of real life had of late driven all other romances out of the mind of Ivan; but the sight of an interested reader awakened his slumbering tastes. He came to the side of Tolstoi — a gay, good-natured youth, to whom he could say anything he pleased. "Is that a new book which you seem to like so much?" he asked.

"I am ashamed to confess it is new to me, or was so until lately," returned Tolstoi.

"What is it? A romance? I should think it a kindness if you would lend it to me when you have done with it yourself."

"Look at it," said Tolstoi, placing it in his hand.

It was in French, as Ivan expected; but its appearance was different from that of any French book he had ever seen before. Although divided into chapters and verses, it was evidently not poetry, and very sacred names were of frequent occurrence. He turned to the opening page, and exclaimed in surprise, "The New Testament!—how strange!"

"Why should it be strange?" said Tolstoi simply. "What better book could I find to read?"

"What is it all about?" asked Ivan. "Of course I know there are the holy gospels, but this book seems to contain a great deal besides."

"Oh! I cannot tell you in a moment. Read it for yourself, and you will soon learn to love it well."

Ivan turned back again to the page with which his friend had been occupied, and which he had kept open with his finger. He read these words: "Love your enemies, bless them that curse you, do good to them that hate you, and pray for them that despitefully use you, and persecute you ; that ye may be the children of your Father which is in heaven : for he maketh his sun to rise on the evil and on the good, and sendeth rain on the just and on the unjust." "That sort of religion would never answer!" he exclaimed indignantly, allowing the book to fall from his hand. "What? *Love the French?* Do good to *them?* Pray for *them?* I think whoever recommended you, just now, the reading of this book, must have gone altogether out of his senses. We should all be ruined if such ideas as these got abroad amongst us, especially at the present moment, when it is our supreme duty to hate the enemies of the Czar and to destroy them."

"Then how comes it to pass that the Czar himself loves this book and reads it daily?" asked Tolstoi, as he reverently took up the volume from the ground.

"I cannot believe that," said Ivan.

"It is quite true. I heard it from my uncle, who, as you know, is always about his person. It was that which made me read it first. Now 1 love it—better than any other book in the world."

"Since you tell me all this, I will buy a copy, and take it with me to the camp. Pope Yefim would be pleased if he knew it. He has sometimes lamented to me that the unlearned cannot have the Scripture narratives in any tongue they are able to understand. There is the old Slavonic, of course, but you might almost as well try to read Babylonish."

"There is French—for *us*," said Tolstoi; "and I own that it seems a better thing to me to read the sayings of Christ than the scoffs of Voltaire."

"Perhaps you are right," Ivan answered thoughtfully. After a pause he added, "Since I have stood alone, like one on a rock in the midst of a raging sea, with death before me, death behind me, and death on each side of me, I have sometimes thought what strength it would give me if only I could look up

and see a Face bent down on me from above, a Hand outstretched to help me."

The next day the Chevalier Guards began their march, and
Ivan with them.   Adrian also returned to his duty ; and soon
they were in the midst of one of the most memorable campaigns
the world has ever seen.

CHAPTER XX.

WEARY, WANDERING FEET.

"There shall be no more snow,
No weary, wandering feet."

IT was one of the early days of a genuine Russian winter. The vast and desolate plain between Moscow and Smolensko was white with snow; bitter winds thick with falling flakes were sweeping over it; and the wintry sun struggled in vain to pierce a dense frosty fog. A regiment of French infantry, weary, dispirited, and famishing with hunger, was toiling through the snow-drifts. Already the ranks were thinned terribly, while the ghastly faces and shrunken limbs of the survivors told the story of their sufferings. All the soldier's pride in his appearance, in the brightness of his arms, in the trim perfection of his accoutrements, had vanished long ago; half the disorderly crowd had thrown away the muskets they were too weak to carry, nor was a dress to be seen that deserved the name of a uniform. Any warm garment found amongst the spoils of Moscow was made to do duty as an overcoat, without regard to the sex of its original wearer. Our old friend Seppel wore a lady's fur-lined dressing-gown, whilst the practical Féron contented himself with a sheep-skin shuba which had once enveloped the ample form of a Russian coachman. But no fur was warm enough to keep the bitter cold of that wintry day from the weakened frames of men whose only food since leaving

Moscow had been a few handfuls of rye soaked in water or a little horse-flesh.

Clinging to the arm of Féron was a form slight and worn, and evidently ready to sink with fatigue. "Peste! Mind what you are about there!" cried Féron sharply, as Henri de Talmont stumbled and sank to his knees in a snow-drift a little deeper than usual. Then, pulling him up again by main force and setting him on his feet—"Can't you see where you are going?" he asked.

"No, I cannot see," answered Henri in a weary voice. "Féron, you have been very good to me. But it is no use. You must let me go."

"I shall do no such thing. Here, my boy, take a pull at this;" and he put a flask filled with vodka to the lips of his friend. "Now you can see a little better," he said with a laugh, as the stimulant brought a momentary colour to the pale cheek of Henri. "Can't you hear too? Listen! there are wheels coming near us, and horse-hoofs. God grant it may be stores of some kind, and if so"—Féron paused a moment and set his teeth resolutely—"the Old Guard themselves, with the Emperor at their head, shall not keep them from us."

The wheels were already quite close, else under the circumstances they could not have heard them at all. A carriage drawn by four horses, and attended by outriders, came dashing by. It had only one occupant, a general of division, wrapped from head to foot in rich furs; but every available spot was crammed with packages and bottles. Some of the men sprang towards it, and clinging to the back or the sides, begged in piteous accents for bread, meat, spirits, even a little tobacco— anything "Monsieur le Général" would be good enough to spare them. The coachman and the outriders had to use their whips pretty freely to get rid of them. It was only surprising that they did not take what they wanted by force; but either the lack of courage and mutual understanding, or perhaps some remains of military discipline, prevented an outbreak of open violence.

"Fools for their pains!" said Féron bitterly. "They might know by this time that the general *never* has anything to spare for the soldier. But I am glad he is gone, for the sight of his luxuries made me mad. May his horses break their knees in the next snow-drift! Sure to do it before long. That's one comfort!"

"And then," said a comrade, "perhaps we may overtake him, and get horses, stores, and all. What a supper we should have!"

"Ay," observed another, "*his* horses are very unlike the last we supped upon. Poor brutes! they were little more than skin and bone."

"Féron," asked a third, "are there no horses in this accursed country—no men, no food, no anything?"

"Not much, I suppose, at the best of times. But remember, my lad, we marched over this very ground ourselves a few months ago, and wasted and destroyed all we could find."

It was too true. In this respect they were filled with the fruit of their own devices; their wanton acts of pillage and devastation recoiled upon their own heads.

"Féron," murmured once more the faint voice of Henri, "I can go no further. I *must* lie down and rest."

"Monsieur Henri, if you lie down on that ground, you rise never more."

"I know it; but I can bear up no longer. My sight is gone, my limbs are failing. Dear Féron, let me go." And in spite of the sustaining arm of his friend, he staggered and fell. Féron bent over him, entreating him to rise, and offering his help.

"O Monsieur Henri, think of your mother—of your sister, Mademoiselle Clémence. If you hope ever to see their sweet faces again, rouse yourself, exert all your strength."

But already Henri seemed half-asleep. A look of rest stole

over his worn features, and his eyes were closed. Opening them for a moment, he murmured, "Féron—my mother—Clémence. Ask them to forgive me. Good-bye, dear Féron God bless thee!"

The others meanwhile continued their march. In those terrible days the fall of a comrade scarcely made a Frenchman turn his head. Seppel called to Féron, "Come along, man! For what are you lingering?"

To stay behind would be to share the fate of Henri, not to rescue him. Féron turned sadly away; but after taking two or three steps, turned back once more, murmuring, "What a fool I am! No good to him, and a sore loss to me. Still, if he *should* awake, even for a moment." Stooping down, he slipped his flask of vodka into the benumbed hand of Henri. "Adieu, comrade," he said. "If ever I see France again, I will tell thy mother and Mademoiselle Clémence."

He rejoined his comrades, and marched on; but as long as it continued in sight, he could not help looking back, every now and then, to that black spot in the snow where a comrade had lain down to die. "Soon enough," he thought, "it will be covered with white, and all trace of my poor friend gone for ever. Perhaps *I* may be the next—who knows?"

But at least there was one sufferer unconscious of suffering now. A feeling of utter peace, of deep content, unknown for many days, steeped the weary senses of Henri. He seemed to be sinking into the heart of a profound and dreamless sleep. Pain and fatigue—cold and hunger of body—aching, feverish unrest of spirit—all had ceased together. The last sounds that reached his dulled ear before he passed into unconsciousness were the words of Féron, "Thy mother and Mademoiselle Clémence." And once again those beloved faces drew near—bent over him—glimmered faintly and yet more faintly—at last vanished into air. But he did not even know that they had vanished. All was oblivion now.

Assuredly never again in this world would Henri de Talmont have awakened, had not a sudden thrill of agony called him roughly back to life. He started up to wrestle with a great half-savage wolf-dog, which had fixed its sharp fangs in his arm. Pain and desperation lent him a momentary strength, and clenching his hand, he dealt his antagonist a blow between the eyes that sent it howling away over the snow. Then he picked up Féron's flask, and having thanked in his heart that generous friend, he drank some of its contents, which seemed to infuse new life into his frame.

Thus strengthened, he rose and stood upon his feet. It was midnight. The snow had ceased to fall, and the fierce winds of winter had dropped into utter stillness. Above his head the moon shone forth from a cloudless sky, and a thousand stars glittered with frosty brightness. Not a living thing was in sight, not a tree, not even a stone. Nothing met his gaze but a broad expanse of stainless white, covering the whole horizon like a veil of silver. How desolate it looked, yet how fair and pure! With what bright softness the moonbeams touched the snow! and how calmly the majestic eyes of those sleepless, starry watchers looked down from on high, as though they would say to the toiling, suffering sons of men, "We have seen ten thousand times ten thousand nights like this since the making of the world. We know the secret of the Lord. He means something by every star and every snowflake; and what he means is very good."

"He telleth the number of the stars; he calleth them all by their names." The words flashed unbidden through the mind of Henri. He remembered that in this solitude he was not alone. God was here. He could not turn to God as his friend, and he *knew* that he could not. Brought up in a religious atmosphere, he was all the more distinctly conscious that he himself was not religious—that he stood outside some sacred enclosure Clémence had entered, that he had not something which she had. But had it been a stranger or an enemy whose presence he felt amidst that immense, dreary, aching solitude, still he would have flung himself at his feet and implored his help and pity. Surely he might cast himself upon the God who counted the shining host above his head; surely that God would look down with pity on the creature his hand had made, who was "wandering in dumb dismay" over the untrodden snow. If He would only bring him home, and let him see his mother's face again, and ask her forgiveness before he died!

He knelt down and prayed; if indeed the words were not a cry of agony rather than a prayer. But they were breathed into the ear of One who heareth the young ravens when they cry and the beasts of the forest when they seek their food. As he rose, he noticed some bright thing glistening in the moonlight near the spot where he had been lying. He took it up, and found that it was a tin case containing preserved meat. No doubt it had belonged to the general of division, and had fallen out of his carriage as he passed. But to Henri it seemed the beginning of an answer to his prayer. He ate a portion of the meat, reserving the rest for future use, and drank a little more vodka. Thus a degree of animation was restored to his exhausted system. "Even yet," he thought, "I may rejoin my companions."

There was no wind, yet so intense was the cold that it seemed to pierce him through and through. He felt as though he were in a bath of ice. He determined to keep moving, to walk on straight before him as long as he had strength to do so. He supposed that he was still upon a road of some kind, because when he diverged to the right or to the left the snow became deeper, while if he kept his direct course it did not reach above his ankles.

Onwards he toiled, and still onwards, weary and footsore, yet not quite despairing. He knew well that if he yielded to his ever-increasing fatigue so far as to lie down again, he should rise no more. It seemed as if years had passed since he parted with his comrades, a lifetime since he quitted Moscow; and as to his old happy life in France, *that* belonged to another and earlier stage of existence, almost beyond his recollection.

Red rose the sun over the snowy landscape, to sink again, after the brief wintry day, in clouds of purple and amber. Once more the stars came out, and still Henri toiled on. But his strength was well-nigh spent; he was ready to sink from fatigue, and his little store of meat and vodka had long since been exhausted. "After all," he thought, "it is hopeless. As well die first as last.—But what is this? Have the stars come down upon the ground? or whence are those lights I see in the distance?"

He tried to collect his failing senses and to think. Could this be a town he was approaching? No; the lights were not numerous enough. Perhaps it might be a Russian village? Scarcely; for that the lights seemed too far apart,—though, even if it were, he would take his chance and go forward. Better to fall, like some of his comrades, beneath the axes of the mujiks, than to perish with cold and hunger in the trackless wilderness.

Suddenly he cried aloud, making his voice ring over the snow, "Bivouac fires!" A gush of joy, long unknown to him, filled his heart, bringing with it, from its very intensity, a kind of momentary pain, as the warmth for which he was longing would bring a tingling pain to his half-frozen limbs. "Bivouac fires!" he cried once more, with a glad, weak voice. "I shall see the faces of my comrades; I shall hear their voices. Thank God!"

Hope and joy lent new strength to his weary feet. As he drew nearer to the lights, he saw that the snow was trampled by footsteps and crushed by wheels. And then the thought occurred to him, "If these should be our enemies? If I should find myself in the midst of Russians?" But as the cheerful blaze of the nearest fire grew clearer and more distinct, and he saw figures moving around it, fear and hesitation vanished. He felt nothing but a wild longing to get close to it, which grew every moment more intense. Running, slipping, staggering along as best he could, at last he threw himself on the ground before the fire, in the very midst of the group that surrounded it.

"Eh! what have we got here?" cried some one with an oath. The words were French, so much at least was plain to Henri's bewildered senses; and at the same time a very savoury odour reaching his nostrils reminded him that he was famishing with hunger.

The next moment he was roughly seized and dragged upon his knees. "What do you want here? You are none of us. Be off with you, and pretty quick too!" cried a fellow dressed in a velvet coat which had once belonged to some Moscow exquisite.

Slowly and stiffly Henri rose to his feet. "Comrades," he said with a bewildered air, "it is you who are making a mistake. I am one of you—a Frenchman—a private in the Tenth Infantry—"

"Hang the Tenth Infantry! It is every man for himself here. You are not one of our coterie.* We cannot feed all the stragglers of the grand army. Begone this instant, or—" A push with the butt end of his musket finished the sentence.

The heartless cruelty of his countrymen filled up the measure of Henri's cup of suffering. His spirit was broken. With no power, with scarcely even a wish to struggle any longer for his life, he staggered slowly away, intending to lie down in the nearest snow-drift and die.

* The French, during the retreat, formed themselves into little "coteries" of twelve or fifteen. If an outsider tried to join himself to one of these, he was pitilessly driven away to die, sometimes even murdered.

Some one took a blazing brand out of the fire and flung it after him. "If you want fire, take it!" cried he, and a mocking laugh rang in the ears of Henri. He turned, and said, "Would that I had met this night, instead of you Frenchmen, a company of Russians—or, still better, a pack of wolves!"

"What is all this about?" asked a deep, hoarse voice, and a tall figure rose slowly from the opposite side of the fire.

"It is a straggler, a *polisson*, who was trying to join our coterie. We have just been sending him about his business," was the answer.

"What a hurry you were in! Bring him to me," said the voice of authority.

There was no need to bring him. Henri himself turned gladly, though very feebly, towards this new arbiter of his fate. But when he saw him, he started in surprise. It is true that part of his uniform was concealed by a long cloak lined with fur, but his great hairy cap, and his white waistcoat and gaiters, showed him to be one of the Old Guard, the very *élite* of the French army. These veterans were objects of envy to all their fellow-soldiers; for while the rest had been treated with cruel neglect and indifference, receiving between Moscow and Smolensko absolutely no rations whatever, the Old Guard were well and carefully fed, and supplied abundantly with wine or spirits. The reason was obvious. Upon them devolved a duty of paramount importance, that of guarding the person of Napoleon. Therefore, when the bulk of the army, demoralized by its sufferings, had broken up into fragments, the Old Guard was still able to keep rank, to present a noble appearance, and oppose a firm front to the enemy. Hence the surprise of Henri at finding one of its number amongst a group of wretched-looking stragglers belonging to various regiments.

Meanwhile the Guardsman surveyed him with a critical eye. "Why, this is only a slip of a lad, un petit jeune homme," he said. "He looks half dead already. Mes enfants, he shall stay with us."

Faint tones of remonstrance began to make themselves heard, but they were silenced in a very summary fashion. The Guardsman laid his bronzed hand, hard as iron, upon the shoulder of Henri. "Sacre!" he cried. "You shall take him and me together. Both of us, or neither!"

This was decisive. The poor, abject, half-starved wretches knew their master; they felt their lives depended upon his care and guidance; and they obeyed him as, in a time of need, the incapable usually obey any capable person who undertakes to direct them. Room was made for Henri beside the fire, and the very man who had flung the brand after him a few minutes before now volunteered to chafe one of his ears, which showed symptoms of being frozen.

Supper was served, consisting of a piece of roasted horse-flesh without bread or salt, and a very small quantity of rum, carefully measured out to each member of the party, and mixed with snow-water. Then every man crept as close to the fire as he could, wrapped about him what garments he had, and tried to sleep; every man, that is to say, except the Guard, who, explaining to Henri that some one must always watch, and that the first watch of the night devolved upon him, lit his pipe with a meditative air, and seated himself beside the fire.

Weary as Henri was, he could not help asking one or two questions. "Garde," he said, "do you know where we are?"

"Somewhere on the way to Smolensko, which, if we live, we may reach perhaps in two days or three."

"Shall we find our regiments again, do you think?"

"I cannot answer for yours, my boy; the new ones seem to be melting like snow-flakes. The Old Guard," he added with a flash of pride, "is always to be found, whether by friend or foe."

"These men around us, who are they?"

"Waifs and strays, like yourself. We are gathering together in coteries of a dozen or so, to try and keep one another alive in this horrible desert."

"Little life they would have left in me, but for *you*, Garde. God bless you for your kindness."

"Thank you, comrade. Blessings do a man as little harm as curses any day. Here, take a pull at my pipe."

"No, thank you. I don't smoke."

"More fool you! That is the way you young conscripts die off, because you never know what is good for you, nor how to keep your souls inside your bodies. Now, when I was in Egypt"—here he stopped suddenly, and a look of emotion passed over his bronzed, weather-beaten features—"ay, Egypt, Italy, Spain,—Lodi, Marengo, Austerlitz, Wagram, Friedland, —why go over all these now? Why recall the past—the glorious past? Why, indeed? Have our eagles floated over all the world to lie buried in a Russian snow-drift! Bah! This confusion is only temporary. You shall soon see the Emperor rise again in his glory, and overwhelm our hounds of enemies with destruction. I tell thee, boy, he is unconquerable. A cloud—a little fleeting cloud—may pass over his star and hide it for a moment, but it will shine out again all the more brightly afterwards."

"But," said Henri sadly, "if he expected us to fight for him, he ought to have fed us."

"My lad," said the Guardsman sternly, laying his hand upon Henri's shoulder, and turning him round away from the fire, "you see that snow?"

"I have seen too much of it," returned Henri. "I think I shall never see anything else."

"Out there you go, to have part or lot with us never more, the first word you speak against the Emperor. With his own hand he gave me these medals, this cross"—touching his breast—"and, moreover, he said to me once when he was reviewing us, 'Pierre Rougeard, I know you for a brave man. It was you—was it not?—who took that pair of colours at Lodi?'"

"Garde, how were you separated from the rest?"

"You will see to-morrow that I am lame. In a skirmish near Moscow I got a ball in my leg and a sabre cut on my shoulder. We who were wounded were all put into waggons by the Emperor's orders, to be sent on to Smolensko; but those in charge of us, thinking our lives less precious than the plunder they were bringing from Moscow, flung us out by the wayside to die." *

"Wretches! May the Emperor punish them as they deserve."

"The Emperor has much more important things to think about. We of the Old Guard do not die easily; what would kill conscripts like you, only hardens us. I contrived to live and to creep along, picking up every day a comrade or two in distress, until we formed the little coterie you see now. I hope to overtake the Old Guard at Smolensko—if not, farther on. All I live for is to rejoin my colours, and to fight once more for the Emperor. But you are almost asleep. Sleep on, my boy; to-night, at least, you shall neither freeze nor starve."

Henri *was* almost asleep. But he roused himself for a moment or two to breathe a thanksgiving to Almighty God for the help sent him in his need; together with an earnest prayer that he would be pleased to bring him through all dangers again to his native land, to see the face of his mother and of Clémence.

All succeeding generations will ask in half incredulous wonder how it came to pass that a splendid army, numbering over six hundred thousand men, and commanded by perhaps the greatest military genius that ever existed, could fall so suddenly and swiftly into a state of utter disorganization and

* A fact.

abject misery. Certainly never, since those ancient days when the Red Sea rolled over the hosts of Pharaoh, or the angel of the pestilence smote the sleeping myriads of Sennacherib, was the arm of the Lord stretched out more visibly in the sight of the nations. Yet it is the glory of Infinite Wisdom, not to interpose amongst the wheels of human action with arbitrary breaks and changes, but so to direct the whole stupendous machine that wrong works out its own punishment and right its ultimate justification by the operation of everlasting laws. In gaining Moscow, Napoleon expected to gain everything—food and shelter for his troops, stores of all descriptions, treasures enough to satisfy the greed of those soldiers of fortune whom the hope of plunder had attracted to his standards. He expected to dictate a humiliating peace to the crushed and trembling Czar, and to make yet one more submissive tributary of hitherto unconquered Russia. But in the flames of Moscow and the heroic resolution of Alexander he found the destruction of his plans. Retreat became a necessity; and it had to be made through a country already devastated by the license of his armies—license for which he made himself responsible, which indeed he forced upon them, by neglecting to provide them with the necessaries of life. This cruel neglect recoiled upon his own head: even before the severities of a northern winter set in* the hosts of Napoleon were *perishing with hunger.* "If he expected us to fight for him, he ought to have fed us," was the mournful accusation that fell from the dying lips of many a gallant soldier, who, faithful to the end, would allow himself to utter no other reproach. What famine and pestilence—the result of insufficient and unwholesome food—had begun, was completed by the arrows of the winter in the hand of God himself. As, on the occasion of another memorable national deliverance, "he blew with his wind," and the foes of his people were scattered; so now he

---

* Not "earlier than usual," as the apologists of Napoleon delight in repeating.

cast forth his ice like morsels, and who was able to abide his frost? Snow and vapour and stormy wind fulfilled his word. Of the six hundred thousand warriors who crossed the Niemen in the pride of their strength, only about forty thousand miserable fugitives—diseased, forlorn, and famished—straggled back again five months later.

CHAPTER XXI.

OVER THE BERESINA.

OUGEARD and his companions succeeded in reaching Smolensko, but only to find it a scene of intolerable wretchedness and unutterable confusion. The Emperor and the Old Guard had left some days previously, and for the disorganized troops pouring every hour into the miserable, ruined city, there was neither food nor shelter, neither order nor discipline. So our little coterie still kept together, and hoping against hope determined to continue their march towards the frontier.

Ten or twelve weary days of marching followed. Always hungry, always cold, always tired, Henri would have given up the struggle once and again, but for the thought which kept for ever

"I must see my mother and my sister again ; I cannot die without my mother's forgiveness."

Usually their only food was a little horse-flesh, but even that failed them frequently; nor could fuel be always found for the fire of their bivouac. From the bodies of their comrades that strewed the way they sometimes obtained articles of clothing— a sad resource, but all, even the gentle Henri, were now becoming inured to sights of horror. Sometimes they would meet with other coteries whose condition was as pitiable as their own, or they would be alarmed by a few stray shots from the "clouds of Cossacks" that hovered about them. Rougeard informed them that the enemy was *beside*, not *behind* them; the Russians having very prudently chosen their lines of march parallel to that of the retreating French armies, which were thus kept from straying to the right or to the left, and sternly restricted to the track their own cruelty had already rendered a desert.

At last a serious misfortune happened to the little band. A long day's march, absolutely without food and in piercing cold, had exhausted them all. Rougeard, who was by far the strongest of the party, said to his companions, "Rest in the shelter of this wall, while I go a little further towards the lights I see yonder. I daresay some of our people are there; perhaps they will respect my uniform, and spare us a little food." He moved away, but turned back for a moment to add, "Keep up your hearts, my lads. If your strength is good for one day's marching more, I think you may see the Beresina before to-morrow night."

That was the last time they looked upon the face or heard the voice of Pierre Rougeard. Whether he was buried in the snow, was murdered or made prisoner by the Russians, they could not tell. His loss dissolved the coterie which his influence had held together. Its members went their several ways, and far too sad a task would it be for us to follow them. Each in his own measure fulfilled the awful doom that had fallen upon the host to which he belonged. For the word had gone forth : "Thus saith the Lord, Such as are for death, to death ; such as are for the sword, to the sword ; and such as are for the famine, to the famine ; and such as are for the captivity, to the captivity."

We may, however, follow for a little way the fortunes of Rougeard. The bivouac fires he saw at a distance proved to be those of a Russian regiment of volunteers. He fell into the hands of the sentries, and in spite of a resistance as desperate as his exhausted condition permitted him to make, was secured, and brought at once to the colonel, a Russian nobleman named Demidoff. To his questions Rougeard replied with proud fearlessness ; but he owned, upon being asked, that he was famishing with hunger. Demidoff, who perhaps had been reading the Book his sovereign loved so well, led the prisoner to his own tent, where an elegant and abundant dinner had just been served. "Sit down, my friend," he said to him, "eat and drink ; you are welcome."

But the veteran did not obey. His brave, proud heart, which no peril of field or flood or wilderness had ever daunted, was melted, was crushed by the unexpected kindness. A great shudder passed over his frame. Trembling "as certainly he never would have trembled before the enemy," he said with uncontrollable emotion, "Can it be that a Russian, an officer, bids me sit down to eat and drink with him, after all the horrors we have committed in his country, and against his Emperor ?" *

But it could not be expected that all Russians would take their revenge after the manner of Demidoff. Many of the mujiks, who had been insulted and plundered, or had seen their relatives murdered by the French, put the prisoners that fell into their hands to a cruel death. Fortunately, reports of these outrages soon reached St. Petersburg, and a ukase was despatched immediately by the hand of a special courier, forbidding all such

* A fact.

practices on pain of the Czar's highest displeasure ; and, as the most effectual mode of preventing them, offering the reward of a ducat of gold for every prisoner brought safely to head-quarters.

Henri de Talmont bore in mind Rougeard's parting words, and determined at all hazards to try to reach the Beresina. He was strengthened in his belief that he was drawing near some point of general rendezvous by the constantly increasing crowds. At length, instead of a vast and solitary plain, he found himself traversing a broad high-road, frozen hard, and thronged with a disorderly rabble of soldiers and camp-followers, amongst whom vehicles of all kinds were moving with difficulty. Some of these were baggage-waggons, but the great majority contained women and children connected in various ways with the French army, and endeavouring with it to make their escape from a hostile country. Most pitiable was the fate of those unhappy fugitives.

As Henri stumbled wearily along, the velvet cap of a little child dropped from one of the carriages and fell at his feet. He picked it up and restored it to its owner, a pretty fair-haired boy about four years old.

"Thank you, poor soldier," lisped the child in soft Italian, a language of which Henri had learned a little from his mother.

"I think, Guido, we could make room for the poor soldier here," said the child's mother, a gentle-looking lady with an infant in her arms ; "he seems very tired."

Most thankfully did Henri accept the proffered help. He soon ascertained that the lady was an Italian singer who had come to Russia, with the band of professional artists to which she belonged, in the train of the fantastic and pomp-loving King of Naples. These poor children of pleasure, dragged un-awares into the midst of a horrible tragedy, seemed like butter-flies caught in a thunderstorm. Madame Leone told Henri, with many tears, that her husband had been made prisoner by the Cossacks, and that she knew not whether he was alive or dead. Henri tried to console her, helped her to take care of the children, and defended her as well as he could from the rude assaults of the famishing soldiers who surrounded the carriage, begging for food, or rather demanding it.

At last they reached the bank of the Beresina, but it was to find themselves in the midst of untold confusion and unutterable horror. The frozen marsh beside the river was thronged with an innumerable crowd, increasing in density as it neared the heads of the two bridges which had been thrown across the current. Hundreds of vehicles were there, vainly attempting to force a passage through the living mass. Oaths and shrieks, cries, groans, and entreaties resounded upon every side. To add to the terrors of the scene, the Russians were pouring a continuous fire upon the troops which were endeavouring to cross the river.

In the midst of all this bewildering, maddening confusion, Henri found himself thinking dreamily of his mother's stories of the terrible passage of the Loire by the defeated Vendéans. "It was like the day of judgment," she used to say. "And what," asked Henri, "would she have thought of *this?*"

He was startled by a voice near him. "Monsieur Henri, is it you? Is it really you?" cried some one in the crowd, seizing his hand and grasping it. "This is indeed a miracle."

"Féron! dear Féron!" exclaimed Henri, springing from his seat in the carriage and throwing himself into the arms of his comrade.

Questions and explanations followed, and each told the other his adventures since they parted.

"Where is our regiment?" asked Henri.

"It has ceased to exist," returned Féron. "'Sauve qui peut' is our only marching order now."

"Ah, friend," said Henri, "I see you have suffered. Your hand —"

"Frost-bitten one bitter night. I could not help thinking when I lost it of that poor Russian whom we branded in the hand before we came to Moscow. Do you remember him, Monsieur Henri?"

"I ought to remember him. I saw him again in the city, and he did me a good turn.—Now, Féron, I want you, if you can, to help me to protect this lady and these two helpless little children."

"*If* I can. But we must be patient. Those who are rushing madly forward to try and reach the bridge only increase their own danger. Already they are trampling one another down by dozens."

"Ay," said Henri, "because they are afraid the bridges will be burned or broken as soon as the effective troops have passed over them, to protect the retreat of the Emperor."

"Fools! Do they think the Emperor will let the bridges be touched so long as one Frenchman or Frenchwoman remains upon this side? They do not know him," returned Féron.

"Perhaps not," said Henri sadly. "Ah, what is this?" he cried the next moment, as a bullet whizzed close by them through the air.

"I believe our rear-guard and the Russians are fighting it out, and we are near enough to come in for a stray shot or two."

"Then help me to turn this carriage over, that we may make a shelter for the lady."

This was accomplished, not without some difficulty. Anxious hours of suspense and forced inactivity followed. Night fell, but an awful light still illumined the landscape. What looked like a semicircle of flame environed half the sky. It was the fiery breath of the Russian cannon.

Suddenly there came a sound of fearful shrieks, and a frantic swaying and tossing of the crowd. One of the bridges—that constructed for the artillery—had broken down, precipitating its

living freight into the freezing waters beneath ; and the miserable multitude on the bank, who were suffering more and
more from the cannonade of the enemy, now rushed forward in
blind terror to gain the only remaining bridge.

Henri lost sight of Madame Leone and the baby in the press,
and it was with difficulty that he saved little Guido from being
trodden under foot, by holding him continually in his arms.

Féron kept by his side throughout. At last, however, he cried
aloud suddenly, " Comrade, I am done for ! That bullet—"

Henri saw it was too true. In great distress he knelt down
beside him and tried to stanch the blood that was flowing from
his breast.

Almost at the same moment a company of the rear-guard
came thundering by, forcing their way through the living mass,
and cutting down without remorse or pity all who obstructed
their retreat.

" Time to go *now*," said Féron with an effort. " Monsieur
Henri, don't stay for me.　I thought *I* would have brought
home news of you ; now *you*—but go, I entreat of you, go at
once.　No time to lose."

" Never, while *you* breathe. Besides, as you said, the Emperor will not leave a Frenchman behind him."　Recollecting
that Madame Leone had filled with wine the flask Féron himself had left with him, he mixed some of its contents with
snow-water, and put the reviving draught to the lips of his
comrade.

" Monsieur Henri," murmured Féron, " can you say a prayer
for me ? You used to pray, though we laughed at you for it
in the regiment."

" There is one prayer I have often prayed since all this
trouble came upon us," said Henri.　" It is good, and it is short ;
you can say it for yourself—' God be merciful to me a sinner,
for Jesus Christ's sake.'"

" God be merciful to me a sinner, for Jesus Christ's sake,"

Féron repeated earnestly; and during the hour that followed—an hour that seemed like a year to Henri—the cry was often on his lips.

But he grew weaker and weaker, until at last he fell into a kind of stupor, while Henri watched silently beside him.

Just about the dawning of the day, a cry, great and terrible, thrilled every heart, and reached even the dulled ear of the dying man. He roused himself, and murmured faintly, "What is it, Monsieur Henri?"

Henri knew too well. All around him were repeating, in tones that expressed every variation of anguish and despair—"The bridge is on fire! the bridge is burning!" So, after all, Napoleon had *not* waited until every Frenchman was safe on the other side!

"'The hireling fleeth, because he is an hireling, and careth not for the sheep,'" thought Henri bitterly. "But *thou* shalt never know, Féron. This pang at least shall be spared thy dying hour."

He bent once more over his friend, who was feebly repeating the question—"Monsieur Henri, what is it?"

"Nothing that concerns you or me," Henri answered firmly. "Do you suffer, comrade?"

"No—no pain. Only I am sinking—sinking. I want to say that prayer again. God be merciful—for Christ's sake."

With these words on his lips, Féron passed away. Henri had scarcely time to close his eyes before he was forced by the strong current of the crowd from the spot where he had been standing. He kept fast hold of Guido: just now he cared but little what became of himself; his only thought was to save the child. He was at last pushed into a position from which he could see the river; but he turned shuddering from the sight, which indeed was horrible beyond description. Men, women, and children were struggling in the icy waters, or sinking for the last time beneath them. Here and there a strong swimmer gained the opposite bank in safety; but the weak, the famished, the wounded perished by hundreds. Pieces of the broken bridge, to which drowning wretches were clinging, floated about amidst *débris* of every conceivable kind; and those on board the few sorely overcrowded boats were violently thrusting away their despairing comrades who tried to enter.

One of these boats was just putting off from the bank when Henri called aloud, "Take this child with you, for God's sake!"

A tall man stood upright in the boat. "Hold him up, man," he cried; "give us a sight of him."

Henri did so.

"The very child we are seeking—eh, comrades?" said the man, turning to his companions. "About three or four years old, fair-haired, with a crimson velvet cap. Well worth our while—a thousand ducats reward." Then to Henri: "Throw him in, my lad."

This was much more easily said than done. Little Guido clung to his protector with all his might, absolutely refusing to be separated from him. Henri found it impossible to unclasp those soft arms from about his neck, though he tried hard to do it.

Meanwhile the men in the boat were disputing with one another. Some were willing to take Henri as well as the child; others objected, afraid of losing the reward or of having to share it with him. But the tall man who had spoken first decided the question. "Let the lad come with us," he said. "Anything to save time."

So Henri stepped into the boat with his little companion still in his arms. It did not occur to him until afterwards that Madame Leone would have been by no means able to offer a reward so large as a thousand ducats for the recovery of her child. Happily during the crossing Guido engrossed all his attention. Terrified by everything around him, he cried violently for his mother, and refused to be comforted ; so that a child's tears drew away the eyes of Henri from the agonized faces of strong men, who were looking up to Heaven with their last appeal for mercy ere they sank to rise no more.

Scarcely had the boat touched the opposite bank of the stream, when a lady ran down to meet it, and stretched out her arms to receive the boy. But the next moment a cry of bitter disappointment rang through the air. This was not *her* child—not the darling for whose recovery she had offered all her golden store. The broken-hearted mother turned away, and Henri saw her no more. Still holding Guido in his arms, he followed listlessly and mechanically the stream of fugitives who were taking the road to Vilna.

CHAPTER XXII.

THE AIDE-DE-CAMP OF ST. PRIEST.

THE miserable fugitives who succeeded, at the cost of so much suffering, in crossing the icy waters of the Beresina, found no " promised land " on the other side. Better had it been if with one accord they had laid down their arms on the banks of that fatal river, and surrendered to the mercy of the enemy. The horrors that awaited them well-nigh cast into oblivion those they had already passed through, and filled to absolute overflowing the cup of trembling put into their hands. Until then the cold had not exceeded that of the ordinary winter of those regions; but during that terrible month of December it grew ever more and more intense, until it reached a pitch of severity almost beyond precedent. A silent, invisible, invincible enemy, it mowed down the ranks of strong men with a pitiless scythe, sparing neither the young recruit nor the hardened veteran who had passed unscathed through all the sufferings of the preceding campaign.

Henri de Talmont was at first only conscious of one definite purpose, that of keeping his little charge from perishing with cold. If he could but bring him alive to Vilna, perhaps he might find Madame Leone there and restore him to her. Seeing that a crowd had gathered about a carriage which had been overturned, and which they were plundering of its contents, he joined it in the hope of obtaining some provisions for the way. With more consideration for Guido's tastes than for his own, he seized eagerly upon a small bag of sugar and a box of chocolate bonbons. He afterwards made use of the chocolate as a bribe to induce the little one to run along by his side, for he was scarcely strong enough to carry him. But the poor little fellow was unable to endure the piercing cold, and cried piteously to be taken up again in his arms. Weak though he was himself, Henri could not resist the appeal; but it hastened the inevitable moment when, utterly overcome with fatigue, he was fain to lie down and rest, even at the risk of rising again no more.

So many broken and abandoned properties of all kinds strewed the way that it was not difficult to contrive a sort of shelter for the night. A disabled gun-carriage and a couple of cloaks served Henri as a tent for himself and Guido, whom he folded to his breast as warmly as he could, and both were soon fast asleep.

The intense, biting chill that preceded the dawn awakened Henri. "My poor little Guido is very cold," he thought; "I must wrap him up better;" and he took the coverings from himself to fold them more closely about his charge. The child did not waken, nor even stir; nor did any increase of external warmth remove the icy chill from those little limbs. Henri grew alarmed, and thought at last that he ought to awaken him and give him some nourishment. But all his efforts were in vain. That wintry night Christ had called a little child to come to him from the frozen plain. Gentle was the call and silent the response,—the young spirit passed away in sleep, without struggle and without suffering.

Black despair fell upon Henri then. There seemed no use in making any further struggle for life. All around him were dead or dying; all whom he had known during the long agony of the retreat from Moscow had yielded to their doom. Féron was dead—Rougeard was dead, as he believed—the dying face of many another comrade rose before him—and now, this child. How was he better than they?

Before he lay down to sleep he had prayed for himself and for Guido. The little one also had clasped his baby hands and lisped in his soft Italian a prayer that they might find his mother on the morrow. But beside that still, fair form—almost as white as the snow around it, and consecrated with the twofold beauty of childhood and of death—Henri breathed no prayer. Not then, nor for many days afterwards. It was no use, he said in his heart.

Still he wandered on — in cold, in hunger, in weariness. Hope was gone, memory had almost left him; nothing remained but that desperate clinging to life, which is scarcely more than the instinct of an animal. The path he had to follow was strewn with the dead bodies of his comrades; and upon these he sometimes found a little bread, or a small quantity of wine or spirits. On more than one occasion he warmed his freezing limbs by crouching beneath the corpse of a fellow-sufferer in whom the vital spark was only just extinct. He could not have survived at all but for the sugar and the chocolate that he had obtained for Guido. These, though he knew it not, afforded precisely the kind of nutriment best adapted to sustain life under intense cold.*

He was seldom conscious of any sensations but those of the body. He was always cold, always hungry, always in pain; only sometimes this never-ceasing, never-ending sense of pain was lightened by a kind of dull satisfaction, as when he found food, or slept, or felt a little warmer than usual. Occasionally a comrade would hail him, and inquire his name and whither he was going. Henri hardly knew what he

---

* The survivors in this terrible calamity were usually those who "happened to have about them a little sugar or coffee."

answered. Sometimes he would talk incoherently; at other times he would reply correctly enough—say he was going to Vilna—and in his turn ask questions about the road. He noticed that some of those whom he met stared at him vacantly, or with the fierce glare of insanity; when he spoke they would give him wild and wandering answers, or perhaps even threaten him with violence. Once a miserable being, looking like a spectre, stood and gazed at him in silence, until he asked him what he wanted. " Nothing," answered he, with a strange, sad smile,—" nothing; I am a dead man."*

There were moments, perhaps hours, when Henri's crushed intelligence seemed to revive, and he regained the power of thought and feeling. But these seasons were the most terrible of all. His soul was fast bound in misery and iron. It was hard with despair as the ground beneath his feet with the frost of winter. If he thought of his mother—he "would never see her again; and what did it matter? She had never for-given—never would forgive him now." Of Clémence—" she was so good! She would be very happy in her religion, in her pious books, in her good works. No doubt she was happy enough even now, though her one brother was dying miserably of cold and hunger by the side of a Polish road. Clémence would only say, ' It is the will of God.'"

The will of God! That was the bitterest thought of all. His will was inexorable. There was no use in prayer. Henri had tried prayer, and had not been heard. God did not care for him. He sat on his throne, far above yonder cold, gray, pitiless wintry sky, — as cold, and yet more pitiless. This was his hand, his vengeance; by his inscrutable decree half a million of men were dying in torture, because he was angry with Napoleon Buonaparte.

Sometimes he thought it was not his will, but only a terrible chance. Sometimes it seemed easier to believe, with most of

* A fact.

his comrades, that there was no God, no Being who shaped the destinies of the human race. Practically, at least, there was none for him; none to whom it mattered whether he lived or died. Then the whole subject would pass from him and be forgotten in the absorbing interest of his quest for food. Something to allay the pangs of hunger had to be sought for, very much as the wild beast seeks for its prey.

How long this dreary life in death continued Henri never knew. But it had an end at last, like all suffering on this side of the grave. One day he found himself in what was evidently the melancholy and abandoned ruin of a once beautiful pleasure-ground. The pitiless frost had done its part to blight and to destroy; but the yet more pitiless hand of man had left its deeper traces. A castle, once fit for a royal residence, but now dismantled and partly burned, completed the picture of desolation.

All at once, as revealed by a lightning flash, Henri recalled the past. Could this indeed be Zakret—the splendid summer residence, with beautiful gardens, which the Czar had purchased just before the war? Only six months had passed since Henri wandered with genuine pleasure amidst its shady walks, and admired its magnificent conservatories filled with rare exotics, its terraces gay with the bloom of a thousand summer flowers. He even remembered the exasperation he had felt at the conduct of his fellow-soldiers, who wasted all that wealth of beauty with reckless, malicious hands, because it belonged to their enemy the Czar. "He is well avenged," thought Henri. "We did not dream that he would have proved himself so strong."

Another thought came then. Zakret was close to Vilna, the goal for the present of his weary wanderings. The idea lent his worn frame a momentary strength; he would get up, and go there immediately. He had thrown himself upon a seat— some broken masonry belonging to what had once been a beautiful fountain—but now he rose quickly, and tried to walk. But the effort proved too much for him; he tottered, slipped upon the frozen ground, fell, and utterly lost consciousness.

When he recovered from his long and deathlike swoon, he found everything changed around him. Instead of the wintry sky, he saw above him a lofty vaulted roof. The light was dim, but sufficient to reveal the scene. The floor was covered, or rather crowded with prostrate forms; in some places they lay in heaps. He stretched out his hand, and touched the form nearest him; it was cold as ice, and in his horror at the thought that he was surrounded by the dead, he uttered a weak, agonized cry.

Several heads were raised at this, and eyes, bright with fever or dim with the mists of approaching death, gazed at him in a kind of dull surprise.

"Where am I?" he asked feebly.

Some one dressed in a ragged French uniform, and carrying a large pitcher filled with snow, approached the place where he lay. "In prison," he said. "They brought you in a while ago with some other sick men."

"Are you a warder?" pursued Henri.

"You insult me! Can't you see my uniform? I am, like yourself, a prisoner and a Frenchman. But those of us who are still passably strong are allowed to go down to the court and gather snow for the rest."

He was prevented from adding more by the clamour of the sick men around. All who were able to speak begged in piteous accents for a portion of the snow, holding out cups and other small vessels to receive it.

Henri was more conscious at the moment of hunger than of thirst. "Is there any food?" he asked in a faint voice.

A piece of hard biscuit was pushed towards him, and he took

it eagerly. Then half-a-dozen hands were extended, and as many voices spoke to him—"Take my biscuit, and give me in exchange your next cup of snow-water."

Henri ate a little, moistening his biscuit with the snow-water; but bitter experience had taught him moderation. Then, forgetting that he was no longer a famished fugitive fighting for the necessaries of life, he began, from habit, to conceal the remainder about his person.

A harsh, bitter laugh, from the man who brought in the snow, made him look up. "No need to hide what nobody wants," said he. "Biscuit is the only thing we have in plenty here—except death."

"Can this indeed be Vilna?" Henri asked with a bewildered look.

His informant nodded.

"Then where is the army—the Emperor? How comes it that we are prisoners?"

"The army?—gone like the snow I brought in just now. The Emperor?—safe in Paris by this time. If it will be a comfort to you in your dying moments to know that his Imperial Majesty 'never was better in all his life,' I have the satisfaction of affording it. He announced the fact in his last bulletin."

Henri stirred uneasily, and cast a mournful glance around him. All that met his senses was foul and loathsome in the extreme. The atmosphere of the place was "at once icy and pestilential;" and the whole, the sick, the dying, and the dead, lay heaped together promiscuously. Dead bodies, or mutilated portions of them, were piled together in the windows, a ghastly defence against the bitter wintry wind; while every noxious odour, every hideous and revolting sight that accompanies disease and death, filled the vaults and corridors of the spacious building, making it one vast and dreary charnel-house.

"This is horrible!" he murmured.

"Nothing could be worse. No beds—no straw even—no fire, no wine, no medicine—nothing but rations of hard biscuit, and the snow we can find for ourselves in the court."

"The Russians, since we are their prisoners, ought to treat us with more humanity," said Henri.

"The Russians, my boy, have as much as they can do to take care of their own sick and wounded. As for us, hundreds of famished wretches are brought in here every day, until there is no more room in which to lay them down to die. This building which is now our prison, the Convent of St. Basil, will soon be our grave. That is one comfort. Our miseries will be quickly ended. The hospital fever has broken out."

"Typhus fever?" said Henri with a look of horror.

"Even so; we are dying fast. Every day we have to carry out the dead bodies, or to throw them from the windows."

"Are there no physicians?"

"Physicians? What should bring them *here?* It is death to enter these doors. Not the very Poles themselves, who were so loud in their acclamations when we came here six months ago—who called us their brothers, their deliverers— would dare to bring us now so much as a cup of cold water. Even the guards die who are stationed to watch us. We shall soon be left unguarded. Then we may go out free if we like —only none of us will be alive to go."

Henri covered his face. He was utterly crushed. He seemed no longer to feel, to care for anything—a numb chill despair lay like a weight of lead upon his heart.

After what might have been, for aught he knew, a considerable time, he was aroused from his stupor by the sound of voices, and interested, in spite of himself, by what reached his ear. Some one was pleading earnestly with another in the accents of a soft musical tongue, which at first he took for Italian, like

Guido's, but he soon found that he could not understand the words spoken. However, the speakers presently relapsed into French, and then he easily gathered that one of them, a Spaniard, dying of the cruel hospital fever, was entreating his French comrade to write for him a letter of farewell to his wife. Evidently the feelings of the Frenchman were touched. Henri saw him tear a leaf from a book which he had with him, and write upon it at the dictation of the Spaniard, and in his language. "Though where is the use?" he heard him say to one near him in a lower tone. "Poor fellow! there is none to send it for him."

By-and-by another pitcher of snow was brought in by Henri's first acquaintance, whose name was Pontet.

When with some difficulty he had distributed the coveted refreshment among its many eager and agonized claimants, he said briefly, as he set down his pitcher, "I have news."

Heads were raised and eyes were turned towards him, but for the most part languidly; suffering had well-nigh killed desire and hope—even fear was scarcely felt.

"The Emperor is come," said Pontet. In that word there was a spell potent enough to arouse the dying. On every side exclamations arose—"Come back! Retaken the town! Stolen a march upon them all! Ah, what joy! What a triumph!" and one voice, weak but courageous, raised the old well-remembered cry, "Vive Napoléon!"

"Hush, you fools!" said Pontet sharply. "Napoleon is far enough away. Do you think there is no other Emperor in the world? I am speaking of the Emperor Alexander."

Bitter was the disappointment, especially to dying hearts. Pontet came in for sundry curses, feeble but emphatic, and one sick man flung his cup at him. "How dare you raise our hopes only to dash them so cruelly?" he cried.

"I had more to tell," Pontet continued; "but if you care not to listen, I can spare my breath."

"Tell us, friend, tell us," spoke two or three voices together.

" I have made a friend amongst the guards who knows a little French, and is disposed to be communicative. He says the Czar has appointed General St. Priest governor and guardian of all the prisoners."

"St. Priest !—Who is he ?"

" A Frenchman in the service of Russia. *Because* he is a Frenchman this office has been given him. My comrades, this looks well."

" Nothing looks well now but the grave," said the man who cried " Vive Napoléon."

" Pontet," he continued, " I don't think much of your news. St. Priest may be a Frenchman, but then he must be a pretty rascal, to fight against France."

" Well, we shall see."

" What is that noise ?" asked Henri, as the loud rattling of an iron chain was heard.

" They are only swinging the great lamp up to its place, where it hangs from the roof. How early they are lighting it to-night ! It will be daylight in the court for another hour."

After this Henri fell into a troubled, uneasy sleep. When he awoke, there was a general stir around him, and a murmur of suppressed excitement. " What is the matter ?" he asked of Pontet, who was sitting near him, resting his head on his hand.

He looked up to answer the question. " The guards say Monsieur de St. Priest is coming to visit us."

" He must be a brave man," said Henri.

" Ay de mi !" murmured the Spaniard. " If I *dare* but ask him to send that letter ! Ah, Teresa mia !" Tears stole into his dying eyes as that beloved face arose before him in its dark, well-remembered beauty ; and once more his little children seemed to climb about his knees, while the orange-tree beside his cottage door shed its fragrant blossoms over him.

"Hush!" said those around—"hush! here comes Monsieur le Général."

St. Priest came slowly, threading his way through the thick ranks of sick men stretched upon the ground. His look was absorbed and anxious; some great care seemed to oppress him. Pontet whispered, "See how he is leaving the work to his aide-de-camp."

For all observed that the companion of St. Priest paused continually, and, bending low over the sufferers, spoke in turn to each, patiently waiting for an answer. Those near him noticed also with surprise that Frenchmen, Poles, and Germans were addressed with equal fluency, each in his own tongue.

As he approached, the good-natured Frenchman who had written the Spaniard's letter for him whispered, "Try the aide-de-camp. He looks kind."

Thus encouraged, the dying man stretched out his worn and fevered hand. "For the love of God, Monsieur l'Aide de camp," he prayed in his broken French, "take this letter and send it for me. It is my last farewell to my dear wife."

"That letter shall reach its destination," was the answer, uttered in a tone of deep feeling; and stooping over the prostrate form, the speaker added some gentle words of hope and consolation.

As his tall figure resumed its erect position, the lamplight shone upon his face, revealing it to Henri. It was a noble, refined, sensitive face, pale with uttermost horror and loathing at the abominations around, though the revolt of the shrinking nerves and senses was crushed down by a strong will, and a look of profound compassion and sympathy effaced every other expression. Instinctively Henri raised himself, and, resting on his elbow, gazed at him with a hungry longing in his heart that to him—even to him also—he would address so much as a single word. At the same moment the stranger's pitying eye fell upon his young, sad, wasted face. "Et toi aussi, pauvre enfant," he said with tenderness, bending down once more and touching Henri's forehead gently with his hand.

Henri seized the hand in his and pressed it to his lips. "Speak to me so again," he cried, "and I verily believe I shall not die, but live!"

His prayer was granted. He was spoken to, or rather spoken *with*, until St. Priest drew near, and with an anxious air *entreated*, not commanded, his companion to hasten onwards.

Then Henri covered his face with his thin hands and wept quietly—almost the first tears he had shed since leaving Moscow. The gentle shower softened the hard soil of his heart, the flood-gates were thrown open, the fountains of the great deep were unloosed, and the shower became a storm. "Mother, mother!" he sobbed piteously, "O mother!" Wild and passionate was the longing that swept him to see her face again, hers and his sister's. He thought of the old days—of his happy childhood, of the love and tenderness that used to surround him; and every thought unlocked afresh the source of tears. He wept until he could weep no more.

Meanwhile, Pontet followed the visitors as far as he could, and then spoke to the guard at the door. He came back with a beaming countenance and a manner full of suppressed excitement. "Wonderful news, my comrades!" he began eagerly. "Guess, if you can, who it is that has been among us—that we took for the aide-de-camp of M. de St. Priest?"

"It was an angel from heaven," murmured one poor sufferer, lifting up a face flushed with fever. "There was light—rest while he was here. Oh, if he could but have stayed! The darkness is coming back now."

"He has left the light with *me*," said the Spaniard. "God must have sent him here, his messenger, to fulfil my last wish."

"But his name, his name?" cried the eager Pontet,—"no one has guessed that yet. Will you try, or shall I tell you? But if I do, you will not believe me."

"Tell us, tell us," cried half-a-score of voices.

"The aide-de-camp of St. Priest was no other than our great enemy—our conqueror, Alexander, Emperor of Russia!"

His auditors were utterly incredulous. "Have you lost your senses, Pontet?" they cried; "or have the guards been mocking you and us? Not a physician, not a nurse even, would enter here were a fortune offered as a bribe; and do you expect us to believe that the Czar, our enemy, would risk his life—*for us?*"

"Listen," answered Pontet; "the guards have told me all. He has spent the whole day going through the other hospitals;—at last he came here. M. de St. Priest, knowing well how the deadly hospital fever is raging amongst us, entreated, implored him not to enter. He would not listen. Then the general, in a kind of desperation, flung himself before the door, and, daring his sovereign to his face, told him he should enter only over his body. The Czar put him gently aside and walked in; and I tell you, comrades, there is not a nook or corner in all this den of horrors that he has not thoroughly explored. There was no hiding anything from him. I take it, things will be altered with us from this time forth. My friends, if there is any man amongst you happy enough still to believe in God, let him thank him this night for sending the Emperor Alexander here."

When the comments made by others upon this speech had died away, Henri raised his quivering, tear-stained face and said gently, but with a new air of courage and firmness, "Pontet, *I* believe in God; and I thank him—as you say." After a pause he added, "Dear comrades, if you will listen, I should like to tell you how it is with me; for, perhaps, some other poor lad may even now be struggling and suffering in darkness, as I have been."

"Say on," cried several voices.

"When I was wandering through the snow, in hunger, in

misery, in despair, almost in madness, I lost my faith in God;
—perhaps because I never had the right kind of faith, because I
only believed that he was great and just, without believing that
he was *my* God. I fainted utterly. I thought either that he
was not, or that there was with him no love, no compassion. I
thought his pitiless hand was sweeping us all from the face of
the earth, because he was angry with Napoleon. I thought he
was like the great fire in Moscow, which burned, blazed,
destroyed, unchecked by human efforts, unstayed by human
prayers. May he forgive me! To-night I can believe in his
forgiveness and in his divine compassion. If the *man* who
was our enemy—whose land we tried to ruin, upon whom we
heaped every insult, every injury in our power—can pity and
forgive us, surely the God who made him will not be found
less merciful than he! Surely none but that God could so have
softened the proud heart of the Czar; and perhaps he has
done it just to show that even for those who have sinned deeply,
wilfully, like me, there is forgiveness with Him. Therefore let
us hope in the Lord; for with the Lord there is mercy, and
with him is plenteous redemption."

There were murmurs of assent from the pale lips of many of
the sufferers around him; and Pontet observed, with a thoughtful air, "The lad speaks well; and perhaps what he says may
be true. Who knows?" *

---

* All that is told in this and the succeeding chapter about the ministrations of
Alexander to the French prisoners is strictly and circumstantially true. Sir Archibald
Alison, who well observes that Alexander terminated "a campaign of unexampled
danger and glory by deeds of unprecedented mercy," had the details from the Emperor's
own physicians, Wylie and Crichton, his assistants in the noble work. There are many
other sources of information from which interesting anecdotes may be gleaned. The
story of the dying Spaniard is one of these. Alexander not only took care to forward
his letter, but sought out all the other Spanish prisoners, clothed them, and sent them
home at his own expense. He described his visit to the Convent of St. Basil to a friend
in these words:—"I was there in the evening: a single lamp illumined those profound
vaults, beneath which piles of corpses had been heaped almost as high as the walls. I
cannot express the horror with which I was penetrated when amongst the dead bodies I
saw creatures moving who were yet alive." On his way to Vilna, he took up in his own
sledge starving French soldiers whom he met with, and brought them to those whom he
could trust to take care of them, leaving money to supply their wants.

CHAPTER XXIII.

THE MOSCOW MEDAL.

"Now glory to the Lord of Hosts, from whom all glories are!"

HE very next day Henri de Talmont was removed from the horrible Convent of St. Basil to one of the other hospitals of the town—in which, indeed, every palace, every public building sufficiently large, was now being transformed into a hospital. As he passed through the streets, he observed that large fires were burning in all the thoroughfares; and the Russian physician who took charge of the party of invalids told them this was done to purify the air and to destroy infection.

A delicious sensation of rest stole over the weary frame of Henri when at last he found himself lying on a comfortable pallet, in a clean, well-warmed room. Nourishment sufficient for his need and suitable to his weak condition was given him with a willing hand. He had escaped the deadly hospital fever, but the prostration of his strength was excessive, the vital forces seemed exhausted. For many days he lay in a kind of contented apathy, slumbering continually, and even when not asleep floating in hazy dreams amongst vague remembrances of the past. Once or twice he roused himself sufficiently to make some inquiry after his fellow-sufferers. "Be at rest," said his nurse. "All are cared for now; just as well as the wounded Russians." But he used to waken up thoroughly whenever the Emperor came to inspect the hospital where he lay. He would watch with pathetic eagerness for a word, even for a look, from him, and live upon the recollection until his next visit. To most of the other French prisoners the person of their benefactor remained unknown ; and as Alexander moved in and out amongst them, listening to their complaints, ministering to their needs, and speaking words of comfort, they took him generally for the aide-de-camp of St. Priest.

One day Henri, feeling rather stronger than usual, observed with interest a handsome, splendidly-equipped young Russian, who had come to visit one of his countrymen in the same ward. The conversation, carried on in their own language, was unintelligible to Henri ; but something in the face of the visitor touched a chord of memory. The Russian, seeing the sick Frenchman look at him earnestly, and as he thought imploringly, came to his side and asked kindly in French, "Can I do anything for you ? "

"No, sir, no ; I thank you. I have everything I want. Stay though," he added with a slight increase of animation ; " I should like to know, if you will be good enough to tell me, how the Grand Duke is to-day."

Strange to say, the eccentric, passionate Constantine, at other times even wantonly cruel, was now so wrought upon by the example and influence of the brother he adored that he emulated his works of mercy, and had actually caught the hospital fever in his ministrations to the prisoners. Alexander himself seemed to bear a charmed life through every peril ; for God fulfilled unto his servant the word upon which he had caused him to hope : " A thousand shall fall at thy side, and ten thousand at thy right hand ; but it shall not come nigh thee."

The Russian answered, " He is much better. Dr. Wylie has pronounced him out of danger. You know Dr. Wylie ? "

"Yes ; he comes here often. He examined me one day, and said he would like to bleed me, only I was too weak."

The Russian could not suppress a smile. " You enjoyed a

most unusual exemption," he said.   "Dr. Wylie's lancet is not easily escaped.   But I hope, as you *have* been so fortunate, that you are growing stronger?"

"I scarcely know.   I ought to be; for I am not in pain, not hungry, not cold.   All that is so strange now, so pleasant.   But, pardon me, have I not seen your face before?   Where can it have been?"

"I do not remember yours," was the answer.   That was not wonderful; for Henri was a melancholy shadow of his former self, with ghastly, shrunken features, and frame reduced to a skeleton.   The hardships of a very severe campaign had told also upon Ivan Pojarsky, but in a different way; he looked bronzed and weather-beaten, and much older than he really was.

"I remember now," Henri resumed after a pause.   "I saw you during the Occupation, in a church in Moscow.   After the service some Russians attacked me, and I might have been killed, but for that brave fellow with one hand.   He appealed to you, and you protected me.   Ah!" he added with a sigh, "if I had known then what sufferings were before me, I might have prayed you to plunge your sword into my breast!"

"I am glad to find you amongst the living," Ivan said kindly.

"And that day," mused Henri, "was little more than three months ago, while it is but two since we left Moscow.   Were there ever two such months since the beginning of the world?"

"Of suffering?—I think not," said Ivan thoughtfully, as he took a seat beside him.

"Of suffering for us, of glory for *you*.   How you must triumph, you Russians!   Five months ago Napoleon crossed your border with half a million of men; and now the miserable remains of that splendid host are dying in your hospitals, pensioners of your bounty.   Surely such an overthrow was never seen since Pharaoh and his armies perished in the waters of the Red Sea!"

"How we triumph, we Russians!" Ivan repeated. "Should you like to know how? Our Emperor said the other day in confidence to a friend, 'This miserable campaign has cost me ten years of my life!'"

"*Miserable!* when it has been for him and his one long glorious victory!"

"True; but the sufferings he has witnessed have well-nigh broken his heart."

"The sufferings *of his enemies*," said Henri, as tears filled his eyes.

"They have so cast our own into the shade, that we ourselves almost forget them. Yet you must not think we have suffered nothing. Remember Moscow, our beautiful, our holy city; remember Borodino and the other battles in which the best blood of our country was poured out like water. Moreover, the ice-king has thinned our ranks as well as yours."

"Ah! not so fatally."

"No; we had wholesome food, and warm clothing, and care and comforts for the sick. As a rule, our invalids recovered, while yours died. Yes, oh yes, God has surely given us a great deliverance; would it had been at less cost to others! Look here, monsieur,"—Ivan took a silver medal, new and bright, from his neck, where it hung attached to a sky-blue ribbon. "The Czar has just given one of these to every man who has borne part in this winter's campaign, from the general to the youngest recruit."

Henri examined it with interest. One side bore a Triangle surrounded by rays, and in its centre an Eye.

"What does that mean?" he inquired.

"It is, with us, the symbol of the Divine Presence," Ivan answered, crossing himself. "It typifies the All-seeing and Ever-present—the Three in One. Beneath, you read '1812,' the ever-memorable year when He himself interposed to deliver us. Now, turn the other side."

Henri did so, and saw, though he could not read, an inscription in the old Slavonic tongue.

"That is, translated literally, '*Not us! not us! but His Name!*' In your French Bible—the same which I use also—the verse reads thus :—'Not unto us, O Lord, not unto us, but unto thy name give glory.'"

"Beautiful!" said Henri; and as he gave back the medal, he looked with interest at the brilliant young Guardsman, who spoke in such a simple, manly, unaffected way of God's Word and Providence.

"To-morrow the Czar leaves this," said Ivan, replacing his medal. "We of the Chevalier Guard go also, of course."

Henri's cry of distress made all the sick men in the ward raise their heads.

"What is the matter?" Ivan asked compassionately.

"The Emperor is going!" Henri said, or rather sobbed, for so weak was he that he could not restrain his tears.

"You need not be afraid that will change anything, my poor friend. He has made arrangements for the safety and the comfort of all the prisoners. Henceforth they will want for nothing."

"I was not afraid of wanting food or shelter," Henri said. "But, M. le Garde, when I lay in that horrible prison, dying in black despair, it was *his* voice called me back from the gates of the grave, and showed me what the mercy of God was like. I would give half the little life left in me to hear that voice yet once again." After a pause he added, with an effort to control himself, "Still, he stayed among us longer than we could have dared to hope. Is he going home now?"

Ivan shook his head. "His work is not half done yet; nor ours," he said.

"What will you fight for now?" asked Henri with a sad smile. "For vengeance?"

"For *peace*," returned Ivan. "Shall I tell you what the

Czar says about that? He speaks without anger or bitterness
of your Emperor."

"Call him not *mine*," Henri interrupted, with a flush on his
pale cheek. "Mine he never was. I am a Royalist."

"Well, then, of Napoleon. 'What a brilliant career,' said
the Czar, 'that man might have run! He could have given
peace to Europe—he could have done it; and he has not.
Now the charm is broken.'"

"At least you Russians cannot regret that," said Henri with
enthusiasm; "for the olive crown of the peace-maker which
Napoleon has put aside awaits the brow of Alexander."

"So said the friend to whom the Czar was speaking.* 'If
only peace is made,' was his answer, 'what does it matter by
whom, whether by him, or by me, or by another?' It is a
good time to think of peace," Ivan added. "To-morrow will
be Christmas day, when peace and good-will upon earth were
sung by the angels."

"To-morrow?" repeated Henri. "Am I dreaming? Surely
I remember noticing that one of the first blessed, restful days
I spent here was Christmas day."

"You forget," said Ivan with a smile, "that we Russians
are behind the Western world by twelve days. Our Christmas
is your feast of the Epiphany. After divine service to-morrow,
the Czar begins his journey, and we follow."

"You do not accompany him?"

"No; he travels with far greater speed than we could do.
For guards he never cares anything."

"Strange," said Henri—"strange; and how perilous! Think
of the country, overrun by war, swarming with stragglers from
the army, with desperate characters of every kind!"

"He has no fears," returned Ivan; "nor we for him. Even
our white-haired general, with all the caution of his seventy
years, answered to some one who spoke as you do, 'Who could

* Madame de Choiseul-Gouffier.

have the courage to harm him?'* But, my friend, I must go now, for it is late. Accept my best wishes for your recovery." He clasped Henri's hand warmly, and contrived to leave in it a few pieces of gold. Henri tried to remonstrate, but was quickly silenced. "Soldiers always help one another; that is a matter of course. If you like," added Ivan, with a touch of playful malice, "you can repay me after the first French victory. Good-bye."

"What a fine young fellow!" thought Ivan as he left the hospital; "so grateful and so patient. And I have forgotten even to ask his name! How thoughtless of me! Too late to return now. But I am sure he is well born, particularly since he calls himself a Royalist. Probably he belongs to one of those noble families of the old *régime* Napoleon delights to oppress and humble."

Over Ivan himself great changes had passed, and were passing even then. Perhaps his share in the foregoing conversation has already indicated these with sufficient clearness; if not, his conduct during the events that have yet to follow may complete the picture.

Amongst the works of faith and love which in all ages have been inspired by the precepts and the example of "the forgiving Christ," the labours of Alexander on behalf of his perishing enemies undoubtedly deserve a place. It is good for the world to keep such deeds in remembrance, although to those who do them the world's remembrance may avail but little. It was not the motive that inspired, nor will it be the reward that crowns them.

A few years later, at Cherson in the Crimea, Alexander stood beside the grave of a philanthropist whose character and work he held in genuine veneration—John Howard, the prisoners' friend. With his own hand he designed a monument to mark

---

* "Eh, mon Dieu," s'écria le maréchal, "qui est-ce qui aurait le courage de faire du mal à cet ange?"

the resting-place of Christ's honoured servant, choosing for its sole inscription those words of Christ himself—" I was sick, and you visited me; I was in prison, and you came unto me." " Where the kings of the nations lie in glory, every one in his own house," the Czar Alexander Paulovitch has his stately sleeping-place; and well might it bear the same inscription. No human hand has placed it there; but we doubt not Divine lips will one day utter the commendation, " Inasmuch as you have done it unto one of the least of these, you have done it unto Me."

CHAPTER XXIV.

ONE YEAR AFTERWARDS.

> " War is mercy, glory, fame,
>   Fought in Freedom's holy cause,
>   Freedom such as man may claim
>   Under God's restraining laws."
>   WORDSWORTH.

ETWEEN the opening month of 1813 and that of the following year a great change swept over Europe. Men of Teutonic race, true-hearted sons of their dear Fatherland, look back upon that era with honourable pride. They talk with enthusiasm of "the war of liberation," telling gratefully beside their hearths, or by the vine-clad banks of their glorious "German Rhine," how prince and peasant armed for the fight, and flung from them the intolerable yoke of the foreign oppressor. Körner's patriotic lyrics thrilled every heart, and many another tuneful voice, then and since, has chanted the pæan of Germany's deliverance,—·

> " How the crowned eagle spread again
>   His pinion to the sun ;
>   And the strong land shook off its chain,
>   So was the triumph won."

But there are other heroes besides the pre-Homeric of whom it may be said,—

> " They had no bard, and died."

In that memorable battle fought long ago in the valley of Elah, we are told how the men of Israel arose with a great shout, and rushing upon their Philistine oppressors, chased them with tremendous slaughter to the very gates of their own fastnesses. It was a glorious victory; but it would scarcely have been won at all if the Hebrew champion had not first slain Goliath "in the name of the Lord of Hosts, the God of the armies of Israel." In like manner the battle of the deliverance of Europe was really fought and won upon the frozen plains of Russia.

The early days of 1813 found the Russian hosts upon the frontiers of their own country. Within that country, through the blessing of God upon their valour and constancy, not an enemy remained except in captivity. By the first month of 1814 the still victorious armies of the Czar had reached the boundaries of France. That unhappy land seemed now about to suffer what she, or her rulers, had once and again inflicted upon others. "Woe to thee that spoilest, and thou wast not spoiled; and dealest treacherously, and they dealt not treacherously with thee! when thou shalt cease to spoil, thou shalt be spoiled; and when thou shalt make an end to deal treacherously, they shall deal treacherously with thee." So has it ever been since the world began: wrong begets wrong, cruelty engenders cruelty; "they that take the sword perish with the sword." It was the hour of retribution. Slavs and Teutons, whose homes and hearths had been made desolate by French bayonets, gazed, flushed with triumph, on the fertile plains of France, and promised themselves and their dead a terrible vengeance. "We will reward her even as she rewarded us, and the cup which she hath filled we will fill to her double," they said in their hearts. It was the voice of Nature.

But in that hour another voice was heard. "Soldiers," said Alexander to the armies of Russia, "your valour and your perseverance have brought you from the Oka to the Rhine. We are about to enter a country with which we are waging a sanguinary and obstinate war. The enemy, entering our empire, brought on us great evils, but suffered for it an awful punishment. Let us not take example by them; cruelty and ferocity cannot be pleasing in the eyes of a merciful God. Let us forget their deeds, and render them, not vengeance and hatred, but friendship, and a hand stretched out for peace. Such is the lesson taught by our holy faith. Divine lips have pronounced the command, 'Love your enemies; do good to them that hate you.' Soldiers, I trust that by your moderation in the enemy's country you will conquer as much by generosity as by arms; and, uniting the valour of the soldier against the armed with the charity of the Christian towards the unarmed, you will crown your exploits by keeping stainless your well-earned reputation of a brave and moral people." This was *not* the voice of Nature, but of Grace.

But these noble words, did they die upon the ears of those who heard them, leaving only an echo, faint though musical, to remind them of the existence of such things as mercy and humanity? or did they really prove strong enough to restrain the excited passions of a hundred thousand fighting men? Strange to tell, the voice of Alexander was obeyed. It was not easy to secure such obedience; it would not have been even possible, had not he whose lips uttered the command been passionately loved, as well as feared and honoured. But a touching proof how well it was secured was given years afterwards. When, through the length and breadth of Europe, the tidings flashed from lip to lip, "The Emperor of Russia is dead," the peasants of the French provinces through which he marched at the head of a victorious hostile army crowded unbidden to their churches to offer their humble prayers, useless indeed but sincere, for the repose of his soul.

Two months of hard fighting brought the Allies from the banks of the Rhine to those of the Marne, which they crossed on the 28th of March, and found themselves in the rich and fertile plain that surrounds Paris. The Chevaliers of the

Imperial Guard had borne their full share in the glories and dangers of the war; for their place was near the person of a sovereign of whom it was said with truth that "the only life he ever exposed without reflection was his own." Their ranks were sorely thinned: one gallant youth had fallen by a shot from the same battery as that which killed Moreau, two at Toplitz, others at Leipzig and elsewhere. But their arms were as bright, their equipages as splendid, as when they left the banks of the Neva; and their massy silver cuirasses reflected the sunshine of France from surfaces as stainless as those which flashed upon the parade-ground of St. Petersburg.

Ivan Pojarsky was an ensign now—he had won his colours on the banks of the Elbe—and he wore besides the Order of St. George along with the Moscow medal on the breast of his crimson tunic. He had escaped without a wound; but his friend Tolstoi was looking very pale, and had his left hand in a sling.

As the Chevaliers rode together towards Paris on the evening of the 29th of March, their party was joined by some noble young Prussian volunteers, their personal friends. One of these, named Schubart, was vaunting to the Russians the courage and ability of Blucher, and telling them the story of some of his exploits.

"All that is very well," said Tolstoi, with a little irritation. "Far be it from me to deny that Prince Blucher is a brave soldier and a good general. But where, I ask you, would he be now, but for his Russian auxiliaries? You know as well as I that his army contains four Russians for one Prussian. Still," he pursued, "there is all the difference in the world between your fine old hero and that Austrian trimmer and time-server, who, I verily believe, would have us all prisoners in the camp of Napoleon, if he were left to himself."

"I am not any more in love with Prince Schwartzenberg than you are," said the Prussian; while Ivan whispered to Tolstoi, with a warning glance, "Take care."

"Oh yes, I'll take care," answered Tolstoi lightly. Then, as a spasm of pain passed across his face, "What a nuisance this hand is! Lucky it is not the right one, though."

"If it had been," said Ivan, "you would have done as Diebitch did at Austerlitz—taken the sword in your left, and fought on."

"I am sorry to see you are wounded," remarked Schubart. "How was it?"

"Oh, it is nothing," returned Tolstoi. "I got the hurt three days ago, in that fight with Pacthod's corps."

"A brilliant affair. We have all heard of it," said the Prussian.

"Ay," answered Tolstoi; "those Frenchmen fought like demons."

"Like heroes, you mean," said Ivan. "Certainly the empire Napoleon has kept over the hearts of his soldiers is no less than a miracle, especially when we know how little he would care if all of them were dead to-morrow, provided he had as good to replace them. It was sixteen thousand men with guns and cavalry against six thousand without either; and yet they would not yield to us. Our guns raked their lines. Still they stood undaunted, resolved to resist to the death. The Czar sent an aide-de-camp with a flag of truce to them. They shot him dead." *

"Not *very* chivalrous that," Schubart interposed.

"No, truly. But how gallantly they fought! They would have kept their places till they were cut to pieces, man by man. And to that it must have come, but the Czar would not have it. He called on us to follow—us of the Chevalier Guard," said Ivan with a look of pride—"and dashed head-long into the midst of them, breaking up and scattering their compact square by the sheer impetus of his charge. It was a

---

* The aide-de-camp was Rapatel, a protégé of Moreau, who had attached himself to Alexander out of gratitude for his kindness to the family of his friend and patron.

glorious *mêlée*—the grandest I have ever seen. Think of Pacthod giving his sword into the Czar's own hand, and not dreaming until afterwards that the gallant cavalry officer whose courage and promptitude averted a massacre was the Emperor himself!" *

"Ach, wunderschön!" cried Schubart. "Herr Tolstoi, I would take your wound twice over to have been in the midst of it."

"Look!" Ivan suddenly exclaimed, pointing to the scene before them. While absorbed in their eager talk, they had been ascending an eminence, from the top of which they now caught their first sight of the magnificent capital of France. The sun had just set, but its parting beams still lingered upon the gilded dome of the Hôtel des Invalides and the stately summit of the Pantheon. "Paris! Paris!" was the exclamation that broke from every lip, and resounded far and wide in lengthened cries of fierce joy and exultation. "Paris! Paris!" was shouted again and yet again, as rank after rank of that gallant army beheld the goal of all their aspirations, the end of all their toils.

After the first involuntary cry Ivan was silent. At length he said quietly to his friend Tolstoi, "When I think of that terrible September, the last but one, and of the flames of Moscow, the wonder and the gladness seem too great, too awful for words."

"Those flames are burning in many a heart now," Tolstoi answered.—"I suppose they will hardly let us in yonder without a struggle," he added in an altered tone. "What will tomorrow bring?"

---

* A distinguished English officer, who was present, says this was the only occasion on which he ever saw Alexander put himself personally forward ; he was usually, though only too ready to share the perils of war, careful to leave its glories to his generals. But this was to save life.

CHAPTER XXV.

" FATHER PARIS FOR MOTHER MOSCOW."

" Lay the sword on his breast; there's no spot on its blade
In whose cankering breath his bright laurels will fade:
It was taken up first at humanity's call;
It was sheathed with sweet mercy when glory was all."

HE passion and the tumult, the glory and the agony of the next day will live in History as long as History herself lives to depict the scenes of blood and violence which earth has witnessed. No battle in that terrible war was more hotly or more obstinately contested than the battle of Paris; although it ought to be remembered that it was not the men of Paris who contested every inch of ground with the Allies, but the corps of Marmont and Mortier, old soldiers of Napoleon, the National Guard, and the youths of the Ecole Polytechnique.

The sun that shone upon that long day's conflict was already near its setting when Ivan, with the rest of the Chevalier Guard, was still straining every nerve to drive the French from the Butte de Chaumont, an important height commanding the city. It is not enough to say that he fought with gallantry: all did that. He fought as one whose whole soul was in the work —who was conscious of no thought, no impulse, no resolve save that Paris must be won for the Czar that day. His horse was at a gallop; his red sabre was driving the fleeing French before him; the crest of the hill was reached; the city lay outspread beneath his feet;—when a well-aimed bullet grazed the top of his silver cuirass, and passed through his right shoulder. Faint and dizzy, he still pressed on. To be stopped *now* would be intolerable. But in another moment his senses reeled; all things grew dim about him. He had barely time to thrust the colours which he held into the hand of the comrade nearest him; then, after clutching vainly at the mane of his horse, he found himself lying under its hoofs. Immeasurably bitter was the thrill of disappointment that flashed through him ere consciousness departed. "I shall *not* enter Paris with my Czar," he murmured with his failing voice. After that he knew nothing.

When he came to himself he was still lying on the ground where he had fallen. Blood was flowing freely from the wound in his shoulder, but no hoof of horse had grazed him as he lay —all had passed him by, sparing the fallen, as those noble and gentle creatures so often do. He heard voices near him, and to his joy they spoke in *Russian*. Then the Butte de Chaumont was theirs yet! He raised himself with an effort, and looked about him. It was night, but lights were blazing all around. A party of artillery occupied the height which he and his comrades had won for them, and the gunners were standing, match in hand, beside their loaded pieces. It was evident that the word of command to fire upon the city that lay outspread beneath them was expected every instant. Fierce and eager was the excitement. The passionate, exulting anticipation which kindled every eye and throbbed in every heart resounded on all sides in "houras" and "vivas," while from lip to lip along the ranks the cry was echoed and re-echoed, "Father Paris, you shall pay for Mother Moscow!"

A voice near Ivan—a voice that Ivan knew—exclaimed, in tones of deepest emotion, "Thank God and the saints, we have our revenge this night for our beautiful and holy city, laid in ashes—ay, and for our dead, our *murdered !* Anna Popovna, in *thy* name I send the messenger of Death into the homes of the infidel Nyemtzi."

" Michael ! Michael Ivanovitch !" Ivan called in a faint and quivering voice.

Fortunately Michael heard the sound, and moved towards the spot whence it came. " Great St. Nicholas !" exclaimed he, " it is Barrinka !"

A good soldier always knows what to do for a wounded comrade. Water, mixed with a little brandy, was quickly borne to the lips of Ivan; and gladly would Michael have bound the wound himself, only he thought it right to yield the privilege to some one who had the use of both his hands. " But what shall we do for linen?" asked the gunner who undertook the surgeon's office.

" Here is the very thing we want !" cried Michael, delightedly producing from his knapsack a clean white cambric handkerchief.

" A token from some fair one, I suppose," said his comrade with a laugh, as he took it from his hand.

" A token from some one harder to find," returned Michael. " From a Frenchman with a notion of justice and mercy in his head."

" The Frenchmen shall learn what justice is before the dawn of to-morrow's sun," said the gunner with a dark and angry look.

He bound Ivan's wound as well as he could, gave him a little more brandy and water, and then, with Michael's assistance, placed him on a kind of couch made of cloaks and blankets. Meanwhile their companions kindled a fire, the warmth of which proved welcome to all the party.

" I feel quite comfortable now," said Ivan. " Thank you, my brothers."

At that moment an exclamation of amazement broke from the entire group. Upon a pole, on an eminence near them, a white flag was visible through the darkness. Bitter murmurs, even cries of disappointment, began to be heard. " Can it be," cried Michael, " that they are dreaming of a truce now—

now—with the city in our very hands? It must be those accursed treacherous Austrians or those fools of Prussians who are showing the white feather. But the Czar will never listen to them—*never!*"

"Never!" eagerly assented all around. "He remembers the flames of Moscow."

They were not left long in suspense. Presently an aide-de-camp, galloping along the lines, brought the orders of the Czar: "Extinguish your matches. Pile your muskets. The city is about to capitulate."

The order was obeyed, but with a great and bitter cry, like the cry of a wild beast that sees his prey escape him. Rage and disappointment filled every heart to overflowing. Michael flung himself on his knees beside his now useless gun, covering his face with his one hand, while the tears rolled down his weather-beaten cheeks.

Touched by his distress, Ivan called him to his side. "What is the matter, friend?" he asked gently.

"Matter, Barrinka? Matter enough to break the heart of a man who has marched from Moscow to Paris with only one thought, one hope in his heart—the hope of vengeance."

"I cannot blame you, Michael. You have bitter wrongs to avenge."

"Ay, Barrinka," answered he, choking down the emotion he did not wish to betray. "I see nothing day and night but that sweet pale face with the look of death upon it. Only killing Nyemtzi makes it go away now and then for a little while. All this time I have been thinking, perhaps if we kill Nyemtzi enough—kill and destroy them utterly—*utterly*," he repeated, sending out the word with a hissing sound through his clenched teeth, "that face may go or change—change back again," he added more gently, "to the old happy look it used to have in the bygone days when she was my betrothed, before the Nyemtzi came and ruined everything."

"I think, Michael, there may be another way to bring the change you long for," began Ivan; but Michael interrupted him.

"No !" he cried passionately—"no way but killing Nyemtzi. That is all the joy left me now upon earth.   And the Czar will not let us do it."

"He will not," said Ivan.   "That is true.   Remember, Michael, that he who forbids it is the Czar Alexander Paulovitch—no one else.'

"If it *were* any one else," returned Michael gloomily, "we should tear him to pieces."

"What do you suppose has made the Czar forbid it ?   Ever since we entered this land of the enemy, he has held back his avenging armies, as one might hold a bloodhound in the leash from springing on his prey.   Is it that *he* has no wrongs to revenge; that *he* has forgotten holy Moscow and the Kremlin and the outraged tombs of his fathers ?"

"'The Czar is God upon earth,'" said Michael, quoting the proverb of his people.   "He does what he pleases.   How could such as I pretend to understand him ?—Are you suffering, Barrinka ?" he asked, as Ivan stirred uneasily and shivered.

"Not much.   I think it is the chill before the morning that I feel.   Wrap that cloak around me, please, and give me a little more brandy."

Michael did so, saying, as he tried to fasten the cloak, "If I had my other hand, I would do it better for you, Barrinka."

"You have done it well, my friend; but you must often miss your hand, and regret its loss."

"Regret it !" cried Michael with the old enthusiasm flashing from his eyes.   "*Never!*   Did I not give it for the Czar ?"

"Michael, listen to me.   As you love and honour the Czar, so the Czar loves and honours *his King*."

"*His* king ?" repeated Michael, wondering.   But a moment afterwards he made the sign of the cross.   "I understand," he said in a lower voice.

Ivan resumed: " The thought of vengeance may have been dear to him—dear as was your hand to you—still at the command of his King, and for his sake, it was surrendered, and that joyfully.   You see ?"

" I see." Michael relapsed into silence, and stood gazing thoughtfully upon the city spread out beneath their feet, and growing every moment clearer in the dawning light.   At last he said, turning once again to Ivan, " Barrinka, it is true I gave my hand for the Czar.   But I never thought he would care—or even hear of it.   He did though; he spoke to me with his own lips.   He thanked me, and said I had been found faithful.   Not *one* hand, but two, would have been well lost for that.   But will his King speak to the Czar and thank him ?"

" Yes," Ivan answered, " he will, though I cannot tell how. God has many ways of speaking to his servants."

In due time the day broke, and the sun arose over Paris. Then came relief and refreshment for the troops, and surgical help and care for the wounded.   Then came also the tidings, flashing from rank to rank, " The capitulation is signed.   The city has surrendered *without conditions*.   At half-past three o'clock this morning, the keys of Paris were placed in the hands of Alexander."

CHAPTER XXVI.

"A poor man helped by thee shall make thee rich;
A sick man served by thee shall make thee whole:
Thou shalt be blessed thyself in every sense
Of blessing which thou renderest."

THE two years so eventful to others had not passed without change over the mother and sister Henri de Talmont left sorrowing behind him in the cottage at Brie. That he had joined the corps of recruits instead of making his escape soon became known to them. Both were stricken to the heart; and because this was so, the grief of both was still and silent. Clémence told her mother Henri's parting words, upon which a mournful light was thrown by what followed. But these brought little comfort, and no tidings since had reached them from the wanderer. As may have been inferred, the letter intrusted to Seppel was never posted; and Henri did not write again.

At length came news of the appalling disasters in Russia. Neither Madame de Talmont nor Clémence indulged the faintest hope that Henri could have survived them. They mourned for the one who "was not," in an utter desolation, beyond words and beyond tears.

Sometimes they murmured sadly to each other, "If only we knew the truth." For it was one of the bitterest drops in their full cup of bitterness that they could not tell in what form death had come to their beloved, while they knew but too well how hideous and revolting were some of the forms assumed by the king of terrors. Horrible details reached them, piercing the thick veil of falsehood with which Napoleon sought to hide the disasters of his army; and imagination—that magician so powerful for good and evil—exercised a fearful ingenuity in torturing their aching hearts to the uttermost.

These were pangs they endured in common; but each had besides her solitary burden of pain. That of the mother was tinged with something like the bitterness of remorse. She had been wroth with her boy for deceiving her and betraying the cause she held dearer than life. Pride and anger had kept her back from obeying the first impulse of her heart when she heard of him as amongst the conscripts who left the village. She thought of hastening after him to Paris, that he might not go forth to die without his mother's pardon and her blessing. But she put the thought aside. The difficulties in her way would have been very great, yet it was not these that deterred her. It was the persuasion that he did not deserve this sacrifice at her hands—that the first step towards a reconciliation ought to come from him. If he wished for it, why had he not written? —But now everything was changed. With vain tears that had no healing in them the broken-hearted mother mourned over " the irrevocable past."

Clémence too had her lonely sorrow. Deeply thoughtful and truly pious, after the strong, stern, self-sacrificing Jansenist fashion, she knew too well that her brother's young heart had never truly surrendered itself to its Creator and Redeemer. The " Except ye be converted" of the Divine Teacher held as real a place in the creed of Clémence as in that of any Protestant; nor, under the circumstances, could the Catholic belief in sacramentary grace interpose its soft, misleading glamour between her eyes and the truth. So her soul went down to the depths of a sorrow without hope; depths that few are strong enough to sound, and those who do sound them seldom

tell what they find there. Some, it may be, bring back
from thence secrets of divine love, "treasures of the deep that
lieth under," worth all they have passed through to learn
them. But it was not so with Clémence. She brought no
pearls with her from the deeps of ocean. It was much if she
herself came back, or rather *drifted* back, forlorn and weary,
because mind and body were no longer strong enough to bear
the strain of intense emotion. She said in her heart,—as
poor Henri thought she would do all too easily,—"It is the
will of God;" but she never truly said, "Thy will be done."
Perhaps she made her heavy burden heavier by asking from
herself what God never asked from her; forgetting that it is
not his will that any sinner should perish, and that Christ himself wept tears of divine compassion over lost souls. So her
own faith grew dim and clouded, until even the sense of personal love to God seemed to vanish away, and with it the trust
in his love to her; for, unhappily, her creed did *not* teach her
that his love to his chosen and adopted is "everlasting."

In the course of time an outward change was mercifully sent
to break up the current of those two sorrowful lives. A
widowed sister of Madame de Talmont's mother had been able
to retain a portion of her property through all the storms of
the Revolution. Madame de Salgues had lost both her sons,
and only one grandson remained to her, the object of her passionate devotion. But the agents of Napoleon kept watch over
the lad, as a scion of the old noblesse; and when he had
attained a suitable age, Madame de Salgues was requested to
send him to the Ecole Polytechnique, such a request being too
evidently a command. She wept, but had to obey; removing,
however, to Paris, in order to be near him. But the superintendent of police, the notorious Savary, had a word to say upon
that subject; and the poor old lady was soon forbidden to reside
within the city. Remonstrance was useless; so she retired to
Versailles, where she was still near enough to receive frequent

visits from her grandson. Finding herself alone and lonely, with failing health and depressed spirits, she thought of Madame de Talmont; and very wisely wrote offering a comfortable home to her and her daughter, if they would come and cheer her declining years.

The invitation was accepted with thankfulness; and the first faint gleams of comfort stole unconsciously into the darkened hearts of Madame de Talmont and Clémence as they sought to soothe the sorrows of another. Poor Madame de Salgues had soon a fresh grief to mourn over. Like all her family, she was a stanch Legitimist, and she had brought up her grandson in the same political creed; but he could not long withstand the influence of his new surroundings. Before he had been three months at the Ecole Polytechnique, his teachers and fellow-pupils had wrought a rapid conversion, and made him as fiery and unreasoning a partisan of Napoleon as he had once been of the Bourbons. Emile de Salgues was not a lad whose opinions upon any subject were likely to be of particular importance to the rest of the world, but to Madame de Salgues the apostasy of her grandson from the good cause was a very grievous affliction.

The invasion of France by the Allies, and the attack upon Paris, caused many apprehensions to the household of unprotected ladies; but, as they themselves would have expressed it, they were "quitte pour la peur," no adversary nor evil of any kind came near them. They all rejoiced at the overthrow of Napoleon, but with trembling, and that for more reasons than one, — they could not yet believe it was real, and they had not the slightest idea of what was to take his place.

On the day following the entry of the conquerors into Paris, Madame de Talmont said to her daughter, "Clémence, the Allies have sent their wounded here."

Clémence looked up from the embroidery upon which she was engaged. Two years of sorrow had changed the young girl into a grave and quiet woman; but there was even a rarer beauty than of old in her pale and sculptured face. "There must be many wounded," she remarked with an air of sadness. "Every one says the fight was an obstinate one."

"The hospital is full to overflowing. Clémence, they are all of them mothers' sons, *also*."

In the last word there was an undertone of pain that went straight to the heart of Clémence. "True, dear mother," she said softly.

"I have been thinking," Madame de Talmont resumed, "that it would do us good to try and comfort some of them, even a little. What should *we* feel now, if we knew that any one had done it for our beloved?"

With Clémence a call to action always found a ready response. "What can we do, mother?" she asked with even a touch of eagerness.

"To some of the sick men fruit may be welcome; to others, a little money to buy the trifling luxuries they may long for; to all, kind words will not be valueless."

"But, mother, they are Germans and Russians. They will not understand us."

"Some of them will. At all events, we can try."

An hour afterwards, two ladies dressed in deep mourning and closely veiled entered the Hospital of Versailles. Each carried a basket filled with grapes and oranges, which they easily obtained permission to distribute amongst the patients.

"These are all Russians who are here," they were told; "the Prussians and Austrians have been provided for in other places."

The sufferers were well cared for, as well at least as circumstances permitted. A liberal allowance was made for their support by their own government; and the Mayor of Versailles interested himself so warmly in their welfare, that the Czar afterwards wrote him an autograph letter of thanks.

Madame de Talmont and Clémence passed between long rows of pallets, distributing their little gifts, which were most thankfully received, especially the oranges, of which the Russians were excessively fond. They tried to show their gratitude by looks and signs; and one poor fellow, remembering a word which is the same in most languages and full of blessing in all, brought tears to the sad eyes of Clémence by looking up and murmuring, "Christohs;" as though he would have said, "We are one in Him.'

They came at last to the ward where the wounded officers lay. Their little store was long since exhausted; and even had it been otherwise, they would have thought the common soldiers greater objects of compassion. So they passed on rather quickly, and without paying much heed to the pale but interested faces which were raised from many a pillow to gaze at the gentle, sweet-looking ladies, the very sight of whom seemed to do the poor sufferers good.

At length one face arrested the eye of Madame de Talmont, and she could not but pause for another look. It was a young and handsome face, with a burning spot on either cheek, and a contraction of the brows that told the story of feverish pain. Yet, in spite of weariness and suffering, the eyes were absolutely beaming with joy, and a happy, satisfied smile played over the parted lips.

She stood for a moment by the side of the invalid. "My young friend," she said kindly, "you seem to be in pain; and yet you look happy."

"Yes, madame, I am indeed happy," answered Ivan Pojarsky, who had just been receiving a visit from his friend Tolstoi. "How can I help it? Yesterday the Czar entered Paris in triumph."

He spoke French as correctly and with almost as pure an accent as Madame de Talmont herself. She was touched and interested by his words. "But," she asked, "do you not feel it hard to be lying here, helpless and suffering, while your Emperor and your companions in arms enjoy their triumph?"

"Oh no, madame," he said with animation; "I cannot think of that. Nor could you, if you belonged to my Czar. If you had seen the flames of Moscow; had heard the thunder when the mines exploded that laid half our Kremlin in ruins; had witnessed the faith and courage that upheld him *then*, had watched the long and weary conflict he has waged from that hour until now—patient, wise, self-sacrificing, undaunted,*— you would rejoice for him in the very depths of your heart that the goal is won at last, that he stands a conqueror in the midst of Paris, and possesses the gate of his enemies!" In his eagerness he half raised himself, his eyes sparkled, and his whole face flushed with excitement.

"Gently, gently, my poor young friend," said Madame de Talmont in a tone of almost motherly tenderness. "I fear you will hurt yourself."

"Oh no, madame;"—but even as he spoke his colour changed rapidly, and his lip quivered with the pain he tried to hide.

Meanwhile, many thoughts were passing through the mind of the silent but observant Clémence. There was a little stand beside the bed, upon which were a phial containing medicine, a small book, and a clean white cambric handkerchief. She saw, with interest and pleasure, that the book was a copy of

---

* He could say all that and more with perfect truth. The conduct of Alexander during the War of Liberation forms a very bright page in his history. He spared no effort to infuse his own courage, energy, and determination into his allies. At the outset, he wished for the chief command of the united armies, a position for which he was well qualified, and to which he possessed every possible claim. But Austrian jealousy interfered; for it must be remembered that Francis of Austria had given his daughter in marriage to Napoleon, so that the infant heir of the common enemy was the grandson of one of the allied sovereigns. Inspired by his cabinet, the Austrian general, Prince Schwartzenberg, opposed the arrangement, and Alexander quietly gave way. He appeased the indignation of the King of Prussia, and reconciled Schwartzenberg with him. He broke up his own enormous armies into auxiliary corps, most of which he placed under the command of his allies; and abandoning the lower ambition of being the nominal head of the confederation, contented himself with being its soul and its inspiring genius. It was he who planned, and urged upon his allies, the march upon Paris that brought the war to a successful termination.

the New Testament in French. Then her eye rested upon the folded cambric, and presently a cry of amazement broke from her lips.

Every one started and looked towards her. Madame de Talmont was terror-stricken. So quiet and self-contained had Clémence ever been, that even in childhood a cry from her lips was a thing almost unknown. And now, with a face as white as that of any of the stricken sufferers around them, she was placing the handkerchief in the hand of her mother. "Look," she faltered—"look, mother!"

Ivan called an attendant, fortunately within reach. "Will you kindly place seats for these ladies?" he said, for he saw that the agitation of the mother was as great as that of the daughter. Both were gazing spell-bound at the crest, worked curiously and skilfully on a corner of the handkerchief, and having beneath it the initials "H. de T." No wonder; for it was the fingers of Clémence that had wrought every stitch, and her mother's eyes had watched the work. In both hearts a horrible dread succeeded to the first rush of uncontrollable and unreasoning emotion. Was this amongst the spoils of the dead?

Ivan watched them with pitying eyes. "Have the goodness to be seated, madame and mademoiselle," he said. "A little nearer, please; I cannot speak very loud. But I think I have something to tell you."

They obeyed mechanically; and Madame de Talmont said falteringly, pointing to the initials on the handkerchief, "He was my son."

"*Is*," Ivan corrected.

From that moment to her dying day Madame de Talmont loved the voice that uttered that blessed monosyllable.

"I have good hope, madame, that God has preserved him to you through many dangers," Ivan went on. "I saw him twice—the last time at Vilna, after the perils and horrors of the retreat were over. He was lying sick in a hospital there.

Not with any malady, only worn out with hunger, cold, and weariness. Every care was afforded him, and every kindness shown that circumstances permitted ; and so, I trust—"

"But," Clémence interrupted, "can we be sure there is no mistake? M. le Russe, how did you become possessed of this?" pointing to the handkerchief.

"In a strange way, mademoiselle," said Ivan, fixing his deep blue eyes on her face. "A young peasant, a friend of my childhood, was made prisoner by the French as they were marching upon Moscow. They branded him in the hand with the letter N, telling him that now he belonged to their Emperor, Napoleon. The brave fellow took out his axe and struck off the hand, saying to them, 'Take what belongs to your Emperor ; as for me, I belong wholly to the Czar.' Then, mademoiselle, monsieur, your—your brother, I presume, stepped forward before them all, like the gallant and chivalrous gentleman he is, and bound up the poor lad's wounded arm with his own handkerchief."

A look of pride and pleasure flashed over the pale face of Clémence—and Ivan saw it.

He resumed, "It was in Moscow, during the Occupation, that I met him first. My friend pointed him out to me in one of our churches. He found his way there, for he said it did him good to see men kneel in prayer to God, though he could not understand their words. Afterwards, as I told you, I saw him in the hospital at Vilna."

Absorbed though she was in the interest of his narrative, Clémence perceived that Ivan was growing faint. "Mother," she whispered, "I fear we are hurting him. Let us go."

"Only one word more," said Ivan. "You wish to know how *I* came by that," again indicating the handkerchief. "My friend Michael treasured it carefully as a souvenir, and when I was wounded the other night, he used it to bind the wound. Knowing how he prizes it, I was careful to have it washed, and kept it by me to give him when he comes to see me. Now it is better in your hands."

Here one of the surgeons. who for some time had been hovering uneasily about the group, interposed and courteously requested the visitors to withdraw. He said. as he attended them to the door, "Pardon me, ladies. for interrupting your conversation, but I must take care of my patient. who will be in a high fever to-night if he excites himself any further. Indeed, I fear mischief has been done already—not by *you*. ladies." he added with a bow, "but by one of his comrades, who came to him this morning full of yesterday's triumphal entry into the city."

"I hope," Madame de Talmont contrived to say. in spite of her extreme agitation,—" I hope he is not severely wounded ?"

"Severely. but not dangerously." was the answer. " He is one of the finest young men we have. madame ; an ensign in the Emperor's Chevalier Guard. and already very favourably noticed by his Imperial Majesty.—Adieu, madame and mademoiselle : we shall be happy to see you another day."

CHAPTER XXVII.

RECOGNITIONS.

" There's a Divinity that shapes our ends."

"IT is enough : my son is yet alive; I shall see him before I die." These were the first words Madame de Talmont found voice to falter, as, leaning heavily on the arm of Clémence, she traversed the short distance between the hospital and the house where they dwelt.

The unutterable joy and thankfulness that filled the soul of Clémence was not unmixed with fear. With the speechless, agonizing dread of a loving heart, she trembled for the treasure left her still. If, after this re-awakening of their hopes, the only tidings that had to reach them were of a nameless grave at Vilna, how could her mother bear the blow? Surely, had he recovered, Henri would have written to them ere this. She could not help concluding, from the young Russian's narrative, that he had met with sufficient kindness in the house of his captivity to have rendered it easy for him to do so.

But she could not bear to communicate her misgivings. She led her mother to the pleasant room they shared together, and persuaded her to lie down and rest, taking upon herself the task of relating what they had heard to La Tante, as they both called Madame de Salgues.

During the long night that followed, bringing sleep to neither, mother and daughter had abundant leisure for the scattered, incoherent, "discursive talk" beneath which over-whelming emotions usually conceal, because they cannot ade-quately express, themselves. Morning had almost come when Madame de Talmont asked, suddenly raising her head from a hot, tear-stained pillow, "Clémence, what about a ransom? We have that to think of now."

"I *have* been thinking of it, mother," Clémence answered gently. "But peace will be made—*must* be made shortly. May we not conclude that something will be arranged in it about the prisoners?"

"If peace were to be made with any one save Napoleon, I should say yes. Some men would think of their followers, and try to make terms for them, were they themselves on the way to the scaffold. But this Corsican adventurer has as little idea of knightly honour as of Christian grace; while who can tell yet what is to come after him? No, Clémence; you may depend upon it those poor captives have no friends save God and their own kinsfolk.—What can we do? Not even a jewel of any value is left us now."

"But, mother, we have still our little pittance in the Rentes. Now that La Tante supplies all our real needs, we can sell what is there."

"Ah, that is not enough, I fear, since the Rentes have fallen so low. Yet it is all we have.—Clémence, I do not like Rus-sians; in fact, as a general thing, I have quite a prejudice against them."

"Oh, mother, why?" asked Clémence, in tones rather more earnest than the case demanded. "They could not help killing our people; they were defending their native country," she added.

"Not for that, of course; but there are reasons which you do not know. I was about to say, however, that young Russian has interested and attracted me in spite of myself. He seems quite a 'preux chevalier;' and," she added more softly, "although he said nothing of it, I doubt not he showed kindness to our dear one when he met him in the hospital at Vilna. Besides, there is something in his face which I cannot describe, but which haunts and troubles while it touches me. It seems to remind me of some other face known long ago. We must go and see him again to-morrow, and bring him some little token of our gratitude. What do you think he would like, Clémence ? "

But they did *not* see Ivan on the morrow ; for Madame de Talmont was too ill to rise from her bed, and Clémence, even if she had been willing to leave her, could not go to the hospital alone. When, after an interval of three or four days, they made their appearance once more, the courteous Russian surgeon gave them quite a warm welcome.

"M. Pojarsky has been watching for you, mesdames," he said. " You will do him more good than any of our medicines."

"Pojarsky!" Madame de Talmont repeated, as one in a dream—" *Pojarsky !* "

Clémence was amazed to find her mother's ready and graceful courtesy fail her completely for once. By way of supplying her unaccountable omission she ventured upon an inquiry for the invalid.

"He has been very feverish, and has suffered a good deal since," the surgeon admitted. "But he is much better to-day. Will you come to him at once, mesdames ? "

"Willingly, monsieur, if you will be kind enough to distribute these oranges amongst those who need them most," said Clémence, placing a large bag in the hands of the surgeon ; for her mother's continued silence forced her to take the initiative. "Mother," she whispered, as they passed into the ward where Ivan lay—" dear mother, what ails you ? "

"That name awakens old associations—not happy ones," Madame de Talmont answered.

Ivan received his friends with a bright, glad smile of welcome.

Since their last visit he had beguiled his hours of loneliness and pain by endeavouring to recall every word, every look of Henri's, as a drop to be added to the cup of comfort he was bearing to the lips of Henri's mother and sister. Very pleasant had the recognition been to him. Well could he imagine how the solitary invalid far away in the hospital at Vilna must have longed for those sweet faces, for the gentle touch of those kind hands. What would *he* give for such a mother, such a sister, to tend and care for him! But then his thoughts would revert once more, with a thrill of thankful joy, to the triumph of the Czar. How could he wish for anything else in the world when Alexander was in Paris, and the flames of Moscow were avenged?

At first Madame de Talmont seemed embarrassed, and a faint pink flush lent unwonted colour to her pale cheek. But Ivan's detailed description of his interview with Henri at Vilna arrested and held her with its absorbing interest.

"M. de Pojarsky," she said, uttering the name with a little hesitation, perhaps even reluctance, "if *you* have a mother living, I pray God to send some one to comfort her, as you have comforted me."

"Ah, madame," returned Ivan, "I have never known my mother; she died in my earliest infancy. I am tempted to envy M. de Talmont," he added with a smile.

Madame de Talmont looked at him with quickened interest. "May I ask," she said rather quickly, "does your father live? It is sad if one so young as you appear to be, stands alone in the world."

Ivan sighed. "I *am* alone in the world," he said. "But the strange thing is, that I cannot tell whether my father is living or dead."

"How is that?" pursued Madame de Talmont eagerly. But Clémence interposed, from a kindly desire to spare the young Russian a painful recital. "We can guess," she said—"we have heard, even in France, of exiles in Siberia. We have pitied their sufferings."

Ivan's white face flushed. "No one is sent to Siberia *now*," he said eagerly, "who would not in any other country than ours be far more severely punished. It was the Czarina who exiled my father," he continued with some excitement—"not my Czar."

"Do not think me unkind or discourteous," Madame de Talmont said gently, "if I venture to inquire what was the offence laid to his charge. I have a reason."

"I can answer without pain or reluctance," said Ivan. "My father's disgrace and banishment, and my mother's death, which quickly followed, took place in my infancy; and the kind but simple people who cared for me and brought me up could tell me very little. But from that little I have gathered that my father, being in Paris at the outbreak of the Revolution, became involved in the crimes of the Jacobins, rather from youthful thoughtlessness than from any deliberate evil intention."

"*Ah!*" said Madame de Talmont.

Something in her tone made Ivan raise himself to look at her. "Madame," he asked quickly, "did you know my father?"

"That is a question I shall be better able to answer if you on your part will tell me — was your mother a Frenchwoman?"

"Yes, madame," said Ivan, looking greatly agitated.

"Have you ever heard her name?"

"Not her family name, madame. Her Christian name I know—Victoire."

Madame de Talmont wrestled in silence with some emotion, and conquered it. Then taking Ivan's hand in hers, she said kindly, even with tenderness, "My dear boy, you must accept us as your cousins."

"My cousins!" Ivan repeated. "Ah, madame, how gladly! But I must entreat of you to explain to me my good fortune. It quite bewilders me."

"I can explain very easily. Your mother, Victoire de Talmont, was my husband's much-loved cousin—nay, his sister rather, for he was early left an orphan, and her father was as a father to him. Her only brother, Louis de Talmont, was as his brother, until that hateful revolutionary madness seized upon him, bringing misery and disunion into the household. It was her brother's influence made Victoire give her hand to his friend, the fascinating young Russian, Prince Pojarsky. I cannot deny that this was a great sorrow to my husband, for Prince Pojarsky had embraced the same opinions as Louis de Talmont."

"And did you know him, madame?" Ivan asked eagerly. "Have you ever seen him?"

"I did not know him well. All this happened before my own marriage. But I have seen him more than once—a fine, brilliant young man, magnificent in dress and bearing, and very handsome. You are like him; yet I think I see in you a stronger resemblance to the features of Victoire."

Madame de Talmont's estimate of the young Russian prince had not been very favourable, though she naturally and properly expressed herself as kindly as she could in speaking to his son. But Clémence had always beheld the half-mythical Victoire robed from head to foot in shining garments, woven in the loom of her own youthful romance. To see the son of Victoire in the flesh seemed to be part of "the stuff that dreams are made of" brought suddenly into the realities of waking life. Breaking silence for the first time, she asked,—

"Have you any portrait of your mother, monsieur?"

"I have never even seen one," Ivan answered. "My father's ruin robbed me of everything. The poor mujiks who sheltered me most kindly and most bravely—indeed at the peril of their own lives—were unable to keep for me, out of all my father's wealth, even the smallest heirloom."

"We have a likeness of our cousin Victoire, a pencil-sketch from the hand of my father," Clémence rejoined. "We must show it to you, monsieur."

Then Madame de Talmont made some inquiries about his early history; and he answered modestly and with feeling. He dwelt with much gratitude upon the kindness of his dear old friend Petrovitch, saying in conclusion, "He taught me what a good father might be like."

At last it was necessary to say farewell. The ladies withdrew, promising a speedy renewal of their intercourse.

"Would that I had a house of my own, even the humblest," said Madame de Talmont to Clémence, as they returned home; "the son of Victoire should not lie ill another day in a public hospital. Thy father loved her well, Clémence."

Perhaps there was a shade on the brow of the widow as she said this; but it was a tender shade—a long-past sorrow touched and softened into the calm of resignation.

When they reached the house of Madame de Salgues, they went at once to the parlour, where that lady always sat; for, kindly and tolerant though she was, she would not readily have forgiven them if a surprising piece of news had been kept from her a moment longer than was necessary. They found her, however, already engaged in hearing quite as much as was good for her, perhaps rather more.

A lad, dressed in the uniform of the Ecole Polytechnique, seemed to have brought a breath of modern air into the quaint parlour, furnished as "petits appartements" used to be in the days of Louis Quinze. Emile de Salgues was seated before a table laden with every good thing in the shape of food that the house contained. When the ladies entered he was dividing his attention between two occupations equally fascinating. He was exploring the depths of a Périgord pie, and driving his grandmother almost to distraction by a graphic account of the exploits and perils of the Polytechnic scholars during the defence of Paris.

Madame de Salgues was really slight and small, but enshrined in her own particular fauteuil, and arrayed with elaborate care in her antique brocades and laces, she looked dignified and even stately, while her manners exactly suited her surroundings, and seemed to lend them an added grace.

" Be seated, my dear Rose, and you too, Clémence," she said to her nieces as they entered. " You will both wish to hear what Emile has just been telling me."

Emile's narrative did not flow quite so easily in the presence of his cousins. He sometimes had a shrewd suspicion that Madame de Talmont criticised and Clémence laughed at him; though this was hardly correct, because Clémence in those days had little heart to laugh. However, he resumed, after due exchange of greetings :—

" I was just telling my grandmother how we manned the guns at the Barrière du Trône, and sent a point-blank discharge into the midst of Count Pahlen's hussars. Then they charged us in flank ; and, outnumbered though we were, I think I may say we gave them enough to do. It was a glorious fight ! But as for myself, I thought my last hour was come. I was knocked down in the *mêlée*, and flung into a ditch. A gigantic Cossack levelled his spear at my breast, and would have run me through with it ; but another Russian turned it aside, and I heard him say, ' Pas tuez le jeune Français.' " *

" May God's blessing rest upon that Russian, whoever he was !" sighed Madame de Salgues.

" How is the Queen of Cities bearing her reverse of fortune?" asked Madame de Talmont, after suitable comments upon Emile's perils and his gallantry.

" In no queenly fashion," returned Emile, with an air of

* A fact.

mortification, which, however, did not appear to spoil his enjoyment of his grandmother's delicate preserves. "The truth is, I am ashamed of Paris. I am heartily glad *I* was born in the provinces. The Parisians have no faith, no constancy, no loyalty. Would you believe it?—nay, I suppose you have heard it already, for ill news travels fast—they have dragged down the Emperor's statue from the top of the column in the Place Vendôme; they have loaded it with the vilest of insults, covered it with a sheet, put a rope round its neck—I know not what besides."

"Perhaps the conquerors desired its removal," suggested Madame de Talmont.

"Quite the reverse. The whole column would have shared the fate of the statue, but for a placard announcing that the Allies had taken it under their protection. The conduct of the mob has been unutterably base; and no whit better are the fine gentlemen of Paris, while the fine ladies are infinitely worse."

"Take care what you say, my dear grandson," spoke Madame de Salgues' correct, quiet voice. "I could wish to see you more chivalrous."

"Chivalry would be wasted upon ladies who demean themselves so far as to beg the gentlemen of the Emperor of Russia's suite to take them up on their horses, only that they may catch a glimpse of him!"

Here Clémence interposed. "The ladies of Paris may not be very dignified," she said, "but at least they have not, like the mob, incurred the reproach of inconstancy. Perhaps we women are not always wise in our choice of an idol, or self-respecting in the incense we burn before it; but at least we seldom choose as the object of our idolatry a man capable of leaving those who fought and bled for him to perish unpitied in the snow, while he warmed himself at his fire in the Tuileries, saying, in the satisfaction of his heart, 'This is better than Moscow.'"

Such an outburst from Clémence was rare indeed. It would not have been possible, had not the newly-found balm of hope taken the sting out of the old wound, and brought the Moscow retreat within the category of things that could be spoken about.

"These are not the grounds upon which ladies form their estimates of character," Emile returned, a little superciliously. "Oh no! When Napoleon wished to see a lady, he simply ordered her to come to him. This Russian autocrat, in the like case, sends his aide-de-camp to inquire whether madame proposes remaining at home this afternoon, as, if so, he hopes to have the pleasure of waiting upon her. After *that*, what fair lady could suspend her judgment for a moment? Trust the dear creatures, one and all, to prefer the finely-polished pebble to the diamond in the rough."

"Does the polish *prove* the pebble, or the roughness the diamond?" asked Clémence demurely.

"The polish, at all events, takes with the multitude," resumed the indignant Emile. "High and low alike have gone out of their senses about this Alexander. The canaille of St. Antoine are as bad as the habitués of St. Germain. Every word he utters flies from lip to lip, as if it were inspired. 'Ah, sire, why did you not come to us before?' ask the deputies of the municipality. 'It was the valour of your armies that detained me,' says Alexander; and all Paris is delighted. I am bound to own he has kind words for all, and kind deeds as well—so far."

"There is but one question of absorbing interest for us, and for France," said Madame de Talmont. "Does he—do the Allies intend to use their influence for the restoration of our rightful king?"

"That I scarcely know," said Emile. "I do know, however, that the streets are full of white cockades; every hour one sees more of them. And I hear that the Emperor of Russia and the King of Prussia have been deep in consultation with that old schemer Talleyrand, who, of course, is turning his coat again. So, my dear grandmother, and you too, my cousins, I think you may indulge a hope that the reign of the antediluvians is about to recommence, and that Moses and Abraham and all the rest of them may be shortly expected in Paris."

Evidently Scripture history was not taught carefully at the Ecole Polytechnique; still there was a strain of reason in the boy's random talk. It was as true of the men before the Revolution as of those before the Flood, that "they ate, they drank, they planted, they builded," heedless of the rising tide of divine and human wrath, until the torrent overflowed its bounds and swept them all away. Would their successors do the same?

"As for me, *I* am not one of your slight, inconstant time-servers, ever ready to swim with the current and to turn towards the rising sun," Emile pursued, with a tragic air and a sublime confusion of metaphors. "I can tell you, very little more would make me go to Fontainebleau and lay my sword and my life at the feet of the Emperor, the great Napoleon, never more truly great than now, in the hour of his overthrow!"

"My *dear* boy!" Madame de Salgues interposed, in a voice of agony.

"Let us suppose you do it," said Clémence very quietly. "Even such assistance would scarcely, at this stage, restore his fallen fortunes; while you, on your part, would lose that mathematical prize for which you have been trying so hard."

Emile looked angry, and the heart of Clémence smote her. She thought of the glow of enthusiasm with which the young Russian said "*My Czar!*" and, after all, Emile's hero-worship too was sincere in its way.

"I think," she resumed, "you have already discharged your debt of honour to Napoleon. If all who swore allegiance to him fought as you seem to have done at the Barrière du Trône, the Allies would not be in Paris now."

The concession soothed his wounded vanity, and he started a fresh subject.

"You have no idea what the city looks like," he said. "To walk down the Rue St. Honoré or along the Champs-Elysées is as good an amusement as going to the play. All sorts of strange beings, out of all nations under heaven, are riding about. Cossacks in sheep-skin jackets, with sandy-coloured, shaggy hair and beards, long lances, and queer little whips with plaited thongs hanging on their necks; Calmuck Tartars, with flat noses and little eyes; Bashkirs and Tungusians from Siberia, carrying bows and arrows. Strangest of all and best worth seeing are the Circassian nobles, in complete hauberks of steel and bright conical helmets. Then there are countless uniforms of a kind to which we are better accustomed, and some of them very splendid,—jewelled orders glittering on the breasts of the officers. All the Allies wear sprigs of box or elm in their caps to distinguish them.—Clémence, you should come into Paris and see the show. You really must do it. I will take care of you," he added magnanimously, and not perhaps averse to the prestige it would give him amongst his school-fellows to be seen escorting his beautiful cousin.

"My dear, you must not dream of such a thing!" cried Madame de Salgues in great alarm. "A young lady to venture into the midst of a city occupied by a hostile army! Who ever heard of such a piece of insanity?"

"Grandmamma, the city is as quiet as if the allied sovereigns had only come to pay us a visit of ceremony," said Emile. "The shops are driving a splendid trade; only I am afraid our clever Parisians contrive to cheat the strangers outrageously. The Rentes have risen already since the Occupation from forty-five to seventy." (Madame de Talmont and Clémence exchanged glances of satisfaction.) "You could run no risk in Paris, Clémence, unless it should come into your head to say a word against the Emperor of Russia; and of that there is no

danger, because ladies always take care to be in the fashion.
Dame Fashion herself has become a Russian just now. We
have bonbons à la Cosaque, bonnets à la Rostopchine, dinner
services adorned with pictures of the entry of the Allies, and I
know not what follies besides. But it is the most wonderful
triumph of Alexander that he is actually bringing into fashion
the very thing most scorned and laughed at in the Paris of our
days. Can you guess what I mean?"

"Good manners and decorum," said Madame de Salgues.

"*Religion*," said Madame de Talmont.

"You are right, ma cousine," answered Emile. "Alexander
ascribes all his victories, not to his own skill or prowess, nor to
that of his army, but to Providence. Strange to say, his
followers do the same. Veteran officers scarred with wounds
and decorated with orders, and brilliant young guardsmen
evidently of the first fashion, hold the same language. They
tell you, apparently with the most naïve simplicity, that God,
not themselves, has done it all.* Our Parisians, who for years
have scarcely uttered the name of God except to scoff at it,
find this piety delightful—for a change. But the clear-sighted
understand that this sort of language is dictated, if not by
policy, at least by a refined and delicate courtesy. They are
gentlemen, these Russians, and they adopt this tone to avoid
wounding our sensitive pride."

"Do you then find it so much easier to believe in chivalrous
courtesy towards man than in piety towards God?" asked
Clémence.

Emile did not answer; and, after a pause, Madame de Talmont observed,—

"But you said there were generous deeds as well as gracious
words. Those, after all, are the most reliable; and at least it is
pleasant to hear of them."

"Then I have one to tell of, certainly upon a scale of im-

* Englishmen who were in Paris during 1814 bear testimony to this interesting fact.

perial magnificence. Alexander has just restored to freedom—without ransom and without conditions—all the Frenchmen who are prisoners in Russia. It is said they number one hundred and fifty thousand. They are to return immediately to France.—How?—what is it, my cousins?—what has happened?" It was no wonder he asked, for at his words Madame de Talmont had fainted.

CHAPTER XXVIII.

"To that new land which is the old."

IVAN recovered slowly from his severe and painful wound. He had just risen from his bed one day, and was sitting, pale and languid, near the table trying to read, when he heard some one inquiring for him. He had received frequent visits from his comrades in the Guards, and from other friends in the army; but now he turned gladly to welcome one whom he had not seen since the night of the assault.

"Michael Ivanovitch!" he exclaimed; "I am delighted to see you."

Michael returned his greeting with respectful and affectionate warmth, and they sat down to talk over all that had happened. The change in Ivan's appearance shocked and grieved his old playfellow.

"You look so pale and worn, Barrinka," he said. "Have they been good to you here?"

"Most kind and good," said Ivan. "I have had the best of care and nursing. But oh, Michael, I have been longing to tell you the luck the bandage brought me which you placed on my wound. It was wonderful!" And he told the story of his acquaintance with the De Talmonts. "Nothing can exceed their kindness to me," he said. "They insist upon my becoming their guest—or rather, I suppose I should say, the guest

of the aged relative with whom they live. They are good
enough to tell me she is eager to make my acquaintance. So I
go to them to-morrow ; indeed, it was with difficulty I contrived
to put it off so long, but I could not bear to burden them with
a helpless invalid."

" Ah, Barrinka, you make friends everywhere !"

" These friends were made for me, first by you, then by the
Czar, who has put all loyal Frenchmen under infinite obligations. But tell me, Michael, what do you think of Paris? I
have not been there yet, you know."

" Well, Barrinka," said Michael meditatively, and with the
air of an old traveller, " I do not think much of it after all. I
would not compare it for a moment with St. Petersburg, not
to speak of holy Moscow. I never saw holy Moscow until just
before the fire,—and that was like seeing a lovely face with the
hand of death upon it,—but this city of the Frenchmen is nothing
to it—nothing ! To what it *was*, I mean," he added with a sigh.
" Where do you see anything like the great beautiful houses,
painted red and green and purple and yellow ; like the roofs
of burnished lead, all shining as if they were on fire ; like the
gilded domes and crosses on the tops of our churches? Napoleon himself had the wit to admire them, and to know he
had nothing half so good in his own country, so he got the
dome of the Hôtel des Invalides gilt to look like one of ours,—
a Frenchman told me that himself.—Curse those Invalids !"
said Michael, with a sudden change of manner and a look of
gloom and ill-humour.

" And why so? What harm have the poor old fellows done
to you?" asked Ivan, half laughing.

" Great harm, Barrinka. Think of their having got hold of
our own Maria Ivanovka and taken her for themselves !"

" Your—*who* ?"

" Our Maria Ivanovka, who was with us from the day we
left St. Petersburg until we entered this same city of Paris—

which is no great things of a city, as *I* shall always say. Poor dear Maria Ivanovka! She may have been rather old,—I don't deny it,—and she *had* a droop in her upper lip, which they say is a bad sign, besides being frayed about the mouth in a sort of general way. But the Invalids will never love her and take care of her as we used to do."

A momentary stupefaction had fallen upon Ivan; he wondered hazily whether Michael was speaking of a hospital nurse or of a favourite sutler. But he prudently held his peace, and Michael went on : " Before the war she used to take care of the Winter Palace,—there are some that say she stood in front of it for fifty years, but that I can't believe. However, not a fight have we had since we left St. Petersburg that she has not borne a part in and done her business *well*, though it is I who say it. At Leipzig her carriage was broken; but we mended it with a cart wheel, which answered famously."

Ivan understood now. " You don't mean to say," he exclaimed, laughing heartily, " that the Invalids have got your gun ! How came that about ?"

" It is no laughing matter, Barrinka. They *have* got her ; and it was the Czar's own doing. He went to see the poor old Frenchmen, and found them sorely cast down and sorrowful, breaking their hearts over their country's disgrace and their Emperor's defeat."

" That was natural," Ivan interrupted. " Think what you and I would have felt, Michael, had this war gone against us. And if we were old and worn out, unable to strike a blow for our country and our Czar, we would have felt it all the more."

" The Czar seems to have thought like you, Barrinka ; for he spoke kindly to the poor old fellows, and tried to cheer them. And when he found they were grieving over the loss of their guns, the trophies of their old victories that they used to be so proud of, he told them to be comforted ; they should have their trophies back again. The Allies had carried off those guns of theirs when they came into the city, so what must he do but send them twelve of ours, Maria Ivanovka being one of them—to my sorrow."

For a moment Ivan wondered silently, "Was there ever such a knight in friendship or in war" as his Czar, Alexander Paulovitch? Then he said: "I think you need not grudge your gun to the poor old Frenchmen. Do you know how many of their cannon they left behind in our country, for *us* to show as trophies of what our arms—no, rather of what our God has done?"

"No, Barrinka, I have never heard exactly; but I am sure they must be many."

"Not counting those they contrived to bury, or lost in the rivers they passed over, we have captured of their cannon—nine hundred and twenty and nine!"

"Great St. Nicholas!" cried Michael, lifting up his one hand in amazement.

"Shall we not show our gratitude for this marvellous deliverance by gentleness and kindness to our enemies, whom God cares for, even as he does for us? That is what the Czar thinks. He has refused to break down the bridge of Austerlitz, —a standing monument of the old triumph of the French over *us*,—or even to change its name. 'It is enough,' said he, 'that I have passed over it with my armies.'"

"Can that be possible, Barrinka? Then no wonder every one is saying now that the Czar is taking the part of Napoleon and of his family."

"And if he is? What is a brave man's duty when a foe has fallen? Should he not think, 'How would *I* wish to be dealt with if the case were mine?' My friend Tolstoi tells me that as the Czar was entering Paris in triumph, he looked up and saw the statue of his great enemy on the top of the column in the Place Vendôme. 'If *I* had been placed so high,' said he,

' my head would have been turned.'   Surely he was not thinking of the lifeless statue on its pinnacle of stone, but of the
living man on the proud summit of this world's dominion and
glory."

"Barrinka, the Czar *is* there now, and his head is not
turned."

"Thank God ; for it is his grace that keeps him safe.
Michael, my friend, do you remember the oath we swore that
morning in the camp at Tarovtino, with the explosion still
sounding in our ears that laid half the Kremlin in ruins?"

Michael's eyes kindled and his dark cheek glowed. "How
could I forget it, Barrinka?" he said. "Did we not swear to
take such vengeance on Napoleon and the French as the world
has never heard of yet? Woe is me! we have had the chance
and lost it."

"Not lost it—used it nobly. Do you not see, Michael, that
the Czar has indeed taken such vengeance as the world never
heard of before? To comfort and help our enemies, to give
back good for evil, is not indeed the world's way, but it is the
way of Christ; and perhaps in the end even the world may
come to see it is the best."

The day after this conversation took place Ivan became the
guest of Madame de Salgues. It was a happy change for him.
Now, for the first time in his life, he was thrown into the society
of good, refined, and noble-hearted women. He enjoyed its
pleasures with keen appreciation ; though, as it happened, the
beginning of his acquaintance with Madame de Salgues was
not particularly promising. When the ceremony of presenta-
tion was over, the old lady began to compliment him upon the
magnanimity of his sovereign in restoring to France her rightful monarch.

"Madame," answered Ivan, who was anxious in his turn to
say something agreeable, "the Czar has only been desirous of
consulting the wishes of the French people. He and his Allies

would have given their approbation to any settled government the nation had been pleased to appoint, excepting that of Napoleon or a member of his family. But Louis Dix-huit appears to be the choice of France."

Madame de Salgues stirred uneasily in her chair. "My dear young friend," she exclaimed in a slightly irritable tone, "do you not see that is as much as to say that if a man takes a purse of gold from the hands of a robber, he is at liberty to give it to whom he pleases? Not so;—he must restore it to its owner, else he himself is a robber also."

Ivan had a dim perception of the fact that France did not belong to the Bourbons in at all the same sense that a purse of gold belongs to its owner, but it was scarcely clear enough to express in words; and had it been otherwise, courtesy would have admonished him to decline an argument with his hostess. So he dexterously changed the subject; and Madame de Salgues afterwards observed to her niece, "That young man is certainly very well bred, and a perfect gentleman. But I fear his principles are rather unsettled. I hope he will not influence Emile."

Madame de Talmont could not suppress a quiet smile at the idea of the scapegrace Emile suffering contamination from Ivan. As days passed on, the young Russian proved a very pleasant addition to the little household, and brightly and swiftly the period of his convalescence glided by. When the weather improved, he often sat in a summer-house in Madame de Salgues' little garden; and here the ladies would bring their embroidery and bear him company, or comrades from the city would come to visit him.

He had one visit from Michael, who was fêted and made much of by the De Talmonts for Henri's sake. He said afterwards to Ivan, "Who would have thought French people could be so good and gentle? May the Virgin bless the young lady's sweet face! If she would just get one of our priests to baptize her into the true orthodox faith, I should like well enough to see *you* lead her up the church, a little farther than the font, Barrinka. I think she is almost good enough."

"Hold thy peace, Michael!" cried Ivan, half pleased, half angry, and blushing deeply. "How little you understand! *I* am not good enough to kiss her feet, or to take up the glove she has dropped and give it back to her."

At an early stage of their acquaintance Ivan discovered Clémence's little store of theological books, and asked leave to study them. It was now nearly a year and a half since he had begun to read his Bible with attention and interest; but books about religion were still quite new to him. He began their study eagerly, hoping to find a solution for some difficulties which had occurred to him; but, instead of this, fresh perplexities were awakened in his mind. He found that he had plunged into a labyrinth of words and ideas absolutely strange to him. It is true that the shallow scepticism of his youth had long since given place to the only real belief he ever knew. The flames of Moscow, the study of the New Testament, the living faith of the man whom he supremely admired and venerated, had been God's way of leading him into a simple, child-like dependence upon Himself, and a genuine desire to serve and follow Him. But of the deeper mysteries of spiritual experience he was still almost wholly ignorant.

One afternoon Madame de Salgues was slumbering in her easy-chair, and Madame de Talmont had been called away; so he found himself practically alone with Clémence. The opportunity was too precious to be lost. He took from his pocket a little book, " Les Pensées de Pascal," which he had been studying with deep and rather mystified attention. Showing her a passage her own hand had marked carefully, line by line, he asked,—

"Mademoiselle, what does that mean? I confess I cannot understand it."

She read—"'I see my abyss of pride, of curiosity, of sin. There is no connection between me and God, or the holy Jesus Christ. But he has been made sin for me; by his wounds we are healed. He has healed himself, and therefore assuredly he will heal me. I must place my wounds upon his, must give myself to him, and he will save me with himself.'"

Clémence paused a while. "I think it means," she said at last very reverently, "that the Lord Jesus Christ has taken our sins upon him, and put himself in our place. We should be quite overwhelmed when we come to see the 'abyss' of sin that is within us, if we did not know he had done so. But he has taken our sin and bound it about him like a robe, that we may take his righteousness and stand before the Father robed in that." This, however, was a height beyond the range of her own ordinary spiritual experience. So she added presently, with an involuntary sigh, "*If* only we are numbered amongst his redeemed."

"It is very wonderful," answered Ivan thoughtfully. "Of course I always knew the blessed Lord died for our sins," he added, crossing himself; "but I never felt that there was any 'abyss' of sin within me. Do you think, mademoiselle, that one must feel that in order to be really religious?"

"I think we cannot know the grace of Christ without knowing our own sin," Clémence answered. "But, monsieur, look at these words also; I think you will find them easier to understand." She turned to another page of the book, and read— "'Console thyself; thou wouldst not be seeking Me, if I had not already found thee.'"

Ivan pondered. "*Found thee?*" he repeated. "As the shepherd in the gospel found the lost sheep? But perhaps the sheep never knew how far he had wandered; certainly he never was able to tell. That is a comfort. I like, too, to think of one of the proverbs of my country : ' The babe does not know God, yet God loves it.' But I fear I am deplorably ignorant, and in every way very far from what I ought to be."

It was not often that the talk of these young people glided into channels so profound.   The bright and varying experiences that lay near the surface of their lives furnished far more frequently the daily bread of their intercourse.

When Ivan grew stronger, his friends urged him to go and see the wonders of Paris, which the elder ladies vaunted to him, exerting all their powers of description to depict them in glowing colours.   They had of course already done the honours of Versailles, with its splendid palace dedicated " to all the glories of France."   Ivan was far too polite to tell them, as Michael would have done, that he was sure Paris could not equal Moscow before the conflagration ; but he seemed less anxious to see Paris than to bring his friends to see the Czar.   At last an expedition was arranged for an early day in May.   A carriage was engaged, in which Madame de Talmont, Clémence, and Ivan were to drive together to the city, where Emile was to meet them, and a long day of sight-seeing was to follow.

Ivan, all this time, was like one who floats dreamily on the calm expanse of a tropic sea.   Now and then a bright land-bird skims by, or a blossom borne from afar sleeps on the surface of the still, clear water.   He is drawing near the shore of a new, undiscovered country ; but as yet he has not seen, has not dreamed of it.   His "eyes are holden," until he feels the coral grate beneath his keel ; then suddenly he looks up—and behold, in one glorious moment all is changed !   Palm trees wave above him, green grasses kiss the water's edge, gorgeous plants trail their luxuriant wealth of flowers, and for him there is a new world created.

CHAPTER XXIX.

"Charity suffereth long, and is kind; charity envieth not; charity vaunteth not itself, is not puffed up, doth not behave itself unseemly, seeketh not her own, is not easily provoked."

THE day fixed upon for the expedition to Paris was bright and sunny, with that delicious and undefinable quality of exhilaration in the air which is nature's promise of summer hours to come. Such days often make sorrowing hearts yet more sorrowful, because the chords of hope and memory are intertwined, and no touch is light enough to stir the one without at the same time awakening the other. But the young and happy—those who are looking before them, not behind—find in the vague gladness of the world without the answer and the echo to voices equally glad and vague in the world within them. Earth, air, and sky alike seem to whisper, "Something good is coming. *We* know what it is, but we may not tell it yet."

Truly something good was coming to two young hearts that day; nay, it had come already, only they themselves were not quite conscious of it. The sharp eyes of the Polytechnic scholar discerned some things which were perhaps not equally clear to those more immediately concerned. Emile felt very angry with Ivan for what he chose to consider his presumption, and he vowed inwardly that, if he could, he would spoil his plans. It seemed a kind of propitiatory sacrifice to his fallen idol Napoleon to disappoint and humiliate one of his conquerors—"ce coquin russe," as he called him in his heart. But he allowed nothing of this to appear during the day; he was assiduous in performing his duty of cicerone to the party, and anxious that Ivan should miss no sight calculated to give him an exalted idea of the glories and resources of France—least of all the Louvre, then rich with the spoils of a vanquished continent.

He only permitted himself a slight touch of malice when Ivan met one of his friends, and was told by him that they could not see the Czar that day, as he had gone out to Malmaison. The evident disappointment of Clémence piqued him almost as much as it flattered Ivan.

"Never mind, ma cousine," he said. "We will show you the camp of the Cossacks in the Champs-Elysées—*that* is something really worth seeing. It is true they are perfect savages, ugly, uncouth, and unclean; but they are sufficiently amusing for all that."

Early in the day Ivan had observed the words, "Ici on dine à la Russe," on the window of a fashionable restaurant in the Rue St. Honoré. He took Emile privately into counsel, saying, "I should like to give our friends a genuine Russian dinner;" and the lad, notwithstanding his private feelings, was glad to assist in a plan that promised a little amusement to himself. Accordingly, when the day was nearing its close, and the eyes and limbs of the little party were thoroughly tired, no one was very sorry to hear Emile say to Ivan,—

"This is the place where you wished me to order dinner, Monsieur Posharky. I have carried out all your directions to the best of my ability."

But ere they could enter the glittering doors of the restaurant, their attention was attracted by a little scene which was passing on the crowded footpath of the fashionable street. A gentleman whom Emile would have called old, Ivan middle-aged, and Madame de Talmont in the prime of life, was bending in evident perplexity over a little girl, who was crying and stamping her small foot in a vehement passion.

"Ma petite, ma chère fillette," he was expostulating, "be wise, I pray thee. Bethink thyself; all the world is gazing at us. Come, come, my child, dry thine eyes. I will buy thee a far handsomer brooch at the first jeweller's shop I can find."

"But it will not have in it the hair of dear mamma," sobbed the child, a slight, black-eyed little girl of eleven or twelve.

Meanwhile Madame de Talmont recognized in the gentleman an old friend, a political exile, who had doubtless accompanied the stream of returning *émigrés* back to Paris.

"Can it be that I have the happiness of seeing once again my dear old friend Monsieur de Sartines?" she interposed, making a most welcome diversion; "and this—is this young lady the little Stéphanie we used to know, whom I have so often held in my arms? Monsieur de Sartines, here is my daughter Clémence," she added. "She too will have grown almost beyond your remembrance."

But Clémence was already making friends with the disconsolate Stéphanie, listening to the story of the lost brooch, and comforting her with a tact and gentleness which Ivan was watching with admiring and delighted eyes.

Madame de Talmont soon remembered him, and presented to M. de Sartines "Our young friend Monsieur Pojarsky, a Russian, an officer in his Imperial Majesty's Chevalier Guard."

After the usual compliments, Ivan presented a request, framed as gracefully as a Parisian could have done it, that monsieur and mademoiselle would do him the honour to join them at dinner. The proposal was found agreeable, and the whole party adjourned to a handsome dining-hall, where a table exquisitely adorned with baskets of rare fruit and vases of flowers fully satisfied Ivan's expectations. Nor did the repast that followed disappoint the young Russian, jealous in the lightest matters for the credit of his country. The enterprising Parisian restaurateur, having secured the services of a celebrated French *chef de cuisine* whom the war had deprived of his lucrative situation in the establishment of a Russian millionnaire, was able to set before his numerous Russian guests just such a banquet as would have awaited them at the table of a Tolstoi, a Narischkin, a Dolgorouki.

The dinner went merrily forward. The names of the dishes were strange, but their quality was unexceptionable. Amongst other specialties, a delicate fish soup gained the approbation of the party, although Ivan lamented that it could only be made in perfection of the sterlet, not to be found anywhere except in the waters of the Oka, the river near which he had spent his childhood. Emile devoted himself assiduously to certain delicious chicken cutlets called " Côtelettes à la Pojarsky " in honour of Ivan's heroic ancestor; although, when he heard the name, he somewhat ungallantly sought to dissuade Clémence from partaking of them. Rare wines, flavoured with peaches, apricots, and prunes, accompanied the little banquet; and the fruits, ices, and confectionery were voted perfectly "ravishing" by Emile and Stéphanie, nor did any one dispute their verdict.

It would have been well if Ivan's guests had been equally harmonious upon other subjects. But it was impossible, in a crisis like the present, not to talk of public events, and just as impossible to talk of them without differences of opinion. The party consisted of three ardent Legitimists, a Buonapartist, a Russian devoted to his Czar, and a clever, observant child, whose sole political creed as yet was that everything done in the world ought to contribute to the amusement and gratification of Stéphanie de Sartines.

Ivan's ideas of politeness, perhaps a little overstrained, led him to say everything he could think of in praise of Paris; and M. de Sartines replied by a tribute to the magnanimity of the conqueror, who spared the splendid city when it lay at his mercy. "Your Emperor," he said, "has shown himself generous to his fallen enemies."

"Monsieur," replied Ivan, "my Czar has no fallen enemies. With him the unfortunate ceases at once to be the enemy." *

"It has been a great disappointment to us," said Madame de Talmont, "that we failed to see him to-day."

Emile had one of his small sharp darts in readiness for his Royalist cousins. "It is not so easy to see the Emperor Alexander since the return of Louis Dix-huit," he said. "It is no secret that the Bourbon is jealous of the Czar. In order not to interfere with his most Christian Majesty's 'divine right' to be the admired of all admirers in his own capital, Alexander appears to efface himself. He even takes his daily walk at four in the morning, before the 'beau monde' is astir and ready to gaze at him."

"Papa," asked Stéphanie, "what is divine right?"

"Inhuman wrong," said Emile under his breath.

"Try this iced pine-apple, mademoiselle," interposed Ivan, afraid of an argument. "It goes very well with these almond biscuits."

"This is the third or fourth time, I believe, that the Emperor has gone to Malmaison," said M. de Sartines a little stiffly. "He is certainly very attentive to the ex-Empress Joséphine."

"Her health is failing," Ivan answered, "and no doubt her heart is broken. In my boyhood I believed, with almost every one about me, that Napoleon owed his successes to her. We thought she possessed magical powers, and used to transform herself into a white dove, that she might hear and impart to him the counsels of his enemies. How amazed I would have been had any one told me that Napoleon would abandon her; and that the Czar, finding her forlorn and sorrowful, would, out of chivalrous pity, plead for and comfort her!"

* "Ses ennemis cessaient de l'être à ses yeux, dès qu'ils étaient malheureux."— MADAME DE CHOISEUL-GOUFFIER.

"Of all the bad actions of Napoleon's bad life," said M. de Sartines with emphasis, "I believe his treatment of that woman is the worst."

"Perhaps so, monsieur," said Ivan. "Still *I* can scarcely think it, because I have never seen the ex-Empress, while I *have* seen the miserable remains of the gallant army which he abandoned so cruelly in the frozen plains of Lithuania."

The next moment he was sorry for his words, for he caught the angry glare in the eyes of Emile. Either he had not heard or he had forgotten that the lad was an ardent admirer of Buonaparte.

"The Emperor is fallen," said Emile, "therefore, of course, every one finds a stone to fling at him. He was not faultless, —I grant it. You cannot expect real greatness to bind itself down to the rules of a timid conventional morality. But at least he was entirely free from petty vanities and small affectations. You would never find *him* laying himself out to gain the cheap praise of a magnanimous conqueror from the lips of the vulgar."

"*Never*, indeed," assented Madame de Talmont.

"True, undoubtedly," said M. de Sartines.

No one noticed Stéphanie's aside : "I see; *very* clever people need not care about being good. I shall tell my governess that."

But every one looked at Ivan. For a moment he grew perfectly white with anger ; then his face resumed its natural colour, and a smile played about his lips. He said nothing, however, and Emile went on : "Consequently he never overshot the mark and made himself ridiculous, as I must say the Emperor Alexander did the other day, when he actually admitted to his own table, and spent hours in conversation with—whom do you think, ladies ?"

As neither Madame de Talmont nor Clémence replied, Stéphanie felt herself called upon. "Perhaps the Director of the

Ecole Polytechnique, or—could it possibly have been one of the boys?—*students*, I beg your pardon," said she with a saucy glance at Emile.

"My dear child," said her father in a grieved and reproving aside, "do not, I pray thee, try to act *l'enfant terrible.*"

Emile did not condescend to notice her. "No one greater," he resumed, "than the Abbé Sicard."

"Who is he?" asked M. de Sartines.

Madame de Talmont and Clémence knew very well, and looked interested.

"An old fool of a priest who spends his life picking up deaf and dumb children out of the streets, and teaching them to read and to say their prayers," replied Emile.

"How can they say their prayers if they are dumb?" queried Stéphanie.

"They speak with their fingers, dear," Clémence explained in a lower tone. "I will tell you all about it another time. I have seen a poor boy examined who was taught by the Abbé Sicard. It was wonderful and beautiful. He knew far more than many a child who could hear, and he *felt* what he knew."

"His Imperial Majesty," Emile was saying meanwhile, "who has all the affairs of the world on his shoulders, and can scarcely find time to be commonly courteous to the fair ladies who adore him, found time enough to hear all the 'methods,' as they call them, of this fanatical priest; and has given him the Order of St. Ladislaus, or St. Laocoon, or something."

"The Order of St. Wladamir, you mean," said Ivan very quietly. "When the Czar returns home, he will probably establish a school for the deaf and dumb in St. Petersburg, like that of the Abbé Sicard here.* I thank you for telling us all this, M. Emile. Do you take liqueur? I can recommend this curaçoa."

"Curse his effrontery!" thought Emile. "Will nothing

* He established *two*; one in St. Petersburg, and the other in Warsaw.

disconcert him?   I will take another way with him, however."

After the party rose from table, the De Talmonts had a short walk to the place where the carriage was to meet them; and their friends accompanied them.   M. de Sartines gave his arm to Madame de Talmont, and Stéphanie clung to Clémence, so that Emile and Ivan were obliged to bring up the rear together, not greatly to the satisfaction of the latter.   To the former, however, it was a precious and longed-for opportunity.

"M. de Sartines is a very well-bred sort of man," he explained to Ivan,—"though I, of course, am not fond of Legitimists and believers in 'divine right.'   It may be four or five years now since he gave offence, in some way or other, to Savary, the late superintendent of police, and was requested to quit the Empire.   He has just come back in the train of Louis Dix-huit, with a great many more who are less wanted.—Peste! the whole city is full of these white cockades; one would think there was snow in May time.—I suppose that by this time *you* know all the family affairs, M. Posharky, and they have told you that long ago, before he left Paris, M. de Sartines was betrothed to my cousin Clémence."

Ivan's sudden, irrepressible start, and the deadly paleness that overspread his face, gave the keenest gratification to Emile. " But he is so old, he might be her father," he said at last.

"That does not matter in the least," returned the spiteful Emile. "He is an excellent *parti*—has a good property, settled principles, and all that.   Do you not see how devoted Clémence is to that amiable and precocious young lady, Mademoiselle Stéphanie?   She will make an admirable step-mother; though I cannot say I envy her the charge."

"But, at the time you say it was arranged, Mademoiselle Clémence must have been only a child."

Emile looked at him keenly.   "I fear your wound is sometimes painful, even yet," he said.

"Yes, it hurts occasionally.—Is it then your custom here to betroth children?"

"It is the custom for parents to arrange all these little matters as they think best, and sometimes they arrange them very early. Madame de Talmont, though she looks so gentle, is a woman of most decided will, quite capable of settling the destinies of all belonging to her. Ah, here is the carriage! I am glad I have made your acquaintance, M. Posharky, and I thank you for a very pleasant day."

Ivan could not certainly return the compliment. The homeward drive was rather silent; only a few remarks passed between Madame de Talmont and her daughter. Ivan looked, and was, exceedingly tired. Madame de Talmont observed this, and kindly, even tenderly, expressed a hope that the fatigues of the day had not been too much for him; nor did the eyes of Clémence fail to express her concern, though her lips were silent.

But all the time his resolve was taking shape and strengthening. Emile's tidings, while they touched him to the quick, had also revealed him to himself. His path lay straight before him now; he could do no less than

> "Put his fortune to the touch,
> And gain or lose it all."

But the gain was so inconceivably precious, the loss so unutterably terrible! A brave man may have the courage to risk his all; yet he knows the extent of the risk, and it is no disgrace to him if his heart trembles. That evening Ivan's heart trembled sorely; nay, it almost sank within him.

But a powerful ally was at hand. The door was opened for the returning party by a young soldier in undress uniform. There was a startled cry, an instant's hesitation, and in another moment Madame de Talmont was weeping in the arms of her son, and Clémence standing beside them with a radiant face.

Ivan silently sought his lonely chamber; "for," said he, "this joy is one in which a stranger may not intermeddle."

An hour later Henri bounded up the stairs, and knocked at his door. "Supper is ready," he said; "come, my friend, and join us." As they went down together he added, "It is one joy the more for me to find *you* here, M. Pojarsky."

While the happy family party sat together over the repast—almost as unable now to eat for joy as they had been for sorrow on the evening of Henri's departure—their talk strayed lightly over the surface of the eventful histories that had yet to be told and heard.

"I must congratulate you upon your recovery, M. de Talmont," said Ivan.—"If you had seen him in the hospital at Vilna, madame," he added, turning to Madame de Talmont, "you would rejoice and wonder at the change."

"Ah, that well-remembered visit of yours!" returned Henri. "In every way it was a happy one for me. Do you know it has saved me a tedious and fruitless journey to Brie, and a long delay in finding my mother and sister?"

"How could that be?"

"I arrived in Paris last night, very late. This morning I chanced to see a young Russian gentleman in a uniform like yours; so I accosted him, and asked for news of you."

"How did you know my name?"

Henri smiled. "Naturally I wished to know to whom I was indebted for so much kindness. So that day, after you left the hospital, I asked those about me, and easily found out who you were. Your comrade in the Chevalier Guard, whom I met this morning, informed me that you had been wounded, and were now at Versailles. Shall I tell you what he said besides?" he added with a comical air of hesitation. "Just this—'He is a fortunate lad, born under a lucky star, and always sure to fall upon his feet. At present he is the guest of a perfectly charming family of the old noblesse, named De Talmont.'"

"O Henri!" cried the half-blushing, half-laughing Clémence. "I fear your residence abroad has not advanced you in the grace of modesty."

"I shall punish you for that speech by deepening your blushes, sister mine," returned Henri, laughing merrily. "For my informant, M. Tolstoi, was good enough to add, 'There are two elder ladies of the most perfect grace and breeding; and a demoiselle with a face beautiful as the Madonna's, and no doubt a soul that answers to her face.' Of course after that I hastened to inform him that the young lady was my sister, and to beg for the address. So here I am."

"But why did you not write to us during all this long weary time?" asked his mother. "Why did you allow us to fear, nay, to believe the worst?"

"I *did* write, dearest mother, from Vilna, no less than four times; and you can imagine how I longed for one word in reply, and how my heart sank as days and weeks and months passed in silence. Of course I sent all my letters to Brie."

"Then the lazy, dishonest, incompetent postmaster of Brie ought to be ignominiously dismissed from his office, as no doubt he would have been under the old régime," said Madame de Salgues, breaking silence almost for the first time. That night she was taking, gladly and contentedly, the place of an interested spectator of the drama of life, in which her own part had been played long ago. If in the thankful little household there still was one anxious and desponding heart, it was that of Ivan—"the young heart hot and restless," not "the old subdued and slow."

CHAPTER XXX.

THE PURPLE BROCADE ONCE MORE.

> " He says, ' God bless him ! ' almost with a sob,
> As the great hero passes ; he is glad
> The world holds mighty men and mighty deeds."
>
> GEORGE ELIOT.

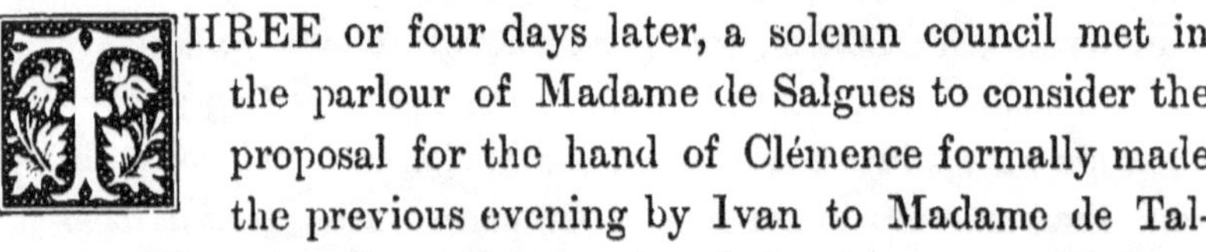

THREE or four days later, a solemn council met in the parlour of Madame de Salgues to consider the proposal for the hand of Clémence formally made the previous evening by Ivan to Madame de Talmont. The council consisted only of three persons—Madame de Salgues, Madame de Talmont, and Henri—the two most immediately concerned being, as a matter of course, excluded. The Czar was expected in Versailles that day; and Ivan, knowing that his only chance of a word from him was to be found in placing himself once more amongst his wounded comrades, had gone to the hospital. Clémence was in her own chamber, on her knees, her hot face pressed down upon the coverlet of her bed. Yet she was scarcely praying. The hopes, the fears, the wishes that stirred timidly in the depths of her heart were too vague to clothe themselves in words. Not even into the ear of her mother could she have found voice to breathe them ; especially since the rigid conventionalities amidst which she had been brought up forbade her to acknowledge that she had hopes or fears or wishes at all. But kneeling there, she felt herself in the presence of One who knew all, who understood each subtle turn and winding of the heart that did not half understand itself; and without too curiously examining her burden, she tried to lay it, just as it was, at his feet. "Our Father who art in heaven," she pleaded, "do what is right and best for me, and for—for *us all*. And thy will be done."

Meanwhile the voices in the room beneath her scarcely paused for an instant. They were calm, well-bred voices, which never interrupted each other, never grew too loud or hasty. But they were the voices of speakers very much in earnest, and with very definite views and opinions. It was with Madame de Talmont that the decision really rested; but she felt it right and fitting to consult the two others, though perhaps she only did it, as persons of a quiet but determined character are apt to do, with her own mind fully made up. "You are aware, my dear aunt," she said, "that the unhappy marriage of our poor Cousin Victoire has created in my mind a strong prejudice against Russians. But this feeling, though it may have its weight with me, ought not to be decisive."

Henri moved uneasily, and seemed about to speak, but restrained himself, and Madame de Salgues inquired, "Does this young man resemble his father?"

"In his figure, yes; and somewhat in his features also; but he is far more like his mother. Victoire was charming; and I am bound to acknowledge that everything I have observed in her son since he came here creates the most favourable impression."

"He certainly seems to be a perfect gentleman," Madame de Salgues admitted. "Un parfait honnête homme," was what she said.

"He is courteous, unselfish, generous," Madame de Talmont added. "His principles appear to be excellent; and although, of course, I greatly deplore the difference of religion, and should much prefer a Catholic, still I believe him to be really pious in his own way, and very scrupulous in observing the rites of his Church. Besides, as Clémence is herself so *dévote*, I have little doubt she will gain him in the end."

"All you say is most true," Henri assented warmly. "Dear mother, if it be your wish to give the hand of my sister to an honourable, noble-hearted, God-fearing man, I think you may search the world without finding a better than Ivan Ivanovitch Pojarsky."

"The young man may deserve all you say of him," Madame de Salgues interposed rather sharply; "but in the meantime I wish to know what are his prospects. What does he intend to live upon?"

"He is an officer—an ensign in the Chevalier Guard," remarked Madame de Talmont.

"We all know that, my dear Rose," returned the elder lady, with just a shade of contempt in her quiet, well-bred accents; "but we know equally well that his pay will scarcely keep him in white kid gloves, tobacco, and pocket-money."

"He does not use tobacco," Henri threw in by way of parenthesis.

"A place in such a corps may be a social distinction," Madame de Salgues continued, "but it is in no sense a provision. It gives prestige, but it absorbs money."

"I believe he has good expectations," Madame de Talmont hazarded.

"Good expectations!" the old lady scornfully repeated. "It would be more to the purpose if he had a good estate. But it appears his father was despoiled of everything, even to his clothes and his jewellery. While as for the young man himself, he has had half-a-dozen civil words from the Emperor of Russia. That is absolutely all. I fail to see how he can set up an establishment and do justice to a family upon *that.*"

"The Emperor, who is in full possession of all his history, would not have placed him in the Chevalier Guard if he had not intended to provide for him," Henri said. "Do you know, my dear mother," he asked rather abruptly, "that M. Pojarsky was in Moscow during the whole time of the Occupation?"

"I know he met you there; but how he came to be there himself I do not know."

"Just like him not to speak of it. I can tell you, however, it was a piece of splendid gallantry from first to last. I heard it talked of even at Vilna. M. Pojarsky, young as he then was, stayed in the doomed city, at the peril of his life, to aid in that terrible work of destruction, which will never be forgotten while the world lasts. He helped to give Murat the warm reception he got there; and he discovered some hundreds of Russian wounded who lay concealed in the cellars, and must have died of starvation but for the food with which he supplied them. I am sure my honoured aunt and my dear mother will both agree with me that these services have established a claim upon his sovereign which no monarch would be likely to disregard, least of all the Emperor Alexander."

The force of this statement was admitted by Madame de Salgues with half-reluctant candour, and by Madame de Talmont with genuine satisfaction. Here the discussion ended, though the conversation lasted some time longer. Finally it was arranged that Ivan's suit was to be favourably received, upon an understanding that the marriage must on no account take place until he had the prospect of an assured and permanent competency.

No one had even alluded to what we should have thought the most important element in the problem—the inclination of Clémence herself. But what is unnamed is not necessarily unconsidered. The heart of the mother beat in unison with the heart of the child, although no words had passed between them. There were tears in the eyes of Madame de Talmont, but a thankful look in her quiet face, when at last she rose and said, "Now I think I may go and speak with Clémence."

"Do so, dear mother," said Henri, rising to open the door for her. "But, I pray thee, do not detain her long. For I have set my heart upon inducing her to walk with me as far as the gate of the hospital, to see the Czar."

"And what need of that, pray?" asked Madame de Salgues. "I understand the Emperor of Russia is to pass through this street on his way to the Castle. We shall all see him from these windows. What more can any one desire?"

"Any one who had a sister as pretty as mine might very well desire to take a walk with her in the town, when all the world is making holiday," returned Henri, laughing.

"Well, that is not so unreasonable. Young people of course like a little pleasure; and the very best people—gens comme il faut—will all be on foot in the streets to-day. But I trust, M. Henri," the old lady added more gravely as the two were left alone together, "that you may never regret having thrown your influence into the scale of this Russian. Even supposing the young man to be the most desirable *parti* in the world, think of the banishment from civilized society, and the frightful climate of St. Petersburg! Clémence might have done better— much better. Not to speak of M. de Cranfort, a very excellent person, *bien rangé*, and with a sufficient property, who is a con- stant visitor here, and I believe not indifferent to your sister, there are others by no means to be despised."

"I suspect M. Ivan has heard something of a certain M. de Sartines which has disquieted him."

"What can he have heard of *him?*"

"I do not know exactly; but the idea seems to have been given that he aspires to the hand of Clémence."

"Oh, as for *that*, it must be a mistake! M. de Sartines has but just returned to Paris after an exile of several years. If in former days he had any *penchant*, I believe it was—do not laugh, Henri—for the mother, not the daughter. My own ideas for Clémence—not that there is any use in expressing them now—pointed, I must confess, in a different direction. I am not rich, but these are evil days, and it is something to have

saved from the wreck of a fine fortune even so much as I have
contrived to do—for Emile." A faint, delicate flush overspread
the furrowed cheeks of the old lady as she uttered the name she
loved best in the world, and added, with a little tender hesitation that was almost touching, "I am very fond of your sister,
M. Henri."

"I know it, ma tante," said Henri, kissing her hand. "I
can never be half grateful enough for all your goodness to her,
and to my dear mother. But I am sure Clémence will be
happy, and that you are kind and generous enough to rejoice in
her happiness."

He went to the door of his sister's room, and knocked. After
a slight pause, his knock was answered by a gentle "Come in"
from Madame de Talmont. Mother and daughter stood together
at the window, and traces of tears were on both their faces.
Henri made his request that Clémence would accompany him
into the town; and Madame de Talmont, who did not like to
deny him anything, decided that she had better go. Clémence
would far rather have stayed at home; but she yielded, as usual,
to the wishes of her mother.

"Have you no dress but that one?" asked Henri with a little
hesitation, as he pointed to the plain black serge worn as
mourning for him, and which, in the three bright, bewildering
days that had passed since his return, she had been too much
occupied to think of discarding. "M. Ivan tells me that the
Czar noticed with sadness 'the number of women and children
in mourning' that he saw on the day of his triumphal entry into
Paris. Do not let him see one in mourning to-day who has
no cause to mourn."

"I have *one* coloured dress," said Clémence; and going to a
closet near at hand, she took out the purple brocade which her
mother had given her before Henri's departure, and which she
had never worn.

"It will do very well," said Madame de Talmont. "Already

the story of *my* life is wrought into the pattern of those flowers.
—And now *thine*."

Henri and Clémence were soon threading their way through
the crowded street, where the inhabitants of Versailles were
making holiday. The brother and sister seemed to have
changed positions, if not characters. Henri had passed
through such terrible suffering of body and mind, that although the one might recover its strength and the other its
tone, still there was something gone from him which could
never return: he had left his youth behind him in the snows of
Russia. On the other hand, a fresh spring-time of life and hope
had come to Clémence; the garden of her sad and careful girl-
hood was beginning to rejoice and blossom as the rose. As in
former days the grave and motherly elder sister had watched
over and counselled the careless, happy-hearted boy; so now it
became the office of the manly brother to protect and shield,
perhaps to advise, the young and timid maiden trembling on
the brink of the deeper joys of womanhood. Yet, though they
had much to talk of, at first few words passed between them.

"We are late," Henri observed to Clémence, as he hurried
her along.—"Here they come!"

The Czar had already left the hospital, and the stately cavalcade was advancing slowly down the street on its way to the
Avenue de Paris. "Let us come to these steps," said Henri,
leading his sister quickly through the throng. "We shall see
well here."

But the senses of Clémence were confused by the glittering
train as it passed along. "Where is the Czar?" she asked in
haste, making her voice heard with difficulty through the shouts
and cheering that filled the air.

"*There*—in green and gold—on the white horse."

"Yes; I see him!" she cried, her eye following the direction
of Henri's finger.

On either side of the Czar rode a handsome fair-haired boy,

and the bright young faces attracted for an instant the eye of Clémence. "His sons?" she queried.

"Would they were," answered Henri. "No, he is childless. They are his young brothers, the Grand Dukes Nicholas and Michael."

But Clémence scarcely listened, so eager was she to see what Ivan's Czar was like.

The face was noble, but care-worn and weary, as of a man who had heavy burdens to bear. Just then, however, he turned towards one of the lads, bending his head to catch some laughing remark of his, and a smile flashed like sunlight over his features, revealing a rare and spiritual beauty unseen by her before. She was satisfied.

Henri, meanwhile, was beside himself with excitement. He took off his cap, waved it in the air, then taking advantage of a momentary pause in the incessant and deafening cries of "Vive Alexandre! Vive l'Empereur de Russie!" that filled the street, he shouted aloud, in his clear, high-pitched voice, "*Vive l'aide-de-camp de St. Priest!*"

Clémence gazed at her brother in amazement. "What do you mean? Who *is* the aide-de-camp de St. Priest?" she whispered.

"He has heard! He understands! He is bowing to us!" cried Henri, without heeding her. "God bless him! God grant me one day to tell him what he has done for me. Or, perhaps, *you* will tell him for me, Clémence?"

"Dear brother, let us come home. This crowd is too much for you," said Clémence in an anxious tone, as she saw his rapidly changing colour and the tears that gathered in his eyes.

"No; it is all right. Thank God I have seen him once again. When they have passed on I will take you home by some quiet way, and tell you why I am so deeply moved."

As he spoke they saw Ivan on horseback, amidst the group that followed the Czar. He saluted them; and as he did so his face lighted up until it grew absolutely radiant with satisfaction. "I told him," whispered Henri, "that if he saw you here wearing a coloured dress he might rejoice."

"O Henri!" cried the horror-stricken Clémence, her face overspread with blushes. "How wicked of you! What will he think?"

"Nothing about *you*, sister mine. He knows you were not in the plot; so be at rest. Now, let us come away; our work is done."

They found a quiet way through streets which were little frequented at any time, and that day were absolutely empty. Hitherto Henri had been very silent about the story of his life since they parted; about all at least except the last year, which he had spent very comfortably at Vilna, recruiting his health, and enjoying the society of numerous friends amongst the Polish nobility and gentry, who soon discovered in the young con-script the scion of an old and good family. The allowance generously given by the Czar to all the French prisoners sufficed for his moderate wants;* and he had wisely devoted his leisure to study. Thus much he had told to his mother and sister; but the horrors of the Moscow campaign had been studiously avoided. Now, however, as they walked slowly along, Henri told his sister as much as he could tell any one of the "weltering abysses of trouble" through which he had passed. He told of the weary hungerings in the snow; of the Berezina agony; of the dazed, half-delirious wanderings over the frozen Polish plain; of the bitter, blank despair that settled down upon him at last. He told of the ghastly Vilna hospital, the lowest depth of all; and of the love, divine and human, which met him there and rescued him from the pit of horror. "My feet were set in a large place," he said; "and I thanked God and

* Domergues, a Frenchman bitterly prejudiced against everything Russian, pro-nounces this allowance really "munificent" under the circumstances, and says the prisoners were able to live upon it in the greatest comfort.

believed in him as I had never done before." He added, after a pause, "And Ivan is the reflection of his Czar. Even unconsciously and in the veriest trifles he copies him. Now, Clémence you know another reason why I am not unwilling to trust the dearest of sisters to his keeping."

When the blush that passed over the face of Clémence had subsided a little, she said softly, "No doubt you pray every day for the Czar. So shall I."

"I do ; but it is hard to know what to ask for him. Already God has given him everything we are wont to ask for rulers of the earth—dominion, power, glory, wealth, victory over his foes."

"Let us ask God to give him his very best gifts, Henri."

"Ay, if only we knew what they are."

"We do know, brother,—love, joy, peace, long-suffering, gentleness, goodness, faith, meekness, temperance."

Henri started, as though the thought were new to him. "Those would be strange jewels for the diadem on a monarch's brow," he said. "Yet, after all, the world—here in Paris as well as where I have been in Poland—can bear witness to 'long-suffering, gentleness, goodness.' Of 'love, joy, peace,' of course I cannot speak, for they are gems whose light is turned God-wards."

"Then let our prayer be for those. The face we have seen to-day does not look joyful, Henri."

When they returned to the house they found guests awaiting them, friends of Madame de Salgues, who wished to congratulate her niece upon the return of Henri, and to make his acquaintance. The afternoon was spent in entertaining them, and was already far gone when Ivan joined the party. Madame de Talmont contrived to say a word to him in private, which sent him with a beaming face to answer M. de Cranfort's multitudinous questions about the Dresden campaign.

By-and-by, when the soft May twilight had fallen, he stole

to the window where Clémence was standing looking out on the little garden. She had wearied of the discussion absorbing all the others, about the time and manner of the new king's triumphal entry into his capital. Ivan in his heart thanked the quick, eager voices which were making just then a welcome "solitude for two."

"Mademoiselle Clémence," he began.

A thrill of terror swept over the girl's heart, like the instinctive shrinking of the sensitive plant which closes up its petals at the lightest touch. She took refuge, not in silence, but in speech. "Monsieur Ivan," she said quickly, " I have seen your Czar."

" Have you ?"

" Yes; and heard Henri talk of him. There is a verse in the Gospel of which he has taught me the meaning—'He that is greatest among you shall be your servant.' "

" How true ! You always seem to go to the heart of every-thing." There was a pause sufficient for Ivan's quick ear to note that the pompous tones of M. de Cranfort were quite filling the room. "Dear Mademoiselle Clémence," he resumed, "one little word from you can make me richer than the Czar himself to-night."

Clémence murmured something inaudible, and seemed to need the hand he tried to take to shade her face, though the room was in darkness now.

Then Ivan's passionate heart flashed out and found its utterance. Since the beginning of the world had no one ever loved as he loved Clémence. It is the old fond illusion: to each young and ardent soul its own experience is a new discovery, undreamt of heretofore by the slow heart of humanity. Each generation sings—

> " We were the first that ever burst
> Into that silent sea."

But the moment's rapture was all too brief. The vigilant

eye of Madame de Talmont discerned a state of things which, if suffered to continue, might possibly imperil "les convenances." She rose softly from her place and drew near, near enough to catch the low-breathed words, "My Clémence." After one sigh-—into which all the memories of her own youth were gathered up—she laid her hand gently on the arm of Clémence. "My dear child," she said, "dost thou know that the little Fanchon is very ill ? La Tante will never be content if she is not well cared for. Go and see."

Fanchon was only a favourite lap-dog, but Clémence lavished a good deal of tenderness that night on the little creature.

Three very happy weeks followed ; then Ivan's marching orders came, and he set his face towards his own country, not without sorrow, but with the hope of a glad return at no distant day to claim the treasure left behind him.

CHAPTER XXXI.

LEAVES FROM LETTERS.

"Umile in tanta gloria."—PETRARCH.

THE bright spring-tide had ripened into a yet brighter summer, when one day Clémence entered the parlour where the two elder ladies sat at work. Her cheeks were glowing, and she held in her hand several closely-written sheets of paper. "Dear aunt and dear mother," she said, "I thought you would like me to read for you part of the letter from—St. Petersburg."

"Yes, dear child," answered Madame de Talmont tenderly. "I am sorry Henri is not here. He was so anxious about it."

Henri had gone to Brie, that he might bring to the sorrowing family of his "true comrade," Mathieu Féron, what comfort he could—at least the mournful comfort of certainty.

Madame de Salgues motioned Clémence to a footstool near her. "We shall be glad to hear of M. Pojarsky," she said kindly, but as if the kindness was not quite without an effort.

From the first sheet Clémence read scarcely anything. "He says that his journey has been prosperous," she explained in general terms, "but that he feels a little solitary without— without *us all*." It must be owned that this was a very tame and inadequate rendering of the eloquent original, which she kept to herself. At length she began to read: "'You will remember our last expedition to Paris on the day of the king's triumphal entry, and Henri's pleased surprise when he found

how completely the Czar kept himself and his Russians out of
sight, only mingling incognito with the crowd of spectators,
that none might say of the son of St. Louis, "Foreign bayonets
have brought him back to his capital." You said to me then,
"Think what a welcome they will give him in St. Petersburg!
That will be a triumph to throw this one completely into the
shade!" And Henri added, "Would that I could see it!
But you must tell us all about it when you write." I must—
so far as I can; but it would be impossible to paint the rapture
of enthusiasm, of loyalty, of gratitude with which his return
was awaited. Think of it! Russia not only delivered from
her enemies, but set upon a pinnacle of glory she had never
known before. In less than two short years, the invader
driven back from our capital to his own, stripped of the power
he had misused, and hurled from the throne he had disgraced.
France conquered, rescued, forgiven.'"

"If there is much more about the conquest of France, you
may pass it over," said Madame de Salgues rather tartly. "Of
course, M. Pojarsky writes as a Russian."

"The honour of France is dear—at least to some Russians,"
Clémence answered with a heightened colour. She went on:
"'Three long days did the Senate spend in debating what
Russia should do to show her gratitude to the Czar Alexander
Paulovitch. Other princes had been given high-sounding titles,
had been styled in their life-time the Great, the Magnificent,
the Invincible, or, still more honourable, the Well-beloved
—and for him surely that would have been appropriate.
But some who knew the heart of our Czar spoke and said,
"Such titles would give the honour to himself alone; let us
find one which brings it back to God. That will please
him best." "Blessed of Heaven" was the name chosen
at last. Would it not have sounded well in the long and
glorious line of our Czars, Alexander Paulovitch, the Blessed
of Heaven? Moreover, they planned to erect in St. Peters-

burg, in the Isaac's Square, a splendid monument, grander than your column of the Place Vendôme, to celebrate his glory and familiarize to every eye the names of his victories. They sent a deputation proposing these things, and at the same time praying him to accept the Grand Order of St. George, the highest and rarest of our military distinctions; and to allow them to organize—or rather to *permit*, for the people were but too willing—public receptions, fêtes, illuminations, on the most magnificent scale.

"'I marvel, Clémence, whether you will be disappointed, as I was, when you hear his answer. In no words but his own can I tell it. This is what he wrote to the Senate: "I most earnestly desire and implore the benediction of the Most High upon the nation he has confided to me, that I may be blessed by my dear and faithful subjects, and, if possible, by the whole human race. But though I desire to attain this end, I cannot flatter myself that I have attained it; nor can I permit myself to accept this surname, for I should give the lie to my own principles in offering my faithful subjects an example so contrary to the sentiments of moderation and the spirit of humility that I am endeavouring to inculcate. Therefore, while expressing my deepest gratitude, I request the Senate to regard these things as though they had never been. Raise a monument for me in your hearts, as there is one for you in mine. May my people bless me, even as I also bless them. May Russia be happy, and may the Divine benediction rest upon her and upon me." "It is for posterity," he said afterwards, "to erect me a monument if they think me worthy of it." The Grand Order of St. George he declined to accept, because it is only given to a general who has saved the country from imminent danger, conducted a successful campaign, or gained a great battle. He had not personally performed any of these things, he said; though it may be that in this particular posterity will not agree with him. "This arm,"

added he, "has done no more than another man's." As for
fêtes, illuminations, and processions, he requested most earnestly
that the money which would have been expended upon these
should be used for the succour of the widows and orphans
made by the war. To insure this as far as he could, he came
back to his capital, unannounced and unattended, some days
before he was expected. He went first to the Church of Kazan
to pray, then to the Winter Palace to see his mother. That
was all. Next day there was a solemn thanksgiving service in
the cathedral. I trust that to many of us it was no empty
ceremony, and that the words, "*Not us! not us! but His
name!*" went up from our hearts as well as from our lips.

"'Yet I will own that at first I was disappointed—and that
bitterly—at the self-abnegation of my Czar. But now I am
more than content; I am rejoiced that he has put aside the
intoxicating cup that was borne to his lips. I am learning to
see more honour in humility than in monuments, decorations,
high-sounding titles.

"'He intends soon to hold a levee for the especial benefit of
the officers who have been wounded during the war; and we
are invited, each of us, to state his wants and desires directly
to himself. I will not say that I long for this opportunity—
nor perhaps could I say it with truth. For I *trust*. I leave
with perfect confidence my future—*our* future, which is
infinitely more—in the hands of my God and of my sovereign.

"'Yesterday I called upon General Soltikoff, who showed
me so much kindness two years ago. He looks greatly aged
and broken; indeed, I fear the days of mourning for the noble
old man are at hand. But he was kind and thoughtful as
ever. He told me he had just had the honour of presenting a
memorial to the Czar upon a matter which nearly concerned
me, but that at present he could say no more, as his Imperial
Majesty had expressed a wish to be himself my informant.
This has piqued my curiosity not a little, as you may readily

imagine. I conclude he will speak to me about it at the levee.' "

This was as much of her letter as Clémence saw fit to read aloud. One more paragraph may, however, be given here : " My beloved, I read every day the little book you gave me." (The parting gifts of Clémence to her betrothed had been the sketch of his mother pencilled by her father's hand, and that treasury of heavenward aspiration, so loved by devout and earnest souls like hers, the "Imitation of Christ.") "It is grand and beautiful, but terrible to me. I feel more and more, as I read, how full of sin, how utterly unworthy and vile I am—how far from being wholly detached from the world and given up to Christ. Then I go back to my Bible, and that makes me feel my own unworthiness yet more deeply ; but it also makes me think of the love of God and the gentleness of Christ, and thinking upon these I have hope. There are some words of yours that often come to my mind. You said that the day you saw me first, lying wounded in the hospital, you were surprised and touched to hear me say I could not help rejoicing in the triumph of my Czar, though *I* had no share in it. You said it made you think that if you truly loved your King and Saviour, you would be able even thus to rejoice in him, however it might be with yourself. When I read his own good and gracious words, and think what he is, and what he has done for us, I seem to understand your meaning. But I am very ignorant ; and oh, how I need you to teach me—you, beloved, so much wiser and better than I. I often marvel how you deigned to care for me at all. I think it could not have come about had not a ray of light reflected from my Czar fallen upon me." The letter did not by any means end there ; but there may fitly end the extracts presented to the general reader. Of course many courteous and grateful messages to Madame de Salgues, Madame de Talmont, and Henri found a place ere it was concluded, and these were duly delivered by Clémence.

About a week afterwards another letter arrived, and Henri had now returned to share its tidings. At first Clémence did not read any part of it aloud ; she only told its contents more or less fully. Afterwards she read some portions of it to her mother. It ran thus :—

"St. Petersburg, Wednesday Night.

"My Beloved,—It is with a full heart—half glad, half sorrowful—that I write to thee to-night. God has been good to me—good beyond my utmost dreams ; for has he not given me *thee?* But in the sweetest cup some longed-for drop of sweetness is still lacking; in the brightest life some brightness is still wanting—some cherished wish ungranted. God wills it so, and his will is best. Since my childhood a strong untold longing has lain hidden in the depths of my heart. Now I know it can never be fulfilled—never on this side of the grave. The old hope, the hope of my boyhood and youth, is gone from me. I cannot help these few tears which are falling on the page as I write. But do not heed them; they are not tears of bitterness—for I have been comforted. I am going to tell you how.

"To-day the Imperial reception of which I told you was held for the wounded officers. It was crowded. Amongst those who were present I saw Count Rostopchine, to whom I shall always feel grateful, because he was the first man who gave me work to do, and bade me go and do it. He looks ill and haggard. It is said he sees nothing day or night except the flames of Moscow. The world gives him the credit of the conflagration ; and I cannot say that in this instance the world is mistaken, although hitherto it has been the fashion here to assume that it was done by the French. The count has made himself very unpopular by his severities towards those who were suspected of favouring the invaders, and it is not thought that he will continue in office. He has nobly refused to accept any compensation for his own enormous losses in the doomed city.

" I suppose I am writing all this just to make you a sharer in my own long suspense and weary waiting. I thought my turn for a word from my sovereign would never come, there were so many present older than I. Besides, on such occasions his Majesty never is in haste. He speaks to each: the words perhaps are few, but they are so spoken that each feels that his own particular case and circumstances are for the time the sole objects of attention. But *my* five minutes came at last, and proved enough to crown my long patience with an abundant reward. A kindly question or two about my wound was asked and answered; and then, without further preface, the Emperor spoke to me of my father. He said that after our first interview he had requested General Soltikoff to ascertain whether he yet lived, and that, 'during our absence,' the general had succeeded in obtaining full information about him. 'He will give you the papers to-morrow,' he added—and paused for a moment. Something in his face told me my father was no more, and almost unawares the words passed my lips, 'He is dead, sire.' 'I wish I could say you are mistaken,' he answered. 'All was different from what we thought. He was never sent to Siberia. At his own earnest and impassioned request—the request of a brave man—his punishment was changed to that of compulsory service in the army as a private.* " Let me show my sovereign," said he, "that although the enemy of Louis of France, I am faithful to Catherine of Russia." Ivan Ivanovitch, he redeemed his word nobly, though not to the Czarina. He was one of the many gallant men whom I led to their death at Austerlitz, on the most unfortunate day of my life.† His regiment kept its place until not a man was left unwounded. Will it comfort you to know that he died a hero's death, and that he died for me ?'

* A well-known form of punishment in Russia. Alexander himself inflicted it upon some personages of the highest rank, for gross acts of peculation and dishonesty.

† Alexander always referred to the day of Austerlitz as "his unfortunate day," and never ceased to mourn the slaughter to which he led his brave army upon that occasion.

"'What more could I desire for him, or for myself?' I said. That was nearly all that passed between us. But it was enough. I am comforted concerning my father.

"I cannot write or think of aught else just now. My dear unknown father! So unfortunate! So young too—scarce older, when the storm burst upon him, than I am now. What agony he must have suffered! what desolation! Yet he kept his sorely-tried loyalty without a taint; only craving, as his last boon, leave to die for the sovereign who drove him from her presence with insult, and doomed him to ruin and disgrace. Surely his heart was true, whatever baseless, fantastic dreams of liberty and equality may have set his brain on fire. The Czar says he died a hero's death, and that he died *for him*. Thank God!

"My Clémence perhaps will wonder that I said nothing to the Czar about our future—about my plans, hopes, or prospects. Truly I had intended, if the opportunity offered, to have spoken of these. But to-day I could not—I could think of no subject save one. Forgive me this delay.

"It is late, but I am still sitting at my desk with that precious sketch before me which your father's hand transferred to paper, and your hand placed in mine. My dear mother's face seems to look upon me and to say, 'I too am comforted concerning all I love. Here or elsewhere they are in God's keeping. Never, even in their darkest days, did he wholly take away his loving-kindness from them.'

"To-morrow General Soltikoff is to tell me more. Not *much* more, I suppose. Few particulars of the life and death of a man degraded to the ranks are ever likely to be known. But had *he* told me what I know now, how different everything would have seemed to me to-night!

"Now it is not late, but early. That is really the light of dawn, our Northern dawn, which is stealing in pale and faint. I must put out my lamp and lie down, first thanking God for all his mercies, and praying him to keep me, and those a thousand times dearer than myself, in the hollow of his hand. Good-night,—my Clémence, my queen, good-night!"

"Thursday Morning.

"I take my pen in haste to add a few lines which will change everything for thee and me, Clémence. No, not *change*, only clear away our perplexities, and make the crooked places straight before us. My last night's vigil made me rather a late sleeper this morning, and I woke to find my servant standing by my side, with a large packet in his hand bearing the Imperial seal. You may be sure I lost no time in opening it. Two separate parchments fell out—one the patent renewing in my favour my father's title of 'Prince' Pojarsky, the other the title-deeds of his estate, Nicolofsky.*

"I cannot to-day write commonplace words about this ; *you* will read between the lines, and share the emotions that fill my heart. Surely God has dealt well with me—infinitely better than I deserve. It only remains now for estate, title, and all else that I have and am, to be laid at your feet by your happy, grateful, and devoted　　　　　　　　　　　　Ivan."

---

* A similar act of imperial munificence, performed in a similar way, drew the comment from De Maistre: "En fait d'élégance souveraine, l'Empereur de Russie est un grand artiste."

CHAPTER XXXII.

TWO RETURNS, ONE OF THEM NOT EXPECTED.

" I keep my master's noble name
For warring, not for feasting."

LTHOUGH every real obstacle to his marriage was now removed, it was several months before Ivan found himself at liberty to return to France and claim his bride. He had to go to Nicolofsky, to see and set in order his new estate. It is impossible to describe the joy of his old friends upon that occasion, and the welcome he received from them all, especially from his foster-parents. One of his earliest acts was to emancipate the starost and his family, making them at the same time a present of their homestead. He bestowed a similar favour upon the mother of Michael; Michael himself, as a soldier, being free already. To Pope Nikita and his wife he could give little that they cared for, except kindness and sympathy. They had not recovered from their deep sorrow for the melancholy fate of his old playfellow, their beloved and only daughter. Amongst these friends of his boyhood Ivan became once more a boy. He would sit for hours talking to " bativshka " and to the company gathered around his hospitable stove, telling them the eventful story of the war, as well as his own adventures since they parted.

He could not make this first visit a long one; although he consoled his " serfs," or rather his friends, with the promise that at no distant period he would come again and take up his abode amongst them. He was obliged to return to the capital in time to accompany the Emperor to the Congress of Vienna, where the brilliant series of fêtes and spectacles in which the assembled sovereigns displayed their magnificence made the presence of such a splendid corps as the Chevalier Guard particularly suitable. But at length he succeeded in obtaining the desired furlough, and early in February reached Versailles once more.

He found Clémence unchanged, except that the months of separation had added, in his eyes, to her grace and loveliness. Madame de Talmont looked at least ten years younger since the return of her son; but Henri himself seemed older, and wore a grave if not a troubled aspect. Madame de Salgues also was ageing quickly: Henri told Ivan she was anxious about Emile, who had more than once been in danger for acts of boyish insolence and bravado, such as tearing white cockades from the breasts of their wearers, and giving a jovial supper to his companions on the 21st of January, the anniversary of the execution of Louis XVI.

"A wise government," said Henri during a quiet walk with Ivan in the park of Versailles, "would disregard these follies, and a strong government could very well afford to do it. But I fear the government of Louis Dix-huit is not either wise or strong. He and his courtiers seem to forget that the world has turned round more than once since 1789. There is not a little discontent amongst the people, and there is much, very much amongst the military."

"Do *you* intend to embrace a military life, Henri?"

Henri shuddered. "*Never*, if I can help it. My experience of soldiering was too terrible."

"I do not think you need anticipate another Moscow campaign," returned Ivan.

"Still," pursued Henri, "if my country were in danger, I

trust I should not be found lacking.   My mother is exceedingly anxious to see me in the army.   But my own tastes lead me in a direction quite different."

"To the bar, perhaps, or the Church?"

"My mother and my aunt think these the only rational alternatives.   They talk grandly of 'la noblesse de la robe;' but I confess I do not care for the career of a lawyer, nor do I think I have the talents necessary to insure success in it.   While as for the Church,—may I speak my whole mind to you in confidence, Prince Ivan?"

"Certainly you may, my dear friend."

"I am a sincere and earnest believer in Christianity," Henri said.   "I have heard the voice of God in the stormy wind and tempest, in the snow and hail which fulfilled his will.   But since I have begun to study that will as revealed in his own Word, a suspicion I cannot dismiss grows and strengthens within me, — I fear some of the rites and doctrines of the Church in which I have been brought up are not in accordance with it."

These words awakened for the first time in the mind of Ivan the thought that any real or important divergence might exist between the different forms of Christianity.   Hitherto the world for him had contained two classes only—believers and infidels.   These he found and expected to find everywhere —in the "orthodox" Church of his own country, amongst the Catholics of France and the Lutherans of Prussia.   The idea suggested by Henri was so new to him that he paused for some moments to consider it before he answered, speaking slowly and with deliberation, "I am sorry you are troubled with such thoughts, Henri ; for doubting keeps us from doing, and it seems to me that there is a great deal to be done in the world, and little time enough to do it.   On the other hand, you would not have the doubts if God had not sent them to you.   You are not doubting *him;* you are only doubting in what manner you can serve him best. So you must face your doubts and answer them, one way or the other. God will be with you, and lead you to the light. But in the meantime you need not sit idle."

"True, most true. I am longing to work for God, who has done so much for me. Besides, what right have I to sit with folded hands, a burden upon my aunt? 'If any man will not work, neither shall he eat.' But it is much easier to say what I can't do than what I can. My mother thinks so few things possible to one who has the misfortune, as I feel disposed to call it, of being nobly born."

"What would you like to do, in your heart of hearts, Henri?"

"If I tell you, will you laugh at me, Prince Ivan?"

"Not I! Why should I? When I was a boy I could plough a straight furrow, and I was a fair hand with the reaping-hook. You cannot fancy any occupation lowlier than these."

"I should like to use, not a plough, but a pencil and pair of compasses. At Vilna I lodged in the house of an architect, and spent much of my leisure over his books. I was always fond of mathematics, which are useful in that line. Prince Ivan, if you want to build a palace on your new estate, I shall be most happy to design it for you."

Ivan made him a profound bow, then turned and laid his hand on his shoulder. "Come to Russia with us," he said warmly. "Never was there a better opening for your genius. Think of all Moscow to be rebuilt! Russia ought to be the El Dorado of architects for twenty years to come."

"Are you jesting, Prince Ivan?"

"Never was I more in earnest. The Czar will give you a welcome; and the rather because he shares your tastes himself. In his brief moments of leisure he often amuses himself by taking up a pencil and drawing a design for a public building. So he knows how to appreciate what is good."

"But—my mother.   Already her heart is torn by the thought of parting with Clémence."

"Why need there be any parting?   I think we could make her happy at Nicolofsky or St. Petersburg.   I have often thought about this, and what you have said to me now gives me the courage to propose it."

"Do you intend to leave the army?" Henri asked in his turn, perhaps with some desire to change a subject upon which he was conscious of having said more than he intended.

"I do, as soon as peace is thoroughly settled.   Of course, until then it cannot be thought of.   At the Congress things sometimes looked doubtful enough."

"That affair of the kingdom of Poland seems to be causing a great deal of trouble," said Henri.   "More than it is worth, *I* should say; but the Czar does not seem to think so."

"When did *not* an old wrong cause an infinity of trouble to the man who tries to repair it?   By some strange fatality, it is upon him the punishment generally comes, not upon the man who did it," Ivan answered.   "Those 'designs' upon Poland, for which many who ought to know better are now loudly blaming the Czar, simply mean two things—to Russia an assured peace, guaranteed by a strong, well-defended frontier; and to Poland the longed-for 'unity,' with as much of the longed-for 'independence' as she is fit to have and capable of using."*

"It seems a strange way of repaying the Poles for having gone away *en masse* after Napoleon," said Henri.

"It is the way of my Czar," returned Ivan proudly.   "Did you ever hear what passed between him and Kosakoski, the most devoted of Napoleon's Polish adherents?   'Is it true that you followed Napoleon to Fontainebleau?' asked the Czar. 'Yes, sire,' returned the Pole who certainly had the courage of his opinions.   'I was with him till he left it; and then, if he had asked me to go with him, I would have done it.'   The Czar

* It is understood, of course, that Ivan speaks from the *Russian* point of view.

was silent for a moment, then he asked him, 'What is it you wish for most?' 'The restoration of my property,' said Kosakoski. The Czar immediately wrote an order to that effect, and gave it to him. It is well known that his heart, since his boyhood, has yearned to heal the wounds and to atone for the wrongs of Poland. The Polish hostage, Czartoriski, was the friend of his youth; and in their long confidential talks they planned together to build the old waste places and gather the scattered members of the oppressed nationality. Now Czartoriski reproaches him with doing far too little; while Russia, loyal but perplexed, suspects him of doing too much; and Europe accuses him of caring for nothing but the extension of his own frontier. And your King, Louis Dix-huit," continued Ivan with some bitterness, " to whom he gave a throne, treats him as an enemy." They had almost reached their home when this was said, so Henri was spared the necessity of a rejoinder, nor did he greatly care to make one, Legitimist though he was.

Many a happy talk had Clémence and Ivan in those days about things past and future—things seen and unseen. Their engagement was now openly avowed; the trousseau of the bride was in preparation, and all was arranged except the wedding-day. Madame de Salgues was becoming reconciled to an alliance which would give her niece the title of Princess, and was lavish in her presents of jewellery and costly laces. Since the Restoration her life had become less secluded; many of the returned *émigrés* frequented her house, and found the young Russian prince, the *futur* of Mademoiselle Clémence, a very pleasant addition to their society.

One evening Madame de Salgues gave an entertainment to a few of her friends. It was a supper, refined and elegant, but unpretending, such as, in her own words, "used to be *de bon ton* before the Revolution and the bourgeoisie spoiled everything, when we did not come together to eat and to drink, but to converse and to enjoy one another's society."

Upon this occasion her guests thoroughly fulfilled her expectations, with the exception of the youngest of the party. Stéphanie de Sartines, like a spoiled child, had importuned her father to allow her to accept Madame de Salgues's invitation ; but having gained her point, she sat absorbed and silent, refusing to eat or to speak, and devoting herself to the contemplation of her idolized friend Clémence, from whom she was so soon to be separated.   Ivan pitied the sad-faced little girl, and remembering her exploits at their first meeting, sought to console her with the most tempting of bon-bons and preserved fruits ; but he could elicit nothing beyond a melancholy " No, thank you, monsieur."

" You should say M. le Prince, my daughter," her father corrected.

" En Russie tout faquin est prince,"* observed the audacious Emile to his neighbour, M. de Cranfort.

The latter, though disposed to regard Ivan in the light of a successful rival, resented the discourtesy of Emile, and showed it by asking coldly, " What do you say, sir ? "

" Don't you know the story ?   Before the war broke out the Czar sent Prince Tufaquin as ambassador to the court of the Emperor, who, during their first interview, called him nothing but 'Monsieur.'   One of the bystanders afterwards told him of the title borne by the envoy.   'J'ignorais qu'en Russie *tout faquin* est prince,' was his answer."

" General Buonaparte was a parvenu," said M. de Cranfort ; "therefore it was not altogether his fault if he mistook rudeness for wit."

Emile " knew when he was beaten," perhaps because he was not an Englishman ; so he turned from M. de Cranfort to Stéphanie, whom he heard deploring that Prince Ivan was going to take Clémence away from them into Russia, where she would be frozen to death in the long cold winter, or eaten by the bears.

* "In Russia every coxcomb is a prince."

He bent over her with a comic air of gallantry, and prayed her to be comforted. "*I* am infinitely more devoted to you than Mademoiselle Clémence could ever be," he said; "and, mademoiselle, *I* am not going to Russia."

But he was scarcely more fortunate here. "Of course you are not," returned the young lady sharply, her dark eyes flashing. "I heard a gentleman tell my father that the Czar is inviting all manner of clever, capable people to go to Russia; but for any one who is—who is, well, just *ordinary*, you know, he has no particular welcome."

In the meantime Stéphanie's allusion to Russian bears had occasioned remark. Ivan told some stories about them which were rather amusing than terrible; for bears, like nobler animals who run away when they are attacked, sometimes make themselves ridiculous. Amidst the laughter which followed, Madame de Salgues's valet made a whispered communication—"Madame, there is an old soldier without, who wishes to speak with the young gentleman."

"With what young gentleman?"

"The young gentleman of the house, he says, madame."

"Then ask M. de Talmont to go to him at once, and see what he wants," said Madame de Salgues with a nervous air. The capital and its environs swarmed with old soldiers of Napoleon, who were needy and discontented, longing for any kind of political change, and in the meantime, if report said true, not always despising robbery and violence as less desirable but still legitimate means of repairing their ruined fortunes.

Henri went into the hall, closing the door behind him. He saw in the lamp-light a tall, gaunt figure, wrapped in an old greatcoat, which covered a shabby uniform, but did not conceal the cross and two medals glittering on the breast of the faded tunic.

"I beg your pardon, monsieur," said the soldier in a voice Henri seemed to recognize. "It was not you I wished to see, but the young gentleman who belongs to the Ecole Polytechnique."

"Surely I know you—surely I have seen you somewhere," said Henri, looking attentively at the bronzed, weather-beaten features of the old man.

The veteran shook his head. "You have the advantage of me, monsieur," he said.

But after another brief scrutiny a light flashed over the mind of Henri, reflecting itself in his face. He advanced cordially and took the soldier's bony hand in his. "Pierre Rougeard of the Old Guard," he said, "I am heartily glad to see you. I thought you were with the dead."

It was natural that the young conscript should remember the old Guardsman who had befriended him in his hour of need far better than the Guardsman could remember the conscript. Henri was greatly changed, while scarcely anything on this side of the grave could change the hard, weather-beaten features of Rougeard. He was obliged to recall the past to his recollection. "Never," said he, "did banquet seem so sweet to me as that repast of horse-flesh to which you bade me welcome by your bivouac fire on the Smolensko road. But we gave you up for lost that terrible day before we crossed the Beresina."

"I was made prisoner," Rougeard answered. "But I fell into good hands, and was kindly treated. At the Peace of Paris I came home with the rest—though it is home no longer without the Emperor," he added with a sigh.

"You must have much to tell," Henri rejoined; and as the valet passed through the hall, he said to him, "Alphonse, this is an old friend of mine who showed me much kindness while I was in Russia. Take the best care you can of him. By-and-by," he said to Rougeard, "we will finish our conversation."

He returned to the salon, and related what had passed to Madame de Salgues. That lady, with the characteristic love of a Frenchwoman for a little scene, must needs have the old

Guardsman brought in, that he might drink the health of Henri, and receive the acknowledgments of his friends for the kindness he had shown him.

So Henri fetched Rougeard, who listened to a little speech from Madame de Salgues, had his hand shaken by Madame de Talmont and Clémence, and emptied a brimming goblet of champagne poured out for him by Emile.

As he gave back the goblet, he bent forward and whispered a word or two, which made the lad—unused as he was to self-control—utter an involuntary cry of amazement, and drop the glass upon the ground.

Of course every one started and looked at him; and Madame de Salgues asked in alarm, "What is the matter?"

"Nothing," said Emile in confusion, stooping to collect the fragments of the broken glass.

"Nothing indeed," repeated the terrible Stéphanie. "You need not be alarmed, madame; I heard every word he said, and it was only this, ' *The little corporal has come back.*' M. Emile, who is the little corporal?"

Well might she ask the question, for "all faces gathered blackness." The party of friends, just before so glad and gay, looked as if a shell had suddenly burst amongst them. M. de Sartines was the first to find a voice. "Garde," he said, turning solemnly to Rougeard, "since you have spoken these words you are bound to explain them. I daresay it is mere rumour," he added, addressing the ladies.

For a moment Rougeard stood irresolute. He had come to impart his tidings to Emile, whom he knew already as an ardent Buonapartist, ready to venture his life in the good cause; but to proclaim them in the midst of a circle of Royalists had been far from his intention. However, he soon recovered his composure. To-morrow all Paris would know the truth ; what did it matter about a few hours? With a simple dignity which was not unbecoming, he answered M. de Sartines, "I have the honour, monsieur, to belong to the Old Guard, therefore I have heard to-day what you will all hear to-morrow. The Emperor has set his foot once more upon the soil of France. He has landed near Fréjus, in the Gulf of St. Juan."

"Then by this time he is a prisoner, if he is not shot, or hanged upon the nearest tree," said De Cranfort; while Emile sprang to his feet, and shouted, "Vive Napoléon!"

"If my grandson cannot behave at my table like a gentleman, I will thank him to leave it," said Madame de Salgues with a sternness that amazed every one, and was not without its effect upon Emile, who was accustomed to nothing from her but extreme indulgence.

Ivan, though his own thoughts were sufficiently sorrowful, felt a compassion for the boy, and a dread, not altogether groundless, of what he might be tempted to do if provoked. Turning to his hostess, near whom he sat, he said to her, unheard by the others, "Madame, I pray of you do not be hard with him. Do not let him leave us in this way. His exclamation was natural. I should certainly have done the same had I heard the Czar was coming."

Cranfort caught the last words, and said with petulance, "It is all his fault."

"Whose fault?" asked a quiet, elderly abbé, invited because Madame de Salgues thought no party perfect without a slight, a very slight ecclesiastical flavour.

"The fault of the Czar, M. l'Abbé," returned Cranfort, raising his voice, for the abbé sat at the other side of the table. "If the Corsican adventurer succeeds in erecting his standard once more, and torrents of blood are spilt, it will be the result of the imprudent generosity of the Emperor Alexander. No one can pretend that he was not warned. M. de Talleyrand and every man of sense knew that Elba was no place for Buonaparte. It was keeping a lighted candle at the door of the powder-magazine."

"It did not require the wit of Talleyrand to find *that* out," said M. de Sartines. "The Emperor Alexander may have had political motives of his own sufficient to explain his conduct. Most probably he had. If not, his championship of the Buonapartes does honour possibly to his heart, but little enough to his understanding."

Ivan was about to speak, but Henri, with a quick motion of his hand, arrested him. "Not one word, Prince Ivan," he said in a voice low and tremulous with suppressed emotion. "Not one word from your lips to-night! It is I—I whose life he saved—who must defend him. And from what? Is it from the charge of sparing the fallen? of being too generous, too merciful, too trusting? There are very few who need exculpation from such charges. And I, who but for that mercy of his would now be lying in a nameless grave at Vilna, will not sit by and hear them.—Messieurs, I am a man of peace; I hate strife and bloodshed; and I thought that never again should this right hand of mine touch sword or pistol. Yet I am ready, either now or hereafter, with sword or pistol, or both, for any gentleman, or any number of gentlemen, who may desire to meet me in this quarrel."

"Quel tapage!" muttered Emile. "One man may raise a fine commotion where another may not breathe a word!"

Madame de Talmont was terrified by a vehemence so foreign to the character of her son. She interposed, explaining that no harm had been intended, and entreating him to recollect himself. M. de Sartines also hastened to apologize. "I was not aware, monsieur," he said, "that you were under personal obligations to the Czar. Still I cannot hold myself excused, for I should not have used so much freedom in the presence of M. le Prince. I hope he will be good enough to pardon me."

"No need of that, monsieur," returned Ivan. "The more freely the conduct of my sovereign is discussed by every loyal Frenchman the more will be his honour. The Czar," he added proudly, "has saved Europe once. If need be, he will do so again."

Shortly afterwards the guests departed. Henri drew Ivan aside. "You will be obliged to leave us?" he said in a low voice.

"Yes," Ivan answered gravely. "After what we have just heard, I must go immediately to my Czar."

Henri's voice dropped still lower, and laying his hand on the shoulder of his friend, he said a few earnest words. Ivan answered in the same tone; then, with a countenance wonderfully brightened, he left the room.

When he was gone, Henri said earnestly, turning to his mother and his aunt, " Clémence and Ivan belong to each other already in the sight of God; why should they not do so also in the sight of man? Months, if not more, may elapse before Ivan can return—a long and dangerous campaign, perhaps two, may intervene—how much better a hasty marriage than the wearing suspense and anxiety of a protracted engagement?"

" What difference can it make?" asked Madame de Salgues. " Clémence must of course remain here until things are settled."

" A very great difference," Madame de Talmont answered. " As a wife, he can send for her and she can go to him should anything untoward happen—which God forbid," she added with a trembling lip. " God alone knows what comfort there is in having the right to tend, or to mourn.—Henri, I entirely agree with you."

" It occurs to me that there is some one else whose consent will have to be obtained," Madame de Salgues observed.

Henri smiled. " I believe Ivan is this very moment engaged in obtaining it," he said.

" That being the case," said Madame de Salgues, " and after the opinion your mother has just expressed, it only remains for us to arrange details."

The next morning Clémence and Ivan were married quietly in the parish church of Versailles. It is possible that the young Russian gave a passing sigh of regret to the touching and beautiful ceremonies of his own ritual, which he was obliged to forego.   Gladly would " Ivan the servant of God" have been " crowned with Clémence the handmaid of God," as it is the use and wont to do with brides and bridegrooms in the Greco-Russian Church.   But what did it signify?   He was more than content—he was unspeakably thankful for all that was given him by God and by man.

There was a simple *déjeûner*, the only guests outside the family circle being M. de Sartines and Stéphanie, who was greatly consoled by her dignity of bridesmaid.   There were brave, loving farewells; and then Ivan rode away to rejoin his comrades and to do his duty in the conflicts that might yet lie before him and them.

CHAPTER XXXIII.

> " Yea, thou wilt answer for me, righteous Lord !
> Thine all the sorrow, mine the great reward:
> Thine the sharp thorns, and mine the golden crown ;
> Mine the life won, and thine the life laid down."

IT is amongst the minor yet very real troubles of life that promptitude, courage, and self-denial so often appear to be wasted. The call to action reaches our ear: we spring up responsive, buckle on our armour, and hasten to the front,—only to hear the bugles sounding the retreat, and to find that the conflict has been adjourned *sine die*. So it happened to Ivan. He was stopped on his way to Vienna by tidings that the Chevalier Guard was now in Poland with the main body of the Russian army. To Poland accordingly he went; but only to linger in enforced idleness day after day, even week after week, first at Wiasma, and then at Prague. He could not dismiss the thought,—Might he not just as well have spent all this time with his bride at Versailles? He certainly might, except for the important consideration that it can never be just as well for a man to neglect his duty as to do it.

Meanwhile the accounts from France added to his perplexity and uneasiness. Napoleon, received everywhere with open arms by the military, swept through the land like an unresisted torrent, and on the 19th of March entered the capital once more. Louis XVIII. abandoned it at his approach without striking a blow—a pusillanimity which made old Royalists like De Sartines and De Cranfort hang their heads with shame. It was natural that Ivan should feel the deepest anxiety about the household at Versailles, and for the sake of those so dear to him he could not be otherwise than thankful that a battle had been avoided, although on more public grounds it grieved him to the heart that Napoleon had succeeded so easily in establishing himself once more in Paris.

During his stay in Prague, Ivan was cheered by a letter from Clémence, bearing the impress of her own true, tender, and courageous spirit. Henri wrote also, giving a more detailed account of public events; and Emile contributed a version of his own, which was by no means unwelcome. The student of the Polytechnique wrote as though the entire glory of bringing back the Emperor belonged to him and his schoolfellows; and he exhorted Prince Ivan not to be in the least uneasy about the family at Versailles, assuring him that they would enjoy *his* powerful friendship and protection, with a naïve simplicity that gave his correspondent a hearty laugh. "But after all," thought Ivan, "some atonement is due to the vanity of Emile, which used to suffer so often from the keen though polished thrusts of his Legitimist friends."

All this time a burden of pain and apprehension lay heavy on the heart of Ivan. It was probable that by the return of Buonaparte from Elba, the great work of the Czar would be undone; it was already certain that his expectations were frustrated and his predictions falsified. He intended to do good, and the good had become the occasion of evil. Every mouth was opened now to reproach him with the untoward results of his chivalrous kindness to the vanquished. "You see, sire," said Francis of Austria, "what has occurred in consequence of your protection of the Liberals and the Buonapartists." "We are far," said Talleyrand, "from accusing that greatness of soul which treated a conquered Power almost like a conqueror; but at least we cannot accuse ourselves of the imprudent generosity we admired but could not prevent, though we have now become the victims of it." Doubtless Talleyrand only expressed the sentiments of all the Royalists of France ; yet it was as well for him that he did not at that time fall in with the Emperor of Russia's Chevalier Guard. But infinitely worse to Alexander than all these reproaches was the imminent prospect of another great war, to water the soil of Europe with blood and tears, and renew the horrors it had been the dearest wish of his heart to terminate. Ivan was not surprised when a report reached him that the Czar was ill at Vienna. He knew—he was not likely ever to forget—that each remembrance of the useless slaughter at Austerlitz touched the chords of a lasting sorrow. He had heard of the terrible months of depression that followed the murder of the Emperor Paul, when the attendants of the new sovereign trembled for his reason or his life; nay, he himself had witnessed a partial recurrence of the same depression at the time of the death of Moreau. The sad face of his Czar, as he had seen it then, haunted him day and night, and from the very depths of his heart the cry went up to heaven, " O God, uphold and comfort thy servant, who putteth his trust in thee !"

At last the long-wished-for marching-orders came, and the early days of June saw the head-quarters of the Russian army established in Heidelberg, under the personal command of the Czar.

To the great joy of Ivan he looked well, and what surprised him still more, instead of the expected depression, there was such brightness in his countenance, such cheerfulness in his whole demeanour, that he thought some specially good tidings must have arrived. Meeting his friend Tolstoi, he asked him if such were the case. But Tolstoi reported, on the authority of his uncle the Grand Marshal, that there were no good tidings, but rather the reverse. Matters, he said, looked very serious. It was to be feared the whole strength of the Allies would be required to overthrow Napoleon, and a plan of united action was being arranged amongst them. The Czar was only anxious to do what was best for the general welfare, and it was probable he would be called upon to make the first attack; but time and place were as yet uncertain. " If I were the Czar," Tolstoi added indignantly, " I would see every Bourbon of them all drowned in the Seine before I would stir a finger to save them. You have heard of the practices of M. Talleyrand—how the old fox induced King Louis to enter into a secret treaty against us with the other Powers before the return of Buonaparte, who found the precious document on a table in the Tuileries, where it had been left behind by accident, and sent it to the Czar, just to show him what sort of friends he had."

" No, I did not hear that," said Ivan, keenly interested. " Well, what did the Czar do?"

" Put it into the fire. 'It is not *I* who am to be thought of,' he said, 'but the peace of the world.' I think, Prince Ivan, something else will be thought of if we take Paris again and M. de Talleyrand sees fit to stay there."

Ivan had abundance of leisure at this time, some of which he spent in wandering about the beautiful environs of Heidelberg, looking at the picturesque old town from the " Angel's Meadow," or watching the sun go down behind the shadowy purple hills. He sometimes prolonged these rambles until late in the evening, enjoying the solitude, for thought was busy within him, and had endless materials upon which to work.

On one of these occasions he strayed into a hilly path, secluded from general observation, and found that it led to a cottage, in the window of which a light was placed. He drew nearer, intending to ask his way; for he was surprised to find himself in a place probably not more than a mile from the town, and yet so entirely new to him. As he approached, he was struck by the singular air of neatness which distinguished a dwelling that in size and appearance was little more than a labourer's cabin. Presently he became aware that two or three other persons were toiling up the pathway. An old man, with a consumptive-looking girl leaning upon his arm, attracted his attention, and after a courteous salutation, he inquired of him in French, " Who lives yonder ?"

" That is the dwelling of the French lady who speaks so beautifully about our Lord Jesus Christ," returned the old man in the same language. " There is to be a prayer-meeting to-night, and Adèle and I are going. Will you come too, monsieur ? It will do you no harm to remember your Creator in the days of your youth."

" I trust I do remember him," said Ivan frankly; " but I shall be glad to come in. I suppose you are all Catholics here ?"

" The good French lady is a Catholic, but the young minister who expounds the Scriptures and, prays at the meetings is an ' Evangelical,' as they call it, from Switzerland. But they both love the Lord Jesus Christ, and talk as if they had seen him face to face."

" Ay, indeed they do," the girl said timidly. " They make you feel him so near."

The old man looked at her affectionately. " The visits of Madame, and the little meetings in her cottage, have indeed been new life to thee, my child," he said.—" You cannot think, monsieur, what a change there is in her—how much stronger and better she is since these happy thoughts have come to us."

" It is true," the girl assented. " Last year I thought I was dying; and oh, monsieur, the grave seemed so dark, so awful ! Now the fear of death is quite gone, thank God. Still I think He means to let me stay here a little longer, and I am glad—if it is his will."

" Come, dear," said her grandfather; " the door is open.— Come, monsieur."

Ivan hesitated.   "Shall I be welcome?" he asked.

"Oh yes, monsieur.   There is a gentleman, the son-in-law of Madame, I believe, who is always there, and another, a tall and handsome officer, who is seldom absent.   He seems to be a devout soldier, like Cornelius of old.   The rest are only friends —people like ourselves."

Ivan went in, took a seat on a bench beside his new friends, crossed himself, and bowed his head for a moment in prayer, then looked about him.   It was now late, and the little room was lighted, somewhat dimly, with candles of an ordinary kind. Fortunately he was placed where he could clearly see the very striking face and figure of the lady whom Adèle pointed out to him with the one whispered word—"Madame."   Her hair was silver, her face worn and haggard, with the look " of one that had travailed sore."   Less than fifty she could not have been—Ivan thought her much more; but hers had been one of those intense and passionate lives which are measured " not by months and years," but by fears and hopes, by joys and sorrows, perhaps by raptures and despairs.   There was fire in her dark eyes, and upon her pale and wasted features an expression at once of dreamy mysticism and of ecstatic ardour.   In youth she had been very beautiful, but no mere physical beauty could survive the storms that had swept over her.   Yet some better thing had come to her in place of her faded loveliness; so at least they said who saw her when she spoke of that which was God's special gift and message to her soul—" the love of Christ which passeth knowledge."   It was this secret whispered in her ear that, in spite of many errors and some serious faults, made Julie de Krudener a power for good in her day and generation. She had this treasure in an earthen vessel—in one that was flawed and well-nigh broken; but she had it, and gave of it to others.

Though Ivan could read little of this in her face, yet he was greatly struck by its expression.   "She ought to be a sibyl or a prophetess," he thought. The persons on either side of her scarcely attracted his attention at all; they were her son-in-law, the Baron de Berckheim, and a young Swiss pastor, whom Adèle called M. Empaytaz.

Just as the clock in an adjoining apartment began to strike, the door opened once more, and an officer of tall and commanding aspect entered the room. He went quietly to what was evidently his accustomed place, close to one of the lights, laid a Bible which he had brought with him on the table, and sat down. Ivan found it as much as he could do to suppress a cry of amazement—for it was the Czar. But he held his peace, and neither by look nor sign betrayed what he felt.

A prayer was offered, in which Ivan was far too bewildered to join; he scarcely even observed that it was unlike any prayer he had ever heard before, being extempore. Then the young pastor opened his Bible, read a passage, and began to expound it. But Ivan heard little; for he could not withdraw his eyes from the Czar, who was listening intently to every word, and who found and read every passage of Scripture referred to, making constant use of the little eye-glass he always carried in his sleeve.*

After some time, however, it occurred to Ivan that what interested the Czar so deeply ought to interest him too. Surely some mysterious power must dwell in the words which could thus enchain a soul already filled with weighty cares, tremendous responsibilities, soaring projects. Of what was the pastor speaking?

A sentence reached his ear that caught and held his thoughts, making him also an absorbed and eager listener. It would not be true to say that he forgot thenceforward the presence of the Czar—*that* would have been impossible—but he felt it only as an influence which added a conclusive weight of evidence and a potent undefinable charm to all that was said.

* All this, as also the account given at the end of this chapter, is strictly historical.

The pastor's theme was the forgiveness of sins, a subject now full of interest for Ivan. He had long outgrown the stage of spiritual life in which he said that he felt no "abyss" within him. Prayer, study of the Scriptures, and intercourse with Clémence had by this time taught him much of the hidden evil of his own heart. Of his sins he could say now in uttermost sincerity, "The remembrance of them is grievous unto me ; the burden of them is intolerable." How he was to be relieved of that burden had never been very clear to him. · He knew that pardon had come to mankind through Christ, and that it was connected in some way with his death upon the cross ; but how it was to reach his own need, to avail for his own sin, he scarcely knew. He supposed that he ought to read his Bible and to pray, to repent truly, to obey God in all things, and to put his whole trust in him ; and this was what for some time past he had been earnestly endeavouring to do.

But this new teacher, to whose voice his Czar was listening with such reverence, spoke of the death of Christ as an atonement not merely for the sins of the world, but for the special transgressions of each and every believer in him. "I can say," he added, "to each one present here, ' *Thy* sin was laid upon him.' Whoso believes in him, accepts the grace he offers, is forgiven and justified through him. Such has, even now, everlasting life, and cannot come into condemnation, but has passed from death unto life."

Ivan listened, wondering. Could this indeed be true ? Might it be possible for him to leave that room, not as he had entered it, hoping, praying, longing to be one day forgiven and accepted of God, but in actual present possession of that priceless boon ? This "glad evangel" would have seemed to him far too glad to be anything more than a beautiful dream, had not the radiant countenance of the Czar given the clearest evidence that *he* believed it. When the lecture was concluded—and to Ivan it seemed far too short—he hastened home to search his well-worn Testament, and to find out, if he could, from its pages whether these things were so.

After some hours of reading and prayer he reached the conclusion that it was he himself who had hitherto been blind and stupid. He marvelled that he had not earlier discovered what now seemed to shine upon him from every page of the Book he loved—the glorious truth of present forgiveness and acceptance through faith in Christ. And thus that night one who had hitherto only "believed" dimly and afar off "on the name of the Son of God" came to "know that he had eternal life," and to "believe" consciously and fully "on the name of the Son of God."*

A strange new joy burst upon his soul, flooding it with sunshine. He knelt down and thanked God for teaching him this truth. He could say now "*my* God" and "*my* Saviour." He knew now what was meant by those words of the apostle, "Therefore being justified by faith, we have peace with God through our Lord Jesus Christ."

At length he rose from his knees, went to the window of his apartment and looked out. The town clock had just struck the second hour after midnight. The scene without was calm and still, sleeping in the soft summer moonlight. It seemed to Ivan a beautiful world, over which God was watching, and which he had so loved as to send his Son to die for it. " To die for *me!*" he said in his heart. "What can I do to show my love and gratitude to him?"

As he stood looking out, a solitary figure passed down the silent empty street. Ivan saw it was the Czar, who was only then returning from the cottage on the hill. His attendants were well accustomed to their master's habit of taking long and lonely walks, and his absence, even for many hours, would occasion neither question nor remark. If, instead of commun-

---

* 1 John v. 13. The twofold use of the expression "believe on the name of the Son of God" in this passage is instructive.

ing with nature, he chose to spend the midnight hours in prayer and study of the Scriptures, none need know it.

But Ivan suddenly remembered that a grand review of the whole Imperial Guard was to take place that morning at six o'clock, so he dismissed the idea of writing at once to tell Clémence the wonders he had witnessed, and wisely threw himself upon his pallet to snatch a few hours of necessary slumber.

When he came to the parade-ground in the morning he felt like one bewildered. There, in the midst of his brilliant staff, their uniforms glistening with gold and jewels, and the costly trappings of their magnificent horses glancing in the sunlight, stood the Czar, at once the centre and the heart of all that martial pomp and pride. As Ivan, in his place in the Chevalier Guard, advanced, retreated, wheeled to the right or the left, in instant obedience to the word of command that issued from those imperial lips, he wondered silently which was the dream— this splendid pageant, or the scene last night in the lowly cottage; but when he looked again upon the calm and joyous face of the Czar he knew that both were real.

It was not until long afterwards that he heard the story of how God had spoken to the heart of the Czar. Madame de Krudener for some time past had been acquainted with the Empress Elizabeth, and other persons belonging to the Russian Court. What she heard from every one of the noble character of Alexander awakened in her mind an intense desire to be of use to him. "I have great things to say to him," she wrote to a friend; "for I have felt much upon his account. My business is to be without fear and without reproach, his to be at the feet of Christ." Such impulses are sent from above.

It was late in the night of the 4th of June. Alexander sat in his quarters at Heilbronn, depressed and weary, trying to read a book of devotion, but unable to profit by what he read. He had heard of the conversations of Madame de Krudener with his wife, and the thought passed through his mind, "I wish she would come and talk to me." At that moment his confidential attendant, Volkonski, entered the room, and told him, with much ill-humour, that there was a lady in the ante-chamber who insisted upon seeing him, notwithstanding the lateness of the hour.

"I cannot get rid of her, sire," said the irritated aide-de-camp.

Alexander inquired her name.

"*Madame de Krudener.*"

"Ask her to come in," said the Emperor. He afterwards told a friend that he felt as though he were dreaming, so strange did the coincidence appear to him.

Madame de Krudener entered. Certainly she did not fear the face of man. She prophesied no smooth things to the monarch of all the Russias. Perhaps she scarcely knew how far God had led him already; for she told him, with uncompromising boldness, that never yet had he come to the foot of the cross with the prayer of the publican on his lips, and that until he did so there could be neither pardon nor peace for him. Much more she added, perhaps not altogether wisely ; but since she held up Christ and his cross before him, there was power in her words to reach and to bless a heart which had been prepared of the Lord to receive them. Seeing him affected even to tears, she apologized for her boldness, and would have paused, but he entreated her to go on. This proved the first of numerous interviews.

Many a quiet talk over the Bible, prolonged into the hours of the early morning, took place in the labourer's cottage at Heidelberg, where Madame de Krudener had established herself in order to be near the Emperor. The young Swiss pastor, Empaytaz, who shared in these conversations, has left a brief record of them. One day he summoned courage to ask the Emperor plainly, "Sire, have you now peace with God ? Are you assured of the pardon of your sins ?"

Alexander was not a man who could hear or answer such a question without emotion. For a time he was silent, apparently questioning his own heart. Then "it seemed as if a dark veil was lifted from his face," and he looked up and answered, "Yes, I am happy—I am very happy. I have peace, even the peace of God. I am a great sinner; but since Madame"—glancing towards Madame de Krudener, who was present—"has shown me that Jesus came to seek and to save that which was lost, I know and believe that my sins are pardoned. The Word of God says that he who believes in the Son of God—in God the Saviour—is passed from death unto life, and shall not come into condemnation. I believe; yes, I have faith." Two words were at this time often on his lips—"I am very happy," and "I am a great sinner." They supplied the double key-note of his inner life. His joy in the forgiving Christ kept pace with his sorrow for the sins that had grieved him; the one grew and deepened in the same proportion as the other.

Years afterwards he said to a friend—tracing his conversion, it is interesting to observe, not merely to his conversations with Madame de Krudener, but to the whole course of God's dealings with him from the time of the burning of Moscow—"Since then I have known God as the Holy Scriptures have revealed him. Then I learned to understand, and I understand now, his will and his law; and the resolution to consecrate to him only, and to his glory, my life and my reign has ripened and strengthened within me. Since then I have become another man; to the deliverance of Europe from her ruin I owe my own salvation and deliverance. It is only since Christianity has become important above all things else to me, since faith in the Redeemer has been manifested in me, that his peace—for which I thank God—has entered into my soul. Ah, but I did not arrive there at once: the path by which I was led stretched across many a conflict and many a doubt."

It was no wonder that now he found it less difficult than

ever to pardon his enemies. It seemed to him something which he could not help doing, because he had been himself forgiven. "Why should I do otherwise?" he said, when Madame de Krudener expressed her surprise at some act of forgiveness extraordinary even *for him;* "have I not the gospel in my heart? I know only *that;* and I think that if any one were to compel me to go a mile with him, I should willingly go with him twain." So glad was his heart in those early days of faith and love.

God had given this man the seventh part of the habitable globe to rule over. He had given him the splendour of a throne, the wealth of an imperial treasury, the command of mighty armaments. He had given him even more—victory over all his foes, success in all his undertakings; at this time nothing that he sought to accomplish was denied him. Yet the man's deep heart was still unsatisfied. "All these things were too little" for him. One thing he desired of the Lord, that he sought after—"to behold the beauty of the Lord, and to inquire in his temple." That also God gave him. The brightest glory, the "crowning mercy" of Alexander's life, was no earthly triumph, no victory in war or diplomacy; it was that God answered him in the joy of his heart, and enabled him to say, with the poorest and humblest of his believing children, "My Father, my Saviour." The secret of the Lord was with him, and He showed him His covenant.

CHAPTER XXXIV

"Forbid it, Lord, that I should boast,
    Save in the cross of Christ, my God;
All the vain things that charm me most,
    I sacrifice them to his blood."

 "GREAT battle! Napoleon is annihilated! Wellington and the English have done it!" Such was the cry with which Tolstoi rushed breathless into the guard-room where Ivan and others were sitting. The tidings were not wholly unexpected, and yet they came with startling swiftness and suddenness. Only a few days before had Napoleon disclosed his real design, and poured his troops into Belgium. So rapidly had this movement been effected, that while Wellington was actually engaged in writing to the Czar to arrange a plan for an offensive campaign, the French had advanced upon the British and Prussian cantonments, and the firing had begun. Wellington's letter was dated the 15th of June, and by the evening of the 18th—one of the most momentous days in the world's history—Napoleon was a ruined and despairing fugitive.

It was only natural if, after the first outburst of exulting joy at the overthrow of the common enemy, the Russians remembered Moscow and the glories of the German campaigns, and said sadly each to the other, "Ah, why were not *we* there?"

"I do not grudge the English their laurels," said the captain of the Chevalier Guard. "They are a gallant race, and have been true throughout to the cause of Europe and of freedom. But why were not *we* at hand, instead of Blucher and those Prussians, to stand by them breast to breast?"

"We can only say, captain, it was the will of God," answered Ivan. "He sent the English and the Prussians to Belgium, and kept us here. He knows—and all the world knows too—that the Czar was as ready for the work as Wellington or Blucher, and would have done it quite as well."

The Czar himself recognized in this event the hand of God, and was satisfied. He had learned a lesson perhaps more difficult than that of being ready to do any work required of him— he was "ready *not* to do." Without an afterthought of jealousy he saw the work he had begun completed by another, to whom was given the crowning glory of dealing the fatal blow to the enemy *he* had first grappled with and overthrown. The heart-felt joy with which he gave thanks for the victory of Waterloo was deepened by the thought that the blood of his Russians, shed so freely before in the cause of Europe, had now been mercifully spared.

Three weeks afterwards the allied sovereigns entered Paris once more, and Louis Dix-huit returned in their wake. A second time had the way to his capital been made safe for him by his "dear friends the enemies," as he sarcastically and ungratefully styled his deliverers.

The Chevalier Guard attended their imperial master, and Ivan had the intense joy of a reunion with his young bride. His return was far more speedy than they had either of them dared to hope, and their hearts were filled with thankfulness. Madame de Salgues had removed from Versailles into the city, where she had taken a small house in a fashionable quarter, and Ivan obtained permission to reside with his friends.

Many things had happened during his absence; he had much to hear as well as to tell. The "Hundred Days" had left their impress upon all the household. Madame de Salgues told him she had come to Paris as much from a determination to defy "General Buonaparte" as from a sense of the insecurity of a town like Versailles in such troublous times. Henri, strange to say, had reaped advantage from the general confusion. When the power of Napoleon was re-established, Madame de Talmont deplored that the army, as a career for her son, was of course out of the question; and Henri thought this a favourable moment for broaching the ideas he had already uttered in confidence to Ivan. They were received much better than he had ventured to expect; and he was now, with his mother's consent, studying under a celebrated architect. "One must sometimes sacrifice one's feelings," she said, "though *never* one's principles. And, after all, what to do? The army is no longer a place for a man of honour; the bar you do not like; and to the Church there is at least one objection,—I do not wish the noble name of Talmont to die with you."

Emile was now a resident under the roof of his grandmother; he had ceased to wear the uniform of the Ecole Polytechnique. With a few other students who made their imperialism very obtrusive during the Hundred Days, he had the honour of sharing in the downfall of his hero by being expelled at the return of the Bourbons. This ended not only his military and scientific education, but, at least for the present, his hopes of obtaining a commission.

A day or two after his arrival, Ivan inquired for M. de Sartines and his daughter, whom he had not yet seen.

"No doubt they will be here to-morrow," Madame de Salgues answered. "They know you are with us. Besides, we are their near neighbours now, and they seldom leave us three days without a visit."

"Wish they would leave us three weeks!" said Emile. "That little girl is a perfect nuisance."

"My dear boy, how very ungallant you are!" Madame de

Salgues observed. "Still," she added, "I must own that Mademoiselle Stéphanie is not by any means improved."

"Not altogether *her* fault, poor child!" put in Clémence.

"Oh, *you* always speak for her, ma cousine, because she is like your shadow," said Emile. "Three mornings in the week, at least, Prince Ivan, she comes here. 'Papa,' she says," and the lad imitated the little girl's tones—"'papa will allow me to go to the Tuileries gardens, or the Champs Elysées, or the Louvre, if Mademoiselle Clémence will be so kind as to accompany me.' She has not even the grace to say, 'Madame la Princesse.' But now *you* have come, we shall have an end of all that."

"Then I am to understand," said Ivan, greatly amused, "that the deterioration in Mademoiselle Stéphanie's character is owing to her intercourse with Clémence?"

"Of course," returned Emile laughing.

"There are those about her," said Madame de Talmont more gravely, "who encourage and applaud her pert speeches; and that, to a child, is absolute cruelty."

"Who *did* encourage them during the Hundred Days, you mean to say," Emile resumed. "While the Emperor was in power, you were all of you glad to hear, even from the lips of a child, whom no one could punish or seriously blame, the impertinences the grown-up Legitimists were longing to utter, but dared not."

"Some of us," said Madame de Salgues with dignity, "never condescended to conceal our opinions. You will do me the justice to remember, Emile, that I gave to every one, as my chief reason for coming into Paris, my desire to show the usurper I was not afraid of him."

"As if the Emperor—" Emile began indignantly, but fortunately checked himself in time, and turned off his annoyance with a laugh. "You forget, my dear grandmother," he said, "that there was another reason yet more potent. The truth is,

Prince Ivan, we came into town to avoid that poor M. de Cranfort. Since the auspicious morning when my cousin became Madame la Princesse, the unfortunate gentleman has not been quite in possession of his senses. It is reported that he carries two loaded pistols about with him, and threatens to shoot first Clémence and then himself."

Every one present laughed heartily, assuring Ivan there was not a word of truth in the story.

" As much, I suppose," said Ivan in a low voice to Emile, " as in another story you told me once—about M. de Sartines."

" I am glad enough now *that* was false," Emile answered graciously. " That child would have been the death of Clémence. I hope M. de Sartines, if he does marry, will marry a dragon, able to keep her in order. But really," he added, " M. de Cranfort is not quite sane. I have heard him say the most extraordinary things ; and, do you know, he was for some years at Charenton ?" After a short pause, he resumed suddenly— " Prince Ivan, how is the Emperor Alexander ?"

" In excellent health," said Ivan cheerfully.

" I am truly rejoiced to hear it."

" Very kind of you," returned Ivan smiling, but with a slight air of surprise at his emphatic manner.

" Because," resumed Emile, in a tone of mystery, " as we are all friends here, I may observe that we have heard rumours— extraordinary rumours."

" Do you mean about his illness at Vienna ? It is true he had a fall from his horse, and—"

" Oh, *that* is nothing. That is not what I mean. But the strangest things are said of him here, and in the best circles too, where you know he was adored last year. In the Faubourg St. Germain all sorts of ' *on dits* ' are rife about him. People say he has become very singular,—a fanatic, a pietist, and I know not what else ; that a certain crazy old lady—"

" Hush, hush, Emile," said Madame de Salgues and Madame

de Talmont almost at the same moment. Clémence looked anxiously at Ivan, and Henri started up indignantly. "I, at least, will not stay to listen to such folly," he said.

"A truce, for once, to your championship of the Czar," said Emile. "I suppose Prince Ivan may speak now."

Ivan might have answered angrily, but for certain words which thrilled through his heart, taking all the bitterness out of Emile's reckless taunts: "Esteeming the reproach of Christ greater riches than the treasures of Egypt"—only *he* said "the treasures of *Russia*," and the magnificent crown jewels he had seen in St. Petersburg flashed before his eyes in a dazzling, bewildering maze of light and colour. For a moment he did not speak; then he asked, with a gentleness that surprised every one, "What were you going to say, Emile?"

"Nothing—at least not much," was the rather apologetic answer. "Rumour always exaggerates things, and most especially the rumour of St. Germain. Perhaps it is *not* true, after all, that Madame de Krudener makes the Emperor Alexander fast and wear sackcloth; or that she has persuaded him he is the white angel of peace, and Napoleon the black demon of war; or that—but, as I say, these may be foolish stories. Still it seems to be undeniable that the consummate artist, who last year played the *rôle* of magnanimous conqueror with such *éclat* amongst us, is now assuming, by way of variety, that of medieval saint. Henri Quatre is masquerading in the guise of St. Louis. Seriously,—what has come over him, Prince Pojarsky? Is his mind really affected, or is it all some deep-laid political scheme?"

"Certainly, Emile, I am amazed at your audacity," Madame de Salgues interposed again. "Prince Ivan has the patience of a saint."

"From *your* lips, madame," said Ivan bowing, "I accept the name as a compliment; though others, it seems, use it for a reproach.—Emile, I am not careful to answer you in this matter.

You have but to watch the course of events, and you will see that there is not a man in Europe of sounder understanding than my Czar. Of what he has already accomplished I need not remind you; and I had rather not, considering *whom* he has overcome. If his religious principles expose him to reproach, it is only 'the reproach of the foolish.' They are not new to him, though of late they have deepened and strengthened. All those stories you allude to about his intercourse with Madame de Krudener are fabrications. The grain of truth they contain is the fact that God has been pleased to send him a message by the lips of a woman;—and why should he not?"

To this there was no answer, and the little party broke up. But Ivan drew Emile aside. "I want a word with you," he said. "Do you know in what temper the minds of men are now?"

"Do you mean the minds of Royalists?" asked Emile bitterly. "That I do. I believe that if they had the power they would put every Imperialist of us all to the sword; or if not, it would only be to reserve us for the dungeon and the scaffold. The Bourbons gnash their teeth upon us. The Duchess of Angoulême says openly, 'Mercy cannot be distinguished from weakness.'"

"Ah, my friend, can you wonder? When that stern, sorrow-stricken woman had a girl's tender heart, it was turned to stone by the cruel murder of both her parents and of her young inno-cent brother. But others who have not the same wrongs to avenge are quite as eager for vengeance."

"They are a bad set, those Bourbons," said Emile.

"Certainly *I* shall not plead for them. They have not used us or our Emperor well. But consider that in the eyes of a German every Frenchman is as odious as a Buonapartist can be in those of a Royalist. The Prussians talk openly of dismem-bering France; and, Emile, who is to hinder them? Not Louis —he is powerless; not Austria—she will share the spoils; not England—she is just, and even generous, but do you expect her to go to war single-handed in the cause of her enemies?"

"*One* man would have hindered them," said Emile—"he who is a captive now. France will soon wish the Emperor back again."

"I respect your faith in your hero, though I do not share it. But, my dear Emile, you cannot deny that, however it has come to pass, the most stupendous genius of modern times has proved, practically, the most stupendous failure."

"Is success always the test of greatness?"

"By no means. But Napoleon has always acted as though it were; has aimed at it, lived for it, sacrificed everything to it, and finally lost it. As he has now left—been forced to leave— his country to the deadly enemies his ambition has raised up against her, what will the end be, Emile?"

"Who can tell? As for me, I feel ready to hang myself."

"Pray for the life and health of my Czar. You will see him stand between the avengers and their prey; between prostrate France and victorious Germany; and even, so far as becomes a foreigner, between prostrate Imperialists and victorious Royal- ists."

"That it should come to this! That France—our proud, glorious France—should have to thank a Czar of Russia!"

"Where is the shame of thanking him, if God has given him the power to befriend her?"

"*God?*" Emile repeated scornfully. "That's your way of talking, you Russians. Don't you see now that it ends in folly and fanaticism?"

Ivan laid his hand on the shoulder of Emile. "My dear boy," he said, "do you know why I am talking with you thus? Not to make you believe in my Czar. *His* glory is in good keeping; and if you prefer Napoleon for a hero, I have no more to say. The cause I want to plead with you is not his, but your own. You call him fanatic and dreamer because of his faith in God and in Christ. I want to show you that it is this very faith which makes him generous, merciful, just."

"I do not see the good of faith," Emile broke in passionately. "I don't mean *religious* faith, but faith of any kind. We had faith—oh, such intense, glorious, undoubting faith—in the Emperor and in his star. And we loved him so! You cannot understand it, Prince Ivan, but it is true. Do you remember Henri's friend, the Old 'Garde' Rougeard, who came to tell me of the Emperor's return? He fell at Waterloo; a comrade of his, who crept back wounded to die amongst his children, told me about it. When all was lost, the remnant of the Old Guard was called upon to surrender. 'La Garde meurt, mais ne se rend pas,' was the proud reply; and those brave men died where they stood.* Poor Rougeard took the colours from the falling ensign, and with his dying hand wrapped them round his breast. 'Vive l'Empereur!' was his last word."

"And the Emperor lived, *after* such followers as these," said Ivan with tears in his eyes. Emile saw the tears, and they did him more good than a hundred admonitions. Ivan presently resumed: "Suppose, Emile, that when your Emperor dies some one were to try to persuade the world that he had never existed,—that his whole personality, life, and career was a fiction from first to last?"

"Any one who tried it would be laughed at for his pains."

"Of course. Every effect must have a cause. Men do not love, trust in, die for that which is not, and never has been."

"What are you trying to say?" asked Emile, a little surprised.

"That the existence of Christ is as certain as that of Napoleon."

"Was. There was once such a Person, I am sure."

"*He is*. In the year three thousand six hundred—if the world last so long—who do you think will die for the name of Napoleon Buonaparte? Who will love him, obey him, follow him as my Czar on his throne to-day is not ashamed to confess

* This story is not true; but it was believed at the time.

that he loves and follows *his King?* Nay, even the glory of my Czar will pass away, the jewels that sparkle in his crown of fame will pale and wane (*that* will not matter, for he will have cast it long ere then at his Redeemer's feet); but the glory of Christ will last for ever and ever."

"I know you really believe in the Christian religion. I cannot, but I respect those who can."

"I believe in *Christ*, Emile; and I want you to believe in him too. I want you to search and look, and never rest until you find out—first that he is, then that he is worthy of all your faith and love."

"Where do you want me to look?"

"If you will, at the lives of those who profess this faith. See if it does not produce better and nobler results than any other principle of action. But I had far rather you looked at the picture of Christ himself as you will find it in the holy Scriptures."

"Well, I will try," said Emile, evidently touched. "At least I can read. I have more than time enough for reading now. I study mathematics with Henri; but he is *so* tiresome that every lesson ends in a quarrel.—Last term I had the second prize at the Polytechnic, and now I expected the first. Was it not hard to be turned out?"

"Very; but you have the consolation of suffering in the cause of your Emperor. If I were you, Emile, I would study hard enough to show the world I was no loser. And, one word more; I would keep away from political meetings, *secret* meetings especially, and eschew plots and intrigues. They are only snares and pitfalls dug for the feet of those who cling to a lost cause."

"Lost!—Oh, Prince Ivan!"

"My friend, Napoleon has played his game and lost his stake. That is plain to every one. But *you* have the cards still in your hand. Do not spoil your chance."

"Do you mean my chance of success? I thought you despised success."

"I mean your chance of a noble life. But I ought not to have said 'chance.' There is none."

"There is destiny."

"There is *will.* Your will, and God's will, which means only good to you, if you will accept it."

"There is something in what you say,—especially about secret meetings," he added in a lower tone. "But it is late ; I must go to those mathematics. Good night." He turned away, softly whistling the air of a song very popular with the Imperialists, "Veillons au salut de l'Empire." "*I* shall watch henceforward over the safety of something else, very dear to Prince Pojarsky," thought the conceited but generous boy. "How little he guesses what plans we have talked of—we Buonapartists—at those secret meetings he denounces ! Such, for instance, as the assassination of a certain great personage, in *his* innocent eyes the greatest in the world ! But if ever again, in my presence, any one dares to drop a hint on that subject, I swear the words shall be his last !"

CHAPTER XXXV.

"THE GRAY SISTER OF HEARTS."

" Why should we dream youth's draught of joy,
   If pure, would sparkle less;
Or that the cup would sooner cloy
   The Saviour deigned to bless?"

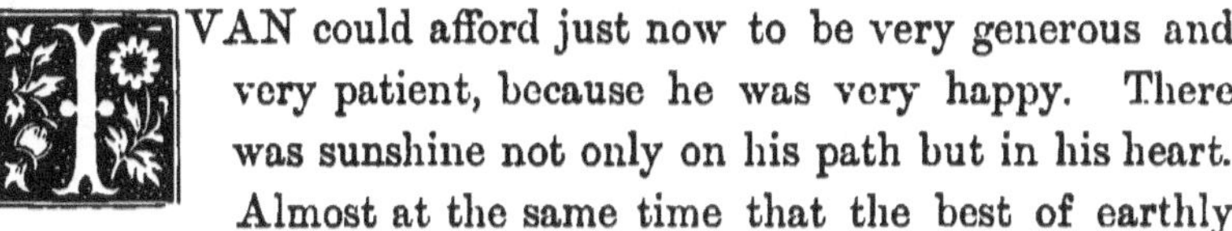

IVAN could afford just now to be very generous and very patient, because he was very happy. There was sunshine not only on his path but in his heart. Almost at the same time that the best of earthly blessings had been given him, he was given also the conscious possession of the love divine; and he received it in thankful, trustful joy. Christ had come to him, not in sorrow, as he comes to many, but making the brightest hours of life infinitely brighter by his presence.

He thought he had nothing to do but to tell Clémence the new happiness he had found, and that she would immediately understand and share it; that she would no longer be content to wait for acceptance with God until some future day, but would henceforth enjoy the glad consciousness of being already accepted in the Beloved. But to her tender conscience and thoughtful mind difficulties presented themselves which had never troubled the eager, impulsive Ivan. Her fears of self-deception, of presumption, of spiritual pride, raised up a host of shadowy disturbers of the peace within, which Ivan had not skill enough to combat. He urged her therefore to come with him and hear the teachers from whom he had learned so much.

Madame de Krudener had come to Paris, and established her-self in a house adjoining the Elysée Bourbon, where she held what would now be called "drawing-room meetings," to which all the rank and fashion of Paris were flocking. It was strange that for once religious meetings became the rage in the very stronghold of ungodliness, vice, and frivolity. Many of the visitors had their curiosity piqued by the extraordinary reports that reached them, and wished to ascertain the truth for them-selves; many more "went to scoff," and of these a goodly number "remained to pray."* But the greatest attraction to these *soirées* was the hope of seeing the Emperor of Russia—a hope, however, not often gratified. Far from parading his religion, Alexander was strongly tempted to conceal it. His sensitive nature dreaded ridicule; and he was well aware that a profession of personal religion would expose him to the most polished shafts of that exquisite Parisian wit, which, keen as the scimitar of Saladin, could divide asunder, with fine, unerring touch, the most delicate fibres of thought and feeling. Even in Protestant London—which he always placed in honourable con-trast to Paris for seriousness and morality—he had observed that religious laymen were looked upon almost with contempt. It was therefore not without much prayer and conflict that he took his stand on the side of God in the face of all the world.

He did not often mingle with the throng that filled the drawing-rooms of Madame de Krudener to overflowing on three or four evenings of every week; but he frequently came later, when his day's work was over, for prayer and quiet study of the Scriptures. These hours of communion were prolonged until far into the night; yet he always rose at five in the morning, so that no man was able to reproach him with any lack of diligence

* "Many a Parisian scoffer, going to hear her in her drawing-room, which was open to all, returned," says Sainte Beuve, "at least thoroughly subdued by her personal magnetism. Those who seriously believe in the intervention of Providence in the affairs of the world should not judge her too superciliously: 1815 was a decisive epoch, and to religious minds it may well have appeared that the crisis was grave enough to demand a prophet."

in business, nor was any part of the heavy burden of care and responsibility that fell to his lot neglected or avoided.

Clémence would gladly have accompanied Ivan to some of Madame de Krudener's meetings; and Madame de Talmont, though she had her objections, might have gone also, but for the determined opposition of Madame de Salgues. "In my time," said the lady of the old régime, "women did not preach; and certainly, if they had done so, 'gens comme il faut' would not have gone to hear them. Why should you need Madame de Krudener to tell you to repent and believe? I suppose you hear those Christian duties inculcated every Sunday and holiday, when you go to church."

"Many people go to hear Madame de Krudener who never enter a church," Clémence observed.

"That is possible," returned Madame de Salgues. "Sick people, who will not eat wholesome food, sometimes take a fancy for extraordinary messes, and a wise doctor gives them their way. But you, my dear niece, are certainly not in that position."

"Madame de Krudener does not always speak; sometimes it is M. Empaytaz, a Swiss pastor, who gives the address," Clémence ventured again.

"Worse and worse, my dear! A *Protestant!*" cried Madame de Salgues in a tone of horror. "I sometimes wonder what the world is coming to. All barriers, all distinctions seem to be swept away in these revolutionary days."

Henri was sitting in another part of the room, occupied with a book; and none, save Clémence, noticed the flush of pain that overspread his face at these words.

Ivan and Clémence agreed that it would not be right for the latter to set aside the expressed wish of a relative to whom she owed so much. Therefore, instead of listening to Madame de Krudener or Empaytaz, she studied the Bible diligently, both alone and with Ivan, and lost nothing by going to the fountain-head, instead of to streams, not always of undeniable purity.

Yet her desire to see and hear the remarkable woman whose words were making so great an impression was very natural, and was destined at length to be gratified. One morning, while the family were seated at their eleven o'clock *déjeûner*, they were honoured by a visit from Stéphanie de Sartines. The little girl was intensely conscious of a new silk dress—green shot with pink, which shone and glistened with each of her quick, restless movements—and of a large Tuscan hat adorned with a wreath of blush roses. She exchanged greetings, in a highly satisfied tone, with every one in the room, and then, coming to the side of Clémence, began as usual, "Papa says he will allow me—"

The smile that passed round the group was not unnoticed by the observant Stéphanie. She looked up quickly, but resumed her little speech after a moment's hesitation. "Papa says he will allow me to go and hear Madame de Krudener preaching to the children, if you will be kind enough to accompany me, mademoiselle,—I mean Madame la Princesse; and if M. le Prince will permit you," she continued, bowing towards Ivan with the air of a little queen.

"If no one objects more than I do, Madame la Princesse is quite at your service, mademoiselle," answered Ivan, with a smile and a bow as ceremonious as her own.—"I am on duty to-day, as you are aware, m'amie," he added in a lower voice to Clémence.

"I thought the old lady kept her ghostly admonitions for those who needed them—hardened transgressors like M. de Talleyrand, for example," said Emile. "Does she lecture chil dren too, for variety?"

"It appears she does. *You* ought to go and hear her, M. Emile," returned Stéphanie gravely. "It would do you good. —But really, madame," she added, addressing Clémence again, "you *must* come. It will be so—so delightful, so exciting, so *amusing*."

"My dear child, one does not go to a religious service to be amused," observed Madame de Talmont.

"Ah, madame, you cannot imagine how delicious it is! My cousin Coralie has told me all about it. Madame de Krudener visited Coralie's pension and preached to the young ladies, and you never saw anything like it! They were all moved—they shed torrents of tears—it must have been grand, beautiful; a great deal better than going to the theatre—even when Talma is acting, as papa would say. I would give the whole world to see it for myself, and to know what it is all about. Come—*do come*, mademoiselle—madame, I mean.—Prince Ivan, I beg of you to send her with me."

"You are most welcome to her escort as far as I am concerned," Ivan answered. "But, mademoiselle, if you or I were going to meet even an earthly monarch, I think we should do so with a little more seriousness."

"Ah, that reminds me—that is the best thing of all. Coralie says that the Czar is coming to the meeting to see the children. —What do you think of *that*, M. Emile?"

"I think he may go wherever he pleases; he is sure to be welcome," returned Emile with unusual graciousness.

Ivan gave him a quick glance of surprise and pleasure, then said, turning to Stéphanie, "May I ask where you heard that, mademoiselle? For it does not look very probable."

"Oh, M. de Berckheim told Coralie's father; for he is a great friend of his. This is not a little meeting in a school-room, Prince Ivan; it will be quite a grand affair. Any children who like may come, and grown-up people too. There will be crowds, no doubt. I daresay we shall find it hard to get seats. It will be altogether delightful. Besides, I am longing to see the Czar."

A few questions about time and place were asked, and the answers showed that Stéphanie had carefully considered every detail of her plan. "We can get a fiacre," she said, "and be there in three-quarters of an hour."

Madame de Salgues, who had been silent hitherto, now spoke in a gracious tone. "If you are to hear this woman at all, Clémence, it appears to me that you could not do so in a manner less open to objection. Go, my dear niece, if you wish it."

"I am at your service, Stéphanie," Clémence said smiling; and she rose to leave the room. As she passed the chair of her aunt she kissed her hand with a grateful look; and the old lady responded kindly, "I hope you will enjoy yourself, my dear." She had been greatly touched, though she had said nothing, by the quietness with which Clémence had given up what was evidently her own and her husband's wish, in deference to her feelings.

"I must own, mon ami," Clémence said to Ivan, who joined her while she was making her simple toilet, "I think it is a pity the Czar should go to a meeting such as Stéphanie expects this to be."

"Why so, if it please you, my princess?" asked Ivan, rather surprised.

"Because," she answered, "the children will all be gazing at the great people instead of listening to what Madame de Krudener is saying to them. Besides, it is bad for them—is it not?—to think themselves objects of attention. The less the religion of children is noticed and talked about the better."

"Oh, you need not fear. The presence of half-a-dozen gentle-men, in a large public room, will be scarcely observed by the children; and who is to tell them that one of them is the Czar? You don't know, Clémence," he added with a change of tone, "how his heart yearns over the little ones. In England, no sight pleased him so well as the annual gathering of the charity children under the dome of St. Paul's Cathedral. And I have seen him myself in Dresden, when he lodged in the Bruhl Palace, come out in the evening to watch the children playing in the gardens, which he would not allow to be closed against them. Three little princesses—'daughters of Russia'—are sleeping in the Church of St. Alexander Nevsky at St. Petersburg, and God never gave him a son."

But Stéphanie's impatient voice was heard in the passage, so, after a tender little farewell to Clémence, Ivan escorted the ladies to a fiacre, and saw them depart.

The room where the meeting was held was crowded when they arrived. However, Coralie saw her cousin and Clémence seeking a place, and persuaded the governess who had charge of her party to make room for them. Clémence at first regretted this, for the girls began to chatter amongst themselves about their dress and other trifles in a way well calculated to put to flight all serious impressions.

Meanwhile she looked with much interest on the face and figure of the person about whom Ivan had told her so much. Perhaps on the whole she was disappointed : the worn and haggard features had in her eyes no charm save one, the charm of intense earnestness and utter sincerity. The thought passed through her mind, " That is a woman from whom I might learn much as a teacher, but I could never trust her as a guide." One thing, however, she learned that day—that the Pietists neither thought lightly of sin themselves, nor induced others to think lightly of it. The "Gray Sister of Hearts" (so Clémence remembered Ivan's calling Madame de Krudener) denounced in scathing accents just those sins of which the world thinks least— the sins of childhood. Conceit, selfishness, disobedience, forgetfulness of God, were exposed in terms that Clémence might have thought exaggerated, had she not remembered that the poison-seed is the poison-plant in embryo. Never before had she felt so thoroughly—

> "That the most childish sin a child can do
> Is yet a sin which Jesus never did
> When Jesus was a child, and yet a sin
> For which he came in lowly pain to die."

By-and-by the speaker's tone changed, and with a tenderness of look and manner of which Clémence felt all the charm, she spoke of "the child-loved Lover of children," of the Shepherd who gathers the lambs in his arms and carries them in his bosom, who gave his life for the sheep and the lambs so willingly, so patiently, so lovingly. "My little child," she seemed to say to every one present, "he died for *thee*, he loves *thee*, he speaks to *thee* and says, 'My son, or my daughter, give me thine heart, and give it to-day.'"

While she listened, the head of Stéphanie had sunk very low, her face was quite shaded by the broad leaf of her hat, and Clémence saw with wonder that tears were falling quick and fast upon the cherished silk, utterly unheeded by its owner. She tried gently to take her hand; but Stéphanie, with a quick, impetuous movement, drew it away.

When the meeting was at an end, any who wished for private conversation were invited to remain.

"Shall we go home, dear?" Clémence whispered. Stéphanie shook her head with a vehement negative. Her slight frame was quivering with convulsive sobs. After an interval Clémence asked gently, "Why are you weeping so bitterly? Tell me, dear. Is it for your sin?"

The child looked up quickly. "Not all—not *most*—for that. Most because I have grieved Him, and He is so good."

Clémence said no more; she prayed in silence for her little friend. Her own deep inward life had taught her great reverence for the soul of another. Even in that of a child there might be mysteries with which no hand but God's could deal aright. Stéphanie prayed too, for the first time in her life.

Meanwhile the "Gray Sister of Hearts" was going quietly amongst the children who, like Stéphanie, had remained, advising, comforting, and instructing them, according to the power God had given her. At last she came to Stéphanie. "My little girl, why do you weep?" she asked, with that peculiar tenderness which in great measure accounted for the spiritual magnetism she exercised.

"I am holding out my hand to the Lord Jesus, and he will not take it," was the answer.*

"That is only because his arms are around you already, dear little one," she said. She added many loving words, to which Clémence as well as Stéphanie listened with deep interest. At length she kissed a farewell to her little pupil, in whose eyes a happy light had begun to shine. "I am ready to go now," said Stéphanie, putting her hand in that of Clémence.

It was late when they reached home. Madame de Salgues and Madame de Talmont were beginning to grow uneasy, and Henri had just volunteered to go in search of the wanderers. They were warmly welcomed; and, as had been already arranged, Stéphanie remained to spend the rest of the day with her friends.

While Madame de Talmont asked Clémence many questions about the meeting, Emile opened a fire of banter upon Stéphanie, about the effect her dress and appearance had produced upon the assembly, and especially upon the Czar, "The very least I expected of his Imperial Majesty," he said, "was to send an aide-de-camp to inquire who was the charming young lady in pink and green silk."

But Stéphanie did not reply with her usual saucy readiness; and Henri, noticing her agitation, quickly came to her relief, making some commonplace inquiry about the numbers who were present.

"Ah, I see what is the matter," said Emile: "the Czar was not there after all. Very unlike him, to disappoint so many young ladies."

Stéphanie gave the surprising answer, "I do not know if he was there. I never thought of him at all."

Then Clémence drew her gently away to her own room, leaving her there in quiet until supper was ready. As she went

---

* Really given to Madame de Krudener by a child of Stéphanie's age, at a meeting similar to the one described above.

out Madame de Salgues observed, "I really think that child is improving—at least in appearance. This evening she looks almost pretty."

"I have always said that Mademoiselle Stéphanie de Sartines will one day be a beautiful woman," Henri answered in a tone of decision.

CHAPTER XXXVI

"The shadow had passed from his heart and brow,
And a deep calm filled his breast;
For the peace of God was his portion now,
And his weary soul found rest."

"YOU must all come, my friends," said Ivan. "I have set my heart upon it." He had been describing the preparations for the grand review of the Russian army which was to take place a few days later in the "Plaine des Vertus."

"Ah, yes; you must all go, certainly," remarked Madame de Salgues.

"Unless Madame de Salgues is obliging enough to be of the party, no one will go," said Ivan. "I know that at least I can speak for Clémence."

"But what to do, my friend? It will take three days at the very least—one to go, one to stay, and one to return. And then, think of the crowds! Who knows even whether we shall find room in any of the hotels?"

"You need have no anxiety about that, madame. The Emperor has engaged all the hotels and posting establishments of the district. I have only to obtain his order, through his secretary, for everything you require, and I know that I can do so. You must stay for the religious service on the day following the review; it will be the Emperor's name-day."

"I should certainly like to witness *that*," said Madame de Talmont.

"I am sorry that my duties must deprive me of the pleasure of being your attendant cavalier," pursued Ivan. "But Henri and Emile will more than supply my place; and you may perhaps wish to invite a friend to join your party."

"If we engage a carriage," said Madame de Talmont, "we can accommodate another lady. Who shall it be, ma tante?"

"It is for Prince Ivan to express his wishes on that point."

Ivan gracefully referred the choice to the ladies, and Clémence pleaded for Stéphanie. "She has been so good lately, poor child," she said. "And this will be a pleasure she will remember all her life."

"By all means. Let us have her father too," suggested Emile. "For I hear that this wonderful Madame de Krudener is to be there; and as she is the only person who has ever succeeded in taming mademoiselle, perhaps a little arrangement with M. de Sartines—"

"Hold thy peace, Emile," said Madame de Salgues. "I will have no jests levelled in my presence at religious persons, be they whom they may; and I suppose this enigmatical old lady is some kind of irregular nun, or at least a Carmelite. I cannot pretend to say what she is :—but, my dear grandson, you must permit me to observe that your tone of late has been very offensive to me. It is entirely that of the Empire, not that in which you have been educated. Your manners, too, have quite deteriorated. They are becoming absolutely bourgeoise."

"Pardon, madame," returned Emile with a bow. "I am sorry they do not please you. But you must acknowledge they are not likely to be mended by the life I am leading," he added a little bitterly. "Idleness is the mother of mischief."

Madame de Salgues relinquished the useless altercation with a sigh; and Ivan for the second time sought a private interview with Emile, following him into the little room where he was wont to indulge his habit of smoking at a safe distance from his grandmother.

Ivan showed him a piece of paper. " I shall not insult you by asking whether you know anything about this," he said.

It was the copy of a letter addressed to the Czar by a person who signed himself " Captain of Regicides," threatening him with instant death if he would not immediately proclaim Napoleon II.

" I should like to hear you do it ! " cried Emile indignantly, as he flung the paper on the ground, and set his heel upon it. " I should like better still to find out the author of that precious document, and to treat him *so*," he added, grinding it beneath his foot. " Such scoundrels bring the good cause into disrepute. But the Emperor Alexander has too much courage and good sense to regard them."

" True ; yet others may be forced to regard them for him. The threat has not been an empty one, Emile. They have tried to poison him."

" *Never !* " cried Emile, starting and changing colour.

" And nearly succeeded," Ivan continued sadly. " All our joy in the present, all our happy plans for the future, might to-day have been turned into mourning. And not ours only—"

" But how was it ? " Emile interrupted.

" It occurred to his cook, contrary to his usual practice, to taste the wine laid ready for his master's use at dinner. The poor fellow's life has been saved with the utmost difficulty."

" That is abominable ! " cried Emile. " If I but knew the miscreant who did it, I would spare the executioner a bad business. Peste ! if we want a victim, we Imperialists—and perhaps it is not unnatural we should—we ought to take Gneisenau who proposed a scaffold for the Emperor, Talleyrand who deceived and betrayed everybody impartially all round, or old Louis himself who ran away from his throne without striking a blow.

We might spare at least the one chivalrous enemy who always spared us."

"It would be better for yourselves," said Ivan. "And for others too. Baron Muffling* says he is longing to get the Czar out of Paris, as, if he is assassinated, or even insulted, no power on earth would be able to avert a general massacre of the inhabitants by the Allies."

"Which *you* would take part in, Prince Ivan."

Ivan was silent for a moment, then he said in a tone of deep feeling, "Do not ask me. I am a Christian, I hope, but I am a *man* also. I know not what I would do. God grant I may not be put to the test."

There was a pause, then Emile asked, "What does *he* say?"

"If I tell you, will you scoff?"

"At him? No; that I can promise you."

"Well, then, he has asked his friends to pray for him."

"Useless, but harmless," said Emile with an air of generous toleration. "Very clever persons have worn amulets; and even the great Napoleon was not free from a superstition or two."

"Not as an amulet against steel or poison does my Czar think of prayer. 'Do not pray,' he says, 'that I may be guarded from the evil that man can do to me; I have no fears on these grounds. I know that I am in the hands of God.'"

"That is like Napoleon's confidence in his star," thought Emile. He had almost uttered his thought aloud, but he checked himself in time. For he reflected that this was not blind confidence in a thing, in some unknown power—chance, fate, or destiny—but rather, what Ivan had spoken of to him before, trust in a *Person*.

Ivan resumed presently, "What he desires his friends to ask for him is protection from the evil influences of the world, and

* The Governor of Paris.

specially *from those of this city.* Emile, you understand something of his meaning, and of mine ? "

Emile turned aside to avoid meeting the eyes of Ivan, for his words had touched a chord within. Thrown in idleness upon the great, unquiet, corrupt world of Paris, the position of the youth was truly perilous. Secret political intrigue was wooing him upon the one hand, while vice was spreading its snares to allure him upon the other. Ivan had succeeded in conveying an emphatic warning at the same time against both.

" I wish I were more like Henri," Emile said at last. " He is sometimes tiresome—a little, but he is as steady as a rock, a perfect gentleman, and a stainless man of honour."

" God will help you, Emile ; then all will be well," said Ivan as he left the room.

The manifold excitements of the next few days put aside for the time all graver thoughts. The unpretending carriage of the De Talmonts mingled with a continuous stream of other vehicles on their way to the Plaine des Vertus, and the striking and amusing sights afforded by the journey were almost sufficient to turn the brain, of Stéphanie at least. But the grand review itself confused and bewildered the imaginations of far more experienced spectators. " Do not ask me what I think of it," said Madame de Salgues in the evening, when at last a happy, weary, excited party sat down to rest in their hotel. " I feel as if for a whole year at least I had not been myself, but some one else, and had been living amidst glare and glitter, bright colours and splendid uniforms. Such masses of men moving as one—such glorious martial music !—such deafening thunder of artillery !—I could not have dreamed of anything like it."

Emile whistled softly to himself. " It has made my grandmother quite poetical," he said.

" That is not wonderful," remarked Madame de Talmont. " It was indeed the poetry of war."

" Yes," said Henri thoughtfully ; " and if *I* had not been

forced to read the stern and rugged prose, I should have looked at it with other eyes.   But all the time I could not help thinking how many gallant men like those I had seen die in misery."

"But did you know what they were doing at the end?" asked Emile.   "That last tremendous charge, that made all the ladies start and change colour, was what is called a charge in line.   It was right well done too, though it has long been thought no one could manage it except the English.   With such material, and under such leadership, nothing is impossible. With an army like that," he added a little sadly, "Napoleon would conquer the world."

Just then Ivan came in to pay his friends a short visit, and to see that they were comfortably accommodated.   Many were the compliments addressed to him and the questions asked of him, especially by Emile.   "The discipline of your army seems admirable," said he.   "I should like to know how it is managed."

"Like all other discipline worth the name," Ivan answered; "by justice and mercy.   The Czar knows how to punish, though he loves to pardon."

"Of course he must punish sometimes; but one does not hear of it."

"He knows how to punish in ways you could not hear of. A word, a look, silence even, he can make a terrible punishment.   But this power he rarely uses.   I have heard it said that he 'can annihilate a man without touching him;' but I have never seen him do it, and I hope I never shall."

"Nor I either," said Emile.

"I know of *one* reproof he administered.   One of our colonels failed to have his regiment ready at the time appointed for reviewing it.   He received a severe reprimand, and was broken-hearted.   The Czar saw it, sought him out afterwards, and comforted him, telling him that 'it was not for one mistake the faithful services of years could be forgotten.'"

"If," said Madame de Talmont, "there was any drawback to our enjoyment to-day, it was the difficulty we found in recognizing the great personages we wished to see amidst all the brilliant confusion. We needed our Chevalier of Malta by our side to point them out to us."

"He would willingly have been there, madame," said Ivan bowing. "But to-morrow you will find it easier to distinguish them. At the grand religious ceremony all will be present. You will see the royal personages assembled in the tent where they are to hear the service."

"Ah," said Stéphanie, "that will be delightful! I am longing to see the great English Duke Vellington, who conquered General Buonaparte,—or the ex-Emperor, as one may say," she added considerately, with a sly glance at Emile.

Their expectations were not disappointed. The solemn pageant of the following day was graced by a glittering galaxy of royal stars, upon which no eye could rest without emotion. Beside Alexander stood the wayward, ungainly Constantine, unlike him in all but brotherly love ; and next to him, the young Grand Dukes, Nicholas and Michael. The King of Prussia was there, with his two sons,—one of them destined to wear hereafter an imperial diadem ; the Emperor of Austria, with some members of his family ; and, most admired of all perhaps, little Stéphanie's hero, the Iron Duke.

But the sense of these great earthly presences passed away and was forgotten in the solemn awe of the scene that followed. "An immense army of conquerors" all at the same instant fell on their knees in prayer and thanksgiving. Each regiment, led by its own chaplain, moved in harmony with the rest. Magnificent vestments, fragrant incense, and the most exquisite vocal music contributed their charms ; until, to those who witnessed it, it seemed as if this worship scarcely belonged to earth. After the breathless, spell-bound silence that followed the last chanted psalm of praise, Clémence faltered tearfully,

"I think it is like that perfect worship in the courts above, where the great multitude, whom no man can number, fall on their faces before the Throne."

"Ah, sister mine!" said Henri with a sigh, "there is no perfect worship here. And this,—beautiful as it is, is far indeed from perfect. I doubt even whether it is quite in accordance with what we know of the will of God. But," he added softly, "'the good Lord pardon every one that prepareth his heart to seek the Lord God of his fathers, though he be not cleansed according to the purification of the sanctuary.'"

The religious service over, the guests strolled through the camp, enjoying the sweet summer weather, and the curious and interesting sights that met their view on every side. Amongst the crowd of visitors there was no happier party than that of Madame de Talmont. Joy had ripened the quiet grace of Clémence into a sweet and rare loveliness; there was a soft and steady light in her dark eyes, and the glow of perfect health upon her cheek. She was dressed that day with unusual care; Ivan himself had superintended her toilet for the expedition, and had chosen the simple exquisitely-fitting robe of silver gray silk which she wore. And that morning, before the service, he brought her the loveliest of roses, crimson and cream colour, and fastened them in her belt, "for the Emperor's fête," he said.

In the course of the afternoon his friends met him; he was walking with a group of officers of distinguished appearance. Coming to the side of Clémence, he took her hand and led her gently forward. "His Imperial Majesty wishes to be presented to you," he said quietly.

If Clémence felt a momentary embarrassment, it was quickly dispelled; for a very courteous gentleman was bowing over her hand, and a kind voice was saying pleasant things of "my friend Prince Pojarsky," and of the welcome which awaited Madame la Princesse for his sake in St. Petersburg. What she answered, or what other introductions followed she scarcely knew, for all that passed seemed like a dream, only far more easy and natural. "*That* the Emperor!" said Stéphanie afterwards. "I should not have been at all afraid to talk to him myself. He was only a gentleman."*

"*Only* a gentleman?" Madame de Talmont repeated. "Such gentlemen are not so plentiful, my little Stéphanie."

"But that Prince Ivan is doubtless well acquainted with the etiquette of his own court, I should say he made a blunder," observed Madame de Salgues. "A lady, were she the highest of the land, would be presented to the King of France, not the King to the lady."

"Yes; and the King would go in to dinner before his guest, were that guest an Emperor," said Emile. "Certainly no one can call Louis Dix-huit 'only a gentleman.'"

"Prince Ivan may be trusted in matters of etiquette," said Henri. He added apart to Clémence, "Do you remember, sister mine, the good things we two agreed to ask for the man who saved my life?"

"Love, joy, peace, God's best gifts. And there is that in his face to-day, Henri, which makes me think God has heard and answered our prayer."

They were not mistaken. A few words, spoken that evening to intimate friends, show how truly Alexander dwelt then in the secret place of the Most High. "This day has been the most glorious of my life, I shall never forget it," he said; but never surely did king or conqueror give so unique a reason for his joy and triumph: "My heart has been filled with love for my enemies. I have been able to pray fervently for them all; and it is with tears and at the foot of the cross that I have prayed for the welfare of France."

Such joy as this is like the name in the white stone, "which

---

* "He 'has the honour of being presented' to a lady; he 'begs that they will excuse' him, etc.; he says, 'will you permit?' as well as others. He is right, for he is a true gentleman, which is not quite so easy as some believe."—*De Maistre.*

no man knoweth save he that receiveth it." It would lose its beauty and its reality if passed from lip to lip as a common thing. Nor was it. It was told at the time in confidence to those who should have held it as a sacred trust; and the confidence was not violated until, for Alexander, all earthly joys and sorrows were no more. His *joy* was his own; but his *faith* was a thing to be confessed before all the world. And such a confession was the real meaning and purport of the celebrated Holy Alliance,—so greatly discussed, ridiculed, wondered over, blamed.

To Alexander, and to Alexander alone, belongs unquestionably the responsibility of this act, in which, not without much difficulty, he obtained the concurrence of his brother sovereigns. There is no doubt that it was his hand which penned the remarkable document itself, as well as the private letter which accompanied it when sent for signature to the English Prince Regent. A few words from this letter may explain his intention. "The events," says Alexander, "which have afflicted the world for more than twenty years have convinced us that the only means of putting an end to them is to be found in the closest union between the sovereigns whom Divine Providence has placed at the head of the nations of Europe. The history of the three last memorable years is a proof of the happy effect this union has produced for the safety of mankind. But to assure to this bond the solidity required by the greatness and purity of the end to which it tends, it ought to be founded on the sacred principles of the Christian religion. Deeply penetrated by this important truth, we have signed the act we submit to-day to the meditation of your Royal Highness. You will see its object is to strengthen the ties uniting us, in forming the people of Christendom into one family, and in assuring to them, under the protection of the All-Powerful, the happiness and safety of peace in the ties of an indissoluble fraternity."

The purpose of the Holy Alliance was threefold. It was firstly, as has been intimated, a solemn confession of faith in Christ, which Alexander, both as man and as sovereign, made for himself, and desired his brother sovereigns to make also. It was, moreover, a solemn declaration of the brotherhood and unity of all Christian nations. And, lastly and chiefly, it was a bond and pledge of peace. A stable, enduring, universal peace had been the dream of Alexander from the days of his youth. He had seen much of the miseries of war; and to his noble, sensitive, romantic spirit, ever full of longings for the happiness of humanity, the vision of terminating all these miseries, and ushering in a glad new period of joy, security, and prosperity, robed itself in the fairest colours. Once and again did he say, at different epochs, that he would willingly give his own life for the peace of the world. It was a poet's dream, to be wrought out, not in the stately march of rhythmic words, but in the more enduring language of golden deeds.

Two good things, which seemed to bring nearer the fulfilment of his dream, happened almost at the same time. His great antagonist, the troubler of nations, who had hitherto made peace impossible, was laid low; while to himself Christ came in conscious, realized presence, saying to his soul, "I am thy salvation." Was it strange if he thought the great work Christ had given him to do was to establish this longed-for peace upon the foundation of a firm and enduring faith in Him? "Oh, how happy I am!" said he in one of those moments of private intercourse with congenial friends in which heart and lips were opened. "My Saviour is with me. I am a great sinner, but he will make me his instrument in obtaining peace for the people. Oh, if all people would understand the ways of Providence, if they would but obey the gospel, how happy they would be!"

That splendid, impossible "if" was the rock upon which the whole project—like a gallant bark richly freighted—foundered

and was wrecked.   As it has been well said, "In desiring to
Christianize the world, Alexander attempted the impossible.
He vainly flattered himself that he could regulate according to
the gospel the transactions of nations and individuals who had
never submitted to the gospel; but it was the error of a noble
heart, and so much the more excusable because, uniting in himself the civil and religious supremacy within his own empire, he
had no means of ascertaining how far the reign of Christ is not
of this world.   Because he misconceived this truth, he sowed
his path with inextricable difficulties, he saw his noble desires
abandoned to ridicule."*

If the leading statesmen of Europe, to each of whom in turn
the Holy Alliance had to be submitted, did not venture to
ridicule it openly, it was not so much because the document
came from an imperial hand, as because they thought it involved
them in difficulties of too grave a character.   It was natural
that Metternich and Talleyrand should hesitate to advise their
sovereigns to sign such a paper; regarding it, as they did, as a
mere rodomontade, with no more bearing upon practical business
than a tale out of the Arabian Nights.   Castlereagh's letter to
Lord Liverpool presents a vivid picture of these perplexities.
He foresees that, "as Wilberforce is not yet in possession of
the Great Seal," there may be some difficulty in passing the
document through the ordinary course of office; but he considerately hopes that no person will blame the Prince Regent
for not refusing to sign it, "when the objection lies rather
against the *excessive excellence* than the quality and nature of
the engagement."

Doubtless from their point of view the statesmen were right.
The Holy Alliance was an anachronism.   The world was not
ready for it.   It was like a spring flower which, opening ere
the frosts of winter have departed, is doomed to wither in their
chill ungenial breath.

* Vie de Madame de Krudener, par M. Eynard.

But the flower, though it perishes untimely, has not lived in vain. It has told its tale and borne its message. It is not only one of Nature's unfulfilled promises, it is also one of her unconscious prophecies. In every age and season there are hints and premonitions and vague foreshadowings of that which is to follow, promises "which are written upon the heart of things." Winter has her prophecies of spring, and spring of summer. It is the very nature of these to be abortive, or at least to bear no fruit unto perfection. In one sense they are failures, but in another they are nobler and more precious than all present successes.

> "The high that proved too high, the heroic for earth too hard,
>   The passion that left the ground to lose itself in the sky,
> Are music sent up to God by the lover and the bard,—
>   Enough that *He* heard it once, we shall hear it by-and-by.
> *For what is our failure here but a triumph's evidence*
> *For the fulness of the days?"*

The music that throbbed and swelled and found an utterance —imperfect, indeed, but genuine—in the Holy Alliance, has not quite died away amidst the laughter of fools, and the clamorous, discordant voices of selfish politicians. "We shall hear it by-and-by," when a harmony serene and perfect—like that of the morning stars that sang together—shall usher in the reign of peace and righteousness for which the weary waiting earth has so long been yearning. For "the earth shall be filled with the knowledge of the glory of the Lord, as the waters cover the sea." "The kingdoms of this world shall become the kingdoms of our Lord, and of his Christ; and he shall reign for ever and ever." "In his days shall the righteous flourish; and abundance of peace so long as the moon endureth." "Nation shall not lift up sword against nation, neither shall they learn war any more."

CHAPTER XXXVII.

AT NICOLOFSKY.

"Do noble things, not dream them, all day long;
So making death, life, and that vast for ever,
One grand sweet song."

"YES, the first snow of winter is falling. Does my Clémence regret exchanging the flowers of France for the snows of Russia?"

"*Do I?*" she asked, looking confidingly into Ivan's face while she leaned on his arm. They were standing at a window in the old castle of Nicolofsky, watching the white flakes as they fell gently to the ground. It was night, but a full moon shed its soft, pure radiance, over the peaceful scene. "Our first night at home, Ivan," she continued. "I shall love this place. I am so glad we came here at once."

"And I am so glad to hear you say so. I have often felt, Clémence, that it was too generous, too unselfish of you and your mother to agree in counselling me to decline the Emperor's offer of a post in the Army of Occupation, which would have kept us together in France, perhaps for years."

"You know, Ivan, that you are needed here."

"I know it. I must get rid of Dmitri at once; and my only way of doing so is by being my own steward. I fear he has used my poor friends here very hardly. Yet, according to his light, he has been faithful; and after Zoubof's letter, pleading his cause so earnestly, I could not well set him aside for another.

It is true I neither respect Zoubof nor like him,—though he has behaved very courteously to me, being evidently well satisfied with whatever arrangements the Emperor made with him about the estate."

"If you are your own steward, Ivan, will you not have to remain here all the year?"

"Not *quite*, m'amie," Ivan answered smiling. "That would be too great a sacrifice. For this winter, indeed, I purpose keeping my princess a captive in fetters of frost and snow; and perhaps next summer we may content ourselves with a visit to Moscow, our martyr city, of which it is indeed true that we think upon her stones. But, if God will, the following winter must be spent in St. Petersburg."

"*I* should be well content to stay here and work amongst these poor, faithful-hearted people, who gave us such a loving welcome to-day. Some of them wept with joy to see you again, Ivan."

"Yes, Clémence, I love them dearly; and they love me with the love they gave poor little Ivan Barrinka long ago. Still— the capital has attractions—"

Clémence smiled. "It was a sacrifice for you to abandon the army," she said.

"How could I do otherwise? God gave me these people. Besides," Ivan added, "my great temptation to remain in the service was the hope of one day becoming an imperial aide-de-camp. But for these posts there are far too many candidates already. It will now be necessary for the Czar to place his army upon a peace-footing, and a very difficult task that will be.—But, m'amie, you have not told me yet what you think of this old, tumble-down owl's nest of a castle?"

"The château is much better than I expected, Ivan. A few judicious repairs will do a great deal; and we can adorn and beautify as much as we like. I mean to have the loveliest of gardens, in spite of the climate; and to induce the good folk here, if possible, to care for and cultivate a few flowers for themselves."

Ivan shook his head. "And share the common fate of reformers," he said. "The mujik is a good fellow, but you will find it hard to move him. He hates change, even change for the better. If he ever learn to read his Bible, as I hope with God's blessing he will, I think his favourite text will be, 'Stand ye in the ways, and see, and ask for the old paths.'"

"And yet," said Clémence, "you tell me he is wonderfully pliable and imitative; that if you take the little mujik from his village you can make of him anything you please—soldier, valet, coachman, musician, even scholar or artist."

"Yes; and you can make anything you please of a bar of iron—under certain conditions. But it would be almost as easy to bend the cold iron with your hand as to change the ways of the bearded mujik under the roof of his own izba.—But I think, dearest, we must rejoin our friends; I hear preparations for supper in the next room."

Ivan had brought with him to Nicolofsky an alert, clever young German doctor, and a gray-haired French priest. It had been his wish, no less than that of Clémence herself, that his wife should enjoy the rites of her own communion; and Henri, who spent much of his leisure in visiting the poor, discovered amongst them an old acquaintance of the family, who seemed exactly suited for the post of domestic chaplain to Madame la Princesse Pojarsky. M. Grandpierre, a relative of the valued and faithful steward of the De Talmonts, was the curé of a country parish in La Vendée when the war broke out. He stoutly exhorted his parishioners to fight for their King; marched with them to the field; ministered to the wounded and shrived the dying, often amidst the rain of Republican bullets. When the cause he loved was lost, he took refuge in Paris; and there, after years of poverty, Henri found him in a garret of the Faubourg St. Antoine. Many sorrows had tamed his fiery spirit; he was now a humble, simple-minded old man, much more likely to be the pupil of Clémence than her teacher. Dr. Krausekopf, a rising young physician from Heidelberg, had been added to the establishment of Prince Pojarsky, because Russian doctors were few and unskilful; and Ivan knew it would be quite useless to introduce a Frenchman in that capacity, at least if he wished the mujiks of Nicolofsky to profit by his skill. With the exception of the priest and the doctor, the household contained only two foreigners, the waiting-woman of Clémence, who was a widow, and her child, a little girl.

The next morning, a deputation from the village came to the castle to welcome their lord. Ivan went to meet them in the great hall; but he turned back again, saying to Clémence as he took her hand, "Come, dearest; I want to show my wife to the man who sheltered my helpless childhood at his own peril. The good old starost is there, Clémence; and Pope Nikita, the father of Anna Popovna."

If anything could have made the mujiks of Nicolofsky doubt the infallibility of their "Barrinka"—their loved prince and master—it would have been his marriage with a Frenchwoman, a child of the accursed race who had outraged the soil of holy Russia. But when the graceful, gracious lady, with her sweet face, came amongst them, and accepted their homage with such cordial and winning kindness, their prejudices gave way; and they vanished entirely when she took in hers the great hard hand of the aged starost, saying in broken Russian, "Let me thank you, bativshka, for all the love you showed little Ivan Barrinka. I must go soon and see your wife, who was his nurse." For the priest too she had a word of kindness; and to each of the rough, bearded mujiks she gave her hand, which they were fain to kneel and kiss. The starost gazed at her with tearful eyes, and said something apart to Ivan. "He tells me," Ivan explained, "that he thinks you so like my mother, whom I never knew. But he prays that your fate may be happier than hers."

The months that followed were spent by Clémence and Ivan in endeavours to benefit their people. Ivan repaired, as far as he could, every wrong of which Dmitri had been guilty; and it was not his fault if any mujik in Nicolofsky lacked bread, kvass, and kasha in abundance, wool and sheepskins for clothing, or a well-built and comfortable izba. He tried to restrict the consumption of vodka, and to promote honesty, cleanliness, and truthfulness; though, it must be added, with only partial success. Clémence did her part; and the peasants soon learned to trust her as their own and their children's friend. They loved her still better when she acquired Russian enough to be an intelligent and sympathetic listener; and in her turn to tell simple Bible stories, chiefly of our Lord's life and death, and most of them to her hearers new and fascinating as a romance.

In the long evenings, Clémence and Ivan, with M. Grand-pierre and Dr. Krausekopf, gave many an hour to earnest, united study of the Scriptures. The individual character and experience of each shed a special light upon these readings. Ivan represented happy, confident, child-like trust; Clémence devout thoughtfulness, rather tending towards asceticism; Krausekopf intellectual doubt; and the old priest a dim and groping faith, which, however, was growing every day more clear and strong. Each helped the other; and the one great, ever-present Teacher, who never fails those who seek him, was helping all.

Letters came to them regularly with tidings of their absent friends. One day in the early spring Ivan entered the morn-ing room of Clémence with a radiant face, and in his hand a large packet. "The post has come. Here, my Clémence," he said, as he shared the spoils with her. "Our friends have been good to us this time;" and he sat down at the window to enjoy his own portion.

But, as he read, his face changed, and he cast an anxious, sorrowful glance towards Clémence. Almost at the same moment a cry broke from her lips, "Oh, Henri—Henri!" Ivan went quickly to her side, and laid his hand tenderly on her shoulder.

"Henri has—has become a Protestant!" she faltered, in tones of dismay.

"So he tells me," said Ivan. "This letter is from him. He writes like the noble-hearted Christian man that he is. Clémence, you must not grieve for him. He has done well to obey the voice of his conscience."

"But our mother—it is such a blow for her," Clémence said mournfully.

"Yes; I am sorry for her—*very*. But, m'amie, God will help her to bear it, and bring good out of it in the end. *I* do not think the change of creed such a weighty matter. What does anything else signify, so long as a man believes in our Lord Jesus Christ?" After a pause he resumed, taking up another letter, "Emile will give us an impartial statement of the case. Let us see what he says."

"Emile has behaved well," Clémence observed, looking over the remainder of her letter. "My mother says Madame de Salgues was so angry, that, but for Emile, she and Henri must have left her house and gone to live in some poor lodging. But Emile reasoned with her, reminding her that he himself was once an infidel and a scoffer, which is worse than a Protestant, yet she never dreamed of forbidding him the house; and so, not being noticed, he grew tired of scoffing, and became in time like other people. He told her Henri would probably do the same; and pleaded, moreover, that his conduct had been always regular and blameless, and could bring nothing but credit to any one."

"He says as much for him here," said Ivan, reading from Emile's letter. "'My cousin is really miserable about the soul of her son, which she thinks to be in peril; while my grandmother is only annoyed at what she considers a social degradation. In the eyes of the one, Protestantism is heretical; in those of the other, it is "bourgeoise." My grandmother fancies that Henri was demoralized by his campaign under the Emperor's standard, whereas Henri himself says that it was only then he learned what religion meant. I cannot profess to understand the matter, not being myself religious; but there is certainly a curious connection, not to say confusion, between saintliness and heresy. Henri is religious—he is "converted;" yet he is called a heretic, and mourned over by your excellent mother-in-law as next to an infidel, and on the highroad to perdition. He has a fast friend in little Stéphanie, who takes his part in season and out of season. I am rather glad of it; for the child had almost ceased to be amusing, Madame de Krudener tamed her so effectually.'—You must write to your mother, Clémence," said Ivan, laying down the letter, "and pray her to be tender and patient with Henri."

"*That* will be needless," Clémence answered. "To my mother Henri will be as a sick child who needs a fourfold share of tenderness. I know her well. Fondly as she clung to him before, he will be closer than ever to her now.—One thing is certain, Ivan. We can no longer hope for a visit from her next summer. Until Henri's education as an architect is finished, no power on earth will move her from his side. Our only hope is that hereafter, through the kindness of the Emperor, some work may be found for him in this country."

"It *shall* be found," said Ivan, in his bright, confident way. "Here, at least, religious differences create no prejudice. A man may profess what creed he pleases, so that he does not outrage public order, or make proselytes from the national Church. We Russians are very tolerant."

"Is not toleration sometimes only indifference under a mask?" asked Clémence. "Ah, when will men learn the secret of holding truth dearer than life, and yet being gentle and patient with those who do not see it through their eyes?"

"Some secrets are only learned in 'the secret place of the Most High,'" Ivan answered softly.

Neither he nor Clémence was at all aware that they themselves were slipping unconsciously from the moorings of their own ancestral creeds, and that their study of the Scriptures was bringing them nearer day by day to the present standpoint of Henri.

Not long after this sorrow, joy came to the household. When the first days of the short Russian summer smiled upon Nicolofsky, a little guest was sent to the old castle. Very proud was Ivan of his first-born child; and to Clémence it seemed as if no one since the beginning of the world had ever been so happy as she. It was agreed that the babe should bear the name of Madame de Talmont; so a little "Rose" budded soft and fair amidst the snows of Russia, giving promise of one day unfolding its petals in full beauty and fragrance.

CHAPTER XXXVIII.

A ROSEBUD.

> " Mais elle etait de ce monde où les meilleures choses
> Ont le pire destin ;
> Et Rose elle a vécu ce que vivent les roses,
> L'espèce d'un printemps."

 HAPPY quiet year passed away at Nicolofsky ; then Ivan and Clémence removed to St. Petersburg, where they established themselves for the coming winter in one of the palaces on the Fontanka. Clémence, upon this her first visit, found the city wonderful and fascinating in its very strangeness. It seemed a thing of yesterday; the magnificent buildings, the stately streets and squares, looked as if they had sprung into being at the touch of an enchanter's wand. Not yet had the hand of time left its impress anywhere. When she arrived, all was life, colour, animation ; every pulse of the great city was throbbing, and the din of its multitudinous and busy noises smote strangely upon ears accustomed to the quiet of the country. But soon a change came. The snow spread its soft white mantle over the crowded thoroughfares, the sounds of traffic were hushed, the steps of passers-by fell silently, and the bright blue waters of the Neva were chained by the genii of the frost. " It is like a city of the dead," thought Clémence.

But she thought differently when Ivan took her, well wrapped in furs, for her first winter drive in St. Petersburg. It was pleasant to glide rapidly through the clear frosty air along the

Neva Prospekt, filled with glittering throngs on foot or in gaily-decorated sledges. Costumes the most various and striking showed that every race and kindred, from Persia and Japan in the far East to the forests of America in the West, had its representatives in that northern metropolis. Tartars in their robes of fur, Cossacks in their hooded cloaks, mingled with bearded Russians in blue caftans, and Englishmen and Germans in the sober attire patronized by modern Europeans. Officers in uniform were without number; and the robes of ecclesiastics, Romish as well as Greek, diversified the scene; while fair ladies, in elegant though slightly exaggerated Parisian toilets, bowed from their sledges to their friends, or alighted at the doors of the handsome and brilliantly-decorated shops.

Their life in the capital was full of interest to Clémence and Ivan. The best and most brilliant society received them with open arms. Ivan's comrades in the late war gathered round him, and many were their pleasant social meetings. Clémence was soon presented at Court, and won the marked approval of the dignified Empress Mother, and—what she prized much more highly — the favour of the gentle Empress Elizabeth. Both the Empresses found their chief enjoyment in assisting the Emperor in his works of mercy. The more active disposition of the elder led her to take delight in the management of the great Foundling Hospital (her especial favourite); also in the establishment for the education of young ladies; in the School for the Deaf and Dumb, where the methods of the Abbé Sicard were being carried out with diligence and success; and in many other institutions, which were either founded or fostered by the benevolence of Alexander. When the Winter Palace set the example, it was no marvel that charity became the fashion in St. Petersburg. Not from fashion, but from a far higher motive, Clémence and Ivan engaged heartily in such pursuits, spending much of their leisure and their substance in the work of serving " Christ in his poor."

There were at this time in the best society of St. Petersburg two distinct religious circles, differing widely, and each in its own way very influential. At the Sardinian Embassy, the "old man eloquent," Count de Maistre,—with his white hair and eyes of fire, his "esprit fin" indescribable in English, his keen, quick sympathies, and his brave, high, chivalrous spirit, —strove hard to turn the stream of religious thought into a strong and steady current leading Romewards. He was worthy to have been the champion of a better cause; but he and those like him never really knew for what they were contending. They were as loyal-hearted soldiers who fight and die heroically beneath the banner of a usurper, honestly believing they are serving their true king. Madame Svetchine, Countess Tolstoi, and other devout women, were just then yielding to the fascination of De Maistre's eloquence; and a colony of Jesuits, zealous, active, and not over-scrupulous, were furthering the work of proselytism after their peculiar fashion.

Around Prince Galitzin, Alexander Tourgenieff, Princess Metchersky, and others of a similar character, there gathered a very different circle—earnest students of Scripture, simple evangelical Christians, with whom faith and love were the fulfilling of the law, and forms occupied a very subordinate place. These were in constant communication with the leaders of the evangelical movement in other countries, and especially with the agents of the Bible Society. They knew themselves the objects of suspicion and aversion, not only to the Romanizing party, but also to the zealous members of the Greek Church, the men of the old school, who were strongly attached to things as they were, and jealous of all reform. But they were strengthened by the knowledge that the heart of the Emperor was with them, though his sense of justice made him endeavour to hold the balance evenly between the contending parties, and his natural attachment to the Church of which he was the head deterred him from any course that he thought likely to endanger its stability or weaken its influence. Ivan from the first, and eventually Clémence also, gave a decided preference to the society of Galitzin and his friends; although they occasionally frequented the Sardinian Embassy, and Clémence found a warm personal friend in the Countess Tolstoi.

The Christmas festivities drew on, and Clémence and Ivan were amongst the guests invited to the grand ball and supper given at the Winter Palace to celebrate the Emperor's birthday. Ivan was extremely anxious that Clémence should be present at one of these magnificent entertainments, which had all the brilliancy imperial wealth and splendour could give, with the addition of what does not always accompany them—the charm of exquisite taste and "sovereign elegance." He returned from the levee, where he had spent most of the day, in high spirits and full of pleasurable anticipation. But his surprise was great to find Clémence, still in her usual dress, bending with a troubled face over the cot in which their little Rosebud lay.

"Surely there is nothing wrong with our darling?" he said, stooping tenderly over the sleeping babe. "It cannot be. She was so bright and full of life when I left you this morning."

"There *is* something wrong," Clémence whispered, looking up, but scarcely stirring, for the little hand of the sleeping child had closed about her mother's finger. "I cannot but be anxious, since that terrible attack of croup she had when the cold weather began. Listen!—her breathing is still quick, though quieter now than an hour ago. But I must be here to do what is wanted—and to do it at once. I *cannot* go with you, Ivan," she said pleadingly.

Ivan was greatly disappointed, but he would not combat his wife's resolve. After a pause, he said gently, "It shall be as you like, dearest. I see little Rosebud is stronger than the Czar."

"Say all that is right for me," Clémence continued. "But

I don't think you will have any trouble there. We have not only imperial courtesy to deal with, but kind hearts and true."

"Hearts that often bleed beneath their purple trappings," Ivan answered. "The Empress Elizabeth does not appear at this ball: she is mourning to-night for the death of a little girl whom she had adopted, and to whom she was tenderly attached. 'Every one dies in whom I take an interest,' she says. Perhaps her own frail health makes her look the more sorrowfully upon all things. Pray for her, Clémence."

"Indeed I will. How the happy ought to pray for those on whom life's shadows seem to fall! *We* have all sunshine, Ivan."

But even then a shadow was falling over their happy home. The little Rosebud, so lovingly watched and tended, was fading quickly. When Ivan returned that night from the Winter Palace, with its splendour, its lights, its music, his own dwelling was hushed and still. The Master had come for their treasure. Unmurmuringly, though with tearful eyes and aching hearts, they gave it into his keeping. They might have said, had they known the words,—

> "God took thee in his arms, a lamb untasked, untried;
> He fought the fight for thee, he won the victory,
> And thou art sanctified."

CHAPTER XXXIX.

> "The lonely glory of a throne
> May yet this lowly joy deserve ;
> Kings may make that a stepping-stone,
> And change ' I reign ' into ' I serve.' "

WO or three weeks later Clémence sat alone one afternoon. A bright wood fire burned on the hearth, and on a little table near her lay a pile of needlework—garments for the poor. But just then she was occupied with a letter from her mother, written in happy unconsciousness of the sorrow which had fallen upon her dear ones ; and she could not help a few tears which dropped quietly upon the page, full of questions and remarks about their little Rosebud.

While she was reading Ivan came in, with more brightness in his face and animation in his step than had been there since Christmas eve. But he saw the tears, and stooping down kissed her tenderly.

" What is it, m'amie ? " he whispered.

" These letters, dear," she answered, looking up with the smile of welcome *his* entrance never failed to win from her. " My mother's is about our Rosebud." After a pause and a little sigh she added, " The only important news she tells us is that our friend M. de Sartines is dead."

" Indeed ! I am very sorry."

" So am I, especially for Stéphanie. She has written to me

herself, poor child — a long letter, but I have not read it yet."

"Does our mother give any particulars?" asked Ivan.

"Only that his illness was a short one—inflammation on the lungs. She says Stéphanie has behaved admirably, tending her father bravely and carefully, and watching beside him to the very end. She is almost heart-broken."

"Poor little one!—How lonely she must be! I wish we could bring her here. *You* would comfort her, Clémence."

Ivan paused; then resumed, with a slight touch of uneasiness in his voice, "M'amie, will it trouble you if a friend comes to visit us to-night?"

A look of pain passed swiftly over the face of Clémence. The sorrowing heart is prone to shrink within itself, and to dread the first breath of outer air, the first touch of common life. "Not if it is only an intimate friend," she said at last, "such as M. Tolstoi or M. Adrian Wertsch; but I should not quite care to see a stranger, Ivan."

"It is no stranger; it is one whom we both love." Then he returned rather nervously to the subject of the letters, asking what would become of Stéphanie.

"For the present she is to be sent to the pension where her cousin Coralie is," Clémence answered. "Her uncle, who is now her guardian, appears to wish it, and she herself is indifferent. La Tante has not been very well of late, Ivan; she seems to be in low spirits, but I am thankful to say she is becoming reconciled to Henri's change; and he, for his part, writes very cheerfully. The best judges in the profession he has adopted think highly of his talent. He has just gained some prize for a design;—but I have not yet finished reading his letter."

So they talked on, until at last Ivan suggested preparations for tea, and rather to the surprise of Clémence interested himself in them in a way quite foreign to his usual habits. She only looked at him wonderingly, and with a little amusement, as he arranged and rearranged the tea-table; but when he actually began to make inquiries about the quality of the beverage itself, her eyes, so lately tearful, sparkled into a smile as she asked,—

" When did *you* become a connoisseur in these things, Ivan? I thought the difference between tea and coffee was the extent of your knowledge on the subject."

Ivan, instead of answering, kissed her; then taking a white camellia from a vase on the table, he fastened it at the throat of her plain black dress. " My Clémence must look her best to receive the Emperor," he said.

" The *Emperor!* " she cried in dismay. " Oh, Ivan, why did you not tell me? "

Before he could reply a sledge stopped at the door, and Ivan hastened down to welcome his guest.

Clémence had scarcely recovered her composure when the Emperor entered the room, saying pleasantly,—

" I must make my apologies to Madame la Princesse for inviting myself. Prince Ivan Ivanovitch is responsible : he gave me permission to take you by surprise, and promised me a welcome."

The promised welcome was given by Clémence, very gracefully and cordially, in spite of a little tremulousness in her voice and nervousness in her manner. One gentle, significant word of sympathy for her sorrow was spoken ; then, all ceremony being waived, they took their seats together at the table, the Emperor declining the " fauteuil " Ivan placed for him, and choosing an ordinary chair instead.

" You know I am deaf," he said; " let me sit where I can best hear the voice of madame." *

---

* In the following conversation not only the sentiments but the words given are all those of Alexander himself. It was his habit to pay an occasional evening visit in the manner described above to those whom he esteemed. He was not particular as to their rank (some merchants' wives had poured out tea for him not unfrequently), but they were always persons noted for piety and good works.

As, with a hand still trembling, Clémence poured out the tea, she remembered the stories she had heard of such evening visits made by the Emperor, "to talk at his ease," and recalled the words of De Maistre when some one criticised this habit in his presence: "It is a touching thing to me to see the ruler of a great empire, in the age of all the passions, find his recreation in taking a cup of tea with an honest man and his wife."

In the meantime her place behind the "samovar" was no sinecure, for the Emperor drank many cups of tea, while he talked earnestly with Ivan upon the things of which his heart was full—schools, hospitals, and prison reforms.   He soon drew Clémence into the conversation.   Her interest in the institutions of St. Petersburg was evidently well known to him, and he asked her opinion on various matters of detail, especially about the school for the deaf and dumb.   Then they talked of primary schools, and of the Lancastrian system, which he had sent commissioners to England to investigate with a view of adopting it in Russia.   This led to the general subject of education, which he remarked ought not to be merely mechanical, but adapted to the development of the intelligence.

"Some teachers would turn their pupils into absolute machines," he said, "by way of levelling their path to knowledge."

Here the soft voice of Clémence broke in.   "Ought not religion to be the foundation of all education?" she asked somewhat timidly.

"If education is, properly speaking, the extension of light," said the Emperor, "surely it ought first of all to extend the true light—the light that shineth in darkness."

As a means to this end, he spoke of the translation of the Bible into the vulgar tongue, a work which he was then urging forward with all his influence.   He gratefully acknowledged the services of the noble British and Foreign Bible Society, and spoke with enthusiasm of that and other agencies which were promoting the cause of Christ throughout the world. The extent and accuracy of his knowledge of missionary work astonished Clémence and Ivan. They learned afterwards that every Saturday morning Prince Galitzin used to bring him, by his own desire, all the information on the subject he could obtain during the week. It was from the study of the Divine Word that he had himself obtained light and comfort; and therefore, as he said, he " reckoned it his most sacred duty " to disseminate that word.

Clémence, who had been a little disturbed by the warnings of De Maistre and other enemies of the Bible Society about the danger of misinterpreting Scripture, ventured to ask whether it might not be well to associate some simple commentary with the text of the Bible.

" Commentaries have this inconvenience," he said in reply, " that they substitute more or less for the text of Scripture the ideas of some one who interprets it according to his own system. These ideas will not be accepted by all. But it ought to be the aim of every Christian, whatever communion he may belong to, to allow the sacred Code in all its extent to act upon him with perfect freedom. This action cannot be otherwise than beneficent and stimulating, as may be expected from a divine book —from the Book of books."

" Where there is faith to receive it," Ivan threw in, " it produces in all alike certain great results, yet with important differences."

" True," he resumed. " Its action will be different in each individual, and just because of this difference is it grand and extraordinary. It makes of each individual whatever it is possible to make of him with regard to his particular nature. Is not unity in variety the grand point at which we seek to arrive, in order to secure the prosperity of Churches and of States? Everywhere in external nature we see this principle of unity in variety, and we perceive it also in the history of nations : only, we must not take for a measure the short space of our own lives ; it is to ages and decades of ages we must look when we seek to judge of the result of a great struggle between opposing forces. Upon all the children of time and of party spirit—such as contradictions, lies, vain interpretations—time itself does justice ; they evaporate like foam, and are gone. Truth remains. But the action of truth is slow ; often centuries elapse before it is accepted. Still it makes way ; the means exist not of sealing it hermetically, as some would do with the Holy Scriptures. Do not the rays of the sun make their way ? and those who live in their brightness are the children of light." *

No one cared to break the silence that followed these eager, burning words. The same thought was throbbing in the heart of Clémence and of Ivan—that it was a grand and beautiful thing, a precious gift of God, to be allowed to work for that great future victory of truth and light. " But how little a woman can do," Clémence thought sadly. " Still, every word and deed of kindness, every message of divine love passed on to one poor waiting soul, helps the cause as truly as does the Czar himself in throwing wide open before the Bible the gates of his vast empire." Almost before she was aware, she had uttered something of her thought.

"Ah, but you would be wrong indeed to think yourself useless," said the Emperor in his courteous way. "Good women are true benefactors of society, by their example and the influence of their virtues. In their presence one seems to breathe a purer moral atmosphere."

" I think, sire," said Ivan, " that every human soul possesses influence, even the soul of a little child."

His thoughts, and those of Clémence also, turned to an empty cot in the next room. Quiet talk followed, of which

* These remarks on the influence of the Bible are taken from the conversations of Alexander with the Lutheran Bishop Eylert.

their little one was the theme,—sweet converse about "the ransom for that baby paid," and the home to which she had been taken. It was truly "from very heart to very heart" that hour. At last the Emperor rose to take his leave; and not until then did Clémence venture to say something that *must* be said—something that she might reproach herself all her life if she lost this opportunity of saying.

"Sire, I have one brother, dear to me as my own soul, and he charged me solemnly, if ever I had the privilege of speaking with your Majesty face to face, to tell you that he will bless until his latest hour *the aide-de-camp of St. Priest.*" Then in a few brief words she told the story of Henri's deliverance.

The Czar was much moved. Not so often did the blessings of the many he tried to bless reach his ears. His successor might well say that he "had before his eyes, in his brother, the example of a sovereign whose whole existence was an incessant sacrifice to duty, and who nevertheless had so seldom succeeded in securing even gratitude, at least from his contemporaries." Yet we have evidence that when gratitude came to him he found it very sweet. After a pause, he said gently,—

"Madame, I have only done my duty. What is called the right of reprisal has always seemed terrible to me. The only revenge we ought to take is in doing good."

By this time the Emperor's famous coachman, Ilya, who had spent the evening with the servants of Ivan, a much-honoured and fêted guest, had in readiness the unpretending sledge in which his imperial master drove about his capital.

"Have you forgiven me, dearest?" asked Ivan, when he returned from attending their august visitor to the door. "It is the first time I ever kept a secret from you."

Clémence looked in his radiant face, and her only answer was a smile.

"He is charmed with you," Ivan went on delighted. "I knew it would be so. He admired you even the first day he saw you—the day of the review in the Plaine des Vertus. How well he looks, does he not, Clémence?"

"Yes; well, but worn; and there is a weary look in his eyes. I think he needs rest, Ivan."

Ivan shook his head a little sadly. "Do you know where he is going now?" he asked.

"Home, I suppose; it is midnight."

"Ilya tells our people he is going to visit the hospitals. He goes sometimes at midnight, to ascertain that the patients are as well cared for by night as by day.* Yet to-morrow morning at six o'clock he will be in his cabinet or on parade."

"The light that shines must burn, and burn out," said Clémence. "But, Ivan," she added with hesitation, "may I say something?"

"What thing is there which you may *not* say, my Clémence?"

"There is one thing which you would not hear from any lip on earth—a word of blame for your Czar. But do not think I mean it so if I ask, could not some life less precious be found to spend itself in these ministrations? Would not he do well to remember the warning of Jethro—'Thou wilt surely wear away, thou, and this people that is with thee; for this thing is too heavy for thee'?"

"Clémence, you do not know our Russians. I love them well, yet I see their faults, which are something like those of clever, ill-educated children, but on a gigantic scale. They are, when they choose it, the most accomplished of deceivers. They can elaborate and carry out a fraud with a patient ingenuity, a consummate dexterity, that one is tempted to call quite artistic. When the Czarina Catherine travelled through the empire, her courtiers of course wished her to imagine it in a state of the highest prosperity; so they erected mock villages along her route, and drove to the neighbourhood herds of

---

* A fact. Visitors to St. Petersburg during the reign of Alexander bore witness to the admirable condition of these institutions.

cattle, and troops of well-dressed peasants to greet her with smiles and acclamations. It takes all the vigilance of my Czar, and all his careful personal inspection, to guard against similar deceptions; and I fear that even he does not always succeed."

"Is not the remedy for this want of truth, as for other evils, to be found in the dissemination of the Word of truth?" asked Clémence.

"Surely it is," said Ivan with a brightening look. "Do you not feel, Clémence, as if the spring were come,—as if every plant were budding with new, glorious life? Amongst the princes of the earth, one says, 'I am the Lord's;' another subscribes with his hand unto the Lord, and surnames himself by the name of the God of Israel. His Word is loved, honoured, scattered broadcast amongst the people. Think of the joy of having it in our common tongue, Clémence—the tongue in which the babe lisps to its mother, and the gray-haired mujik tells his stories of the past as he sits beside his stove! Soon, I hope, in the izbas of every village throughout the length and breadth of our land, the father will be reading to the children the story of their Saviour's love. I learned to-day two things which rejoiced my heart about the home I have never ceased to love —holy Moscow, the city of our solemnities."

"Tell them to me, Ivan."

"One is a joy to me upon grounds purely personal, and I think it will please you also. As an ornament for the restored city, the Czar is about to raise a stately monument to the memory of my patriotic ancestor and his brave associate. ' To Prince Pojarsky and Citizen Minim, from grateful Russia,' so runs the simple and noble inscription. But, what is far better, he has just given to the Bible Society, for its storehouse and head-quarters, that great old building which was formerly the office of the secret police. Think of Bibles being laid up in what used to be the torture-chamber! How quickly and how gloriously the rays of the Sun of Righteousness are rising upon us! They are flooding with light even those dark places of the earth which used to be the habitations of cruelty."

"But is there not something else still to be wished for, Ivan? Those free Bibles you speak of, should you not wish to see them read and loved by free peasants?"

"That is coming too," said Ivan, with rapt look and confident voice. "Every one who knows the Czar knows that his cherished dream—his favourite, his ruling idea—is now, as it has ever been, the emancipation of the serfs.* Through the facilities he has afforded and the encouragement he has given, many have been freed already. Count Sergius Romanzoff, for instance, has given liberty to all his serfs."

"And why not Prince Ivan Pojarsky?" asked Clémence in a low voice, as she laid her hand on his arm and looked earnestly into his face.

"You utter the voice of my own heart, Clémence. Often have I thought of this. But—" He broke off his unfinished sentence, and began to pace the room with rapid footsteps.

Clémence took up the last word. "But—there are many difficulties," she said.

"One is quite sufficient, for the present," Ivan pursued. "The people of Nicolofsky are not fit for greater freedom than they have now; they would not know how to use it. Let us train them for it," he added as he stopped before her chair.

"Which already we are trying to do, are we not?" asked Clémence.

"Yes," he said. "That is God's work for us. Part of it. There is work here, too—noble, blessed work. How good it is of our Father in heaven to cast our lot in such times as these, Clémence. Surely they are the last times, when ' the mountain of the Lord's house shall be established in the top of the mountains, and shall be exalted above the hills, and all nations shall

---

* "Emancipation is one of his ruling ideas. A great part of the acts of his government bear the impression of it."—*Dupré de St. Maure.*

flow unto it;' when 'they shall teach no more every man his neighbour, and every man his brother, saying, Know the Lord : for all shall know him, from the least to the greatest.'—Surely we shall live to see that blessed consummation, you and I."

In the bright enthusiasm of their youth they forgot the words of Alexander, "It is to ages and decades of ages we must look ;" nor perhaps did he always remember them himself. But the next thought of Clémence was one very natural to the still aching heart of the bereaved mother. "If only our little Rosebud could have lived to see it too," she said.

"Ay," said Ivan. Then after a pause he added, "But she sees Christ, which is far better."

CHAPTER XL.

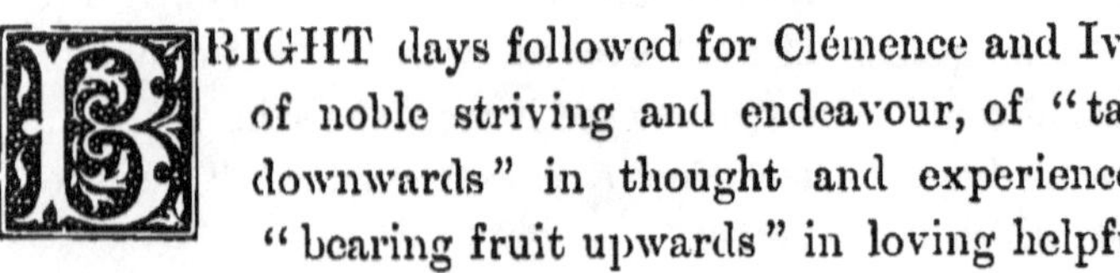

> " Waft, waft, ye winds, His story;
>   And you, ye waters, roll,
> Till like a sea of glory
>   It spreads from pole to pole ;
> Till o'er our ransomed nature
>   The Lamb for sinners slain,
> Redeemer, King, Creator,
>   In bliss returns to reign."

BRIGHT days followed for Clémence and Ivan—days of noble striving and endeavour, of "taking root downwards" in thought and experience, and of "bearing fruit upwards" in loving helpful toil for others. Their little Rosebud was not forgotten. The baby guest whose visit was so brief that it seemed to come and go like a dream left an abiding blessing behind her. Heaven looked nearer and more real to the parents whose treasure was there already ; and labour felt more sweet for Him who had her in his keeping. Thenceforward the tender, introspective spirit of Clémence grew more and more into the glad undoubting faith of Ivan. Nor did the little cot remain empty ; for God sent them other gifts—in the course of the next three years two baby boys came to gladden their home.

Meanwhile the stirrings of new life seemed to pervade ever more and more the land in which they lived. It was something like what the early Reformation era had been in the elder lands of Europe. Nor was it only the rich and great who shared the blessing; to the poor also the gospel was preached. One morning late in spring, when the frost and snow had at last disappeared and the Neva was navigable again, Ivan stood on the quay watching what was then to the inhabitants of St. Petersburg a strange sight and new. Amidst the numerous boats that cleft the blue waters with the aid of sail and oar came an unfamiliar monster, panting and puffing on its rapid way with an air of conscious power, while a dense column of steam issuing from its funnel bore witness to the triumph of modern science. Ivan gazed and wondered, until his attention was distracted by an exclamation in a voice he knew—"*Great St. Nicholas!*"

Turning a little, he saw beside him a sergeant of artillery, who was lifting up one hand in amazement.

"Michael Ivanovitch!" he cried. "I am heartily glad to see you. And so you have got your promotion," he added, touching his epaulette.

"Yes, Barrinka; and two orders," returned Michael, proudly showing the badges to Ivan. "We have just been sent here from Moscow, where we were stationed since September twelve-months."

"You must come home with me," said Ivan. "My wife will be delighted to see you. She will send an account of your visit to your mother; for she writes a long letter every fort-night to Pope Nikita, with messages for half Nicolofsky."

"I shall soon be able to write to my mother myself, Bar-rinka," said Michael with an air of pride as he walked beside Ivan to the Fontanka. "It only takes one hand to do that," he explained.

"But it takes learning," returned Ivan laughing. "I did not know you were a scholar, Michael."

"Oh yes, Barrinka; there is a school in our regiment now, and we are learning to read and write. Barrinka, is it true that the words of the blessed Lord," he asked, crossing himself, "will soon be all turned into Russ and put into a printed book, which any poor man like me will be able to read if only he knows his kirillitza?" *

"Quite true; I have myself seén the translation of the Four Gospels."

"I have a little bit of it already. See, Barrinka." He took from his pocket a printed copy of extracts from the New Testament. These had been selected by the excellent Quakers Allen and Grellet, printed by the Emperor's express orders, and distributed for use in all the primary schools which he had established in the army and throughout the empire.

"It is full of the most beautiful things about the blessed Bog Sŭn," continued Michael: "how he healed the sick and gave sight to the blind; how he died for our sins, and rose again the third day; and how every one who believes in him will get a free pardon for his sake, and have part in the resurrection of the just. What a wonderful thing it is for a poor man to be able to read all this for himself, just as well as if he were a pope or a monk! One of my comrades has a book too, written by an Englishman, which the Czar himself got turned into Russ— it is called 'No Cross, no Crown.'† Besides telling how the Son of God bore the cross for us, it tells how we must bear any cross he sends us for his sake; and how, if we follow him here, we shall have a crown of glory by-and-by in his kingdom,—a crown of glory, like the Czar! Only think of that, Barrinka! I can scarcely make up my mind to believe it; and I am longing to get *all* the words of Christ to read for myself, that I may know if it is true. But, to be sure, the Czar must know."

"To be sure he knows! It is all true, Michael; I can show you the words myself in which it is promised, and read them with you."

"Oh, how good of you! Still, I am thinking that rather

---

* The Russian alphabet; so called because arranged by Bishop Cyril.

† By William Penn. At the special desire of Alexander, the Countess Metchersky translated it into Russ.

than be a king myself up yonder—which is what I am no way fit for—I would like to go on serving the Czar there, as I do here. Would not you, Barrinka?"

"I think so *now*. But how it will be with me then I cannot tell. 'It doth not yet appear what we shall be.' Christ's promise is enough: 'I will give thee a crown of life'—'To him that overcometh will I grant to sit with me in my throne.' Yet is it said too,' They serve him day and night in his temple.'"

By this time they had reached the gate of Ivan's palace. Clémence gladly renewed her acquaintance with the friend of her husband's boyhood; she gave him a hospitable welcome, and, to his intense delight, showed him her two lovely boys, the elder just able to lisp his father's name, the younger a three months' babe in the cradle.

From that time Ivan's old playfellow was a frequent visitor. Clémence helped him in the studies of which he was so proud; and they had many a quiet happy talk together about Him of whom the Book they loved so well testified in every page. Eventually, however, the current of their lives divided, and swept them apart, never probably to meet again on this side of the grave. But the lessons they had learned remained with both, and both in their several spheres sought to pass them on to others. Many years afterwards, a German traveller* in Russia visited the churches of St. Petersburg, as an interested spectator of the touching Russian custom of the reading of the Scriptures on Easter eve by the people for one another. He tells us that in one of these churches he saw a veteran soldier, scarred and weather-beaten, standing at the desk with a taper in his hand reading the story of his Saviour's death to a company of little children who clustered around him, listening to the sacred words with absorbed and breathless attention. Perhaps he failed to notice, or perhaps he did not think it worth while to chronicle, that the reader had lost a hand.

* Kohl.

Never can it be known, until the great day of revelation, how many hearts at this epoch received life and blessing from the Word of God, scattered broadcast throughout the great Russian Empire, not only with the approbation, but with the earnest personal co-operation, of its monarch. "For," said Alexander, " I consider this undertaking not merely worthy of my attention ; no, I am penetrated by it to the inmost recesses of my soul. And I reckon the promotion of it my most sacred duty, because on it depends the temporal and eternal happiness of those whom Providence has committed to my care. Blessed are those who take a part in it; for such gather fruit unto life eternal, when those who sow and those who reap shall rejoice together."*

But he who uttered these noble words in all the glow and ardour of his first love, had soon cause to remember that the bearer of the precious seed too often goes on his way weeping. As time wore on it became apparent that the hand of the enemy was busy sowing tares with it. Religious activity began to fulfil its inevitable condition by engendering religious dissension. Doubts and perplexities arose, and the noise of angry controversies filled the air. Many devout and noble spirits, alienated by the stiff mechanical formalism of the Eastern ritual, turned their longing eyes towards the West, where stood great Babylon with the golden cup in her hand wherewith she deceived the nations by her sorceries. They knew her doctrines very imperfectly, her history not at all. Hence they yielded too readily to the baleful fascination ; and at length the perversions grew so numerous that even the tolerant Czar was obliged to interfere. He banished the Jesuits—the most active promoters of proselytism—first from the two capitals, eventually from the empire. This step cost him some dear and valued friends ; nor were all as generous and discriminating as De Maistre, who could say, even when he thought he had lost the

* From a speech made by Alexander at a meeting of the Frankfort Bible Society.

favour of Alexander, "I am as sure of his justice as of his existence."

From Madame de Krudener and her coterie he was also forced to separate himself. They criticised his public policy, and endeavoured to prescribe to him the line of action he ought to pursue, especially with regard to the Greeks. Alexander never forgot the past : he treated Madame de Krudener with great gentleness and forbearance, and never ceased to show her thoughtful personal kindness ; but he had to tell her that he could allow no interference with his duties as monarch.

Nor was this the worst. All was not sunshine in the path of evangelical reform ; and even the dissemination of the Word of truth did not seem to bring with it the unalloyed blessing that had at first been anticipated. On the contrary, there appeared to be some foundation for the gloomy forebodings of De Maistre, who, as a Roman Catholic, saw in the Bible Society only a means for overturning the whole ecclesiastical establishment of Russia. "Protestants on one side and Raskolniks* on the other," said he, " are two files which saw the religion of the country at each end, and they must soon meet." Everywhere the new wine was fermenting and threatening to rend the old bottles. . Ignorant soldiers and peasants rushed into wild forms of fanatical dissent, or tore down and destroyed sacred pictures, justifying their acts out of the Russian Testaments their Czar himself had distributed amongst them. Photi, and other zealots of the Greek Church,—who had their own reasons for dreading the influx of evangelical light,—eagerly took advantage of these disorders, not only to denounce such men as Galitzin and Tourgenieff, " who defy us the heirs of the apostles," but to ask the official head of the national Church whether he intended to stand by and see her torn to pieces, nay, himself to assist in the work of destruction ?

This was a question Alexander certainly could not answer in

* Dissenters.

the affirmative. It is evident that he loved the Church of his fathers; that he thought her superstitions mere excrescences which might be removed without seriously endangering her fabric; that he believed her maintenance necessary to the welfare of his people; and that he knew there was nothing ready to replace her. Hence his course of action satisfied no one; he earned the envenomed abuse of the bigots of the Greek Church, who traced all the disorders of the country to the translation of the Bible and the education of the poor; while at the same time he did not quite fulfil the sanguine expectations of the friends of evangelical light and progress. But after all, this does not matter so greatly. The important question is, how far he satisfied the Master in whose presence he tried to walk. This is not for us to decide; but at least we know that no influence, no persuasion, ever moved him to withdraw his help and countenance from the Bible Society, or to allow its work to be impeded in any way.

As for Clémence and Ivan, the Romanizing party had never possessed any attraction for the latter, while the former was gradually receding from the creed in which she had been brought up. But the conflict between the Evangelical and what was called the "Orthodox" party was of deep interest to them both. They went heartily along with Galitzin and his friends; Ivan was even sometimes tempted to go beyond them, and altogether to snap the cords that bound him to the national Church. The superstitious practices which prevail in the Eastern Church, as well as in that of the West, cost him many keen and bitter "searchings of heart." He was especially troubled about the adoration of saints and angels and of sacred pictures. Often did he talk upon these matters with Clémence, and earnestly did they pray that they might "perceive and know what things they ought to do."

Ivan's search after a pure form of faith might have led him further had not a bond, invisible yet most strong, held him to the Church of which his Czar was the head. Ivan thought that if reform were really needed, he would surely be her leader also. His soul refused, in its tender, passionate loyalty, to pass beyond that of the man he loved. Therein he erred. To each one of us who closely follows the Divine teaching an hour is sure to come when, in the true spirit of Christ's command, we learn to call no man our father upon earth—when we can no longer take truth upon trust, even from the dearest and most venerated of human lips. Moreover, Ivan expected from Alexander what from his position alone, if from no other reason, he was incapable of performing. King Arthur could not ride forth along with his knights in quest of the Holy Grail; the place in which God had put him, the work to which He had called him, rendered it impossible.

> "The king must guard
> That which he rules, and is but as the hind
> To whom a space of land is given to plough,
> Who may not wander from the allotted field
> Before his work be done." *

For three or four years Ivan and Clémence continued to spend the winters in St. Petersburg, the summers for the most part at Nicolofsky. Here their labours were amply rewarded. From year to year they observed a satisfactory change in the condition of their people; and so great did this appear at last that Ivan said, "I think, my Clémence, they are almost fit for freedom now."

"But, Ivan," said Clémence, "I am not sure that we are fit to give it to them now."

"Why not, m'amie?"

"For whom would we do it, Ivan? *For Alexander, or for Christ?*"

Ivan was silent; the shaft had struck home. At length he answered, "It is for Christ we must do it, Clémence. And he

* Let the thoughtful student read the whole passage from which these lines are taken. The story of Arthur, as the Laureate has transfigured and interpreted it for us, sheds a ray of light upon that of Alexander.

will help us." After another long and thoughtful pause, he added, "It is better, perhaps, to wait until the village boys whom we have put to school have completed their education."

"That will take five or six years."

"Well," said Ivan with a smile, "before then, perhaps, all the mujiks throughout the land may be free men, and my Czar have won the desire of his heart! Who knows?"

CHAPTER XLI.

"Here have we no continuing city, but we seek one to come."

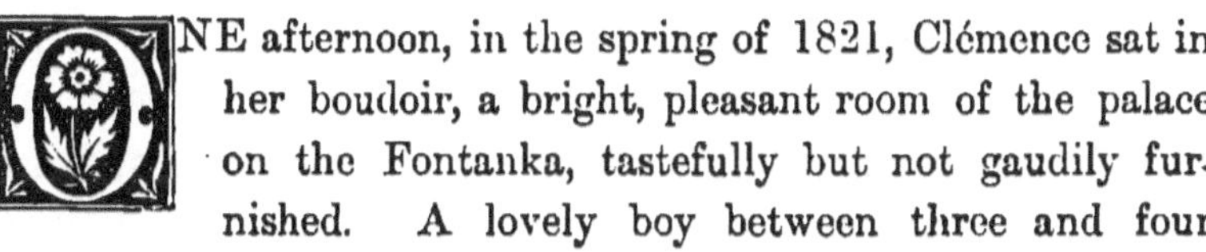

NE afternoon, in the spring of 1821, Clémence sat in her boudoir, a bright, pleasant room of the palace on the Fontanka, tastefully but not gaudily furnished. A lovely boy between three and four years old lay on the floor playing with an ivory alphabet. He was dressed à la mujik, his long curls of gold fell over a miniature caftan of fine blue cloth, which a sash of crimson silk bound about his waist. A younger child, in a white frock of some warm soft material edged with fur, sat on his mother's knee; and a great deal of baby chatter went on, which was rendered still more unintelligible by being half Russian and half French.

On the table beside Clémence lay a pile of books, with which she had been occupying herself. They were copies of the Four Gospels in Russ; and it was her pleasant task to write in each the name of a mujik of Nicolofsky who had been enterprising enough to learn the art of reading, and also to mark such passages and verses as she thought would be particularly profitable for study. But little Feodor's fancy for suddenly grasping the pen in her hand had put a stop for the present to her labours.

Some one knocked at the door; and, thinking it was the

children's nurse, she said, "Come in," without looking up. An attendant entered instead, announcing a visitor—"M. de Salgues."

In delighted amazement Clémence stood up, placed Feodor on the ground, and hastened to welcome a guest who seemed a part of her dear native land. "This is an unexpected pleasure, and a very great one," she said, warmly grasping the hand of Emile.

But Emile, with his old effrontery, saluted her on the cheek, saying, "Permettez-moi, madame ma cousine."

A few explanations followed. Clémence and Ivan knew already that Emile intended to visit them; for he was about to make the tour of the European capitals, and had, as he himself expressed it, every possible inducement not to omit St. Petersburg. But the time of his visit having been left uncertain, it had pleased him to surprise his friends by travelling rapidly and directly from Paris to the city of the Czar.

"You will be glad to hear that my grandmother's health has improved," he said in answer to the inquiries of Clémence. "Madame de Talmont also is very well; and your brother is flourishing, in every sense of the word. I have a portmanteau full of letters and packages for you. How is Prince Ivan?"

"Well, thank you. I am sorry he is out just now; but I expect him home in an hour or two.—My little son, ring the bell for thy mother."

The little mujik, who had been looking at the stranger with large, blue, wide-open eyes, instantly obeyed.

"Come here, my little man," said Emile, stretching out his arms to him. "What a fine boy! Ma cousine, is this your eldest?"

"My first-born is in heaven, as you know," said Clémence in a voice low and gentle, but not sad. "This is our eldest boy —Alexander."

The little Alexander came willingly to Emile, and considered it quite the proper thing to be kissed by him ; for had he not just seen him bestow a similar attention upon " Maman "?

Emile looked admiringly at the child's handsome face, as he seated him on his knee and gave him a bunch of seals to play with. " He is like his father," said he; "while his brother resembles you," he added, glancing at Feodor. " There is no mistaking those soft dark eyes with the long silken lashes. What is his name, ma cousine ?"

" Feodor; in memory of the noble old man who was to his father as a father."

Just then a servant entered; and Clémence, finding that Emile had left his luggage at a hotel, had it sent for, and gave the other directions hospitality required. Meanwhile, Emile carried on a conversation with the little mujik on his knee ; who, not in the least shy, put his hand on the breast of his coat, and then tried to unbutton it, saying, " Where is your star—the beautiful, shiny thing, all made of sparks of fire ?"

" That must be a star of diamonds," laughed Emile. " Is that the sort of plaything *you* are accustomed to, my little prince ?"

" That is what my godfather wears on his coat, and he gives it to me to play with when he comes here," said the little fellow, adding some unintelligible semi-Russian, which quite baffled Emile.

" He has the honour to be the Emperor's godson," Clémence explained.

" Then, my boy, you have a splendid godfather," said Emile.

" Et bon,"* the child added quickly.

At this moment the nurse appeared at the door. She was a stately personage in full Russian costume—a velvet " sarafan," or wide open robe, showing beneath it a close-fitting silken gown, its long sleeves clasped at the wrist with bands of gold, while

---

* This answer was really given by a child of his age, the little son of Madame de Choiseul-Gouffier.

the national head-dress, a kind of crescent-shaped diadem called a " kakoshnik," added to the magnificence of her appearance. She was a person of great importance in the establishment, and much beloved by the children, as they showed by going to her without reluctance even from their idolized " Maman " or " Matinka," as they called her indifferently.

Whilst Emile was doing justice to a repast, which, although prepared upon short notice, proved that Clémence had forgotten none of his boyish tastes, he gave her various items of family tidings, which were new to her, as she had not heard very recently from home.

" My grandmother has been rather fortunate," he said. " Some mines in which she invested a portion of her salvage from the wreck of the family fortunes have proved a grand success.   So the good soul was desirous of purchasing an estate in the country upon which a certain ' mauvais sujet ' of a grandson, who has given her more trouble than he is worth, might settle down at last and ' range himself,' as she says.   By a singular piece of good luck, the ancestral estate of your branch of the Talmonts happened to be in the market, its late republican possessor having made the country too hot for himself."

Clémence uttered an exclamation of surprise and pleasure. " Has La Tante succeeded in obtaining it?" she asked eagerly and with sparkling eyes.

" Yes, ma cousine.   And the first work undertaken by the promising young architect, M. de Talmont, is to be the restoration of the old château."

" Where we were born, he and I—where my mother spent the brief, bright days of her wedded life!" said the delighted Clémence.   " Mon cousin, I rejoice to think that a place so dear to us all will be your home.   You must soon bring a fair bride to grace it," she added with a smile.

But Emile's brow darkened.   " I have no such thoughts at

present," he answered hastily. "Nor ever will," he added in a lower voice.

Clémence saw that she had touched an open wound ; and, to change the conversation, began to ask about Henri.

"He goes on splendidly," said Emile. "Some folk are born on the sunny side of the world, like your little lad, who plays with diamonds from his cradle."

This tone surprised Clémence. An ordinary observer would have thought both the past and present fortunes of Emile far more sunny than those of his cousin. "Henri has known much trouble," she said.

"He always gets out of his troubles on the right side," returned Emile. "He passed unscathed through that terrible Moscow campaign, which slew its tens of thousands, and ruined Napoleon himself. Then he changed his religion, and took the worst time to do it, too,—just after the return of the Bourbons and the priests ; but he only made a nine days' wonder for all his friends, who ended by being more attached to him than ever. He chose a profession which every one thought beneath his birth and his talents, and he is likely to find a career and a fortune in it. Finally, he is affianced to a beautiful young lady, with excellent prospects."

"You amaze me, Emile," said Clémence with a changing colour. "Who is it ?"

"Some one you know very well. Guess," returned Emile, with a cheerfulness which Clémence thought a little forced.

As she paused for a moment before replying, he continued, like one in haste to finish the story, "I may as well tell you at once. It is Mademoiselle de Sartines."

"*Stéphanie !*" Clémence exclaimed. "She is only a child."

"She is a very beautiful young lady," said Emile with emphasis. Going towards the window, he observed, "I am surprised to see so much snow on the ground at this season. Does it always linger so long ?"

"No; this spring is an unusually late one," Clémence answered mechanically, while her thoughts were busy with matters far more interesting. An electric flash passed through her mind, linking together scattered hints, and transient, half-suppressed allusions. The boyish quarrels of Emile with clever little Stéphanie used to be the amusement of the household; and that a serious attachment had sprung out of them was not by any means improbable. A genuine compassion for her cousin awoke within her.—And Henri? So far as he was concerned, surprise as yet swallowed up every other feeling.

"Ah!" cried Emile with a brightening face, "here is Prince Ivan alighting from his drosky. I will go and meet him;" and he hastened from the room.

Emile was not demonstrative; but a warm and genuine friendship for Ivan had a place in his heart since the day when the young Russian answered his scoffs with generous words of counsel and expostulation. Ivan's advice and influence had saved him from much evil, and Ivan's character had unconsciously become his model of excellence.

But they had scarcely exchanged salutations when several guests came in also to share the family dinner. It was the habit of the "grands seigneurs" of St. Petersburg to hoist a flag over their palaces when they intended dining at home, as a sign that their friends would be welcome to join them; and Ivan adopted the hospitable customs of his class, while he avoided much of its lavish and ostentatious expenditure. His guests however departed early, as most of them were going to a ball at Gateschina, the residence of the Empress Mother; and after a whispered word to Clémence he said to Emile, "No doubt you smoke, as of old? I have a smoking-room for my friends, though I am not myself a votary of the fragrant weed. Come with me."

Emile was soon stretched at full length on a velvet-covered divan, and accommodated with a long amber-tipped pipe filled with the choicest tobacco. Ivan seated himself by the fire, and the friends talked together of many things; nor was their communion hindered by the fact that each had a secret care in his heart. Some things were said, or hinted, by Emile which Ivan rejoiced to hear. It soon became evident that the man was not the scoffing sceptic the lad had been: Ivan's words of counsel had gone home to his heart and been the means of keeping him from those " paths of the destroyer " into which there was once terrible danger his feet might wander.

After many other subjects had been discussed, Emile observed, " I am curious to know what you have been doing with the Army of Occupation, since its return from France." *

" It is difficult to know what to do with it," Ivan admitted candidly. " Our enormous military forces threaten to become a perplexity, now that a European peace, which God grant may be enduring, renders them superfluous."

" I should think that army of yours something worse than a perplexity," said Emile laying aside his pipe, " at least to the Czar." His tone was so ominous that Ivan looked at him anxiously.

" I knew in Paris many of your countrymen, ' Messieurs les officiers russe ' we used to call them," Emile resumed after a pause. " You remember, Prince Ivan, what an ardent Imperialist I used to be; and I think still that the exile of St. Helena would make a better ruler for France than any effete Bourbon or Orleans of them all. I should have plunged madly into the wildest intrigues of the secret societies of Paris had not a decanter of poisoned wine stopped me at the beginning."

" Poisoned wine, Emile? Oh yes—I remember."

" But do you remember the lecture you read me with that poisoned wine for a text?—To use assassination as a weapon against political foes is abominable, and all those who do so are

---

* The army which Russia, in common with the other Allied Powers, left in France after the peace of 1815. It was withdrawn in the latter part of 1818.

cowardly villains! The murder of the Duc de Berri shows to
what a length those knights of the dagger and pistol are prepared to go, and ought to frighten all honest people away from
their intrigues. I am sorry to say, Prince Ivan, the army that
has come back to you from France is deeply tainted with the
spirit that has prompted such crimes. Most of your officers are
members of secret societies; and the wildest talk is rife amongst
them. I have heard it said, by one who ought to know, that
it would have been better for the Czar to drown his fine army
in the Baltic than to bring it back to his own country."

Ivan grew visibly pale, but suppressed the emotion he felt.
"The Czar is quite aware of the existence of these secret societies;
he knows, too, that they have extended ramifications even in
Russia," he said. "But have you any idea, Emile, from so
much of their talk as may have reached your ears, what it is
that these gentlemen really want?"

"Scarcely more than they have themselves, I dare say,"
Emile answered with a rather bitter laugh. "I suppose they
would tell you, if you were admitted to their councils, that
they want a constitution for Russia."

"What kind of a constitution?"

"Oh, every one differs as to that. I have heard it said that
every Russian officer carries a constitution about in his pocket.
I suppose, for the most part, they are like those constitutions of
revolutionary France, which were excellent on paper, only they
would not 'march.'"

"And, of course, every one of these gentlemen expects the
Czar to satisfy his own particular aspirations. Suppose he fail
to do it?"

"Suppose he fail to do it—" Instead of finishing his sentence, Emile heaved a long and bitter sigh, flung the ashes out
of his pipe, sat up, and gazed sadly into the fire. Presently he
resumed: "The iniquities of Alexander are twofold. He has
not, as yet, bestowed upon Russia a perfect liberal constitution,

as new and as faultless as a louis d'or fresh from the mint ; and he has used, and is using, his enormous influence to repress in other countries the party of progress,—or of revolution, which you will,—such as the insurgents of Spain and the Carbonari of Italy. He even hesitates to assist the Greeks, who, by the way, seem really to deserve assistance and compassion."

" Ah," cried Ivan with excitement, " there indeed the Czar's perplexity is great. Every true Russian longs to trample in the dust that abominable Ottoman tyranny—cruel, cowardly, treacherous as it is—and to deliver our suffering fellow-Christians, from whom there is going up daily to the throne of God ' the cry of the oppressed that have no comforter ; and on the side of their oppressors there is power, but they have no comforter.' Need I tell you that the first of Russians longs for it more than any of his subjects ? But hitherto it could only have been done at the price of another European war. And even then it might have been done in vain."

" Why so ? " asked Emile.

" Because unless the Czar had a fleet in readiness to support his army, every Christian in Greece might be massacred before our troops could reach Constantinople."

" His position is a difficult one," said Emile.

" *Difficult ?* " Ivan repeated with a heavy sigh. " Would it were *only* difficult ! Sometimes it seems to me as if his way were so hedged about that it is impossible for him to do anything at all. First look abroad, upon the perplexed field of European politics. There his unceasing efforts to maintain the peace of the world have already cost him dear. While he endeavours with the one hand to repress the spirit of lawlessness and anarchy, he is trying with the other to move the ' powers that be' in the direction of justice, mercy, and moderation ; and consequently he is misunderstood by both. Liberals revile him as a friend of tyrants, a renegade from the cause of freedom ; princes accuse him of opening the flood-gates before the torrent of democracy, and say he has none but himself to thank if his own dominions are overwhelmed. Then look at home. *There* is raging the conflict of religious opinion ; Photi, Seraphim, and zealots of their type, are for ever besieging his ear with the accusation that his own hands have undermined the Church of his country by giving his people the Scriptures in the vulgar tongue, and the education necessary to read them. *There* are going forward the plots and intrigues of the active, unscrupulous secret societies : if he tolerates these as the pardonable follies of harmless enthusiasts, he may be as one who stands idly watching the conflagration which will consume his own dwelling; if he allows Aratchaief and Miloradovitch to repress them with rigour, he will assuredly be execrated as a despot. Nor do his difficulties end here. The corruption that has eaten like a canker into every part of the administration of this enormous empire is the worst and sorest of them all. We are still but half civilized. Great as are the strides we have made, and are making, in the path of improvement, the faults of semi-barbarism cling to us yet. In the reign of the Empress Catherine everything was bought and sold, as too many things are even now—in bitter shame and sorrow I say it. ' That they may do evil with both hands earnestly, the prince asketh, and the judge asketh for a reward ; and the great man, he uttereth his mischievous desire : so they wrap it up.' When these things reach the ear of the Czar, he visits them with swift, sharp punishment ; and so men begin to call stern, hard, and suspicious the tenderest hearted man that ever walked God's earth. Yet he cannot stay the evil."

"God help him !" said Emile.

"Amen," responded Ivan. He seemed about to add something more ; but with a look of sadness very foreign to his bright young face he checked himself, and kept silence.

" When did you see him last?" asked Emile.

"I saw him to-day," said Ivan briefly. There the conversation ended: Ivan shortly afterwards accompanied his friend to his apartment, bade him a cordial good-night, and then went at once to the dressing-room, where Clémence was awaiting him, and reading meanwhile the letters Emile had given her.

The accounts of Stéphanie were particularly interesting to her. How the approbation of that young lady's guardian had ever been obtained by a suitor who had so small a portion of this world's goods to offer as Henri de Talmont, was certainly a mystery. The letters only solved it indirectly. That of Madame de Talmont was the most satisfactory. She observed that the will of Stéphanie's guardian was very weak, while that of Stéphanie herself was remarkably strong. When M. de Galmar informed her of Henri's proposal, adding, as a matter of course, that he would decline it for her, she was far too decorous and well-bred to make the smallest objection; but she told him very quietly that she had often thought of embracing a religious life, and that as her friend Madame de Krudener was now about to found a missionary community—she believed among the Tartars on the Danube—she wished to signify her intention of joining it as soon as she came of age. "Your cousin is a strange girl," M. de Galmar observed afterwards to his daughter Coralie. "But, after all, a Protestant is not as bad as a Tartar. Nor is dining upon three courses, instead of twelve, quite as bad as being dined upon oneself by cannibals in some of those savage countries. She had better take the young architect."

Clémence looked up from her letter with an air of amusement, which changed into one of grave anxiety as she saw the serious face of Ivan bending over her. She drew a chair for him near the fire, and said, "I am longing to hear all, Ivan. Why did the Czar send for you? How did you find him?"

Ivan answered the last question first: "Looking depressed and weary, and his deafness more apparent than ever. I had to sit quite close to him, and to raise my voice to make him hear. He spoke very mournfully of the state of things in Siberia, whence the Governor-General, Speranski, has just returned, bringing sad accounts of the prevalence of corruption and dishonesty in the public service. For the present the vigorous measures of Speranski have checked these evils, though at the expense of removing the governor from every province save one. He has sent these unfaithful governors here for their trial; and most of them will probably be sent back to Siberia as convicts. But now his own health has broken down, and he is obliged to quit his post. There is need—great need—of faithful and active men to continue and carry out the reforms he has begun."

Here Ivan paused, took the hand of Clémence in his, and with a look full of tenderness continued his narrative—" The Czar said to me sadly, ' There are so few that I can trust. Will *you* help me in this thing, Prince Ivan Ivanovitch ?' "

Clémence started, and her sweet face glowed with a sudden colour, then grew pale again as rapidly. " *O Ivan !*" she exclaimed. " And what did you say to him ?"

" What *could* I say ? Is it amongst things possible—conceivable—that my Czar should ask me to help him, and be refused ?"

" No ; nor that I should wish it. But, Ivan, this will bring a great change into our happy life."

" These were nearly his own words. He was very kind, he was even tenderly considerate for me and for you, Clémence. He would not, he said, ask from me more than a few years of my life. And for that time, could not your mother come to you ?"

" Come to *me* ?" Clémence repeated a little proudly. " Does he—or do you—suppose for one moment I would let you go to Siberia alone ?"

" I don't believe he does," Ivan answered with a dawning smile upon his serious face. " He added, that should you prefer accompanying me, which indeed was what he expected, every possible comfort and luxury should be provided for you and for

the children. 'A residence in Siberia is not so great a hardship as many men think,' he said. Still, Clémence, I tremble
for our children. They are so young and tender."

"Children born in St. Petersburg are not likely to suffer
much from the severity of any climate short of that of the
North Pole," returned Clémence cheerfully. "God has made
our way plain before us, Ivan. We cannot hesitate."

"So I told the Czar. He would have given me time to
reflect, but I said it was needless. I know that in this I was
doing no wrong to you, Clémence, since your heart ever beats in
mine."

"Did he say anything about the time of our departure?"

"Only that the summer is before us now, and that we must
not lose it. He spoke with much feeling of the Siberian
exiles, and also of the native tribes which are still heathen, and
of the missionary work going on amongst them. He said that
where he is sending me I would find many ways of promoting
the kingdom of Christ."

"How did you answer him?"

"Just as I should have answered *you*, Clémence ;—but such
words do not bear repeating. I said something about the joy
of winning souls for Christ, and I shall never forget the sudden
brightening of his sad face as he responded—'You are young
now, but if after a long life of labour you should only succeed
in leading one sinner to Christ, you will have reason to bless
God, and to rejoice at it throughout eternity.' "*

There were tears in the eyes of Clémence as she said, "He is
right, dearest. We will go bravely and cheerfully, in the name
of our God; for has He not said, 'My presence shall go with
thee, and I will give thee rest'?"

---

* Words used by Alexander to a young Protestant missionary whom the Englishman,
Lewis Way, brought to see him.

CHAPTER XLII.

"Where the frost king breathes on the slippery sails,
And the mariner wakes no more,
Lift high the lamp that never fails,
On that dark and sterile shore."

FIVE years have passed away. To Ivan they have been years of toil and conflict, and yet happy years. In the land of his exile he has laboured earnestly to introduce order, good government, civilization, and, above all, to sow the seeds of Christianity. A district, or "circle," in the north-east of Siberia, immense in extent, but sparely peopled, has been his charge; and he has had to travel many a weary league over snow and ice, and through dense forests of pine and larch. In order that every portion of the wide area intrusted to his care might enjoy the careful personal superintendence indispensable to its prosperity, he established his head-quarters, for six months or a year at a time, in the different settlements within his circle, and thence he made journeys through the surrounding districts.

Clémence seconded all his efforts; and her wise and loving ministrations made each of her temporary homes a little spot of light amidst the darkness. In selecting the numerous retinue who accompanied him from Europe, Ivan had endeavoured to make choice of the persons best fitted to aid him in his philanthropic labours for the improvement of his people. The most useful of these were the able and energetic German, Dr. Krausekopf; and Pope Yefim, the friend of his youth, and one of the earliest fruits of the Evangelical revival in Russia. He was now the sole chaplain of the household, since the venerable Grandpierre had gone to his rest, and Clémence did not desire a successor of the Roman Catholic faith. Ivan found him a zealous and devoted helper, especially in missionary work.

Meanwhile the cheerful prophecies of Clémence about the children had been amply fulfilled. They grew in strength and beauty as well and as quickly as they could have done beneath the beams of a southern sun. Alexander and Feodor had now a little fair-haired brother Henri to play with and take care of, and, to their great delight, a baby sister also to admire and caress. She had recently been baptized by the name of Victoire, because, as Clémence said, "the eldest daughter of the House of Talmont used always to be called Victoire."

A winter of very unusual severity, which surprised Ivan and his household in one of the most northerly settlements of his circle, for the first time since he left Europe cut him off completely for some months from the world of civilization. Towards the end of January violent snow-storms set in, continuing for weeks with little intermission, and rendering impassable the poor apologies for roads which were all that he as yet had been able to construct. So the great fast before Easter found him still sending out fatigue parties to clear the paths, and watching anxiously for the first adventurous sledger who should make his way across the fields of ice and snow with despatches from Tobolsk.

Easter eve came at last; and still isolation and solitude reigned at Novoi Nicolofsky,—as Ivan, in memory of his early home, had named this settlement, of which he was the founder. The short day had closed; and Ivan, robed in furs from head to foot, came in from his manifold labours to enjoy a quiet half-hour with Clémence. He was now about two-and-thirty, and looked even older; for thought and toil and the habit of command had set their seal upon his broad, open forehead. Yet he had lost nothing of his frank, cheerful air; and when he flung off his furs, and seated himself at the fire by the side of Clémence, they looked as handsome and as happy a couple as could have been found in any land or clime.

With a smile of welcome Clémence laid aside her work —a little pair of reindeer-skin moccasins. "I am glad you have come so early, Ivan," she said. "We can have a few minutes' quiet talk before we go down to the church to listen to the reading. How pleasant it is to keep, here in the far north, our dear Russian custom of the Easter evening Bible reading!"

"Yes; our little church is crowded to-night. I have just been looking in. Vanka the huntsman was reading the story of our Lord's Passion according to St. John, and I saw many a tearful face and heard many a sob in the stillness. I meant to have read for them myself, but I would not disturb him. I can read by-and-by, when we go there together."

"What a beautiful custom it is, this reading of God's Word for his brethren by any poor man who is able to do it!" said Clémence. "Where is Pope Yefim?"

"In his own room, I believe. You know that on Easter eve our priests usually leave the churches to the people."

"The poor lads who are out on duty miss something."

"True; but they will have their turn by-and-by. We all must miss something," he added, smiling. "But then we all have our compensations."

"I think the want of tidings from our dear ones is our only *real* trial," Clémence answered. "I sometimes long to see my mother's face, Ivan, and to show her our darlings. What a happy little visit that was which she paid us in St. Petersburg before we left! But for that I should have felt the long separation far more."

"It was very good of her to come such a distance on such

short notice ; and it sent us on our way with lightened hearts. And does not the thought that Henri is at Tobolsk help to break the sense of separation ? "

" Really it does : compared with Paris, or even with St. Petersburg, Tobolsk seems close at hand."

" How well he is getting on there, too," said Ivan. " In a year or two, God willing, he may settle near us in Moscow or in St. Petersburg ; and our dear mother can then divide her time between her son and daughter."

" What a happy dream ! " said Clémence. " And yet *not* a dream, but a sober, practicable plan, a hope that may soon be realized. How good God is to us, Ivan ! "

A handsome boy of eight or nine bounded into the room, his fair hair streaming over his fur jacket, and his bright face glowing with exercise and excitement. " Softly—softly, my boy," said his father.

" Papinka, they are coming !—they are coming ! " he shouted, confident that the importance of his tidings justified any amount of haste and clamour in their delivery.

" Who are coming, my dear boy ? "

" Sledges, papinka, sledges ! Three of them ! " he cried breathlessly. " From the south ! "

" Do not let us be too sure," Ivan said quickly to Clémence. " They may be only, after all, from some neighbouring settlement."

" They are from the south, papinka," the boy repeated. " They have signal-flags. Matvei saw them in the moonlight, quite plainly."

" *I* must see them too," said Ivan, hastily putting on his furs again.

It was true. Their long isolation was over. Tidings and letters and friends from the outer world had reached them at last. Much more and better—Clémence sprang forward with a cry of joy as a rough, sealskin-coated figure entered the room.

"Is it thou,—is it really *thou*, Henri?" she asked between smiles and tears.

"Yes, my own sweet sister, it is I," said Henri de Talmont. "My work in Tobolsk is finished, so I have come to visit you."

CHAPTER XLIII

"The King hath laid his hand
On the watcher's head,
Till the heart that was so worn and sad
Is quiet and comforted."

LTHOUGH the fast of Easter eve is the strictest known in the Greek Church, yet on this occasion willing hands quickly prepared a meal for the travellers, since, as Pope Yefim observed, "Mercy is better than sacrifice." Whilst Ivan's retainers took care of the companions of Henri, he himself was waited upon like a prince by Clémence and Ivan in person, with the assistance of Pope Yefim and little Alexander. In reply to their eager inquiries, he told them the incidents of his journey, which had not been without its dangers and vicissitudes. But, through all that he said, Clémence thought she perceived the shadow of some great sorrow. Her foreboding heart turned at once to what was to both of them equally and intensely dear. Three times she tried to shape the inquiry, "Henri, how is our mother?" and three times the words died upon her lips. But at last she summoned courage to ask the question.

His answer relieved her at once: "Never better, thank God. Such at least is her own report. I bring you letters from her, which she enclosed to me."

Then her anxious thoughts turned to his betrothed, the bright, brave-hearted Stéphanie; but she shrank from uttering her name, lest haply it might have become, for him, the saddest sound upon earth. Ivan, however, had no such misgivings, and approached the subject gaily. "Remember, mon ami," he said, "we are all impatience to hear of la fiancée, la belle Stéphanie."

"I wish you could *see* her," answered Henri brightening. "I do not think any one could deny *now* that she is surpassingly beautiful—and good. She finds all her recreation, all her delight in works of love and mercy. Wherever she goes, her energy and vivacity open the doors wide before her. And then her sound practical sense and loving spirit make her more than welcome."

"I knew it would be so," said Clémence. "I knew my little friend Stéphanie would grow into a noble woman."

"You are a fortunate man, Henri," Ivan added. "How happy we shall be together when you bring your bride and settle amongst us! You must always spend your summers at Nicolofsky. But now it is *my* turn," he said lightly, as he rose and stood beside him, laying his hand on his shoulder. "You must tell me the last tidings of my Czar. I am thirsting to hear of him, and not once have you named him yet."

Henri paused a moment; then he said, in a low, quiet voice, "He is well—*very.*"

Clémence looked up surprised, but Ivan observed nothing. "Tell me more," he went on eagerly. "Where was he when you heard last? What has he been doing?—There is one thing I long, yet scarcely hope, to hear. Has he won the desire of his heart? Are the serfs free yet?"

"The serfs are *not* free;—but, dear Ivan, your Czar *has* won the desire of his heart."

Now first his tone arrested Ivan, who looked at him amazed. "How?" he faltered, with a face growing rapidly white.

"Be calm, dear friend. Alexander has but exchanged the crown of Russia for one more glorious."

At that moment little Alexander rushed in weeping. "Father, mother," he sobbed, "they are all saying the Czar is dead—the dear, good Czar, my godfather. Father, is it true?"

Ivan did not answer. No word passed his lips, no cry; he only tottered and sank as one struck by a fatal bullet. From Clémence just then his white death-like face shut out all sorrows, all losses far away.

But the strong man wrestled with his agony and overcame. After a few terrible moments, during which life changed its aspect to Ivan Pojarsky, he regained a measure of outward calmness.

"Tell me all you know, Henri," he said at last,—"*all*, from the beginning."

The sorrow-stricken group drew close together. Clémence had placed her hand in that of her husband, and was watching him with anxious eyes. The weeping child stood beside his father's knee; and the aged priest covered his face to hide the emotion he could not restrain.

"I have one fear, too dreadful to utter," said Ivan with pale lips. "Can you guess, and remove it, Henri?"

"I can. No hand touched him, except the hand of God. It will be written in history that the Emperor Alexander died of fever, at Taganrog in the Crimea."

"Will it not be true?" asked Clémence.

"Not all the truth. Before the fiery shaft of the fever smote him he was already stricken, I think to death."

"Ever fearless, he was wont to brave the danger of infection as readily as other dangers," Pope Yefim said.

"My life witnesses to that," returned Henri, almost losing his self-control. After a pause he resumed: "Before I left Tobolsk, I met an Englishman who had seen his physician, Dr. Wylie, and heard from his lips a full account of every particular. He told me all. And this, indeed, is what has brought me here."

"It was so good of you to come," said Clémence tearfully.

"He was looking ill when we parted," Ivan said. "Ill and worn. But he was so strong, and only forty-three. I never dreamed of death for him—never once."

Henri answered sadly: "During the years that passed since then, those who loved him have thought of it often—have sometimes almost *wished.*"—but his voice failed; to end *that* sentence was beyond his power. After a pause he resumed: "Repeated attacks of erysipelas wore out his strength,—especially one, desperately severe, two years before the end. He never fully recovered from its effects. His nerves were shattered; sleep forsook him; he could not bear light or noise, even the taper which burned all day on his table to seal his never-ending despatches, had to be carefully shaded. Still he toiled on, rising sometimes as early as half-past three, and allowing himself no time for rest, except such as he could snatch in his rapid journeys, often over rough roads and in bad vehicles. One who had a post in his household,* said to my English friend, 'After two or three days passed in a carriage the uncrowned traveller gives himself up to rest and refreshment, but the Emperor relaxes himself from one fatigue by another. A regiment is reviewed, government officials received, military colonies visited, an establishment created, plans examined, and so forth. Sleep and food have great trouble to glide into the leisure of so busy a life.' Yet, after all, it is not toil which usually strikes at the roots of a strong man's life. Nor is bodily suffering the hardest thing to endure. 'The spirit of a man will sustain his infirmity, but a wounded spirit who can bear?' Again to use words other than my own, and all too sadly true, 'He saw his noble desires abandoned to ridicule, and those to whom he devoted himself rewarded him with ingratitude; until at last the silent but unceasing struggle he had to maintain against those who pretended to second him

* Dupré de St. Maure.

only to paralyze his action, and to enter into his views only that they might the better betray them, filled his days with bitterness, and eventually shortened their course.'" *

"Ah!" said Ivan with a shuddering sigh that was more than half a groan of pain.

"The shadows fell ever dark and darker over that grand, silent, solitary life—how dark those who stood outside could only guess," Henri went on. "He bore his burden alone. Now and then a few sad words falling from his lips almost unawares, or perhaps a look, showed what was passing within. Once a valued friend, a lady, asked of him a favour which in justice to others he could not grant. He couched his refusal, as he was wont to do, in terms so gentle that she was greatly touched ; and when they parted she expressed her earnest wishes for his happiness. At the word 'happiness' a change passed over his face, and he turned away with a sorrowful gesture. In one of his rapid journeys, his favourite aide-de-camp, Volkonski, was his companion. The road was bad ; and in ascending a steep hill the carriage stopped, the horses being unable to draw it. Instead of awakening Volkonski, who had fallen asleep, the Emperor himself got out and gave the coachman the necessary assistance, helping to push the carriage up the hill. As he resumed his place, Volkonski awoke. 'Ah, sire, why did you not call me?' he said. 'It is all right,' returned the Czar. 'You were asleep, and sleep is too precious to be disturbed,'—adding in a lower tone, as if to himself, 'It brings forgetfulness."

"How like him !" said Clémence.

"Too sadly like him," resumed Henri. "It was all Alexander—the unselfishness, the profound melancholy, the reserve that only betrayed it unconsciously in taking thought for another. But I suppose the most direct disclosure he ever made was in a few words spoken to an old and intimate friend

* "Vie de Madame de Krudener." Par M. Eynard.

who asked about his health. 'In body, I am well,' he answered; 'but in mind I suffer always, and my suffering is the greater because I cannot speak of it.'"

There was a pause. Clémence bent down over the fair head of her little son to hide the tears which were dropping slowly. "My child had better go to his rest," she said.

The child's eager face was upturned, and the request to stay was on his trembling lips, when Ivan interposed. "No," he said. "Let him hear all, Clémence. He has the right.—But, Henri, was there no one near to ask whence all this anguish and sorrow of heart?"

"Some at least of its hidden sources were not hard to guess. Had he not tasted all the bitterness of failure—worse a thousand times than the bitterness of death? Which of all the plans, the hopes that his soul hung upon, had found its fulfilment? Which had not disappointed him? The Holy Alliance had become the tool of selfish politicians, perhaps even the instrument of tyrants. The dissemination of the Holy Scriptures, from which he hoped so much, had proved, *apparently*, a cause of discord and confusion; his people, so loved and toiled for, had 'shown themselves insensible to the benefits he sought to confer upon them;' and secret societies and plots for his assassination had answered his unceasing efforts to do them good. Well might he say, with one of old, 'I have laboured in vain; I have spent my strength for nought and in vain.' And with another, 'Now, O Lord, take away my life; for I am not better than my fathers.'"

"But oh, Henri," asked Clémence, struggling with her tears, "did he not know, all through, in whom he had believed? Did not Christ, in the darkest hour, stand beside his suffering servant?"

Henri's face grew sadder still. "Clémence—Ivan, must I tell you all I *think*?" he asked.

"All," said Ivan. "Keep nothing back."

"Then I think the face of his Lord was hid from him.

Wherefore I cannot tell.   There are secrets in His dealings with His own with which a stranger may not intermeddle."

"The evil one has fearful power," Pope Yefim said.   " How would the great adversary, the accuser of the brethren, assault such a noble foe, and wound and harass, since he knew he could not destroy him !"

"There is no doubt he used for the purpose," Henri continued, "that strain of hereditary melancholy which flows through the life-current of his race, and which might—might have— God dealt tenderly with him, after all, though it is hard to see it now."   After a long pause he resumed: " Even when he walked in darkness and had no light he ceased not to trust in the Lord, and to stay himself upon his God.   In the darkest hours his word was his comfort ; and those who feared his name, however poor or lowly, were the men he delighted to honour.   You remember doubtless, before you left St. Petersburg, the visit of those noble-hearted philanthropists, Grellet and Allen ; and you may have heard of their interview with the Emperor ;—how the three, the great monarch and the two obscure travellers, knelt side by side, and poured out their full hearts to God, feeling themselves truly one in that love of Christ which passeth knowledge.   Allen saw him once more, at Verona, when the shadows of the grave had already begun to deepen over him.   Finding him weary and oppressed with work, the Englishman spoke of mental prayer, and said that even in the midst of engrossing occupations a man might lift up his heart to God.   ' It is my constant practice, and I know not what I should do without it,' was Alexander's answer.   To an appeal made to him by the same friend on behalf of the suffering and indigent Waldenses, he responded with a prompt and sympathetic munificence which evidently had its root in the sense that they were his brethren in Christ Jesus.

"The last year of his life was marked by peculiar sorrows. A terrible inundation of the Neva destroyed a great part of

St. Petersburg, and brought death and desolation to thousands of families. While the inundation continued, he spared no effort to rescue the perishing; and for weeks afterwards he went every day to the homes of those who had lost their relatives, relieving their necessities, and speaking words of hope and comfort about the 'city which cannot be moved.' Then another and a deeper sorrow came to him—but of that I will not speak."*

Here the child's clear voice broke in. "Oh, father," he asked wondering, "why did not God comfort him?"

Ivan could not answer, nor could he meet the searching gaze of the boy's young eyes. In broken-hearted silence he turned away. But Henri put his arm around the child and drew him close to him. "God *did* comfort him, at last," he said. "The way was rough, rough and long, but the end was peace.—That journey to the south, from which he returned no more, was undertaken partly for the benefit of the Empress Elizabeth, whose health for some time had been failing. Her physicians had recommended her to pass the winter in Germany, but she entreated them not to separate her from her husband; and, to avoid this separation, he fixed upon a residence for her at Taganrog, in the Crimea, the climate being accounted favourable, resolving to make it his own headquarters for the season. There they spent a few quiet, restful weeks together. Elizabeth wrote to her own family that she had never been so happy in all her life. She drove and walked with the Emperor, who watched over her with all the care and tenderness of which he was so capable. Whenever he walked alone, he visited the poor in their humble homes; and many a touching memory of his kindness will linger long on their lips and in their hearts.†

---

* The death of his only child, Sophie Narischkin, a beautiful and most amiable girl, about to be married to one of his aides-de-camp. The whole story is deeply touching.

† "His face showed care and sorrow, but the remembrance of these walks, and the acts of benevolence resulting from them, is the most touching of my recollections in Russia," writes a Frenchman who happened to be at Taganrog at the time.

"But that peaceful breathing space had an end too soon. During a toilsome journey through the Crimea, filled with the usual details of business, the deadly fever and ague smote his frame; while, just at the same time, tidings no less deadly reached his heart. The vaguely treasonable projects of the secret societies had ended in a desperate and deliberate plot, of which his own assassination was a leading feature."

"*His* assassination!" cried Ivan. "Impossible! They could *never* have done it."

"So it seemed," Henri answered. "For the deed was often purposed, never once attempted. Still the shaft struck home. Many of those who plotted to take his life owed all that made their own precious to his bounty; every one of them had received favours at his hands. 'But what could I expect? It is a just retribution,' he cried, unconscious in his deafness that he spoke aloud. 'Almighty God, let thy judgments fall on me alone, and not on my people!'"

"A just retribution?" Clémence repeated. "How was it possible to him, even for a moment, to imagine *that?*"

"It could only have been possible to shattered nerves and a mind unstrung by suffering. The remembrance of the dark tragedy that began his reign—the thought of his father's horrible fate, perhaps soon to be his own—came back upon him in the hours of pain and weakness. Moreover, a stern duty was laid upon him. Before treason such as had been now disclosed to him no monarch on earth could remain passive. The ruler 'beareth not the sword in vain.' But to Alexander it was easier to suffer than to strike.

"So he returned to Taganrog with fever in his veins and the bitterness of death in his heart. For some days he struggled on, refusing to yield to his ever increasing malady, and rejecting the severe remedies his physicians pressed upon him. They thought he wished to die; and so it may have been, still I am persuaded he would not have thrust the cup of life aside by any act of his own.   He really believed their treatment mistaken.   'My malady is beyond your skill,' he said to them; and again to Wylie, 'Ah, my friend, I think you are deceived as to the nature of my illness; it is my nerves that need a cure.'   Wylie bore witness afterwards that throughout those days, so sad for the watchers, and to the very end, he 'continued to rest upon Christ as his only hope.   His greatest pleasure was to have the Scriptures read to him; and he often requested his attendants to leave him alone, doubtless that he might hold communion with God in prayer.'*

"One loving, tireless watcher scarcely quitted him night or day.   New strength seemed poured upon the feeble frame and timid spirit of the gentle Elizabeth.   Rising almost from her own bed of sickness to watch beside his, yet she never failed, never faltered; even in the most terrible hours of agony no entreaties could win her from his side.   And strength was given her to the end.   His last word, his last look was for her.   She had her reward."

"Thank God!" murmured Clémence—"thank God!"

"When at last Wylie told him his danger,—'Then you really believe I am dying?' he said, looking him earnestly in the face.   Wylie assented.   'The best news I have heard for many years,' returned he, pressing Wylie's hand.   The Archimandrite Fedotof was summoned to act as his confessor.   Their interview was very brief; but the priest said that 'he had never seen more Christian humility, or a dying man more thoroughly prepared.'   Afterwards, with Elizabeth, he partook for the last time of the memorials of his Saviour's love.   No doubt Christ drew very near him then; for a look of exceeding peace and rest came over his worn, suffering face, and he said to Elizabeth that he had never been so happy in all his life.   Summoning the physicians again, he gently told them to do what they pleased, he would no longer object to anything.

* Life of William Allen.

But their treatment, if ever it would have availed, was worso than useless now.   Increased suffering and violent delirium were the result.   Still there were intervals of consciousness, in which he thanked those around him for their services, spoke to Elizabeth with the warmest gratitude and affection, and earnestly commended her to the care of his friend Volkonski, entreating him not to leave her until he had brought her to his mother at St. Petersburg.

"Calm returned at length.   It was early in the morning. He opened his eyes, fixed them with full recognition on the face of Elizabeth; took her hand, pressed it to his lips and his heart; and then greeted Volkonski, who stood beside him, with a smile.   Overjoyed at the recognition, the faithful servant bent down over the hand of his beloved master and tried to kiss it; but Alexander had long ago forbidden him this act of homage as too ceremonious for so dear a friend, and now he drew his hand away with a slight, loving gesture of reproach.   The curtains had been pushed aside from a window near the sofa where he lay, and the morning sun was streaming brightly in.   ' Ah, le beau jour !' he murmured with a look of pleasure.   Then looking anxiously and tenderly at Elizabeth, 'Que vous devez être fatiguée !' he said.   They were his last words, although for another day and night of weakness and suffering life lingered on.   The following morning he again knew those around him, pressed once more the hand of Elizabeth, looked at her with expressive eyes full of affection, and tried to speak—but in vain.   Then, at last, Christ took his weary servant home.—So you see, my child," said Henri to the little Alexander as he drew him closer still, " God comforted him."

There was a long silence.   The aged priest and the little child were weeping bitterly, and the quiet tears of Clémence were falling.   She was the first to speak.   " And Elizabeth ?" she asked softly.

" Elizabeth closed his eyes, knelt down beside him, and in a few words of prayer gave him up to God.   Then she added to a letter she had already begun to the Empress Mother, 'Our angel is gone from us into heaven.   My only comfort is that I shall not long survive him.   I hope soon to be reunited to him.' And I think her hope will not be disappointed." *

Another silence, then Ivan rose slowly, as if to leave the room.   "Stay, dear Ivan," Henri said.   "I think it will comfort you to know with what a passion of grief he is lamented."

"Scarcely," Ivan answered in a trembling voice.   "In this world love and understanding always come too late."

"The long journey from Taganrog to St. Petersburg was made amidst the tears of a sorrowing people, who paid the precious dust every tribute of love and reverence their grateful hearts could devise," said Henri.   "The honours the living would never accept were heaped upon the dead.   In many places the crowds drew the funeral carriage themselves, forgetting how he who lay there used to say he 'could never endure to see men doing the work of beasts of burden.'   The faithful heart of Ilya was well-nigh broken, because, on account of his original rank, which was that of a mujik, he who had driven his lord for eight-and-twenty years would not be permitted to drive him now.   Nothing could separate him from the hearse; by day he walked beside it, at night he slept beneath it, wrapped in furs.   But when he came to the capital the Grand-Duke Nicholas allowed him once more to take the reins.

"In St. Petersburg, his own bright city of the Neva, the sorrow is profound and universal.   There is scarcely a family, from the highest to the lowest, of which he has not been personally the benefactor.   The first three days after the tidings came seemed like the three days' darkness of Egypt.   A deep, silent gloom brooded over all.   To some true hearts that loved him the grief has proved too heavy to be borne.   One such I

---

* Nor was it.   Alexander died on the 1st of December 1825, Elizabeth on the 16th of the following May.

know of—a merchant of retired habits, noted for his munificent charities.   He heard the tidings when walking on the Neva Prospekt, reached his home with difficulty, uttered no words but these, 'The Emperor is dead,' and expired in the midst of his family.*   Nor is it in St. Petersburg alone that he is missed and mourned.   There is weeping in the vine-clad valleys of France as well as on the frozen plains of Russia.†   Wherever his armies trod he has left behind him a track of blessing.

"Of funeral pomp and splendour, of the outward, visible signs of a great nation's pride and sorrow, I have no heart to speak.   The priceless jewels of the seven crowns of Russia which were laid upon his bier could be scarcely less to the senseless dust than they had been to the living man."

"What need of them?" Pope Yefim said.   "Now he wears the crown of glory that fadeth not away, he walks amidst the splendours of the New Jerusalem, with its streets of gold and gates of pearl, its walls of jasper and foundation-stones of living fire."

"He sees the face of Christ," Henri answered; "for it is written, 'His servants shall serve him; they shall see his face, and his name shall be in their foreheads.'"

* "He was said to be no solitary example of a broken heart for the loss of Alexander.   Many were mentioned both in St. Petersburg and in Moscow; and a Russian assured me that he would venture any wager that if all the deaths from this cause throughout the empire were reckoned together, they would amount to above a hundred."—*Kohl.*

† "J'aimais à voir partager ma tristesse jusque par les habitans de cette Champagne où Alexandre était entré en vainqueur.   Il n'y eut pas un pauvre vigneron d'Epernay ou de Vertus qui ne se fut écrié en apprenant la mort d'Alexandre, 'Ah, quel malheur; il avait sauvé la France!'   Une paysanne me disait un jour, 'Hélas, madame, il était aussi aimable qu'il était beau!'"—*Madame de Choiseul-Gouffier.*

CHAPTER XLIV.

"CHRISTOIIS VOSKRESS."

IVAN "entered into his closet, and shut his door;" not to hold communion with his Father in heaven, but to wrestle in solitude and silence with the anguish of his soul. Never before had a sorrow touched the roots of his nature, the very ground and core of his being. He was stricken to the heart, but he was not stunned by the blow. He had been able to hear and to comprehend every detail; and now—far from telling himself, as men often do in the first strangeness of a sudden grief, that this thing was not, *could not* be, true—he felt as if he had known it for years, as if it had already become part of his life. "The Czar Alexander Paulovitch is dead," said Ivan—"dead in the very prime of his days, in the very zenith of his power and glory."

From the first hour he knew him, the soul of Ivan clave to that of his Czar. His love for him was a passion of loyalty and hero-worship, blended with deepest personal affection and gratitude. And now it seemed to him that the world, from which that grand presence had departed, was henceforward a dull, cold, sunless world; where, indeed, there might be much to do and much to suffer, but which could never more be kindled by the light of morning, by the glamour of romance. All was changed, and changed for ever.

He laid before him on the table two memorials of the past which he always wore—the Moscow medal, and the golden coin Alexander's hand had given him long ago by the Oka. The medal he looked at with a sigh and put down quietly, the coin he pressed once and again to his lips. Clearly, as though it were but yesterday, he saw the noble form of " his boyar "— the stately head, the young face, so full of manly beauty and deep concern—bending compassionately over the mujik's prostrate form. Then, unawares, the vision changed. The low, distant chant of sweet voices in the chapel, performing the midnight Easter service, fell upon his ear, and turned aside the current of his thoughts, though it could not break the isolation of his sorrow. Instead of the banks of the Oka he saw the vine-clad plains of France, and heard the thrilling harmony, almost awful in its solemn majesty, of that thanksgiving service in the Plaine des Vertus. In what joy and glory had his Czar walked that day—so grand and peerless amongst men—so full of lowly, reverent gladness before his Saviour and his God !

A flood of bitter pain swept over him. " O God !" he cried, " why didst thou not take him thus to thyself ?" If a heroic, triumphant death had stopped him in the midst of his career of victory, Ivan almost felt as though he could have borne the blow. Or if God had made him to prosper in all he put his hand to, had given him to see the glad fruition of all his hopes and dreams, and then gently taken him, full of years and honours, from an earthly to a heavenly crown, Ivan could have comprehended his ways with his servant; he could have said, " Thy will be done."

He did *not* say it now. His soul rose up in rebellion, and from its seething depths there came the bitter cry, " Was this thy word unto thy servant, upon which thou didst cause him to hope, ' I will be with him in trouble; I will deliver him, and honour him. With long life will I satisfy him, and shew him my salvation ' ? "—*Was* he satisfied ? What had he gained ? Failure, disappointment, sorrow marked every step of his way. Almost had he fainted utterly; almost had his feet stumbled on the dark mountains, while he looked for light, and behold, darkness and the shadow of death. Until at last, worn out and weary, " with shattered nerves and sinews all unstrung," and with heart broken by the ingratitude of those he loved and trusted, he " laid himself down in the grave and slept the sleep of death." " Could any death have been more sad?" cried Ivan in his agony. " Rather would it have seemed a fitting end for a life spent in the service of self and sin, than for one which was laid as an offering at the feet of Christ." Numb, blank despair stole over his heart, and a low half-broken moan arose from his lips—" No use in conflict, no hope of victory ! The noblest, brightest lives only end in the worst bitterness of failure. God is great and good, and there is his heaven still to look for ; but' all things here below are a dark sad mystery. This world belongs to the powers of evil, and they prevail."

Fast bound in the trance of his sorrow, he did not see the red light of the northern morning steal slowly in. Nor did he hear an approaching footstep, nor a gentle knock at the door ; which, however, was not fastened on the inside, so Clémence opened it softly, and came towards him. Bending down, she pressed upon his white lips the Easter salutation, saying, " Christohs voskress " (Christ is risen).

" Voyst venno voskress " (He is risen indeed), Ivan answered mechanically, after the beautiful custom of the Eastern Church.

" My husband," she said softly, laying her hand on his arm, " dost thou believe it ? "

He looked up: her face too was pale, and bore the traces of many tears. " I *know* it to be true," he said.

"Do you believe it, my Ivan? Do you believe, in your heart of hearts, that Christ has burst the bonds of death, not for himself alone, but for all whom we love?"

"Yes; I believe in the resurrection of the just," said Ivan with trembling lips.

"Then why sorrow for our Czar as those that have no hope?"

"Do not speak to me, Clémence. I cannot bear it yet. My heart is breaking. Not so much because God has taken him from us, as because of all the darkness—all the seeming failure."

A still, calm smile passed over the quiet face of Clémence, kindling it with a radiance more than that of the morning. Ivan looked at her wondering. "What is it?" he asked, taking her hand and drawing her to a seat beside him.

"*Christ is risen,*" she said again. "That word folds up within it all comfort, Ivan."

"I see no comfort now."

"You will see it soon, dearest. You will see that His resurrection from the dead—the ending of his bitter agony in endless joy—means the resurrection of all our hopes; and assures us for evermore that life, not death, joy not sorrow, fruition not failure, is his purpose for all who trust him."

"But how bitter the way !"

"Who thinks of the way when the end is won? Was the Master's own way an easy one, Ivan? Yet it is said, 'He shall see of the travail of his soul, and shall be satisfied.' And as the Master, so the servant."

"*Satisfied?*" Ivan repeated. "With what? Surely not with the results of his own work. I thought God meant him to do such great things, Clémence ! Almost to bring in the earthly reign of righteousness and peace. And I believe he thought so too himself. It was the deepest longing of his heart. It was what he tried to do—tried and failed."

"Do you remember, Ivan, the day our little Alexander tried

so hard to make a bow—'a real bow to shoot with,' as he called it? He failed in every effort, until at last he grew discouraged, and cried bitterly, refusing to be comforted. Then *you* came, took the wood and the knife from his hand, and made the bow. I shall never forget his bright glad face as he stood beside you, watching while you worked. He was so proud of your strength and skill, and your success in doing what he could not do; and when the bow was finished, he bore it off triumphantly, to show every one in the settlement how well his father made it for him. Ivan, our child's trust and joy have been a parable for me to-night. I seem to see him for whom our Easter festival is turned into mourning, standing thus by the side of Christ, in full, restful, glad content. What matter if the work dropped unfinished from his own hand? He no longer heeds it now. It is *Christ's* work he is watching. He sees Him preparing the true reign of peace and righteousness, the grand, final victory of right over wrong, good over evil. He is satisfied."

Ivan's sad face brightened a little. "You bring me comfort, Clémence," he said. "I begin to see that even failures—"

"*If* failures after all they were, which I doubt," Clémence interrupted. "Perhaps the seeds he has been sowing will spring up in flower and fruit when not we alone, but our children too, have gone to join him in the resting-place within the veil. Indeed I think no real failure possible to the child of God, except failure in trusting him."

"And there he did *not* fail," Ivan said. After a pause he added, "Yes, there he won the victory;—and yet Christ's victory is more to him than his own."

"As *his* glory was ever more to thee than thine, Ivan."

A patter of little feet and a sound of childish voices broke in upon their quiet talk. There was a loud shrill burst of laughter from the baby lips of Henri, checked by low words from Alexander. "Hush! we must not laugh loud—not *this* morning."

Then the half-closed door was pushed open, and at once three little voices spoke the Easter greeting—"Christohs voskress." Who should be the first to claim Papinka's Easter kiss? Alexander hung back, and putting his arm round Feodor, held him back also, that sunny-haired little Henri might spring triumphantly to his father's arms, never doubting that his own active limbs had won the race for him.

"Voyst venno voskress," said Ivan, as he fondly kissed, first the baby brother, then the two elder boys. There was magic in the touch of those little lips to soothe the heavy sorrow at his heart. But something in the thoughtful face of Alexander made him draw the boy close to him. "My child has been weeping this Easter morning," he said.

For a moment the child did not speak. Then he said falteringly, "I meant to serve the Czar, my godfather, when I grew to be a man."

"Serve instead *his* King, whom he loved," answered Ivan. "And take this thought with thee to keep all thy life, 'The Lord is *good* to the soul that seeketh him.'"

"Yes, father," the boy whispered, winding his arm about his father's neck. "Yes, he is good; for he comforted him at last."

"He did, my child. However dark his ways with his own may seem to be, yet are they all mercy and truth—*all*—when we see them from the end to the beginning. 'Though he cause grief, yet will he have compassion.' He will make the heart of his own to rejoice, and that joy no man taketh from them."

"Papinka, are these our Easter gifts?" asked Feodor, laying his rash little fingers on the silver medal and the golden coin so temptingly near him on the table.

"Nay, my boy; these are too precious for thy father to give away even to his dear little son. When he is laid in the grave, these shall be laid there with him. But to-day, my children, we will not talk of the grave, but of Him who came back from it, and opened our way to the happy home beyond."

So the current of those lives flowed on;—little lives of children, like bright, glad mountain rills, laughing as they tripped along; larger lives of thoughtful men and women, moving towards the sea in ever broadening channels, and bearing precious freights. Sorrow might come to them, but not despair; conflict, but not defeat. Life to them was "a cordial Yes, and not a dreary No," for the same reason which makes it worth while for each one of us to live and work to-day—because " Christohs voskress," Christ is risen indeed.

THE END.

Young Lady's Library.

The Heiress of Wylmington. By EVELYN EVERETT-GREEN, Author of "True to the Last," etc. Crown 8vo, cloth extra, gilt edges. Price 5s. *Cheaper Edition*, 4s.

"There are some remarks in its pages with which sensible people of every creed and every shade of opinion can scarcely fail to sympathize....It is pleasantly and prettily told."-SATURDAY REVIEW.

Temple's Trial; or, For Life or Death. By EVELYN EVERETT-GREEN, Author of "The Heiress of Wylmington," etc. Crown 8vo, cloth extra, gilt edges. Price 5s. *Cheaper Edition*, 4s.

An interesting study of character, going mainly to show the beauty of a quiet, manly Christian life; on the other hand the terrible moral degradation to which selfishness unchecked may lead.

Winning the Victory; or, Di Pennington's Reward. A Tale. By EVELYN EVERETT-GREEN, Author of "The Heiress of Wylmington," etc. Post 8vo, cloth extra. 3s. 6d.

A very interesting tale for young people. The charm of a thoroughly unselfish character is displayed, and in one of an opposite description the idol Self is at last dethroned.

Rinaultrie. By Mrs. MILNE-RAE, Author of "Morag: A Story of Highland Life," etc. Crown 8vo, gilt top. Price 5s. *Cheaper Edition*, 4s.

"We heartily commend this fresh, healthy, and carefully-written tale, with its truthful and vivid pictures of Scottish life."—ABERDEEN FREE PRESS.

On Angels' Wings; or, The Story of Little Violet of Edelsheim. By the Hon. Mrs. GREENE, Author of "The Grey House on the Hill," etc. Crown 8vo, gilt edges. Price 5s. *Cheaper Edition*, 4s.

"Is interesting from the intensity of human feeling and sympathy it develops."—LITERARY WORLD.

Mine Own People. By LOUISA M. GRAY, Author of "Nelly's Teachers," etc. Crown 8vo. Price 5s. *Cheaper Edition*, 4s.

It is a work of great human interest, and all the more is it human because it recognizes the supreme human interest—namely, that of religion, and the strength, purity, and gladness which religion brings to them who receive it in its simplicity and power. A wholesome, suggestive, and wisely-stimulating book for young women.

Nelly's Teachers, and what they Learned. By LOUISA M. GRAY, Author of "Ada and Gerty," etc. Post 8vo, cl. ex., gilt ed. 3s.

A tale for the young. Alice and Lina, while themselves children, trying to teach on Sunday evenings a very young and ignorant child, become learners also in the best sense of the word.

Ada and Gerty; or, Hand in Hand Heavenward. A Story of School Life. By LOUISA M. GRAY, Author of "Dunalton," etc. Post 8vo, cloth extra, gilt edges. 3s.

A touching story of two girls, giving an interesting account of their education and school experiences.

The Children of Abbotsmuir Manse. A Tale for the Young. By LOUISA M. GRAY, Author of "Nelly's Teachers," etc. Post 8vo, cloth extra, gilt edges. 3s.

"This is a book we should like to see in the hands of children. It will help them to be both happy and good."—DAILY REVIEW.

Dunalton. The Story of Jack and his Guardians. By LOUISA M. GRAY, Author of "Nelly's Teachers," "Ada and Gerty," etc. Illustrated. Post 8vo, cloth extra, gilt edges. Price 3s.

"A well-conceived, well-told, and deeply interesting story."—PRESBYTERIAN MESSENGER.

Books for the Household and Library.

Handbook of Practical Cookery. New and Enlarged Edition, in which special prominence is given to the preparing of New Cakes, Jellies, etc.; to very simple recipes for Cottage Cookery; also to various modes of preparing food for the Sick-room. By MATILDA LEES DODS, Diplômée of the South Kensington School of Cookery. With an Introduction on the Philosophy of Cookery. Crown 8vo, gilt roan back. Price 3s.; cloth extra, 2s. 6d.

Domestic Cookery, formed upon Principles of Economy, and adapted to the Use of Private Families. By Mrs. RUNDELL. With 30 Diagrams. *New Edition.* 348 pages, 24mo, cloth. 1s.

This volume contains about 1,500 recipes and directions.

Book of Medical Information and Advice. Containing a Brief Account of the Nature and Treatment of Common Diseases; also Hints to be followed in Emergencies, with Suggestions as to the Management of the Sick-room and the Preservation of Health. By the late Dr. J. WARBURTON BEGBIE of Edinburgh. *New and Improved Edition.* Post 8vo, cloth. Price 2s.

Adam Smith's Wealth of Nations. With Introduction and Notes by J. S. NICHOLSON, Professor of Political Economy in the University of Edinburgh. 8vo, cloth. Price 4s.

"Professor Nicholson's Introductory Essay is a very able critique on the 'Wealth of Nations,' in its relation to the political economy which it formed, and to the larger and more exact theories which it has developed."—BRITISH QUARTERLY REVIEW.

The Graphic History of the British Empire. By W. F. COLLIER, LL.D.; Revised and Continued by W. SCOTT DALGLEISH, M.A. Illustrated with Maps, Plans, and Tables. Crown 8vo, cloth extra. Price 6s. 6d.

The title, THE GRAPHIC HISTORY, is justified not only by the picturesque style of the work, but also by its contents and its plan. It consists of a series of pictures showing, on a broad canvas and without too many details, the great movements— political, social, educational, and religious—which embody essentially the history of the British Islands and the British people. The narrative ends with the Jubilee of Queen Victoria.

The 19th Century. A History. By the late ROBERT MACKENZIE. Crown 8vo, cloth. Price 3s. 6d. [New Edition.]

Presents in a handy form a history of the great events and movements of the present century, in our own country, throughout the British Empire, on the Continent of Europe, and in America.

America. A History. By the late ROBERT MACKENZIE, Author of "History of the 19th Century." Crown 8vo, cloth. Price 3s. 6d. [New Edition.]

"America" gives in a succinct form the history of the founding and development of the various States in North and South America. It is divided into three Parts:—

I. The United States.—II. Dominion of Canada.—III. South America, etc.

Right at Last; or, Family Fortunes. A Tale. By EDWARD GARRETT, Author of "Occupations of a Retired Life." Crown 8vo, cloth extra. Price 4s.

A story in which are depicted the ups and downs in the domestic life of a Scottish family; showing how great trials may be overcome by consistent faith and invincible strength of will.

www.ingramcontent.com/pod-product-compliance
Lightning Source LLC
Chambersburg PA
CBHW031051110726
47900CB00003B/892